TABLE OF CONTENTS

AGENTS
&
ANGELS

BY J.T. RATH

CHAPTER I
FAMOUS LAST WORDS

THURSDAY JUNE 22ND, 2017
TIMES SQUARE, NEW YORK CITY

The bullet entered cleanly into the President's head. His body went rigid as the hot metal exited and an empty stare replaced the small grin he had had moments before. A collaborative shriek echoed through the crowd he had been addressing as the limp body connected with the ground. Secret Service had their weapons already drawn and all of security was now on high alert; a pity they had no idea where the bullet had come from.

Before the bullet, the President had been giving an uplifting parable about patriotism and why the country must put aside all differences and experience unity, hope, freedom; the usual political cocktail that was supposed to form a legendary American moment. The President had chosen to give this particular speech in Times Square, a place where he believed that American dreams were represented to the highest degree. It was a place known throughout the world as the "heart" of the United States, a place where hope could never die. Now it would be known forever as the place where the 45th President of the United States of America was violently assassinated.

Pandemonium was spreading like wildfire across the streets as reporters ran everywhere trying to get the explicit images of a lifeless President lying in a pool of his own blood. They were brought to a halt about forty yards from the body and the sky lit up with flash after flash from their expensive cameras. A few of the more professional ones gathered themselves and began to get their corresponding camera crews ready as they figured out what they would say to a now-leaderless nation. The Secret Service was frantically looking at every corner and window of every building hoping to catch a glimpse of the shooter, communicating with each other through earpieces and wrist microphones.

Many of the tactical snipers who had been present on the roofs of the nearby buildings felt as if they had failed their nation and were also scanning the entire area for activity with binoculars. Pedestrians were running away from the scene, afraid they might be next, and people across the world sat stunned as they learned the news that the President had just been assassinated. It was a moment in history that many knew would change the face of the world much like September 11th had, if not more.

The assassin was amused watching the events unfold. He found the frenzied pedestrians and bystanders particularly entertaining. *As if I would want to waste any bullets on you*, he thought to himself. He had come here for one purpose and one purpose only: to send a message to the rest of the world that the Aqarab Mayta was now a very serious threat. The incidents which had unfolded in Australia had not been serious enough for the world to take notice. The failure that had been experienced at the hands of the N.E.T.S organization put a large impediment on the plans of the terrorist organization, and they would not fail twice. However, the previous image created by failures was about to change after the very public assassination of the most important man in the world had been carried out. Nearby, the assassin could hear of his successes on the TV.

"Cecil Young here for CNN reporting that the 45th President of the United States has just been murdered while addressing the nation in Times Square. As of right now, no additional shots have been fired and NYPD, the Secret Service, and the FBI are evacuating all personnel from the area. Times Square is being shut down indefinitely and we will bring you more news as it comes to us. Again, this is Cecil Young for CNN reporting that the President is no longer with us."

The television station went on to cover the events that were unfolding in Times Square with live images of the scene and the evacuation, and the assassin got up to get a bottle of scotch and pour himself a glass. As the golden brown liquid crashed against the ice, the assassin pondered his existence. Killing was not something he particularly enjoyed, but it was what he was good at in life. He took a small sip and felt the liquid burn as it slid into his chest. The most important man in the world was dead because of him; that solidified him as a near-god. He took another sip.

He looked into the glass to see how much was remaining and swallowed the rest in one last sip. Outside he could hear helicopters flying low, and countless sirens scattering all throughout the NYC floor, however, not one ounce of fear or adrenaline was flowing through his body. He was confident that he would never be revealed as the killer, and even once the group responsible was known, his role will have been long complete. As he poured a second helping of scotch, he reveled in how he had just killed a world leader without the slightest possibility of being caught. He had made sure his bullets were untraceable by custom ordering them from a "special" source in South America. The same story was true of his sniper rifle; there were no possible tracing mechanisms within the rifle - no serial numbers, no brand name, no signs of aging, not even fingerprints on the gun itself or the bullet pushed into the clip.

A day earlier, the assassin had posed as a high-rise window washer and commandeered one of the window washing elevators that are often seen on the outside of buildings. Playing his part, he pretended to wash windows by himself for several hours while working on the side of a skyscraper located very near to Times Square. After he was about three-quarters of the way up the building, he stopped, looked inside the nearby windows he was washing to make sure he was not being watched (the rooms directly next to him appeared to have vacant office space), slipped on a pair of gloves, and unwrapped the sniper rifle that had been laying hidden under a large dirty rag on the floor of the elevator.

He glanced over the Cheytac .408 cal that would change the world. Black, sleek, long, and lethal; this particular weapon would have more impact than most all others throughout history. He majestically held the gun and felt the sound and flash suppressor to make sure it was secure. It added considerable length to the weapon and made it look all the more lethal. *A shark with longer teeth* the assassin thought softly. It was equipped with a tripod mechanism on the front, and the assassin unfolded it while at the same time wiring the barrel to the sides of the cleaning elevator. Looking down the sophisticated scope, he planned out where the target was going to be and adjusted the height of the tripod and length of the wires accordingly. Once the assassin decided the sniper barrel was dead-on target where it was supposed to be, he finalized the wiring by securing the ends and making the wires taut so that between the tripod and the wires, the sniper rifle could not budge if a sudden gust of wind or some other force of nature occurred. A briefcase was also lying on the floor of the elevator and at this point, the efficient assassin opened it, revealing a large remote control with an LCD screen in the middle, as well as a miniature camera equipped with a small antenna device.

The assassin removed a small screw from the right side panel of the sniper rifle. He then removed the panel itself which underneath contained a port for the camera in the suitcase. The camera was then connected with the lens pointing straight down the barrel. The assassin flipped a switch on the side of the camera. A small green light on the side of the device began blinking rhythmically every few seconds signaling that the camera and gun were now armed and the two were in sync with the remote control. He turned on the remote control in order to check the operation of everything, and as he did, a zoomed-in image of the center of Times Square appeared on the LCD screen of the control.

He waved his gloved hand in front of the sniper barrel twice and at the same time a blur covered the screen he was looking at. *This is really all too easy,* the assassin thought to himself once more. After the gun and remote control device were completely set up, the assassin continued his "window washing" duties until he reached the roof of the skyscraper. He got off of the elevator and onto the roof, then lowered the elevator manually back down to exactly where he had set up the gun, if final adjustments needed to be made with the aim, he would be able to do it via remote control which could also raise, lower, or tilt the tripod. Now that his set-up was complete, he figured he would see the city for a day before the President's speech. He *had* always wanted to see a Broadway play…

There were only three hours until the President gave his speech and the assassin was just finishing up his dinner. He had decided to indulge and eat at a nice steak restaurant while sipping on a glass of expensive red wine. As the waiter brought him his check, he wiped the corners of his mouth with the napkin that had been lying in his lap. Despite the check being formidable, the assassin cared little; in only a few days' time he would be much richer than the man he was right now. He paid the check, left a decent tip, and got up. As he walked out of the restaurant the cute hostess smiled at him and he winked back. He had always been a very attractive man, equipped with strong facial features and long brown hair which slid back behind his ears. He was clean shaven and dressed sharply in a cream suit accentuated by a deep burgundy tie. He thought to himself that maybe he would return in a couple days to woo the hostess; women around the world always seemed to be defenseless to his underlying charm.

He exited through the revolving doors, and began the walk back toward his apartment. New York City was always busy, but it was obvious to anyone that had spent any time here before that today was different. There were far more people crowded on the sidewalks than usual, and the traffic in and around Times Square was being heavily monitored by NYPD and numerous Secret Service vehicles. A crowd was already starting to gather where the President would give his speech, and there was a palpable aura that something special was about to happen in the city.

It was right before sunset, and the air was a perfect temperature to be outside. The sky was cloudless for the most part, and the wind was nonexistent – a shooting condition which the assassin had hoped for. A grin emerged on his face as he came to the entrance of his apartment complex and entered. He took the elevator up to his room, entered, and sat down on his couch in front of the TV.

Relaxed and calm, he turned on the television and was greeted with a reporter standing in Times Square with a podium decorated with the Presidential seal in the near foreground. He was in mid-report, " – are expecting a historic moment tonight. The President has made it clear in recent weeks that he believes that it is time to put the 'United' back in the United States. In about two and a half hours' time, we will find out how he intends to accomplish that goal on top of monitoring the recovering economy as well as the war on terror. Back to you Jim."

"Thanks Cecil. We will come back to you as time gets closer to the President's speech tonight," the indoor correspondent commented as the camera transitioned away from Times Square back into the studio. "That was Cecil Young reporting LIVE from Times Square where the President is about to give what many are predicting to be a 'game changing' point in time for his Presidency." the TV volume seemed to drown out as the assassin began to ponder the last few words that came from the reporter: *a 'game changing' time*. A game changing time indeed.

When the President's speech began two and a half hours later, the assassin opened up his briefcase on the chair next to the couch and took out the remote control. He turned it on and was greeted with the familiar image of Times Square on the LCD screen. However this time, the screen was filled with seated people, a podium placed on a platform covered in red carpet, and a focused man giving the most important talk of his life. He pressed forward on an analog stick to the right of the screen and the image zoomed in and blurred. Rotating a small knob under the analog stick cleared and focused the image received from the camera and the assassin was now staring at the President's left shoulder which was moving slightly as he used hand gestures during his speech-in-progress.

Noticing that he was slightly off target, the assassin touched the screen with his right index finger and dragged the image up slightly and to the left. He removed his finger from the screen once he was centered on his target and the image snapped back to where it had been on the shoulder. Slowly, the image, as well as the gun that was a quarter-mile away, began transitioning to the new position indicated by the assassin's touch: the President's forehead. Now that the barrel was collinear with its target, the assassin listened in on the TV to the words the President was almost done spewing as he gently placed his finger near the black button linked to the trigger of the gun.

"I wanted to give this speech in Times Square today to remind everyone of what this country is about. It is not about the dirty politics often seen in Washington D.C. and that is precisely why I did not want to present this there. New York City is a place where our ancestors came to begin a new dream and where thousands still come in order to begin that same dream. It is the gateway to the 'land of opportunity' as some call it, and it can lead to both the successes and failures seen throughout life that make us better people." He paused as he surveyed the crowd around him. His brow was straight and he looked determined to do something great.

"My fellow Americans: society has become split and I fear we are no longer United. The gap between Democrats and Republicans has become too vicious, the arguments between atheists and Christians too great, and the stereotypes of minorities too harsh. These are all differences that were once welcome to our shores, but in the last decade they have felt like curses that are defining and burdening our nation.

"I am not exactly sure how to change this; I am hoping that you will help me. I believe that so much more could be accomplished as a country if we come together and instead of disrespecting each other's differences, we honor them. Instead of placing ourselves on a pedestal, let us invite others, both different and similar, to join our pedestal. Let this be a historic day and the start of a monumental change for the great country of the United States of America." Cheers began to erupt from the crowd as the President continued, "I want to enact this change together, as a nation united under one goal, and do not think for a second that I will let up on this 'reform'!" He was shouting over the crowd now as they continued to support what he was saying. "I am not going anywhere!" The assassin pressed the button, thus solidifying the President's famous last words.

Chapter II
Soaked

His tears were invisible to the others at the funeral due to the steady sprinkle of rain. The sky was dark with charcoal clouds, but silent as if in respect for the dead. Bryson Cooper still felt as if his world had crashed around him the second his wife, Elena, had died in his arms five days ago in Australia. She had been injured, captured, and then tragically murdered in the midst of Bryson's rescue. The man responsible was still alive, Bryson had spared him against better judgment, because of his desperate reveal of a new terrorist threat. *That bastard took everything from me.*

Now he stood here, placing her in the ground, dressed in black, standing openly in the rain. The rain felt good, cold and shocking on his bare skin. He felt he deserved the rain somehow, as if to clear him of his sins from a higher presence. The bandage around his hand was soggy and eerily he could feel rain water seeping through the now-healing hole in his palm where a knife had entered during his rescue efforts just a few day earlier. It stung sharply and Bryson quickly put his hand in his coat pocket.

All he could think about was his dead wife's last words: "*...I'll always be with you. I love you, Bryson Cooper.*" She had spoken them softly and angelically as the light had left her green eyes. Bryson had been holding her in his arms as she bled out in their extraction helicopter. The memory now created a painful phantom sensation. He couldn't bear to relive that final moment without breaking down. It had happened to him many times lately and he feared that he would never get over it. He had never felt so torn inside before; he felt empty and emotionless, but at the same time he felt like his head was full of thoughts about the future, about memories with her, about all the times they would never share…these thoughts stung more to him than any physical injury ever could. They had been partner agents at N.E.T.S., lovers, husband and wife, and best friends – all descriptions of their relationship that were no more.

As he focused his consciousness to the present he realized he was staring at the ground. The blades of grass with clinging rain beads were so green and full of life, and as he slowly brought his eyes up to the immediate horizon, they were met with death.

Elena's casket was beautiful, but at the same time so ugly. Contained inside were Bryson's life and his heart, both dead and in the eternal dark. The casket itself was a stunning deep burgundy oak, almost black in color, with silver handles and latches. Etched into the wood was a rose which covered the full length of the casket with a curved, thornless stem, intricate leaves, and perfectly sculpted petals near the head. It was truly a shame that this piece of art would never be seen again once it was buried deep in the ground. It seemed unfair, just as unfair as the way Elena was taken from him. Shot right in front of his own eyes, he saw the pain consume her face as the bullet had entered her back. Bryson had sworn to the man who killed her that he would someday kill him, but that fateful day he had let her killer live in hopes that his information would save thousands if not millions of lives. Elena would have wanted to die for something, and had Bryson killed Abd Al Aziz on that roof in Australia, nothing would have come of it. Bryson could feel the hatred and anger physically gripping his heart and the tears flowed once more.

This funeral was a small one. Only friends and immediate family were allowed to attend. They had been told that she died in a scuba diving accident while she and her husband had been diving in the Great Barrier Reef. Her funeral was not military based; no N.E.T.S. operative would ever have the sendoff they deserved in order to keep the agency in total secrecy. The agency, which stood for Non Existent Task Squad, was an unknown of the American government, even to the President himself. It was an off-the-books operation that wasn't tied down by the red tape of the visible judicial hammers of the U.S., resulting in a lack of appreciation for the operatives lost, which now included Elena. Instead, she was being buried in a civilian graveyard in a patch of land that her devastated parents thought that they would have filled first. They too were wrecked like most everyone at the funeral, completely shocked at the events that had taken their loved one's life. Elena had not left a mark on many people since her involvement with N.E.T.S. had kept her secluded, but the ones she had interacted with would never be the same again. Her spirit had been infectious to those around her, always brimming with confidence yet filled with compassion. Bryson had known after the first day in training with her that she was an incredible human being and he had fallen instantly in love with her.

The first time he met her he had already been through two weeks of training with N.E.T.S. when his class was told that they were receiving a new recruit that day. This was highly unusual because there had never been a recruit that joined late into training; they normally would just have to wait for the next semester. Bryson's class began to wonder what was so special about this new recruit that he or she was able to skip two full weeks of training. Some were even upset that this new person was exempt from part of the grueling program.

When Elena was introduced to the class, a pathetic round of applause could be heard for a few seconds before it scampered away. She was obviously beautiful and the men in the class weren't complaining in the slightest.

"Elena, your partner for today's exercise will be Bryson Cooper." The captain said aloud. Looking back on it, Bryson realized that was the moment destiny had been set in motion. Elena had walked over to him, and stuck out her hand for a formal introduction.

"Elena Noel, pleased to meet you." She said with a gorgeous smile on her face.

"Bryson Cooper." He replied as he shook her hand softly.

He could not stop looking at her eyes; they were captivating and seemed to be talking for themselves. He was so drawn to her that once the instructor began describing the next drill, Bryson found his mind racing a mile a minute. *Should I ask her out? Should I show her up to impress or let her look good on her first day? Damn she is beautiful. How'd she get in this business…*

"So you need to be able to do all of that within 5 minutes. No mistakes ladies and gentlemen, not on this exercise. Got it?" The commander was just finishing his explanation when Bryson came back to earth.

Elena looked over at him and smiled. "Shouldn't be too hard! Are you ready? We're up first."

Bryson didn't want to let her know that he hadn't been listening so he simply replied, "Yep, let's do it."

They approached the hangar doors where the exercise would begin and were handed live ammunition rounds by the assistants. *Shit, I should have listened.* They were fitted with tactical vests and extra clips before the commander began to speak.

"All right you two, remember it's gonna be dark in there so keep your laser sights on and don't shoot civilians. That will really piss me off. You have 5 minutes to save and disarm, and remember, if you get touched by a blue laser, you are dead…figuratively speaking of course. Good luck." At least Bryson had somewhat of an idea of what they were headed into now, or so he thought.

The hangar doors creaked open slightly as they entered, and then immediately closed. It was pitch black in the hangar.

"Laser sights going live." Bryson stated first. He pressed inward on a button on the side of his pistol and was blinded. "What the hell?" At the same time a commanding airy noise had overtaken the hangar.

"Strobe lights! Everywhere! I think the noise is a wind tunnel or something!" Elena replied. Once Bryson's eyes adjusted to the flashes he looked at Elena and she looked back. She was gorgeous and her radiance seemed to penetrate past the darkness that followed every flicker of the strobes. They both looked around the empty hangar. Between the flashes they could see it was huge and knew they could easily lose each other if they got separated. Ahead of them was a recreated and deserted Middle-Eastern market. Bryson looked at his watch and saw his timer change from 4:31 to 4:30.

"Ok we got four minutes! We are going to have to stick together, but we have to be cautious because these are live rounds! Turn your laser sight on and let's move forward until I say stop!" Bryson was yelling over the noise. Elena nodded and turned on her laser sight. Hers was green while his was red. It seemed to be the only saving grace in this training exercise. Bryson began walking briskly with his gun pointed forward. About three feet in front of the "market" a metal outline of a person popped up from the ground. Bryson instinctively began to pull the trigger as his eye caught a glimpse of the image at the end of his laser sight: a baby. He released the trigger and realized he was looking at a fearful mother holding her crying child. "Check your targets, civilians are present!"

"No shit! Weren't you listening to the brief?" Elena replied. Bryson pretended like he hadn't heard her. They kept walking forward through the market and left and right metal targets were popping up, but they were all civilians. 3:30…3:29…3:28. The red line emitting from Bryson's gun seemed to clash with Elena's green one as they swept over the market with their sights. The strobe lights made everything seem like stop-motion causing them both to exaggerate their movements. They were nearing a fork in the road, each side looking identical.

"Ok!" Bryson continued yelling. "I'll go left, you go right! Keep your laser up in the air so that we can see where the other person is. We'll meet up when it forks back together!" Bryson pointed to Elena then to the right fork as he continued on to the left. As he got deeper into his side he looked up and saw his laser in the sky and looked right and saw Elena's. He watched it move and made sure he was keeping pace with it, trying to imagine where she was in relation to her side and stay parallel with her. Suddenly, her laser was no longer visible and despite the wind noise, he was sure he heard gunshots. It was at that moment that he heard at least six metal figures pop up around him all equipped with lasers as well: blue lasers. As they popped up, their mounted lasers went from being aimed at the ceiling to being closer and closer to head level with Bryson. Quickly, he fired off three separate rounds at three separate targets. CLANK! CLANK! CLANK! The three bullets found their mark and consequentially, three blue lasers turned off. Bryson hid behind the cover of a fake fruit stand as he watched the blue lasers swivel around him. He could no longer hear gunshots from Elena's side and hoped that she hadn't been "killed".

Bryson pulled out one of his extra magazines from his tactical vest and slid it out from behind cover on the floor. After a few milliseconds, all three of the remaining blue lasers were targeted on to it. Bryson took advantage of the situation, popped up from behind cover and focused on where the blue lasers were coming from. The strobe lights made it hard to find the origins of the lasers, but Bryson fired anyway. Once again, three shots, three lasers off. He rushed forward around a corner where he hoped the roads would meet. He could see Elena in the distance and continued to run towards her. 2:00…1:59…1:58. She turned to look at him and an expression of shock cascaded over her face as she raised her gun towards Bryson. He dropped to the ground and began to slide towards her when he saw a blue laser emerging from behind her. It was almost down to her head. He fired. She fired. All that he could see was her standing over him and the strobes continually blinking.

"Enjoying the view?" She asked as she reached down to help him up. "What took you so long?"

"I…uh…encountered some hostiles." Bryson was embarrassed. He was his class' top operative and this new girl had just shown him up, not to mention his slide had ended right under her long legs. It was a good thing the strobes were active or she would have noticed a cloud of blush on his cheeks. "One minute and thirty seconds left! Come on!" He grabbed her hand instinctively and they began to run to down the now single-path market street.

They arrived at the end of the market and nothing was there. They each began to scan the area, their lasers decorating the surrounding area and piercing through the inconsistency of the strobe lights. A faint noise could be heard from behind them and they both swiveled around, greeted by two additional metal figures. One was a hostage with a bomb strapped to its chest and the other was a hostile figure behind it. The hostile figure's laser mounting was off, but pointed directly at the head of the hostage. Bryson began to assess the situation but before he could make an educated decision, Elena had fired a shot and the hostile figure fell backwards. Bryson looked at his watch: 0:30…0:29…0:28…

"Less than thirty seconds!" He yelled as Elena quickly approached the bomb.

"Bryson, these explosives are real!" She exclaimed as she looked over them.

"All the more reason to disable them! Disconnect the power source of the timer and the cable leading to the explosives at the same time! It has to be perfect so that no current flows into the explosives!"

"I'm not sure I can do that! These are REAL!" Elena said with a panicked look on her face.

"We'll do it together then! Take this wire!" Bryson was shouting as he pointed to her wire. There was hardly any time left. He grabbed the other wire. "On three! Ready? One!" 0:04 "Two!" 0:03 "Three!" 0:02…Bryson watched as the time on the counter faded with only one second left. Immediately the strobe lights and the noise in the hangar stopped.

The normal lights turned back on and voice was heard over the intercom as they both adjusted their eyes, "Good job you two. Cutting it a little close, but good teamwork. Ms. Noel, not bad for your first day." Bryson looked at her and a small smile came across her face; he figured she was still slightly embarrassed for freaking out.

"Yeah not bad, newbie. I know I couldn't have done that on my first day," He shot her a quick smile.

"Thanks. Sorry for freaking out over the explosives, I just didn't think there was any real chance of death in this training."

"That's how we learn here at N.E.T.S. It teaches you to deal with the adrenaline and shock your body experiences in real life or death situations…but I'll tell you what, you can make it up to me by going out to dinner with me this evening, how about that?"

His mind wandered back to the present. She wasn't really gone…she just couldn't be. It was not fair for him to have his entire heart murdered while his physical body remained alive. The feelings he was experiencing caused him to seriously doubt if he would ever be able to get over Elena Noel. She had been the love of his life and had he been able to, he would have taken the bullet that day.

The funeral group was now walking up and placing white roses on top of the nearly-black casket. Bryson reluctantly got his legs to begin walking and he gently grabbed a rose from the Father. The raindrops were still falling and causing the casket to become a mirror, or a window for Elena to see all those who loved her. All noise seemed to leave Bryson's head as he approached the final resting place of his wife. He was slowly greeted by his reflection and he stared back at it for what felt like eternity. It was a depiction of a broken man, screaming on the inside. The pain he was feeling was evident in his relaxed facial muscles. He stared into his own eyes and was met with more pain. They were glossy and filled with anguish. He couldn't bear to see his own pain anymore so he brought the rose to his lips, kissed it, and laid it on top of the casket. He tried to stare through the wood where Elena's head was gently resting to get one last glimpse of the world's most beautiful woman and his best friend, but was again met with his pathetic reflection. Angry, he turned around and returned to where he had been standing as the funeral progressed.

The next hour seemed to occur without actually happening. After all the roses were placed on the casket, a few kind words were said by the Father, the casket was lowered into the ground, church songs about life after death were sung sadly, the rain kept falling, and finally everyone filtered back into their vehicles and left. Bryson had physically been there through all of this, but his mind had been so engulfed in thoughts and pain that he mentally had not been present. He had even moved his lips to the words of the hymns, but no actual effort had been put into them.

Thirty minutes had passed and the rain had let up slightly when Bryson felt a hand rest on his left shoulder. Secretly he was hoping it was an angel of death coming to take him back to his wife, but as he slowly tilted his eyes he was greeted with a familiar face. It was David Harper, the head of the N.E.T.S. organization. He was African American, with an athletic build and a strong presence, but his age was beginning to show. He had a few gray hairs around his head and he looked more stressed than usual. He was wearing a black suit with a black tie in honor of the funeral, and was holding an umbrella to protect himself from the rain. Bryson respected this man more than any in his life; he had tutored both him and Elena and taken them under his wing when he realized they were special. Over the last few years, they had all grown as associates, peers, and as friends, and even though Bryson didn't want to admit it, David was exactly who he wanted and needed to see right now.

They stood in silence for a while, just the two of them in the rain, with David's hand still on Bryson's shoulder. Bryson's gaze had not broken from the hole in the ground for even a second after he had looked at David. It felt good to know that he had someone to care about him and despite the cold rain; he felt a surge of warmth from the presence of his friend and mentor.

David was the first to break the silence, "Bryson I can't imagine what you are going through. She was my friend too, but I know she was your life. I will help you get through this however you need, even if that means a little vacation from all of this…"

"No." Bryson replied simply. N.E.T.S. was the only thing he had left, and it was the only thing that would keep his mind off his loss.

"I was hoping you would say that because as you may know, we have a situation. The President was assassinated two nights ago and we have very reliable intelligence suggesting that it was tied to the Aqarab Mayta, the same group you met –"

"I know who they are."

"Yes of course, sorry Bryson. Anyway," he reached into his coat pocket and pulled out what looked like photos, "sorry we have to do this here, but we have several photographs of who we believe killed the President. Unannounced to the public, the murder weapon was found on a high-rise window washing elevator just a few hours after the incident. No fingerprints were left anywhere at the scene and no serial numbers to track the weapons or ammo; it's as if a ghost killed the President. Until a few hours ago that is." David handed Bryson the photos and continued, "These aerial photos of Times Square were taken by a photographer in a helicopter one day before the President's assassination for a tourist brochure and post cards. It looks like a normal photo peering down on Times Square, but if you look in the lower left corner, you will see a 'dash' on the side of one of the skyscrapers."

"I don't see what you are getting at sir."

"Look at the next picture." Bryson flipped to the next picture and was greeted with a zoomed-in, high definition photograph of what appeared to be a busy window washer.

"This man is washing the same building on which the weapon was found. In and of itself, that fact isn't particularly compelling to condemn him, but we ran his image through a facial recognition program which scans all of the traffic cameras, building security cameras, and ATM cameras in the surrounding areas and we found some interesting results." Bryson continued to flip through the remaining pictures as David continued to explain, "There are photographs of him roaming the city days before the President's assassination, visiting tourist attractions, eating at expensive restaurants, and entering in and out of this apartment complex." David pointed to the building the man was entering as Bryson looked at the picture. By the photograph alone, it could be seen that it was certainly no hole-in-the-wall building.

"Window washers don't get paid that much do they?" Bryson asked already knowing the answer.

"No…no they do not and that apartment complex you're looking at has a base rent of $20,000 a month. Not to mention, the restaurant he came out of the same day as the assassination is $120 a plate. For a modest window washer he's either up to his neck in debt, or not who he appears to be."

"So where do we go from here sir?" Bryson was ready to get back into the field; he knew it would be the only way to forget about the pain he was going through.

"Are you sure you're ready?"

"Yes." Bryson replied coldly as his eyes wandered back to his wife's soon-to-be-filled grave.

"Well let's get started then." David replied. And with that, the two of them started from the cemetery and left the dead to soak in the rain.

CHAPTER III
EXTRACTION PLAN

Bryson and David were on a plane to New York City within the hour. They sat together in coach and carried no luggage. Bryson had changed out of his sopping wet suit in the car ride over and was now wearing a long-sleeve T-shirt with a pair of jeans while David still had on his suit from the funeral. To the rest of the world they appeared to be an aging businessman and a pretty face that were on a half-filled flight to the big apple.

For the most part they sat in silence, except when the stewardess came by.

"Can I get either of you two something to drink?" She asked politely.

David responded first, "I'll have a scotch with ice, I think a uh…Glenlivet will be good thank you"

"Same but hold the ice please." Bryson stated. He could use a good drink about now; it would help to ease the pain.

"Two Glenlivets, one with no ice, coming right up gentlemen." The stewardess pulled out two plastic cups, placed a scoop of ice in one, and handed both of them a shooter of scotch.

"Thank you." they both said in unison, and the stewardess nodded and then moved on to the row ahead of them. Bryson downed his drink without really enjoying it and welcomed the small amount of numbness that followed. David noticed this but chose to say nothing; he knew Bryson was in a dark place and they had talked about the death of his wife enough already. What was important now was focusing Bryson on catching the President's killer.

Forty-five minutes later the plane landed at JFK international airport and the passengers slowly filed out like cattle. Bryson and David caught a taxi van and instructed the driver to head towards Midtown. Much like the plane ride, the taxi ride was uneventful, as per usual, the ride took longer than expected because of New York traffic. When they finally arrived at their destination, Bryson recognized the building. It was a tall skyscraper, black in overall color, and it was the headquarters for N.E.T.S. for the northeastern U.S. sector. From the outside it appeared to be a normal building, filled with various companies renting out different floors, a food court, and even underground parking. They walked through the main entrance and were greeted with a busy main lobby. Ordinary citizens were coming and going, talking to each other, spilling coffee on themselves, and engaging in other mundane activities contained within corporate America. David and Bryson joined a large crowd near the center of the lobby where six elevators were transporting people up and down the massive building. An elevator signaled it had arrived with a small "Ping" and the crowd filtered inside the metal box. Once the high-speed contraption was moving, Bryson noticed that everyone was going to three different floors; 34, 56, and 60. As the elevator opened for each floor, the businessmen and women hustled off, eventually leaving the two agents alone.

Now that they were the only two inside the elevator, David approached the long row of buttons located at the front right, pulled out an ID card and held it in front of the button indicating Lobby: L ♦ . A few seconds later, a panel to the right of the buttons on the side of the elevator quietly slid back revealing a hidden one labeled 'N'. David pressed it and it lit up in the center. The elevator recognized the button press and continued its ascent upwards. Within a few seconds, the doors were opening and the familiar site of floor 'N' greeted Bryson and David. Front and center was an extravagant frosted glass desk with the large initials N.E.T.S. etched with blue into the front of it. Behind the desk was a very attractive secretary, and one of the most familiar faces in both Bryson and David's life.

"Hello Mr. Harper, Mr. Cooper. I hope your flight and ride over were enjoyable." She commented with a soft voice.

"Yes Rachel, it was manageable, thank you. How have you been?" David answered.

"Oh I have been great thank you." She switched her gaze from David to Bryson and smiled. "How are you doing Bryson?"

"I'm getting better, slowly but surely." He glanced down at his bandaged hand but knew she was more inquiring about his psyche.

"I'm really sorry for your loss, Bryson." The sincerity in her comment could be seen in her big brown eyes. "Elena was loved by all of us and will be missed."

"Thanks Rachel." Bryson sadly replied. David quickly cut to the chase.

"Rachel, are there any updates on our John Doe assassin near Times Square?"

"No sir, we have various field agents acting as surveillance on him 24/7, but he hasn't gone anywhere except to eat, at least to our knowledge."

"Is there any indication that the CIA or FBI knows of this man? The last thing we need is a media frenzy scaring this guy back to the hole he crawled out of." Bryson had always been amused by Harper's soft discontent for the other intelligence branches in the U.S. He had always claimed that all they were good for was letting the world know that they were always two-steps behind, which oddly seemed to have a biting tinge of truth to it.

"No sir." Rachel replied with a smile. She knew of his grudge too. "According to our reports and, of course, the media reports, the CIA and FBI think that this is another terrorist attack by Al Qaeda. From what we have gathered, the only piece of information they have correct is the murder weapon."

"Ha, figures. Something happens that changes the face of history and they decide to recreate a monster like Osama Bin Laden in order to give the media a story and keep the public living in fear." He paused and shook his head in disgust. "Ok…thank you Rachel. Let me know if the situation changes on our assassin. Bryson come with me." David started to walk down the hallway and Bryson followed.

"Bye, Bryson." Rachel smiled and waved slightly as Bryson looked over. He returned the gesture with a small smile; he had always liked Rachel; she was a very nice girl and a true asset to the agency despite the fact she wasn't a frequent field agent. It didn't hurt that she looked like a supermodel; looks and brains were always an asset in this line of work.

Walking down the hall reminded him of how amazing all of the offices on this floor were. The walls for each room were glass, but for privacy there was a switch which automatically dimmed the glass, preventing others from looking in. Each office was equipped with a table and a whiteboard of sorts (although it was more of a glass board) that had the ability to transfer images, videos, documents, etcetera from the user's computers to the surface. From there, the control was completely touch-sensitive and all in high definition. Bryson remembered the first time he had seen the technology in use, and to this day was amazed by it. It really streamlined the debriefing process. On top of the stylish walls and the slick technology, each room was equipped with a breathtaking view of the bustling metropolis, especially David Harper's room, which the two of them were now entering.

David turned and flipped the switch on the left wall, and the glass around them darkened by several shades. Despite this, the two of them could still see out into the hallway, much like a one way mirror. David sat down at his desk as Bryson walked over to the window and was greeted with the image of the Empire State Building in the distance. Once again, New York City appeared to be the city that never stopped moving as he could see hundreds of people scurrying on the sidewalks and cars jam packed in the streets. It was about four in the afternoon, right at the start of rush hour, and the sun was gradually getting lower in the sky. For some reason Bryson found himself captivated by the image of life outside and David sat there and studied him as he studied the world. Bryson looked down at the sidewalk hoping he would find answers to what his heart was longing to know…*What if she and I had met under different circumstances? What if we had been a normal couple? Would any of this have happened? I don't remember what normal is any more…*

Almost as if Harper knew what Bryson was thinking, he said, "Bryson, it was her time to go. I know it is hard to hear, but it's time to start moving on. You have a career for which you are perfect, and I know deep down that you would not trade that for anything." He let the words resonate for a second before continuing, "You and Elena were never supposed to be a normal couple; none of us here were ever supposed to be normal. We have a greater purpose in life and that's what you have to live for now. Elena would want you to move on." Bryson turned his head towards him, but was looking at the floor, and deep down in his heart and mind he knew David was right. Normal was not a luxury, it was a punishment. He loved what he did, the adrenaline, the service, and the sensation of living for something greater.

"Yes sir." Bryson finally replied. It was time to get down to business. "So what's next? Where do we go with this guy?"

"I don't know…that's what I've been thinking about for the past few hours." David was seated in his chair rubbing his chin and staring off in to space. "We are taking a huge risk here by going after this guy. On one end we have the possibility that he didn't have anything to do with the assassination, the possibility that we made a mistake, and then we have to cover our asses. Then on the other end, we have the chance of him getting away and us losing our only strong connection to the Aqarab Mayta." It was the Arabic name for the newest terrorist organization that Abd Al Aziz had claimed to be remarkably and frighteningly powerful during their altercation days ago in Australia. Even more worrisome was that Bryson believed him. 'Dead Scorpions' was the English translation, almost as eerie as the mystery that surrounded what little N.E.T.S. knew about them.

"Don't we have custody of Abd Al Aziz sir?" The name stung like poison in Bryson's mouth. He loathed the man who had taken his wife from him. *That fucking bastard.* "I would think that he's a pretty strong connection to the Dead Scorpions since he's their supposed leader…"

"Yes, one would think that, but it seems that they have been well trained in the ability to keep their mouths shut. Al Aziz has hardly said anything to us, and we are almost beginning to believe that he is nothing more than a simple pawn…there might be someone higher pulling the strings here. I think that if we capture this guy he'll certainly have some valuable information about who the Aqarab Mayta are, what they're doing, when they plan to do it, and just how the hell they got this powerful under our radar." The two of them sat in silence for a minute or so. Bryson could tell that David was worried, and honestly he was as well. This organization had been ridiculously resourceful in Australia with guns, helicopters, cars, bikes, and manpower. Now they had just murdered the most powerful man in the world without the slightest hint of being caught and brought to justice. Worst of all, Bryson had a sinking feeling in the back of his mind that all of this was just the beginning. As Bryson continued to think about the situation they were in, David started talking out loud to formulate a plan of action, "We know where the assassin is living, at least for the time being. The question is: does he know that we know?"

"I don't think so sir. Rachel mentioned that he had been leaving to eat at restaurants and such. Frankly, if I was an assassin that had just completed *that* high-risk of a kill and I had *any* suspicion that someone was on to me, I would jump the country, not go out for a nice seafood dinner."

"Good point, but where do we go from here?" David seemed confused. "We can go in and apprehend him, but that will look suspicious with a SWAT team knocking down his door, not to mention if we are wrong…"

"Sir, we aren't wrong. N.E.T.S. has never been wrong – "

"There's a first time for everything, Bryson." David cautioned. "We have to go into his apartment quietly, get him, and bring him in for questioning and detainment. Nothing goes wrong this time."

"That's easier said than done, especially when trying to capture a trained assassin…" Bryson knew he was more than capable though. One versus one, he was undefeatable, and this guy was no different. "Do we have the layout of apartment on hand?"

"Yeah, hold on, I'll put it on the board. Just give me a second." David turned to his glass desk, placed his index finger on top, waited for a moment, and the table lit up with a slick operating system. Bryson could see David moving his hands across the desktop at a quick pace, opening folders, scrolling down through files, and finally tapping one. A 3D layout of New York City filled the desk and David conducted some more hand work, bringing up a keyboard near the bottom. He typed on the glass and soon the image was being zoomed in to a specific location. David placed his hand on the far edge of the table and with a giant swipe he "threw" the image to the glass board in the front of the room. The image was much larger here, making it easier to compose a plan of attack.

Bryson walked over to the board and began to examine the building he was looking at: the assassin's current residence in New York City. The apartment building was very nice, and near to Times Square, which probably increased the rent price exponentially. According to the image, it was sandwiched between two taller buildings, although it was about 14 stories itself. The uppermost apartments had fairly large balconies overlooking the busy street in front of the building. David noticed as Bryson's eyes followed up to said balconies.

"We believe that the left corner apartment on top is the one where he's staying. I'm sure the balcony adds to the hefty price tag that our window washer is paying per month." Bryson looked back and smiled at David.

"Yeah and it's also the weak spot of his operation. I could easily get on the roof and consequentially onto the balcony." Bryson was starting to envision how this would begin to go down. "We would wait until he leaves, and I'd get to his balcony, infiltrate the apartment, and then investigate. If I find some suspicious material, I stay until our agents on the outside inform me he's coming back. Once he is back, I'll have the element of surprise, and capture him alive. If we are wrong and he's somehow an actual window washer, I leave before he ever gets back."

"What about once you have taken him down? You can't exactly walk onto the streets of New York with a knocked-out prisoner over your shoulder."

"That's where the alleyways on the side of the building come in…" Bryson began to talk slowly, somewhat making this up as he went, "Once he's in my custody, we go out to his balcony and I raise him to the roof of the complex. From there I lower him into the alley, then lower myself into the alley, put him in a car and bring him back here. Simple as that."

"Sounds like we need to get you a cable reel of sorts and a new car." David said, half smirking.

"If you insist." Bryson joked. He could have conducted the abduction without a car, but he figured it was worth it to add it in to the explanation to see if he could get a new one. They both sat there in silence once again, thinking over the plan Bryson had just laid out. Both of them knew that nothing could go wrong on this operation; this was the man who had killed the President. Bryson thought for a second of the effect that the last few days had had on the world…the nation was crushed; this last President had been very popular among the people. He had been getting agendas accomplished both in the mainland and overseas, and he had managed to stabilize government spending and reverse the recession. Things had been looking up for America until a few days ago when millions had seen their leader shot and killed and the havoc that had ensued. Now they were being told by the remainder of their leadership to believe that the same group who had conducted 9/11 had accomplished the impossible. The American people were not stupid, and Bryson felt sorry for them to be lied to like they were; however, maybe it was for the best that they not know of the power of the Dead Scorpions.

Bryson and David were snapped from their trance when a knock came at the door of David's office. It was Rachel, and she looked to be in a hurry. David looked at Bryson and nodded toward the door and Bryson walked over to open it. He no sooner got it open and Rachel rushed in, panting slightly.

"You guys are going to want to see this."

CHAPTER IV
TWO TYPES OF SLEEP

FRIDAY JUNE 23ʳᵈ, 2017
THE PENTAGON

The luxurious suit demanded attention from both males and females alike. It was all black with subtle silver pinstripes accentuated by a deep turquoise and navy blue tie. The suit was fitted perfectly; showing off the man's toned physique consisting of a strong core, broad shoulders, and large arms and legs. A spotless pair of mirror-like aviators covered his baby blue eyes, and the sun reflected on his dark tan skin as he walked from the parking lot to the visitor's entrance. There was a slight breeze on this cloudless day in Washington D.C., yet it didn't cause his short hair to move an inch. With him, he carried his cell phone, car keys, and a briefcase containing a single envelope. The envelope contained the reason he was here today.

It had been one day since the American President was assassinated and as he had suspected, Washington D.C. was on especially high alert. Every national landmark had obvious Secret Service patrol around it and snipers could be seen from many of the rooftops around the White House and the Pentagon, aiming down into the crowds, scouting for potential attackers. To get into the Pentagon visitors parking lot for his meeting, it had taken nearly two hours and three different proofs of identification. Every single one of the identifications had been forged weeks earlier and contained no true information about who the man was besides height, weight, hair color, and eye color. The man's IDs claimed that he was Thomas Henry from Washington D.C., age 30, and an organ donor, but in reality his name was Ian Tract and he was an operative for the Aqarab Mayta. He was at the Pentagon to deliver a very important message without raising any cause for suspicion, at least not during his visit.

Approaching the door with the Pentagon seal on it, he reached for the handle, pulled outward, and walked inside. Luckily there wasn't any line for visitor's passes and he approached the reception desk calmly and smiled.

"Hi there." he seemed to have startled the receptionist,

"Oh hello! Sorry, I was just…uh…anyways, what can I do for you sir?"

"I should have a meeting scheduled with Ms. Crooms today in about 10 minutes. My name is Henry…Thomas Henry." The receptionist scanned the computer for a quick second, reached to her left, and presented Mr. Henry with a visitor's badge that had his name on it.

"Ok. She has been notified and should be here in a couple minutes. You're welcome to have any food or beverages you see behind you." She pointed straight behind him where there was a table with coffee, cookies, and water next to a couch facing a large flat screen HDTV tuned to CNN.

The receptionist went back to whatever she had been doing before and Ian grabbed a cookie, took a sizeable bite, and sat on the firm couch. As he enjoyed the somewhat dry chocolate chip cookie, he watched the report on TV covering the history of the recent President's shortened term. A small sensation of success swept over him knowing that everything was going to plan. Abd Al Aziz had failed in Australia just like it had been planned (although the additional kill of an N.E.T.S. agent was a plus), the assassination of the President had been carried out perfectly, and the assassin who had carried it out was of little importance to the organization.

The amount he had been promised to be paid, while substantial, was penny change to what the Aqarab Mayta were worth. It almost seemed too easy to him, but then again, the country of America had let itself slip a long ways since 9/11. They had been graced with the notion of being a world superpower for too long, and consequentially let their guard down again.

Despite this, Ian could not have cared less about the American people or the Aqarab Mayta's goal for that matter. He did what he did for the challenge of it all. Civilian life bored him and he had little confidence or sympathy for most of the human race. Americans, British, Russians, Chinese, Italians…all filled with sheep never living up to their full potential. Ian was no sheep and he took commands from the Aqarab Mayta only because of the daunting tasks it presented him with. He did it for the thrill of knowing he was on the verge of his limits, and the violence aroused him. And the money. *Ah yes, the money…*

"Mr. Henry?" A soft female voice from behind him called out.

"Yep. Right here." He responded immediately standing up and turning around. His eyes were met with the sight of a small woman. She was not exceptionally gorgeous, but very cute; she had a sense of innocence still about her. Being the man he was Ian figured that in different circumstances he would have enjoyed robbing her of her innocence. However, he didn't have time for that today and would just have to bury that thought for later. He stuck out his hand as he approached her. "Hi there, Thomas Henry. Thanks for meeting with me today." She returned the gesture and shook his hand. She had a surprisingly strong grip.

"Oh no problem at all, sir. Please." She motioned to the door with her hand. "Follow me." She had been suspicious of this meeting ever since it had been arranged a couple days ago. Hardly anyone knew that Abd Al Aziz existed, and this man had called claiming he could help get answers from their speechless prisoner using a special form of new-age psychology. The only reason he had been successful in getting this far was because he had name-dropped someone who was above her clearance level and been approved almost immediately. Regardless, she was still cautious and was going to be sure to keep an eye on him throughout the whole process.

They were both walking in unison in spite of the fact that he was much larger than she. Around the next corner was a security checkpoint and both were required to remove their shoes, all metal objects, and belts. The guards who were present frisked both of them, and once they were cleared, they one by one entered a detector which showed them nearly nude to the operator. This detector was able to sense anything odd located on the person's body; they were both clean. Ian watched as his items went through the scanner in front of the security guard. He kept a close eye on his briefcase as it passed through the machine without issue. Ms. Crooms was already halfway through putting her shoes back on and Ian sat down and followed suit. Once they were both fully dressed and had all of their items, they continued onward.

"This way please." Ms. Crooms began to walk off while Ian was still tying his dress shoe. He hurried and tightened it and briskly walked to catch up. Ms. Crooms looked back and eyed him. "So what exactly are you going to do to get this guy to talk that we haven't already tried? You mentioned psychology on the phone I believe?"

"Well yes, somewhat," Ian had been expecting these questions, "see, each human being is like a computer waiting to be programmed, or in this man's case already programmed. In order to rewrite a program, you must go back to basics and delete old code."

She interrupted. "So what does that have to do with him answering questions?"

"He is programmed to not answer your questions ma'am. He has been programmed to realize that whatever offers you make him are lies, whatever threats you raise are going to happen anyway, and whatever pain you submit him to is just temporary before death."

Again she budged in, "So how do you intend to re-program that? What are you going to do that we haven't already done?"

"I'm going to become his friend, Ms. Crooms." She shot him a near-laughing glance as he continued, "I have learned that trust is much like a password for a program. Trust gains you access to the program's hardcode and you learn things about the program that you could not tell from the surface. Using this trust, I'm hoping I can gain some insight as to why this man did what he did, where he came from, maybe even future plans he knows about."

"Hmmm. Well for your sake I hope it works. This is our last attempt with this guy. He won't even tell us his name, despite the fact we already know it." They had been walking down the same hall for a while now, finally rounding a corner that led to another extensive hallway.

"Are we almost there yet, miss?" He asked politely. She just kept walking as if she hadn't heard him so he assumed that was her version of 'yes'. After passing by some rooms filled with students and employees quietly taking tests, a global communications room filled with older looking men arguing back and forth, and a room filled with TV's covering news feeds from around the world, they came to a dark empty room near the end of the hallway. As soon as Ms. Crooms walked inside, the lights turned on to reveal a long aluminum table fitted with two seats on opposite sides of each other.

"This is where you will be conducting whatever it is you need to do in order to get him to talk. Be warned you are monitored by cameras equipped with microphones, so don't try anything you shouldn't." She motioned to the table with her hands. "Have a seat. He will be here shortly and I'm off to watch you from another room."

"Ok, thank you."

She exited the room and left the door open as he sat in the comfortable leather chair stationed at the long, reflective table. Ian contained a private smile as he sat, amused that N.E.T.S. would take the Dead Scorpions for such fools. Rather than bringing their prisoner to their headquarters in New York, they had, like a bunch of scared children, sent him to their small, extremely discreet location buried deep beneath the Pentagon for security purposes. Just the simple fact that Ian was there as an "expert psychologist" proved that they were utterly confused and desperate.

He sat his briefcase on the table and began to survey the room with his peripheral vision. One camera that was behind him he had noticed when they entered the room. From where he was sitting he figured that it was at a 30° over his left shoulder. *That works.* As he sat and waited he noticed a second camera by the door. He figured that it would be at a 70° to Abd Al Aziz's left shoulder once he sat across the table from him. *And that works too.*

Ian enjoyed the chair patiently until he heard footsteps coming from outside the door. He turned to look and saw exactly what he thought he would; two somewhat tall agents walking on either side of a prisoner handcuffed at the arms and legs. The dirty man was walking with his head down and slumbering along as if he were headed toward death row. In fact, he might as well be. Once he realized that Ian was sitting ahead of him, he raised his head and glanced at his old friend who was deep undercover at the moment. The two agents sat him in the chair, uncuffed his hands and feet, and then recuffed his ankles to the table that was anchored into the ground. They glanced at Ian as if to wish him luck and he returned a small smile as the two men turned to leave the room again. After the door had closed leaving the two of them alone, Ian, still acting under the persona of Thomas Henry, struck out his hand towards the prisoner across from him.

"Abd Al Aziz I believe it is? I am Thomas Henry, it's nice to meet you." Abd Al Aziz glared at him, refusing to return the common gesture of shaking hands in greeting. "I hear that you are not cooperating with the people in this place, and causing them some frustration?" Ian waited for a response; it was all a great big act between the two of them from here on out. He just hoped that Al Aziz would do his part. "Well let me just tell you that you have been lucky thus far. I can assure you that by the time I am done with you, you will be telling these people everything they want to hear."

Abd Al Aziz smiled at Ian and replied. "I will never tell of anything. Death does not frighten me and neither does torture. I welcome the pain…it is a faster way to Allah and a reuniting with my fallen brothers."

"Hmmm, interesting. Well maybe we will change your mind about that." Ian reached into his briefcase and removed the single manila envelope which he then opened up. Inside was one single sheet of thick, letter paper with a page-long message written on it. "Could you read this please?" Ian handed the tan piece of paper to Abd Al Aziz and sat back as he read the message:

Do not show any emotion while reading this letter, they are watching and listening. Hold the paper directly in front of you.

Your actions in Australia were just, and will never be forgotten. However, you are now a liability and your part is complete in this organization. Our ideals are now achieved and the plan is now in motion thanks in large to you and your team. Everyone in the Aqarab Mayta thanks you for your dedication and soon, your sacrifice.

Contained in the paper of this letter is a compound that remains inactive until it comes in contact with human saliva. Once this happens, it spreads through the blood quickly and stops the heart peacefully and permanently while releasing large doses of melatonin to the brain to cause a deep sleep. It is untraceable and causes the victim to die in their sleep. The last task that we ask of you is to rip off a small corner of this letter, hide it, and administer your death tonight before you fall asleep.

Good luck, and may you rest forever in peace in the glory of Allah.

Sincerely,
You Need Not Know

Two rooms away, Ms. Crooms was ordering the other two persons in the room to zoom in on the letter that Abd Al Aziz was reading. Unbeknownst to her, the letter was not made of just plain printer paper. Ian had created the letter to reflect something other than what the person directly in front of the letter saw. The prisoner was reading one thing, but the molecular makeup of the paper allowed Ian to "project" a different letter 10° to either side of the main user.

"What does it say?" Crooms calmly asked. The guard zoomed in a little further and she squinted as she made out the following letter:

Mr. Abd Al Aziz,

I know that you are in an unfortunate predicament right now, but as a psychiatrist I would like to help. All is not lost for you and I believe you can still lead a very satisfying lifestyle. In order to do so however, I will need you to trust me. I am here to help!

These people want you to answer the questions they have about your organization, and I believe it would be in your best interests to do so. I believe this should be on your own accord though. Take your time. When you are ready to talk, I will be ready to listen. You have many deep secrets that I know are weighing you down and I want you to be able to enjoy life without the burden of keeping them to yourself.

I hope that we can work past our differences and come to an understanding!

Sincerely,
Thomas Henry

As Al Aziz finished reading *his* letter in the opposite room he felt a wave of pride sweeping over him. This was his last honorable task in order to ensure the success of the Aqarab Mayta, and it would certainly be remembered by his colleagues as the ultimate sacrifice. *I will surely earn a spot amongst the clouds.*

"So…what do you think about my proposal?" Ian asked Al Aziz. He was pretending that the paper he had handed him had been an opportunity to talk rather than a death letter. "I think it's fair don't you?" Al Aziz stared at Ian for a long while, studying him, peering over him, and feeling like a towering man of god. He felt sorry for his fellow brother that their positions were not reversed, that he would not be the one to make a noble sacrifice. After this spiritual examination, Al Aziz picked up the letter with two hands and ripped it half, all the while smiling at Ian. As he slowly tore the paper, acting as if he was insulting Ian's "offer", he inconspicuously removed a small corner of the paper and kept it clenched in his fist.

"I see…" Ian paused for a while making sure not to break the persona of the psychiatrist Thomas Henry. "Well then, I guess we are done for today." He stood up and pushed his chair in under the table as Al Aziz remained seated. Reaching over, he grabbed the two halves of the letter and placed them back into the leather binder which he then placed back into the briefcase. The same two agents who had escorted Al Aziz in had now returned and Ian shot them a small nod as he passed them exiting the room. As soon as he was through the doorway, he was greeted with the sight of Ms. Crooms who appeared frustrated.

"What the hell was that?" She was clearly not happy. "You spend five minutes in there and then decide that you are done for the day? You are supposed to make him talk!"

"I was attempting to get him to cooperate Ms. Crooms…like I said earlier, I need to build his trust. Today was merely the acquaintance. The hope is that each day he gets a little more used to the fact that I'm not going anywhere and that I want to help him. I apologize if you thought this was going to be a quick process, but it's not."

She gave him a stern scowl. "Fine. You do what you have to, but I want to see progress within the week. Next time you will not be leaving here within five min – " She was cut off by the ringtone on her cell phone which she immediately answered. After a couple nods she stormed off and Ian caught the slightest tidbit as her voice trailed behind her: " – on a window washer!?"

How the hell did they find him? Ian knew of the assassin's cover story, but how had it been blown? He kept the discovery to himself as he was escorted back through the maze in which they came. Finally, Ian and one of the guards who had been with Ms. Crooms were back at the lobby where they had met, and Ian turned around holding out his hand.

"I look forward to working with you more in the next few weeks." He returned the favor and grabbed his hand and shook it tightly.

"Be here at 10:00am on Monday. We want some time with him again. And we will count on you to continue from there."

"Yes sir." He smiled and then exited back outside into the sun, placing his aviator sunglasses back over his eyes. He got into his car, pulled out of the parking lot, sending the guard a small wave as he left, and began the drive home in Washington D.C. traffic.

As soon as he arrived at the high end hotel room he was occupying, Ian pulled out his cell phone and called the assassin in New York. The phone rang three times and he heard a small click on in the receiver.

"Hello son, how are the toys that I sent you?" The assassin answered, speaking in code.

"Hi dad. Thanks for the toys, but they broke yesterday. I am not sure how, but they all broke." Ian replied in a somewhat childlike voice. They had a general consensus that if things were not going as planned that this meant that the toys were 'broken'.

"Now son, how did they break? Should I go and buy some more?"

"I told you dad I don't know. You can stay there, I will try to fix the toys on my own…just buy better ones next time."

"Will do son. Thanks for the advice. I'll see you and your mother in a few days. Be good."

"Ok, dad. See you soon." Ian hung up the phone quickly and ended the unemotional conversation. The assassin they had hired to kill the President would be fine. He was trained for this kind of thing and would be able to deal with any resistance that he would run into; at least until he had to deal with Ian.

After a nice dinner in the luxurious hotel lobby and a long warm shower, Ian was ready for bed early. It had been a long day and if everything stayed according to plan, the next few days would be even longer. He laid his head on the comfortable pillow and reached over to turn off the lamp light. A small click was followed by darkness and he closed his eyes while letting out a small sigh. Within minutes he was asleep.

Ten miles away, a lonely, proud man sitting in his high security containment room under the Pentagon unclenched his fist revealing a small scrap of paper. He reflected and prayed for several moments and finally laid his head back onto his thin, uncomfortable pillow. After saying one final prayer, he placed the scrap of paper on his tongue and immediately felt it begin to dissolve. Slowly he closed his eyes for one last time. Within minutes he was dead.

CHAPTER V
DISTANT SHADOWS

SUNDAY JUNE 25TH, 2017
N.E.T.S. HEADQUARTERS, NEW YORK CITY

Rachel hurried over to the glass board which Bryson had been studying and began to exit out of the presentation of the assassin's apartment complex. David and Bryson remained silent as they watched Rachel navigate through the program on the glass board; they trusted her to have a perfectly good reason to interrupt them and their planning. After some more hand motions upon the glass, she had brought up a live news feed.

"…the following video was sent to us earlier today. We have attempted to trace the video's origins, but have not been successful. However, the message presented is clear." And with that the commentator was taken off the air and after a slight pause, a clip of an older Middle Eastern man began to play. He was sitting in what looked like a hotel room and immediately Bryson recognized him. There had been a reason Rachel had barged in on their meeting and it was because the man staring back at them was Abd Al Aziz.

Immediately Bryson was filled with rage, hatred, sadness…*had he escaped from N.E.T.S. detainment?* As the man on the TV began to speak, Bryson focused in.

"Your President is dead, America." Abd Al Aziz began with the harsh statement and let the effect simmer for a moment. "He was shot through the head by an assassin working for the same organization that I do. Your media has mislead you to believe that this organization goes by the name, Al Qaeda, the same terrorist group that successfully killed 3,000 people 16 years ago. This is not true. The organization that killed your President, and the organization that was the cause of the violence in Australia days ago is *not* Al Qaeda." Bryson, as well as Rachel and David, could not figure out why they would be broadcasting themselves like this.

"We are no religious extremist terrorist group, nor are we constructed of any particular race or ethnicity. We share one common goal amongst ourselves. This goal is what defines us; it is what has built us to be what we are today. We want the arrogant to become the submissive; we want the United States to die.

"Now…how do you kill a country you might ask? Well it's simple really, but I wouldn't want to ruin any surprise here on television. I'll leave it up to your 'top officials' to figure that out. They did such a good job catching the President's killer that the efforts towards preventing us should be nearly complete." Al Aziz let out a disgusting chuckle and Bryson wanted to rip his head off through the glass board image, "Yes, people of the United States, you *should* be afraid. We have people everywhere, in almost every one of your government organizations. CIA? FBI? Secret Service? *N.E.T.S.*?"

"Damn him!" David exclaimed abruptly. Abd Al Aziz had just addressed his invisible intelligence agency on live television and now they were out in the open.

"All of them have an associate of mine deep within them," Al Aziz continued, "and they answer to one man and one man alone. I am not that man, nor will you ever see that man. But trust me when I say that he has a plan that will cause America to go from the land of the brave, to the land of the beaten.

"Thank you for taking the time to listen. I hope that you enjoy the next few weeks of your life. Soon, the world power known as America will cease to exist and we will fascinate the masses…ma'a salama." And with the cold, Arabic goodbye, he gave a smile that only an insane man could have accomplished and the screen went blank. To the three people standing in the room, it seemed to stay that way for ages; for they realized that they were now up against an opponent which they knew nothing about and had only a short amount of time to prevent what sounded like the worst terrorist attack in world history. Their intense silence was interrupted when the newscaster returned onto the screen.

"And as you just saw, that was a direct threat to the people of the United States. Our sources believe that the man seen in the video is Abd Al Aziz, an oil mogul who was supposedly killed in a car accident several days ago in Rome. No word yet – " the anchor was cut off as Rachel turned off the screen on the glassboard.

"Damn it." David stated quietly. Once again the three of them sat in silence trying to piece together what had just happened and what steps should be taken next.

Finally Bryson spoke, "We need to talk to Al Aziz now and get information out of him. I don't care if we have to kill him to get it."

"Well, there is something else that I haven't told you yet…" Rachel said timidly. David and Bryson both turned their heads to look at her and hear what she had to say, "Before I rushed in here to show you this, I had just gotten word from our headquarters in the Pentagon that Abd Al Aziz just died in his sleep on Friday night."

"Son of a BITCH!" David's fist came down on his desk with a thunderous boom that caused Rachel to jump slightly.

"I'm sorry, sir. According to them, his death was completely natural. They are looking into a psychiatrist that visited him that day though. No word on that yet."

"There's no way." Bryson interjected. "The timing is too perfect. Somehow, someway, the Dead Scorpions killed him because they didn't need him anymore." He paused to think, looking around at the air as if the answers were floating in front of him. "That tells us two things. First, this video was made a while ago, possibly before the incident in Rome even, which means they have a very strict master plan. They knew they would be successful and they knew Al Aziz would be caught in Australia. Second, it clearly means that Abd Al Aziz was nowhere near the top of the food chain in the Aqarab Mayta. I think he was a pawn talked into his death by promises of glory." David nodded slightly, acknowledging that he agreed with everything Bryson had said.

David continued, "Then that means our assassin here in New York is most likely a low player too. He may know nothing."

"True, but he might have something that connects us to them…I mean he has to get paid somehow. That right there is a bank account." Bryson continued to think of reasons that this guy would be worth their time. "He has to have some contact in the Aqarab Mayta; someone he gets updates from or instructions…"

"I agree, sir. I think the assassin is our last bet to stopping these guys. The CIA and FBI are going to be background checking everyone in their departments and by the time they find anything it will be too late. As for N.E.T.S., no one in our agency is rogue like that, I'm certain of it. We have people whose jobs are dedicated to finding moles and double agents 24/7. They would have found out a long time ago if someone in N.E.T.S. was not who they said they were." Rachel's explanation to the both of them seemed solid, and David was sold.

"Ok, then we gotta get this guy. I don't care how, we've just got to get him."

Later that day, New York City was abuzz. People walked about normally, but a whiff of tension could be felt on every sidewalk. The United States had just been openly threatened and the on-air verbal attack had left everyone tense and afraid. As expected, the media had hit the ground running with the footage of Abd Al Aziz, and it was almost continuously playing on every news station. Inaccurate speculation was rampant among anchors, each discussing the situation as if they were educated experts.

"This is pathetic…now they're suggesting that Al Qaeda and the Aqarab Mayta are working together for some 'master plan'! How stupid can they get?" David had belted out to Bryson. He had no choice but to just shake his head and move on. The truth was, ever since he had learned that Abd Al Aziz had died a peaceful death, Bryson was furious and became intensely focused on catching the assassin and getting answers from him in any way possible.

Traffic was terrible, but Bryson was slowly making his way over to the assassin's ritzy apartment complex. This morning he had received his final orders: to capture the assassin alive and bring him back to headquarters. After his briefing, he was given a special grapple device which would allow him to get up and down the side of the apartment building from the alleyway, as well as the keys to a black Chevy Camaro. While he didn't love it as much as the Audi R8 he had driven, and subsequently destroyed, in Australia, Bryson was still excited. He understood that for this extraction he needed a car that would not draw too much attention to him, especially being in a crowded city like New York. So far, he enjoyed the tight handling and gentle roar of the engine as he methodically turned corner after corner to get to his destination.

Police cars and armed officers could be seen on every block. Security was definitely heightened after the events of the last couple of days, and anything suspicious was being acted upon immediately. Left behind backpacks were all being looked at by bomb squads being worked overtime, any fast moving person was met quickly with a string of police questions, and pedestrians were eyeing each other, suspecting something to happen with each passing glance.

The light turned from yellow to red as Bryson and the three taxis in front of him slowed to a stop. Sitting still in the Camaro reminded him of the last time he had been behind the wheel of a car...when he had been going to save his wife. *"Thank you for coming back for me."* Bryson was remembering some of his last moments with Elena; her beautiful green eyes staring at him for the last time...her brown hair blowing in the wind of the helicopter...her final smile...the white glossiness that covered her eyes...the man who had killed her...his decision to let that man live. Pain boiled up inside of Bryson again as he pictured Abd Al Aziz falling asleep to die peacefully, while his wife had been gruesomely mangled with a bullet. It was not fair that such a monster was allowed to close his eyes with no pain and never wake up. It was not fair that Elena had to have died. It was not fair that he was left behind with so much anguish.

HONK! HONK, HONK! Bryson jolted out of his thinking and shot a glance at the light; it was green. The three taxis that had been in front of him were a ways away and he was slowing up traffic. The kind people of New York and their car horns were making sure that he knew of that, and with a quick jolt, Bryson put the car back in motion.

After ten more minutes of driving, Bryson came up to the apartment building where the assassin was believed to be residing and turned left, unnoticeably, into the alleyway on the side of the building. It was a deserted alley, save for a stray cat in the distance. It would tell no secrets, much less pay attention to Bryson. Now all he had to do was sit and wait until he got the go ahead to proceed.

Thirty five minutes had passed when Bryson received a text message from the observation team, reading:

"This is observation squad Juliet Tango Romeo. Target has left premises, proceed with caution. Will text back when target is sighted returning."

He got out of the Camaro, grabbed the handgun lying in the passenger seat, as well as the grapple device that had been given to him that morning. Leaving the car running, Bryson walked over to the side of the apartment building and stopped near the wall. He tucked his handgun in the back of his pants and lifted the cable reel up towards the wall. As he placed the circular device on the wall, he pressed a button on the side of the reel. Slowly and quietly, four small screws began to enter the brick and secure the device in place.

Once Bryson heard the sound of metal entering through brick come to a stop, he turned a numbered dial on the front of the reel. He had to get to the top of 14 stories, but he did not want to overshoot his target so he turned the dial to 137 feet. He pressed another button located on the side of the reel and watched as the cable of the reel shot up through the air, similar to a small rocket. At the end of the cable was a pronged hook, and as soon as the cable had shot up around 100 feet, the hook turned inward and a small burst shot the hook towards the building. Along with the momentum of shooting upward, the hook latched securely into the wall at exactly 137 feet high, sprinkling some debris down towards Bryson, informing him that the process was complete. He walked over to the half-inch diameter cable and pulled outward on it to test its security. It hardly budged, and, looking upwards, Bryson could tell it was taut the entire length of the building.

Upwards he climbed after the cable was worked through a pulley device which had come with the reel. The pulley wrapped around his waist and clipped vertically onto the thick wire, supplying a large amount of friction, preventing Bryson from sliding down unless he pressed inward on the clip on the side of it. Despite the climb being easy with the assist of the pulley, the healing knife hole in Bryson's hand continued to be a nuisance. Every time he grasped the cable to pull up further, a slight tinge of pain began in his palm and shot up his arm reminding him that he was not invincible. Surprisingly, the wound had begun to heal rather quickly and all that was required to cover it up was a white bandage around his palm. Pushing through the pain, Bryson noticed that the top of the building was approaching and when he looked down to gauge his success; his eyes were treated to the dizzying image of a skinny alleyway containing an indistinguishable black car, 130 feet below him.

Once Bryson had climbed the last few feet, he reached up and grabbed the edge of the building, unhooked the pulley device, and pulled himself up. At the top of the apartment complex, Bryson reached over the edge of the building and pressed a small button on the side of the pronged hook embedded into the brick. The button sent a signal through a wire contained within the cable and after a short while a faint whirring noise could be heard in the distance. The circular reel device which had been screwed into the brick near the bottom of the building had since unscrewed itself and was now slowly reeling itself upwards. As soon as the reel reached the top, Bryson grabbed the end of the pronged hook and released a small latch on the lower side. The hook was permanently left in the wall, so Bryson opened the center of the circular grapple device to reveal a small compartment that contained three additional hooks. He proceeded to attach one of the extra hooks to the end of the cable by securing the latch which he had just released, and gently laid the reeling device down on the roof; he would need it later to get him and the assassin to the alley below.

Now that he was on top of the complex, Bryson checked his phone to make sure the assassin was not returning yet: no new text messages. Realizing he still only had a short amount of time, Bryson quickly walked over to the nearby front edge of the building and looked down. About eight feet below him was the balcony of the assassin's apartment, and even further down was a busy New York street filled with the sounds of horns, hums of car engines, and far-off sirens. Bryson sat down, put his feet over the edge and pushed off the ground, jumping the short length down to the balcony. He landed with a soft thud, using his training to distribute the fall to the balls of his feet rather than his heels; it was much quieter that way. Instantly, he crept over to the balcony sliding glass door and pulled on the handle. It was unlocked and Bryson walked right in, officially in the assassin's territory now.

The apartment complex was extravagant, spacious, and way too expensive for a window washer. Bryson was standing in between the kitchen and the living room, noticing every detail around him. The living room had a luscious leather couch, a leather chair, and an appropriately sized HDTV all arranged in front of the window feeding to the balcony. The kitchen was nice, complete with black marble counters, oak cabinets, and a half filled bottle of scotch near the sink. *Hmm…well at least he's got good taste in alcohol.* Bryson cautiously walked further into the apartment and took a left behind the couch. At the end of a small hallway was a room with a closed door and Bryson assumed it was the assassin's bedroom. As he walked towards it, he checked his cell phone a second time: again nothing. The lack of updates was making him a bit nervous, but perhaps the killer had gone out for a long lunch.

He grabbed the handle of the door and was disappointed to feel the lack of budge in his turn of it. The door was locked. With his non-injured palm, Bryson slammed down on the handle and broke it off the door frame. Once he was in the room, he wedged the handle back into the hole of the door. It was dusky in the room, with the only light coming from the sun shining through the spaces between the closed blinds. Walking over to the bed, Bryson noticed a briefcase lying on a chair, and changed course to go investigate it. He picked it up and tried to open it, but it too was locked. Slightly discouraged, Bryson paused for a second and looked around. Honestly, nothing looked out of place to him in this apartment, and he was starting to wonder if they did have the wrong guy. Besides this place being ridiculously expensive, nothing seemed out of the ordinary, and Bryson had yet to find anything to cause him to believe that this was the man who killed the President of the United States.

Trying to shake off doubting feelings, Bryson walked over to the walk-in closet and turned on the light inside. Once again, nothing out of the normal; a few suits were placed on hangers and a couple pairs of shoes were underneath the suit racks. Bryson pushed a couple of the suits apart from each other and was surprised to see another black suitcase that had been lying, hidden, underneath the suits. Even though he assumed it was locked, he grabbed for it anyway and was surprised to see that it was unlocked. As Bryson laid the briefcase on the ground, knelt down, and slowly opened the lid, all of his previous doubts were quickly eliminated. This was definitely someone suspicious' apartment. Inside the briefcase were numerous passports, each with a very separate identity: Christian Hastings...Igonav Svelt...Perry Erett...every passport was a different person that shared something in common: the same picture. Underneath the passports were stacks of several different types of currency including the dollar, peso, pound, and euro. There were pockets on the inside lid of the briefcase and in each one there were identical, cheap cell phones. Bryson quickly opened the backs of the first few and noticed that each one had its own SIM card. He continued to skim over the briefcase and after rummaging for a short while he came across a scary discovery near the bottom, underneath all the money: an extra magazine for a handgun.

BZZZ! BZZZ! Bryson jumped, startled, and immediately reached in his pocket and pulled out his phone to see that he had one new text message. He opened the text and noticed it was from David instead of the observation team:

"Watch squad Juliet Tango Romeo not responding...proceed with caution."

"Shit!" Bryson whispered to himself. He packed up the briefcase as quietly and quickly as he could, placed it back underneath the suits, shut off the light in the closet, and whipped out his handgun from the back of his pants. He exited from the closet with the gun pointed straight and his knees slightly bent. *How the hell would the assassin know N.E.T.S. was watching him and why the hell wasn't squad JTR responding?*

Now that someone very dangerous was on course to where Bryson was, the bedroom seemed much eerier than it had before. The small yellow spots of sun shining through the tightly closed blinds landed on the opposite wall with a strange straight-lined pattern and the dark colored paint on the walls caused the ambient light to have almost no effect on the hole-like atmosphere of the room.

Bryson had almost left the bedroom to continue into the living room when he noticed a shadow cross over a column of the sun spots projected on the wall. The motion only lasted as long as the blink of an eye, but nonetheless it had caught his attention. He froze and attempted to use his peripheral vision to see if there was anybody behind him, but could not see anything. He wrapped his finger tightly around the trigger of his gun, lifted slowly onto the balls of his feet, and swiftly turned around in one smooth motion.

The very black barrel of a gun was staring back at him and he focused his vision past the cold metal on his forehead. He was looking at the window washer who had been under N.E.T.S. surveillance for the last few days.

"Hello." The assassin said confidently despite the fact that he had a gun pointed at his chest. He glanced down at the weapon and returned his cold gaze back into Bryson's blue eyes. "I'm ready to die…so I guess the only question that remains is…are you?"

Chapter VI
A Painful Jump

It seemed to never end. The dark, long tunnel of the barrel of the assassin's gun was infinite to Bryson's eyes, and he had never seen anything *so black*. Then again, he had never been staring *this* close to the exiting end of a gun before…

"What the hell are you doing in my apartment?" A deep, but quick voice demanded. Bryson didn't respond right away and the assassin studied him closely. The man whom he had found in his apartment was not just a run-of-the-mill burglar. There was no sense of fear in this man's eyes, even with a fully loaded gun and a half-cocked trigger pointed at his skull.

"What did you do to the surveillance team?" Bryson demanded back, his gun still pointed at the assassin's heart. He was 100% sure that this man was the President's killer. He had snuck into his apartment without alerting Bryson and there was a sense of past battles in his low voice. This was not the first time that he would have to kill.

"You mean the two armed men across the street in the blue sedan, the guy who tried to call for help at the grocery store, and the man with a mole on his chin who was on the roof of the building across the street? I believe they're dead…sorry." Bryson had figured as much. In this line of work, if a team wasn't responding it was usually not because of malfunctioning radios. "So I repeat myself; why the hell are you in my apartment?" The assassin sounded angry, but looked as calm as if he was reading a newspaper. "I suspect you are part of a government organization, the CIA or FBI perhaps, who somehow discovered that I was the man who killed the President"

"So you admit you are the one who did it then?"

"Well technically speaking an unmanned rifle on the side of a high-rise killed him. I just pushed a button that sent a signal to the rifle that pulled the trigger. So yes, I confess that much. Now, I swear to God if I have to ask one more time why you are in my apartment, I will pull this trigger and spend my night cleaning this floor."

"What if I pull my trigger first?" Bryson was treading on thin ice, but he needed to figure out how to get this guy back to N.E.T.S.

"You won't pull your trigger first because I'm guessing that I'm the last link you know of to the organization that planned all of this." Bryson knew he had just been called out on his bluff and he needed to think fast. The assassin was right; there was no way that Bryson would kill him. A whole country was depending on this guy spilling his guts.

"What makes you so sure?" Bryson asked back. "How do you know the only reason I am in this apartment is because I followed a lead that could possibly lead to the President's killer? And now that I have found him, I could shoot and kill him and be a hero to the American people…" The two of them were in a deadlock. Besides their guns being aimed at each other's vital body parts, their wits were unsure of the other's intentions.

"So how much did they pay you?" Bryson tried to continue the conversation until he could figure something out. "It had to have been a ridiculous amount."

"Who says they paid me? Maybe I'm some type of crazy idealist who didn't like the guy."

"If you were an idealist, you would have identified yourself as one by now. I'm guessing they paid you enough to never have to work again?" Bryson was slowly getting used to the sensation of talking with a gun near his head. Every time he had to move his eyebrows while speaking, the cold metal of the tip of the barrel brushed his skin, sending a chill down his spine.

"They paid me well enough. What the hell do you care anyway? You're going to be dead in a few seconds."

"What makes you think that?" Bryson had a plan now.

"What makes me think that is the fact that I'm sick of your voice and my finger has slowly been pressing inward on the trigger this whole time. It was nice meeting you, asshole."

"How about a deal?" Bryson said quickly, but calmly.

"A what? What do you think this is…a game show?"

"No. I just know there is a second team on their way here right now. They are under strict orders to not enter the premises until I give them any reason too. One of those reasons would include my vital signs ceasing to exist." Bryson had confidence with where he was going with this. He just had to get the assassin to lower his guard, and his gun, for a second. "If you kill me, they will know, and they will be here within 20 seconds."

"Who's to say I can't take them all on?"

"You could try, but I should warn you that they are both heavily armed and armored. I'm not sure you would last too long using drywall and closet doors as cover. Not to mention, that's a lot of noise that I'm sure you don't want…having just killed the President and all."

"So what's the deal then?"

"Well, I *am* a man so therefore I am corruptible." Bryson explained. He could tell the assassin was interested now. "I know you were paid a handsome sum to take out the President, and I want some of it. In fact, I want 40% of it. In exchange, I'll walk out of here, tell them we got the wrong guy, tell them that the reason a window washer is in such a nice apartment is because he inherited some money, create fake files proving this, and then have your personal file deleted from our records."

"How about I blow 40% of your head off right now?" The assassin reacted to Bryson's fake proposal.

"You could. The choice is yours. Take the majority of your money and retire, or kill me and most likely die within two minutes. Your choice." The assassin's eyes revealed his dilemma as they darted back and forth in panicked thought. Gears were turning and Bryson knew he had him. Just a few moments longer…

"Damn it!" The assassin pulled the gun off Bryson's forehead and wheeled around in vexation over the fact that he was about to lose $40 million. It was in this instance of misjudgment that Bryson attempted to strike.

As quickly as he could, Bryson raised his gun in the air while taking a step towards the killer. Once he was close enough, he brought down the butt of the gun directly on the back of the assassin's head, causing a small spurt of blood to erupt from the point of impact. The assassin was dazed, and crumpled forward onto his knees while reaching to grab the wound on his head. As he reached to nurse his gash, he blind fired three shots behind him.

Bryson dropped to a prone position based on his fast auditory reflexes hearing the gunfire and the assassin spun around on his knees. With Bryson's head less than a foot away, the killer lifted one of his knees and brought it down on Bryson's head. THWACK! The pain seared in Bryson's neck as the knee connected with the side of his head. THWACK! Another knee blow directly to the head made his cranium sound hollow after the hit. The assassin brought up his knee for another hit, but Bryson rolled to the side and swung his right leg over his head, kicking his attacker straight in the mouth. The assassin reeled from the hit, instantly clutching his mouth, with blood visibly seeping through his fingers. Both men immediately got to their feet in order to defend themselves.

The killer, staggering and wiping blood from his lip, still had his gun in his hand and turned around to raise the gun at Bryson. All that was in front of him was an empty, dark bedroom with three bullet holes in the wall that had missed their target. Bryson was nowhere to be found so he proceeded to crouch down on his knees slightly and begin searching.

Slowly he walked to the closet where Bryson had investigated just moments ago and flipped on the light in a swift motion: nothing. He turned around; gun still pointed out in front of him and exited the bedroom into the living room. Walk slowly…point gun over couch…*nothing*…keep walking…*where did he go*…swing around chair…*nothing*…*did he leave*? The assassin was in a mechanical thinking mode now: *stay calm and think straight and you will stay alive.* He continued his hunt throughout his apartment with his gun ready to fire this time. There would be no second conversation.

Bryson had made his way to the roof of the apartment complex from the balcony and was crouched, waiting to strike. As soon as the assassin stepped out on his balcony he would tackle him from above, hopefully knock him out, and take him home as planned.

The recent events had gotten out of control but Bryson should have expected it; this organization always seemed to be a step ahead of N.E.T.S. *At least I know for sure that this is the President's murderer* Bryson thought quietly.

Suspense for both parties was tense and each man was getting antsy to attack. Inside, the killer was searching left and right for Bryson's hiding spot, and on the roof, Bryson was trying to hide while keeping an eye out for his enemy. After an anxious wait, Bryson finally heard the sliding glass door to the balcony slowly pulling back. Quickly, he peered over the edge of the roof and saw two arms clenching a handgun, moving forward as they exited the doorway. Bryson ducked back down so he wouldn't be seen and closed his eyes; his ears would instruct him as to when to strike.

The assassin was sweeping over the decently sized balcony very slowly. He was positive that the man whom he had found in his bedroom had to be out here. There was no other place that he could have gone, except out the front door, and that was unlikely because that man still had an objective to complete. However, as he scanned the balcony, he still couldn't see the elusive agent.

"Where the fuck are you?" The assassin whispered angrily to himself as he approached the center of the balcony. He stood still for a moment, holding on to the handgun, muscles loose and ready to pull the trigger. Glancing around, the balcony railing caught his eye. *Maybe he jumped over it and is hanging on the other side, or even dropped down to a lower apartment's window?*

Bryson could hear the assassin below him, starting to walk away from him. Focusing harder, he noticed the footsteps were not going back inside, but further outward on the balcony. *He must think I'm hanging from the railing...* Peeking very slowly, Bryson stuck his head up and was rewarded with the sight of the assassin bending over his balcony railing, pointing his gun down the side of the front of the complex. This might be the only time that Bryson would have the element of surprise and he took advantage of it.

He slung his feet in front of him over the side of the roof, ready to jump down. As soon as his feet hit the balcony, he would drop to his butt and kick out the back of the assassin's knees. From there, he would hopefully knock him out over the side of the head with the butt of his gun. At least that was the plan…

Bryson pushed himself off the roof with a strong sense of determination, but before he had fallen halfway to the balcony he sensed something was wrong. While Bryson was in mid-air the assassin began cranking around with his gun held in his straight arms. Luckily, Bryson also had his gun in his grasp and as he was falling he raised it up, pointing it straight at the assassin.

Both men were caught up in the moment. The assassin's vision was still blurred as he rapidly turned around, but he could make out the sight of a man above him, dropping downward. Bryson's balance was non-existent from the stunt. He was relying fully on instincts. The assassin's gun was making its way round towards pointing straight at Bryson. Bryson's gun was falling with his body, pointing directly at the assassin. The assassin fired his weapon but its sound was instantly deafened by the sound of Bryson's gun firing.

The two opposite guns had been directly lined up, with barrels touching, at the point of fire. The resulting phenomenon caused both firearms to be ripped from their user's grasp due to the sheer force of impact the colliding bullets produced as they exited the barrels.

Both men let out a short yell of pain as their hands deflected backwards and less than a second later, Bryson's feet had landed on the balcony.

"Son of a bitch!" The assassin shouted, bringing his feet around and kicking Bryson's out from under him. Bryson, still in shock of what had just occurred, broke his fall on the balcony floor with his face and winced as he heard the soft thud of his skull on the stamped concrete. His eyes were open but his world was blurred from the impact. The assassin reached down, grabbed Bryson by the throat with both hands, and began to pick him up off the ground. Bryson latched onto the man's wrists as his knees began to lift off the ground and pressed his thumbs as hard as he could inward on the underside of the killer's wrists. The action triggered an often forgotten pressure point in both of the assassin's arms, and he reluctantly let go of Bryson's neck out of shocking pain. Now stable on his feet, Bryson readied for a fight.

Two quick punches from Bryson collided with the man's stomach and he bent over, absorbing the blows. Bryson followed the short combo with a roundhouse to the face leading the killer to stumble back towards the entrance of the patio.

Bryson audaciously approached the wounded dog and brought his leg back then forward with force.

His foot collided with the target's chest and launched him backwards several feet through the open patio door and into the apartment. Bryson hurried in after the nearly-beaten man and clenched his shirt as he began to lift him off of the ground.

He had always found it odd that most fights often mirror themselves throughout the course of the struggle. Just a few seconds ago he had been beaten and picked up, while now he was returning the favor in a sense. Bryson brought the battered man's face to within a half foot of his own.

"It's time you come with me." Bryson studied the assassin a moment; his hair was hanging since his face was looking down and it seemed he had run out of options.

"Not yet, asswipe." The assassin promptly delivered his knee to Bryson's groin as he answered Bryson's command. Bryson was forced to let go and crumpled to his knees in pain. His stomach was in his throat and he could feel the urge to vomit coming closer. The fight was mimicking itself again, but not in Bryson's advantage as the assassin walked over to the kitchen counter and grabbed the half full bottle of scotch. Reeling out of agony, Bryson could do little but attempt to stumble to his feet as the killer walked back to him and seized the bottle by the neck.

Darkness became Bryson's new world. He was in a peaceful place now: a simple dark abyss where no N.E.T.S. existed and no President's killer was attempting to murder him. Just him and the airy floating of nothingness. He felt like he had been there for years, or maybe seconds. Who knew? He had no body in this world, just hundreds of thoughts. It was relaxing, pure, empty, smelly…there was something pungent floating around in the air now. It was a distinctive odor, but Bryson couldn't put a finger on it just yet. His thoughts were too hollow to organize them into an idea. The smell was getting stronger by the second and now there was a second sense coming into play: pain. Bryson could feel a terrible pain coming from somewhere, but once again he didn't know exactly where. Both were getting more intense and ruining the darkness.

Light was creeping back into the picture and soon consciousness regained itself. Bryson felt his eyelids slowly creep open and tried to piece together what happened. The last thing he remembered was a half clear, half brown bottle being swung at him…*Shit! How long have I been knocked out?* The smell had been the odor of a fermented alcohol known as scotch and it was obvious why he was feeling epic amounts of pain at the moment. A glass bottle had just been swung like a baseball bat at his head and shattered on impact.

Bryson could hear footsteps in the distance and slowly tried to focus his vision in a particular direction. The scotch was everywhere and stung his nostrils, throat, and eyes. Every time he took a breath, his lungs were met with a fierce burning that only further escalated his pain. Lying in the pool of alcohol, Bryson's hair was soaked with the brown liquid as well as what he assumed to be his own blood.

The footsteps were coming closer and Bryson kept one eye slightly open while remaining still. Although blurry, he could make out a figure walking from the bedroom, past Bryson's body, to the balcony door. There was red on his face, most likely blood from the previous fight, and he was carrying two black briefcases as he briskly rounded the exit to his balcony. The assassin was leaving for good and Bryson knew he had to pull it together and act fast. He gathered all his strength while keeping an eye out on the balcony for where the killer was going.

It seemed as if his muscles were unresponsive as he tried to get his legs and arms to move. Meanwhile, he noticed the assassin toss one briefcase up onto the roof, soon followed by the second one which Bryson had been able to get into. *Does he think I'm dead?* Bryson asked himself, silently confused as to why the assassin hadn't just killed him. He remembered his bluff about the second team storming the apartment if he died. *Guy must not want to take his chances. Lucky for me.*

A tingling sensation was surging through his legs and arms as he could feel their nerves and abilities kicking back in. Slowly, Bryson was able to place his arms on the floor and push his chest off the ground as his feet began to move too. He glanced outside again and saw the lower half of the assassin's body scrambling onto the roof just as he was coming to his feet. All around him was broken glass, some stained with blood, and a large puddle of the rich liquid that had been inside the bottle.

Bryson hurried out through the door and although his legs were still not fully awake yet, he jumped high enough to grasp the edge of the roof of the apartment complex. Luckily, his arms were operational and Bryson used his strength to pull himself onto the flat, barren roof. Just a few feet away lay the device which he had used to get up here in the first place and as Bryson focused his vision past the device, he saw the assassin running full speed towards the opposite end of the roof of the complex.

"Shit!" Bryson could not let the killer get away. He owed it not only to the people of the United States, but also to David, to catch this man. Grabbing the grapple, Bryson scrambled to his feet and began chasing after the man. His feet were pounding through the white, chalky gravel that covered the roof like so many other buildings in New York. Each step kicked up dust behind him and created a loud crunch informing his target he was in pursuit. He saw the assassin look over his shoulder as he neared the edge of the building and both men ran harder than before. Bryson knew he wasn't going to catch up; he was just too far behind and the assassin was just as fast as he was.

Still sprinting, Bryson got an ingenious idea and began to judge the amount of distance between him and the assassin. 50 feet? 65? Bryson looked down at the grapple and grasped the dial that was set to zero feet. Desperately he turned it to 70 feet and clutched the device with both hands, meanwhile aiming it at the assassin. Bryson pressed inward on the ignition button.

The cable shot away from the device towards the sprinting assassin. He was going to try and jump from the roof of the apartment complex to the building behind it. Bryson heard a small pop and noticed that the pronged hook had deployed from the horizontally-shooting cable and shot its momentum slightly downwards just as it had when he was using it to scale the building.

Step. The assassin knew something was coming but he had to keep running. *Step.* If he could jump to the next building's roof he just might get away. *Step.* His heart was pounding and all pain was eliminated by adrenaline. *Step.* All he needed was three more steps and he could jump and clear the gap between the buildings. *Step.* What was that noise? *Step.* He clenched his calf muscles and prepared to jump. *Step.*

"Arrghhh!" The pronged hook had shot through the assassin's lower right leg as he had prepared to jump. Bryson, still running and holding onto the device could see a mist of blood explode out the front side of the leg as he jumped off the building. The impact and absolute pain from the hook entering his calf had caused the killer's jump to be weak and off balance. As he soared through the air, both men knew that he was not going to clear the gap, but plummet straight down between the two buildings.

"Well, shit." The words had no sooner left Bryson's lips then the mechanism to which he was holding onto locked in place at 70 feet and nearly ripped out of his arms. The assassin hooked onto the other end had gravity on his side and was falling faster than Bryson could run. It was all Bryson could do to not let go of the device and stay on his feet, but he was fast approaching the same edge of the building that the President's killer had just fallen off. Bryson had to think fast. If he let go of the device the man would plummet to the concrete below and if he attempted to stop, the hook would most likely rip out of his leg and leave him falling anyway. Bryson could not let this man die, he was too valuable. Still sprinting, trying to keep up with the yanking device, Bryson committed to what he was about to do: jump down with the grapple. It was suicide but he was hoping that he would get lucky and maybe catch onto something…

Nearly two strides away from the edge the device stopped pulling on his grip. He skidded to a halt and stopped just inches from the corner of the apartment complex roof. Sliding had caused a small plume of white gravel from the roof to shoot over the edge and quietly fall down the side of the fourteen story building. Bryson dreaded looking over the edge; the only reason the tugging stopped was because the assassin had come undone from the device's hook. Slowly he leaned forward and focused his vision downward. He traced the 70 feet of cable with his eyes and holding his breath, hoped against hope that his adversary was still bloodily attached to the opposite end. He breathed a sigh of relief to see the killer below him hanging on to the railing of the fire escape of the opposite building. The cable was still in his leg, with the barbed hook forbidding it to exit the way in which it had come resulting in a look of complete agony plastered on his face. Bryson laid the device down on the ground and sat on top of it, weighing it down with his own force. He pressed the second button on the device causing it to attempt to bring the 70 feet of cable back into the reel.

"Arghhh! Son…of…a…bitch!" The assassin screamed as the hook started pulling upward on his leg. He was still clinching onto the fire escape railing, trying to fight the horsepower of the pulling cable.

"It will hurt a lot less if you let go!" Bryson joked as he yelled down towards the man. After a few more seconds of trying to stay where he was, the assassin let go of the railing and swung over, smacking into the side of the apartment complex's brick wall. The device was working hard, whirring loudly as it pulled up its heavy load. Slowly, the cable rolled up length by length, carrying with it its struggling victim. The grapple had never been designed to be a functioning weapon, but in a time of desperate need it had served its purpose well.

As Bryson sat there waiting, the assassin's foot appeared from just over the edge of the building so he pressed the button a second time, stopping the reeling motion. Still sitting on the device Bryson reached out and grabbed the spot where the hook joined the cable just on the outside of the assassin's bloody, maimed leg.

"It's funny," Bryson started to say, "This isn't really a weapon…or a torture device for that matter." He gave the cable a quick yank upward.

"DAMN IT!" The assassin was fuming through the pain now. "I swear I will ring your fucking neck!" His teeth were gritted together and spit was coming out of his mouth with each syllable as he hung upside down, 14 stories in the air.

"Oh really? Hmmm…well that's interesting because I could easily end your life right now." Bryson grabbed the latch securing the hook to the cable as he continued, "You see, all I have to do…"

He yanked a second time resulting in a second outburst of pain, "is unhook this latch right here and you will fall right on your head."

"Argghhh. DO IT THEN!" The assassin screamed in reply. Both men knew Bryson was bluffing so each of them backed off significantly. Bryson reached out, grabbed the assassin by the uninjured leg and pulled him up onto the roof. The man's pants were soaked with blood and the crimson coloring had started a trail downwards on the silver cable. Bryson laid the man face-up on the gravel as he writhed in agony.

"Welcome back." Bryson stated as if greeting a friend. The heel of Bryson's left foot connected with the forehead of the killer leaving a small imprint of the sole. He then got down on his knees and grabbed the man with both hands around the throat. Squeezing, he focused on the man's vital signs as he attempted to struggle. Bryson wanted him to pass out long enough so he could bring him back to N.E.T.S. headquarters but not die from lack of oxygen.

The assassin had little energy left to struggle. Breathing was not possible and soon his vision of a bloodied villain against a blue sky began to fade into blurs. Despite the fact his attacker's hands were wrenched down tightly on his throat, the assassin noticed the lack of expression coming from his opponents face; even as he took the life out of a man: nothing. Finally after less than a minute of panic he closed his eyes and allowed the darkness and dreams to swallow him whole.

CHAPTER VII
A MORNING AT THE OPERA

MONDAY JUNE 26TH, 2017
DOWNTOWN WASHINGTON D.C.

A light filtered in slowly between his eyelids and soon a blurred image greeted his vision. After laying there, accepting the hazy scene, he brought his fists up to his eyes and gently rubbed them back and forth, clarifying the dream of the beige painted ceiling peering back at him. The bed in which he was lying was remarkably comfortable; large and elegant with cream and burgundy sheets. It had been three days since he had visited the Pentagon.

He sat up slowly, letting muscles adjust to being out of their slumber, and stretched his toned, muscular arms above his head. The suite's complimentary 42-inch HDTV was in front of him, looking as if it were a glossy black portal to another life. After stretching all of his appendages, Ian Tract reached over to the nightstand on his left and grabbed the remote control, pressing the power button as he shifted his feet to the side of the bed and got up. Standing in nothing more than his compression shorts, he walked over to the large window on the other side of the bed and pulled a cord on the wall. The blinds covering the window turned ninety degrees and sunlight shot across the room, landing on the opposing wall.

On the TV Ian could hear exactly what he knew he would hear: talk about the terrorist threat that had aired yesterday. His fellow associate in the Aqarab Mayta had delivered a powerful message to the United States and served his purpose to the fullest potential. It was strange, Ian thought, that the man plastered all over the news, the man whom he had just encouraged to commit suicide, was most likely dead by now. The world was holding its breath over threats from a ghost…he ignored the rest of the broadcast.

The Washington Monument stood strong across the horizon. It almost looked as if it were an ancient weapon; a giant sword for the behemoth of the United States. It pierced the blue sky and defeated any sunlight that came near it by reflecting it back for miles on end. Ian looked down, saw the busy street filled with traffic and pedestrians, and then returned his gaze to the famous structure at the heart of D.C. It was truly a gorgeous day at the nation's capital. The weather seemed to be mocking the American citizens below. Terrified with fear and not knowing if the future was even certain, they were treated with a day which they had no time or energy to enjoy. Ian cared little. He wasn't doing this to prove some religious point or to carry out the whims of a madman. He did this because it was fun. *I guess that makes me a madman…*

Slowly, he took a step back from the window, sunlight drenching his flawless core. He bent over gradually and placed his fingers underneath his feet, making sure to keep his knees straight and breathing even. Ian began to count in his head while quietly mouthing the words. *One*…exhale…*Two*…inhale… *Three*…they were so close…*Four*…the lactic acid was beginning to swim in his upper calves…*Five*…he had to be ready for what was coming…*Six*…a shower and some breakfast sounded good…*Seven*…*Eight*…*Nine*…did they figure it out yet?…*Ten*. His body unfolded as he stood straight, and turned around to walk away from the window.

The shower he was in had a powerful stream; Ian thoroughly enjoyed it. Hands against the wall, leaning over slightly, he stood there accepting the liquid massage coursing over his skin. The water was hot and left a soft singeing sensation as it came in contact with Ian, but he didn't care. The amount of pain was small and soon his body became accustomed to the temperature causing him to turn up the heat a little more. Straightening his neck underneath the stream of falling liquid, he let the spray hit the top of his head. Despite it running down his face, he kept his eyes open and head straightforward. As the water fell over his eyes his vision got glossy; it was distorting his reality. It was an awkward feeling, having something flow over his open eyes. Instinctively, he wanted to close his eyelids but fought the temptation and let the water continue to enter in. Ignoring instincts felt soothing.

After washing up and spending a few more minutes under the heavenly showerhead, Ian got out of the shower, dried off, and wrapped a towel around his midsection. He exited the bathroom and was in front of a large mirror behind two sinks surrounded by granite countertops. The mirror returned a pleasing image and Ian took a minute to admire all the hard work which had paid off. His body was not only near-flawless, but dangerous. Trained in numerous forms of close-quarters combat, gun service, explosives, hacking, and seduction, his body was a weapon that effectively completed any task set for it. As he looked in the mirror, he caught a glance of the clock by his bed in the reflection. He deciphered the backwards numbers in his head and the clock read 9:37 A.M. Towel still wrapped around his waist he decided to go to the small kitchen in his room and make some breakfast. He would need some nutrients and an able mind for later.

He turned the stove top from HIGH to OFF and with a small "click" the electricity ceased and the surface began to cool. The small, double-egg, ham-and-cheese omelet remained in the frying pan as Ian reached in the refrigerator, grabbed some pears and strawberries, and shut the door. The cool breath of the inside of the refrigerator iced his skin, which was still warm from the hot shower, and the tingling sensation caused the hairs on his arm to stand up for a short moment. As soon as the door closed the feeling fled. Placing the fruit on a cutting board, Ian simultaneously reached for a sharp knife and began to start slicing.

Small. That's how he liked his fruit. Eating whole fruits had never really appealed to him; he liked to chop them up into small bites. He figured this was because that way he could combine flavors of fruits together easily. This morning, for example, he would enjoy the combination of juicy, stern pears, with sweet, vibrant strawberries. Along with his omelet, which he now dropped onto a plate, and his fruit, Ian poured himself a glass of pomegranate-orange juice. He sat down at the table in the middle of the living room of his suite and picked up the remote at the center. Sun powered through this room, similar to the way it did in his bedroom; it truly was a perfect day outside. He considered himself lucky that he was on the top floor of the seven-floored establishment, that way he could see the environment rather than the other buildings. Ian rocked his fork back and forth quickly on a corner of the omelet, stabbed the separated piece, and placed it in his mouth. *Delicious…although it needs some salt.*

Remote still in hand, he pointed it at the far wall near the main window and pressed the power button. A quiet humming could be heard coming from the stereo system located in the corner, so Ian held down his thumb on the volume button and it increased until the room was as filled with music as it was with sunlight. The classic opera that was playing engulfed his senses. Thoroughly enjoying the surrounding sounds, Ian continued his breakfast. On one side of his fork he had a plump section of pear with light green skin, and on the other side, a healthy, bright red strawberry. The combination of flavor on his taste buds was ecstasy as he closed his eyes while he finished chewing. With the opera still playing on in the background, Ian quietly finished his breakfast, still sitting in nothing more than his towel. He took the last sip of juice, grabbed his plate, and stood up out of his chair. The music was conducting his movements, the beat and rhythm of the song seemed to be guiding him to his next morning chore. He washed the plate, the frying pan, fork, and glass that he had just used and stuck it back into the cabinet from where they had come. The microwave read 10:14 A.M.; he figured they were coming soon given that he was fourteen minutes late for his follow up "psychology" appointment at the Pentagon…

He could have left by now. He *should* have left. Somewhere deep inside of him his conscious begged the question: *Why did you stay in the same city these extra days? They will come for you! They ARE coming for you!* Many years ago, Ian would have known that he was crazy for staying. The Pentagon officials would know by now that he was somehow tied to Al Aziz's death, even if they couldn't prove it. *I'm sure they are coming here expecting a vacant hotel room.*

But Ian was looking forward to it. *It* was the challenge that they brought when they came knocking on his door. *It* was the violence that would ensue. *It* was the adrenaline that came with performing feats well above average means. Ian had no trouble admitting it; he was addicted. Addicted to this lifestyle and everything that came with it. In anyone else's hands it would have been a reckless addiction, but Ian knew he was more than capable.

He returned in front of the mirror and placed both hands on the countertop leaning forward, looking deep into his own, returning gaze. As much as he wanted the delicious taste of his breakfast to remain on his tongue, he decided against it and reached for his toothbrush. The opera still resonating in background allowed for him to relax as he brought the bristles of the brush back-and-forth over his teeth. The hot water running from the sink in front of him was creating a rising steam that caused tiny droplets to form on Ian's rippled core as they came in contact with his skin. He spit the remnants of the toothpaste out, cleaned his brush, and turned off the steamy water. He returned to his bedroom, still plastered with sunlight and still in the range of the opera melodies. 10:19 A.M. Ian walked over to the closet and pulled back the sliding white privacy door. There were two silver suitcases on the top shelf; one was about three feet in length while the other was normal size. Standing in his bare feet, Ian reached up and grabbed the handle of each, pulling them down and placing them side by side on the bed. Each suitcase had two simple latches and Ian swiftly unhooked each latch with a nearly inaudible "click". The spring loaded tops of the briefcases swung up to a 90-degree position revealing the tools of Ian's profession: guns.

In the larger briefcase, placed precisely in the foam cushioning, were two Spectre M4 sub-machine guns, equipped with silencers and slings. Lying in the middle of the case were extra magazines and a pair of sleek, compact goggles. Ian grabbed each Spectre one by one and removed the silencers; it was going to get loud anyway, no reason to muzzle the velocity of the bullets. He grabbed the goggles, stretched the elastic headband, and placed them on his head. Because he didn't need them just yet, he moved the eyepieces to the top of his forehead.

Moving on, Ian shifted his attention to the smaller briefcase. Although less significant, this case packed just as big of a punch, containing two Beretta M9 handguns, also equipped with extra magazines. Underneath the padding of the M9's were two holsters that clipped onto the Spectre slings. Ian quickly grabbed the M9 on the left, cocked it with a "chhhhick-chick" and placed it back down, repeating the task with the second M9 on the right half of the suitcase.

The opera continuing in the background still soothed him; it kept his inner beast in check and allowed his nerves to stay calm. Calm nerves led to smooth movements. Smooth movements led to good concentration. Good concentration led to impeccable accuracy. And impeccable accuracy led to deaths. This is how Ian operated; this is how he did his job. Focused on the task at hand, Ian grabbed the extra M9 clips and stuck them in the waistline of the towel. The cold, black medal was shocking to the skin at first, but soon the temperatures between Ian's body and the clip met at equilibrium. *Maybe I should put some clothes on?...Too late now.* Ian reached for the Spectre M4 magazines and attached them to the pouches on the slings. Grabbing the sub-machine guns themselves, Ian placed the slings over his chest, with one Spectre hanging on either side of him, followed by the M9s entering their holsters. The adrenaline was beginning to flow now and he hardly even felt the weight of the four guns hanging underneath his armpits. The towel and ammo clips merged into one and felt like they became a part of him. The sound waves coming from the opera were entering his ears, but he could not *hear* it. This was where he needed to be: concentrated.

Ian left the bedroom and entered back into the living room, scanning over the layout and planning his defense. The large double doors that were the entrance to the hotel hallway were located in front of him and to the left slightly. Gripping the arm of the white couch, he rotated it so that the front of it was facing the doors and did the same with the champagne colored armchairs on either side of the couch. Analyzing his newly created 10-foot long source of cover, Ian realized there was more he could do. He jolted over to the kitchen where he had recently made his breakfast, and threw open one of the drawers. Inside were four cutting knives, but as they stood now, they were additional ammo. Knives in hand, Ian went back behind his cover, laid them on the floor, pulled the goggles over his head, and crouched down behind the white couch, both hands stuffed with the trigger of a Spectre. He gazed forward and saw his reflection in the fireplace window that linked the living room to the bedroom. Lethality now had an image. Squatting down so his bottom was sitting on his heels, jet black goggles covering his eyes contrasting the white towel hanging from his waist, six-pack scrunched up, and sub-machine guns pointing upward on either side of his face; these were the aspects that molded the portrait of a warrior. *10:30 A.M....any second now...* He could have left by now. He *should* have left by now.

His attention subconsciously turned towards the opera still blaring. It was one of his favorite songs – a true classic: Por Ti Volare. The soft sound of the beginning orchestra was all that filled his head, and he closed his eyes, soaking in the notes echoing throughout the large hotel suite.

"Cuando vivo solo
sueño un horizonte
falto de palabras"

The quick words were sung with such confidence. The song was beautiful and epic, perfect for what was about to happen…
KNOCK! KNOCK! KNOCK!
"Thomas Henry!" A strong male voice called out. "We need to speak with you. You are needed for questioning at the Pentagon immediately!"
Ian pressed a button on the side of his goggles and his world turned blue. Thermal imaging was his new vision, anything with heat ranged from green (low heat) to red (high heat). Everything else was blue. He could have left by now. He *should* have left by now.
"Sir we can hear your music!" A second male voice added, "We are not asking! This is an order. Come out now and quietly come with us to the Pentagon or we will be forced to make you!"
Ian placed one of the Spectres over his head and fired a single shot at the door.
On the other side, splinters of white-painted wood scattered across the hall.
"Well then. I guess we have our answer." The Pentagon official out in the hall grabbed his sidearm and looked to the heavily

armed four-man teams to his right and left. "Alpha, smoke and clear. Beta, clear after Alpha. Agent Garrison and myself will provide support from the hall. Go silent people, we don't want to draw attention from the street." All the men quietly screwed silencers onto the barrels of their machine guns while the leader of Alpha pulled a smoke grenade off of his combat vest and drew the door ajar.

Ian loved this song, it was just about to come up on the best part…a small "*clink*" hit the ground between the couch-cover and the front entrance. Soon after, a faint hissing could be heard as Ian sensed the air around him becoming more dense. *Smoke grenades, so amateur.*

"Por ti volaré"

"Breach! Breach! Breach!"

"Espera"

Ian popped up from behind the couch with the Spectres pointed forward. The billowing smoke was only discernable to him by the sense of smell. Through his goggles, all that remained was blue, with a speck of red emanating from the smoke grenade canister on the floor. He watched as the first four-man team filtered in the door; two went right towards the living room, and the other two went left towards the kitchen. Their yellow, orange, and green bodies stood out easily against the blue atmosphere.

"Que llegaré"

Pressing inward on the triggers of the Spectres, Ian targeted two separate men and released an axis of bullets in their direction. Both of the colored blobs plummeted to the floor while the two left alive began to fire in the direction where they had heard the shots.

Smoke continued to pour from the grenade as Ian heard, "Beta team – breach!"

"Mi fin de trayecto eres tú"

Ian ducked for cover behind the couch as he pointed both the sub-machine guns over the back and blind-fired across the room. He knew now that they did not have thermal vision like he did, the purpose of the grenade had been to "smoke him out" so to speak. After all, he was just a psychiatrist for all they knew. Sensing that the clips in the Spectre's were almost up, he immediately pressed the release button on the side of the guns, and slammed them inward on the extra magazines wedged tight between his towel and skin. Again, he raised the guns over his furniture barricade and blind-fired away.

Shots were slamming into the walls around him: some burst from an M16 plummeted into one of the chairs he was using for cover, a SPAS shotgun spread destroyed the mantle on the fireplace, and he could hear a couple of powerful handguns firing from the hallway. His adrenaline was up and he was in his element; he couldn't help but smile.

"Para vivirlo los dos.
Por ti volaré"

Ian continued to hold down on the triggers of the Spectres until they were out of ammo.

"He's out! He's out!" He overheard one of the soldiers say. Immediately, he dropped the guns and allowed them to hang from their straps by his side. He reached for the knives on the ground next to him, and stood up from behind his cover. Smoke was still billowing from the grenade on the floor, and Ian could see three men running towards his position through the smoke…

The soldier knew that Thomas Henry was out of ammo and also that he was not the psychiatrist he claimed he was. He was closing in on him right now through the smoke with two additional men right behind him. Although he could not see well, the smoke was not bothersome because they had been provided with breathing apparatuses and clear goggles to keep their eyes and lungs clear. *He must be fortified in his bedroom. Based on the layout of the room,*

he should be right in front of …The soldier never finished his thought. Instead, a short gleam of silver entered his vision before a screaming pain took over his head for a split second. His already-deceased body hit the floor just moments before the other two men's bodies that had been behind him. They all shared one thing in common: a single knife lodged deeply in between their eyes.

Ian tallied up the deaths and realized that he was halfway done. Five men were down, three remained, with two Pentagon agents in the hall. He had a single knife left, he was out of sub-machine gun ammo, and he still had the two fully loaded pistols.

Por Ti Volare continued to blast in the background. The man singing was expressing his love and the distances he would go for the woman he adored. It was a passionate battle between his voice and the orchestra accompanying him, not at all similar to the bestial battle that was occurring in the hotel room between man vs. man. Spectres still dangling by his side, Ian grasped a Beretta in each hand and stood up from behind the couch with arms extended and barrels facing forward. Goggles still in use, he saw the three soldiers still in the room, and the two agents in the hallway; all five men were taking cover waiting for the next move. The remaining five were waiting to see what had become of the three that had gone into the smoke, but were oblivious to the fact that they had been ended with silence.

Ian unloaded both clips of the Beretta M9s into the various items of cover that the three men in the room were using. A few bullets into the kitchen table, a few into the counter, a few into the door of the guest room…none of the shots injured the men, but that was the point. Out of ammo, Ian quickly reloaded both guns and focused them back at their targets.

Having had their cover shot at, the men knew now that Thomas Henry was not dead and that their colleagues most likely were…somehow. They had to return fire and end this now.

Ian had fired numerous rounds into their cover to get them out of it. *Fire into cover always returns fire out of cover*…the smoke was starting to dissipate now. It still covered most of the room but pockets were now missing sporadically in what used to be a solid wall of grey. The man behind the guest room door crouched down and swung out to return fire. Ian fired a single shot that hit the man in the mouth, instantly following that shot with one directed at his head. Both of the remaining men in cover turned to look as the blood splattered the walls and their teammate found a comfortable position on the white and gold tiled floor. Ian fired a third shot that made contact with the hand of the man behind the counter, resulting in screams of pain from the loss of multiple fingers. His counterpart stood up from behind the kitchen table to return fire and three bullets entered his body.

Shots began to ring in from the hallway, signaling the agents still very present in the situation. After removing the Spectre straps from across his chest, Ian moved out from behind his cover, being careful to keep the remaining smoke between him and the doorway. Nearly at the kitchen counter, he peeked over the top and was greeted with the butt of a SPAS shotgun headed straight for his head. Reacting at an un-human speed, Ian sidestepped, grabbed the small stock handle of the gun, wrapped his finger around the trigger and pulled. There was a resounding boom as the man who had tried to hit Ian flew backwards into the wall from the impact of the nearly-point-blank shotgun burst to the chest.

The agents in the hall were about to make their move. There were a few final wisps of smoke floating around and from the sound of it, one of their soldiers had ended the shootout with a shotgun blast. The man known as Agent Garrison was on one side of the entrance, leaning strongly against the wall with his gun held tightly in both hands. Agent Drake was on the other wall, mirroring Garrison's stance. Drake lifted a hand from his handgun and with two fingers gave a "let's go" motion and both men swung out from behind the door frame. They entered the obliterated room. It still exuded a sense of glamour and elegance with its large walls and stylistic features, but regardless, the bullet holes and bodies on the floor detracted from the elegance. Both men, guns extended and ready to fire, swept the room with their eyes.

Abriendo los ojos por fin
Contigo viviré.

"Garrison…" Agent Drake nodded at the stereo still blasting the god-awful opera song in Spanish.

"Yeah." Garrison understood the nod and headed toward the stereo. Drake continued to look around the room for Henry while Garrison reached out for the power button on the stereo.

Por ti volaré…

CLACK! Garrison crumpled to the ground, a bullet stuck firmly in his back. Drake spun around, gun in hand, and saw his target across the room. Thomas Henry was standing there in nothing but a bath towel wrapped around his waist and a pair of black goggles resting on top of his head. In his hands were two handguns, one pointed at the most-likely-dead Agent Garrison and the other pointed at Drake's chest.

Drake's head filled with the sounds of the opera. It was terrible music; he was more of a classic rock type of guy. This crap was just an orchestra playing with some strong voiced guy singing in a different language.

Ian's head filled with the sounds of the opera. It was beautiful music; a gorgeous song. The voice of the artist was absent during this orchestral swing during the approach to the climax of the song. It was so moving, *Por Ti Volare…For you I'll fly*. The man in the song echoed one final, emphatic note:

VOLAAARRRREEEEEEEEE!!!

Drake wondered if he should take his shot now. Both men were locked in a standstill as the song ended. Ian raised the gun that had been pointed at Garrison, backwards, and shot at the stereo behind him. A small explosion of sparks shot out and littered the floor as Ian dropped the handgun, one still pointed at the agent.

"You aren't a professional psychiatrist are you?" Drake asked, already knowing the answer. The man he believed to be Thomas Henry looked back up at him and shook his head. It was anybody's move, but destiny had already made its choice: Ian had a plan. Reaching down with his one empty hand, he slipped the thumb on the inside of the towel around his waist. In one fluid motion he gripped the towel, pulled, and threw it upward towards the Pentagon agent. Drake, by instinct, glanced up at the towel now flying through the air at him. By the time he returned his gaze to Henry he realized he was dead. He saw the flash of the handgun as the bullet travelled across the room. It entered and exited through the falling towel, leaving a small, black, and burnt ring along the white fringes of the hole. Moments later, the towel landed on the ground, stained red by the blood of a failed and dead Pentagon agent.

Ian stood alone in his room, naked, and marveled in his accomplishment. After a second of self-indulgence, he realized that he had to act quickly. The agent he had just killed was a similar height to him, so he quickly went over and took the man's clothes off. Ian ran back to his bedroom, grabbed a pair of compression shorts, and threw them on. Within two minutes he was dressed in Agent Drake's black and white suit. Ian bent down and grabbed the handgun from the man's lifeless fingers, placing it in his beltline. The suit coat had some weight to it and reaching in to the pockets, Ian discovered a set of car keys and a pair of sunglasses. With a small smile, he placed the sunglasses on his face and noticed he still had the thermal goggles resting on the top of his head. He yanked them off and stuffed them in his inner jacket pocket. *Who knows? They might come in handy.*

The white double doors to his suite closed behind him as he exited into the hallway. He went to the end of the hall and called the private elevator that served his floor exclusively. The elevator arrived and Ian rode it silently down to the main lobby of the hotel. The lobby was just as extravagant as his room, equipped with numerous chandeliers, distinctive brown marble flooring, and elegant gold trim. There was a large analog clock above the revolving door exit that displayed the time: 10:45 A.M. Ian stopped in amazement. Everything that had just taken place, from the moment they had arrived to him standing alive in the lobby right now, had been over the small lapse of fifteen minutes.

Shrugging off the awkward feeling of time, Ian continued through the revolving door. He was greeted with the warmth of the sunlight, the sight of a cloudless day, the hustle and bustle of a busy city, and the sound of sirens. In front of Ian, there was a black SUV, a Chevy Suburban, parked along the curb, and completely empty. Grabbing the car keys of out of the coat pocket, Ian pressed the unlock button. The lights on the front of the Suburban blinked once and small clicking could be heard from inside the car. Ian could hear the sirens getting closer, so he casually walked around to the driver side of the car, got in, stuck the keys in the ignition, and pulled into the camouflage of Washington D.C. traffic.

MONDAY JUNE 26TH, 2017
N.E.T.S. HEADQUARTERS, NEW YORK CITY

The assassin's name was Daniel Brody and he was running on an endless rooftop. The sky was unusually vivid, not even blue; just bright, and the ground felt as if it was solid and liquid at the same time. He didn't know why he was running or even why he was on a rooftop, but it strangely felt very familiar to him, almost like déjà vu. Every time his foot struck the rooftop, no sound could be heard. Instead, it sent a tingling sensation all the way up his body. He could see the edge of the roof that he was running towards, but could not discern as to whether or not he was getting any closer to it.

Daniel tried running faster in order to gain ground on the edge but the faster he ran the further and further away it became. Slowing up his pace significantly, he felt like he needed a rest and as he did this the edge of the roof zoomed into reach. There it was. The edge which he thought he had been chasing for hours (or was it seconds?) was just…there. A strange urge coursed over Daniel's mind, an urge to just jump off the edge. There was clearly nothing else to jump to, no other platform or roof was visible; just the annoying sky and the flat roof under his feet.

Without really controlling his bodily movements, Daniel was suddenly flying through the air as he had jumped headfirst off of the rooftop. This phenomenon felt like falling, but different. It was *controlled falling*. Tears began forming as the air rushed past his eyelids, and the world he was in went from obnoxiously bright to a fading dimness. Behind him, he could *feel* something getting closer…some *thing*. Daniel turned his head over his shoulder to see what it was but he couldn't make it out. It was a long, thin shadow, twisted and bent, falling in pursuit behind him; possibly a cable or a wire? It was steadily gaining on him when he noticed it seemed to have an infinite length. There was clearly an end approaching him, but the other end was nowhere in sight. He noticed it moving, writhing, from side to side, as if it was…*slithering* through the air.

Terror slowly rose up in Daniel's gut as the nearing end of the object made its appearance. It was a snake, but not one he had ever seen before. This snake seemed to be made out of metal: metal scales, metal eyes, and a metal tongue. Besides the gleam of the shining silver, the only color on the snake's body was its sharp crimson eyes and the deep red blood that was dripping from the tips of its enormous fangs. Daniel could sense a rage within the snake; he could feel its need to consume him. He tried to fall faster, away from the beast that was quickly gaining on him, but it was not possible. He watched, terrified as the snake unhinged its metal jaw and let all of its bloody, silver teeth sink into his right calf muscle. Blood began to pour out of the muscle and trail the sky behind them, causing the sky to acquire a menacing burgundy hue. Black clouds littered the now-angry ether as Daniel and the serpent continued to fall.

There had been no initial pain when the snake had sunk its fangs into the abundant amount of flesh available in Daniel's calf. But as the pair fell the pain kept getting worse, exponentially worse in fact. What had started off as nothing more than a tickle was now coursing through his body as a signal of extreme pain. The searing, screaming noise in his leg was causing his head to feel as if it was splitting in half. This falling was never going to end; he would be falling for eternity and his pain was just going to get worse until he gave up and died. He was defeated.

Daniel felt something. He was not sure what it had been, but it had been cool and shocking, right in the center of his forehead. He felt it again, this time on his right cheek. A single drop of wetness. Soon the sensation was happening on a very frequent basis, as if it was raining upward as he was falling downward…it was a downpour now. He squinted through his eyelids to try and see what was in front of him and saw a tidal wave headed straight towards his face. It too had a red hue as the water actively reflected the current color of the sky. The wall of water crashed into his face and encased his body as well as the metal snake's. The impact had jerked his neck back causing him to begin to realize that he had been dreaming.

The liquid engulfed his vision and the dream began to collapse. Daniel felt as if he was being pulled from the nostrils and he leaned forward and flexed the muscles behind his eyelids. Unwillingly, his eyes opened, to the real reality, not the dream reality. The nightmare had ended. A new one was about to begin.

A solid chunk of matter came swinging around into Daniel's left cheek and his head was sent reeling. However, he hardly felt the pain from the punch and as his vision cleared he could see that he was staring at the man whom he had found in his apartment. The man's face had slight traces of stubble, and numerous small bandages around his forehead and eyes, most likely from where Daniel had hit him with the bottle of scotch.

"What is your name? Your real one?" The man asked as calmly as if he were asking for the time of day. Daniel couldn't really comprehend the question; his body was still adjusting to everything that was going on.

Both men were sitting in a brightly lit, white room with a mirror on one end. Surprisingly, Daniel was not handcuffed or restrained in any way, but he still felt weak for some reason. There was a bucket by the man's chair that had been previously filled with the water that was now dripping from Daniel's hair onto his clothes and the floor beneath him. Daniel still had to answer the question but before he could, the man punched him on the lower portion of his right leg. His eyes rolled to the back of his head as the pain almost caused him to pass out. It was easily the most intense pain he had ever felt and it was still hurting just as badly seconds after the punch. He looked down and saw a white bandage wrapped around his lower leg, stained deeply with his own blood. A single stream of blood was trailing down from the bandage into his shoe.

"What is your name?" The question was asked a second time. "Who are you? Why did you kill the President? Who are you working for? What are they planning?" The questions were rattled off faster than he could answer.

"Where…am…I? Turn the…goddamn…lights down." Daniel's questions were met with a thunderous smack to the forehead from the cold, steel butt of a gun. "AGRHHHH! Stop hitting me!" Daniel felt as if he could hardly get the words out of his mouth, he was almost having an out-of-body experience. He was watching himself get beat up, but still feeling all of the pain of his merciless interrogator. "What have you…done to me?"

"You have been heavily drugged. It's a special concoction that permits you to be coherent and feel most pain, but you have lost all motor skills from the neck down." The explanation was as calm and clear as possible. This man clearly knew he had the upper hand. "Now, who are you and who do you work for?"

"Why the…hell would I…tell you?" The words were coming a little easier now as he was slowly coming back to full consciousness. He glanced down at his legs and tried to move his uninjured leg: nothing. He tried to move his foot, just a little bit: still nothing.

"Alright, well then let me answer some questions for you. Your name is Daniel Brody. You are one of the best assassins-for-hire in the world and have been linked to numerous high-profile deaths. Some of your aliases have been: Iganov Svelt, Perry Erett, and Christian Hastings, to name a few. Recently you killed the President of the United States while you were under contract with the Aqarab Mayta for $100 million."

"How…do you know my…name?"

"Shut up and keep listening. Now I'm going to tell you a few things that you don't know." The man's demeanor was still as calm as could be. "You are being held by a secret organization of the United States government. Whether your contact with the Dead Scorpions informed you of us or not, I don't care. All you need to know about us is that we are completely off the radar. That means we can do whatever we want to you, and I can guarantee you we will.

"You killed the President of the United States. That fact right there means you will get the death penalty, easy. I can personally guarantee you that you will be dead within the year. Now…" Bryson changed his tone as if to offer a proposition, "if you cooperate with us, and help us to stop whatever the Aqarab Mayta are planning, your chances of a less painful execution rise slightly."

"I…don't know…anything…I just know that…they were paying…me well…so I took the…job." Words had never been such a challenge to him; it was draining what little energy he had left.

"Bullshit!" Bryson placed the muzzle of his gun directly on the assassin's left kneecap. "You killed the President because of orders from somebody! Who was it?"

"I don't…fucking…know!"

"Fine." Bryson replied calmly and slouched back in chair. He pointed the gun downward and the room filled with the "*POP!*" of a fired shot. The bullet travelled through Daniel's left shoe into his foot and the pain of the wound combined with his maimed right calf caused him to pass out immediately.

This time Daniel dreamt of nothing. He was in a world of pulsating darkness. Every throb of pain caused the black world around him to resonate in waves. Although he could not see the physical peaks and valleys of the blackness, he could *feel* it…like a person walking past him in his hole, again, and again, and again.

Bryson had been sitting in his chair patiently for five minutes and thirty-seven seconds when the assassin regained consciousness. During this time, a team of medical officials had come in to tend to his wounds, as well as setting up an IV to help keep the pain at a tolerable level without him passing out again. They had just shut the door as the assassin reopened his eyes to the interrogation room.

"Welcome back." Bryson stated. "Now…are you going to cooperate this time around? Remember the little talk we had before my bullet accidently found your foot?"

"I'm telling you the truth…I have no idea who my contact was."

"I see you are speaking better now, that ought to speed things up considerably." Bryson mocked the assassin.

"I have only spoken to the guy once or twice…it was always in code."

"Is his number in your cell phone?" Bryson looked behind him towards the mirror, made a waving gesture with his hand, and a few seconds later a short man with circular rimmed glasses walked through the door and handed Bryson the phone. Immediately he turned around and left, shutting the door securely behind him. "Answer the question. Is his number in your cell phone?"

"I…I want a lawyer. I want my lawyer." Daniel reiterated. He couldn't give up the Aqarab Mayta for fear of what they would do to him. The pain he was in now would be nothing compared to what he would endure if he was to fall back into the hands of the organization.

"You don't get a lawyer." Bryson calmly responded.

"What? Yes I do! This is Am –"

"You don't get a FUCKING LAWYER! You will *ANSWER* my questions, or so help me God I will end you!" Bryson was fuming. The worthless specimen of human in front of him was truthfully anything but. The man's skills were superb, as well as his brain and body. But he was a terrorist, plain and simple, and the United States was on a strict deadline that was fast approaching. Bryson didn't have time for all the bullshit that the assassin was spewing and he was going to get answers one way or another.

Daniel sat there quietly for a few moments. He figured the man across from him was bluffing; they still needed him and his connection to the Aqarab Mayta. *What else is the Aqarab Mayta planning?* Daniel had thought it was just a simple assassination…either way his life was over. He would be put on trial as the President's assassin and his death would be dragged out through the judicial process of the U.S. government. He wanted to be dead now.

"I'm not going to tell you shit." His glare toward Bryson was sinister and the will to die was displayed clearly in his eyes. "Whatever the Aqarab Mayta are planning, I hope that they succeed. The United States is a disgusting, self-centered, and hypocritical country. Its time has long passed."

"What's it matter to you, so long as you get paid?"

The assassin ignored Bryson's question, "You got a girlfriend? Or a wife? Yeah…you look like the type of asshole who falls in love." The words were flowing much easier for the assassin now as the drug began to wear off. A tingling began in his fingers as the feeling slowly returned to his upper torso. "Was she hot?"

Bryson didn't reply, just stared at the assassin. He was trying to get a rise out of him, but it wouldn't work, not against Bryson.

"Hmmm. I guess not." Daniel answered his own question. "Doesn't surprise me though. I bet she was a *bitch*." Bryson winced as he heard the word in unknown reference to Elena. "I bet she dumped you huh? Weren't good enough in bed? That's a shame…I would have fu –"

"Is the number on your cell phone?" Bryson cut him off. He aimed the gun right between Daniel's legs. "You have five seconds: FIVE…"

"I would have made her do unthinkable things." Daniel's arms could move now, and his chest was beginning to tingle.

"FOUR…"

"Did you like to cuddle? Were you the sensitive type?"

"THREE…"

"What was her name?" Daniel could feel sensation creeping downward from his pectorals to his abdominal region.

"TWO…" Bryson was going to enjoy relieving Daniel of his manhood in a moment.

"I bet her name was *cunt*." He left a nasty emphasis on the despicable final word.

"ONE." Bryson began to pull inward on the trigger as he had promised five seconds ago.

The assassin used the last reserves of his energy and dove forward in his chair placing his head in between the gun barrel and his own groin. The signal had already been sent to Bryson's brain, and the trigger finger pulled itself the rest of the way. Like the earlier shot delivered to Daniel's foot, the noise filled the room as the bullet left the barrel and entered the top of Daniel's head. What was once a deadly assassin and the President's killer was now a lifeless organ slouched in a chair. The bullet never exited the body, so there was very little blood displayed around the white room.

Bryson, after realizing what had just happened, frustratingly placed his gun back in his waistband and leaned forward to check Daniel's vitals. His two fingers came in contact with the killer's still-warm neck and Bryson already knew what had happened: Daniel Brody had just executed himself.

"Shit…" Bryson turned and faced the mirror behind him and began talking to it, "Get medical in here to clean this up." He stated as he turned back around and looked at the dead body. The only link known to N.E.T.S. was now slouched over with his head in his lap and the threat was still very much out there. Bryson picked up Daniel's phone off of the floor by his chair, turned it on, and was greeted with the home screen. Medical personnel entered the room with a stretcher and began to move Daniel and his IV out of the room.

Bryson scoured through the phone looking for anything and everything that had to do with the Aqarab Mayta. There were no text messages, no contacts, no previous calls, no reminders, no voicemails; the phone was empty and Bryson was back to square one. He leaned back in the chair still holding the cell phone and thought to himself. *There has got to be some way to track the calls on this phone. Get the techs on it? But that could be a three-day process…I should have seen this coming! Damn it!*

"Sir?" The short man with the glasses entered the room. "Daniel is dead. Was there anything on the cell phone? Would you like us to hack it?" Bryson sat there for a moment, lost in the obsession of what would happen next. There was a twinge in the healing hole in his hand and he glanced down at the bandage covering it…*Abd Al Aziz was just a pawn…Now he is dead…Daniel was just a pawn…He's dead now too…Who is next?* "Mr. Cooper?" The short man asked again seeing that he had been ignored, "Would you like us to examine the phone?" Bryson's focus came back to the room.

"Hmmm? Uh, yes. Examine the phone, do whatever you need to do. I want to know every call made from that phone and every call that came in. Pictures, contacts, pings, texts, anything you can find. And I needed all of that info by yesterday, you understand?"

"Yes sir, we will work on it right away." Bryson handed the short man the phone and he turned on the spot and exited the room, closing the door behind him. Bryson stood up, figuring that all he could do now was to wait for them to find something on the phone. Walking over to the door, he reached for the handle, but before he reached it the door swung open, revealing the short man with glasses breathing heavily and holding a glowing phone in his hand. He looked as if he had just seen a ghost, or a miracle.

Bryson looked closer at the phone and instantly understood the expression on the man's face. It was ringing:

RESTRICTED NUMBER.

Bryson snatched the phone out of the man's grasp and pointed to the mirror in the room then pointed to the phone, signaling for the people on the other side to begin tracking the call. The short man returned to the room located behind the mirror while Bryson accepted the call on the fourth ring and brought the phone to his ear.

"Hello?" Bryson spoke first.

The voice on the other end replied sounding frantic, "Tell mom I'm going to be late for dinner…"

Chapter IX
Street Sweeper

Monday June 26TH, 2017
N.E.T.S. Headquarters, New York City And Interstate 95

"Hello?" an unfamiliar voice answered the phone.

"Tell mom I'm going to be late for dinner…" Ian recited as he piloted the Suburban through the busy streets of D.C. "The toy store was really busy but I took care of it. I think some angry parents are following me home though."

On the other end of the line, Bryson was speechless as to what to say. He was silent, but realized he had to speak quickly.

"Ok…so besides telling mom that you are going to be late for dinner…what should I do?" The question came out carefully.

"I'm not sure son. I think you should come meet me." Ian knew he would have a tail soon and didn't care that he switched the roles of father and son in the code that he and the assassin had. Ian had to get a point across and he had to get it across fast.

"Meet you where…Dad?" Bryson half felt like this was a prank call or a misdial, but then again…it could be an established code.

"I'm in Washington D.C. now," Ian was speaking calmly now, he was focused again. He wove in and out of traffic effortlessly, slowly making his way to the highway. "I'll keep you updated. But I gotta go now son…I've got to go kill the other parents." A small click ended the call and Bryson shot a glance towards the mirror in the room. The short man bolted out of the door.

"We got him sir. He is in Washington D.C. heading towards Interstate 95 it seems." The short man continued. "Also sir, we just got word that an entire team sent by the Pentagon to apprehend a Dr. Thomas Henry at a hotel in D.C. has been eliminated. The target left the scene in what they believe to be one of their own government Suburbans. They are tracking the car now."

"They're the same guy!" Bryson interrupted. It had been a code the whole time; they had been avoiding the Patriot Act by acting as a casual father and son. "Get teams after the Suburban. I want the son of a bitch taken down within the hour!"

HONK! The sound grew louder and faded as Ian swerved the Suburban between two hybrid cars, cutting one of them off and getting onto the ramp to I-95. His foot pressed the pedal clear to the floor and he merged into the surprisingly-light traffic, making his way over to the left lane and placing the vehicle in cruise. Now that he was on the highway he drove by the law; there was no reason to attract attention to himself. The tracker implanted on the inside of the gold Chevrolet symbol on the steering wheel was giving away his real time position to everybody who was soon-to-be in pursuit. Ian remembered its location from his training he had received on each agency and their unique nuances.

As he drove north, Ian reached over to the glove compartment, yanked it open, and pulled out the extensive medical kit it contained. His eyes checked the rear-view mirror…nothing but a red sports car two lanes to the right and four car lengths back, and a semi one lane to the right and eight car lengths back. *Good.*

He opened the medical kit and immediately he saw the scalpel that he desired. Having grabbed the scalpel in his free hand, Ian plunged it into the steering wheel front. For a second the horn echoed from the vehicle, and Ian began to cut around the Chevrolet symbol. Twenty seconds later the hard plastic cross with frayed leather around the edges fell into Ian's lap and he threw the scalpel back into the kit and placed it back into the glove compartment. He picked up the company symbol and rolled down his window, patiently observing all the cars driving the opposite way on the interstate.

Up ahead was a white Acura MDX driving relatively slow and with all the windows down. This was his target. Ian placed his elbow on the inside door rest and held the tracker slightly out the window. The white car's front bumper was collinear with the black Suburban's. Ian, his gaze focused forward, flicked his wrist and tossed the tracker across the median towards the white SUV. It entered the back left window of the car, quietly hitting the back of the seat, and bounced to the floor under the driver's seat. Ian felt a relief of pressure from his chest as he released a large breath. The Suburban was tracker-free, and quickly gaining mileage between it and its pursuers.

Meanwhile, a housewife running errands and listening to Celine Dion in her newly cleaned Acura was unknowingly attracting just about every government agency vehicle in the vicinity.

"Sir, they are closing in on the vehicle. He recently switched directions and is now headed southbound, straight towards the team. ETA: two minutes."

"Good. Tell them to apprehend him. Do not shoot to kill, only to wound. This may be our last chance." Bryson explained.

"Sir." The short man nodded and spoke into his headset, "Teams: shoot to wound, suspect is to be taken into custody."

"Yooou're heeeere, there's NOOOTHING I fear and I knowww that my heart will go oooooooooonnnnnnn…" Celine's powerhouse hit was being belted out by the housewife in the car as she drove on the Interstate. *Such a moving song*, she thought, *one of the greatest hits of all time*. "Weeeee'll staaay forEVVVER this waaaay, you are saaaafe in my heart and my heart will go on and ooooooooooo – OH MY GOD!" The housewife slammed on her brakes; in front of her was a road block of black government SUVs along with 10 armed men: their weapons pointing at her vehicle.

"Ma'am, please exit the vehicle slowly. Place any weapons you may have on the ground and walk slowly towards us." Breathing heavily and in a slight stage of shock, the woman in the Acura threw the door open, bolted out screaming and ran towards the men hysterically. "Weapons down men, this clearly isn't our guy. Get her under control and we will send her on her way. Jackson, search the car for the tracker."

"On it." The armed squad member ran over to the SUV and began looking it over for the tracking device.

The squad leader broke the news to his commanding officer over the radio, "Sir, this isn't the right vehicle. We are looking for the tracker now but somehow it was ditched. This car is just a civilian."

"Damn it!" Bryson cursed as he reacted to the news. "How in the hell could he have gotten away from them with his car being tracked the entire time?" He thought for a moment. The thoughts were blurred. He was frustrated and desperate. The only man left who could divulge any information had just escaped. Bryson thought of potential next steps...*call in local law enforcement? The man was a trained professional; he had probably changed vehicles by now. Send the teams northbound after the SUV? Wild goose chase. He could have gotten off on at least ten different exits by now...Shit! I might as well just call him back and ask him to politely tell us where he is –*

"Wait a second!"

"Yes sir?" The short man calmly replied as he returned his attention to Bryson.

"He called us on a cell phone and he thought that I was his associate. He said he will keep me updated, meaning he still has the phone. We already tracked the phone earlier so lock onto the same frequency as before and track the phone now!"

"Sir." The short man quickly left the interrogation room and returned within the minute, holding a tablet, and handed it to

Bryson. Displayed on the screen was a black box travelling upwards on a satellite image of I-95.

"That's him! Get those teams on him ASAP. Send them this feed so they can track if he changes directions."

"Team! Listen up! We are moving out: new target! The position is being transmitted to your navigation systems. Same rules apply! Shoot to wound! Let's move, MOVE! MOVE!"

Within seconds, all teams were back in the SUVs, crossing the median of the interstate, and speeding off northbound.

"Am I free to go?" The housewife quietly asked herself as she cautiously wandered back to her Acura.

Ian was cautiously, yet casually, driving. Getting rid of the tracker had been easy, and his pursuers were now facing the opposite direction and at least twenty minutes behind him. All that was left to do was to meet with the assassin, Daniel Brody, and kill him. He had been compromised and the Aqarab Mayta couldn't risk a leak this late in the game. Not to mention they had never planned on paying him $100 million in the first place.

Traffic was getting steadily heavier as Ian drove north, but still not much of a concern as he continued to cruise ahead in the left lane. He took a quick glance at his phone just to make sure he had no new calls or messages and reached over to turn on the radio. His eyes caught the rearview mirror and he noticed a black SUV creeping through traffic, followed by five additional SUVs. Ian felt a chill travel down his spine as his body released a high amount of adrenaline into his bloodstream. *How could they have found me? I'll just have to deal with this now.* He knew that he should have left D.C. earlier, but deep down he knew he loved this lifestyle. The violence. *I'm obsessed with it.* His foot pressed down on the gas, and he began to weave through traffic when necessary. Going well over the speed limit, Ian confirmed his worst fears as the SUVs were still on his tail and closing in.

A quarter mile back, the team leader confirmed the suspect to what he believed to be a Pentagon official. N.E.T.S. had intercepted the communication instead, and they were calling the shots now.

"Sir we have a visual confirmation on the target: driving a stolen black SUV at high speed. Orders are shoot to wound and capture alive. Those still stand?"

"Confirmed. Orders still stand. Call in local law enforcement if necessary." The short man directed as Bryson watched the nearby satellite image, now displayed on a large computer screen.

"Sir!" The team leader switched to his local radio. "Local law enforcement, this is Delta Squad seven-zero-three. In pursuit of a black government Suburban travelling north on I-95, request assistance and road block."

"Confirmed Delta Squad #703. Assistance in form of road block on their way now. Helicopter support not possible, experiencing engine problems for the last week." The female police dispatcher responded. The Delta Squad leader spoke into the radio again, this time to his squad mates.

"Delta Squad, this is our guy! Once again, we need him alive, he is a Priority Alpha! Local law enforcement will issue a road block up ahead: keep your eyes peeled!"

Ian kept increasing his speed. The other SUV's were still on his tail, and he knew he would have to shake them…or eliminate them. As he drove in the left lane, he reached behind and pulled the gun out of his waistline, as well as the thermal goggles out of the coat pocket. *Alright…let's go.* The steering wheel was thrown to the right as Ian made his move to the middle lane and broke out the driver window with the butt of the gun. Glass rained and bounced down the pavement behind the vehicle and Ian stepped on the gas. The Suburban lurched forward, its modified engine gladly working at full power and Ian zoomed past a blue Ford Fiesta, travelling slowly in the left hand lane. Ian leaned out, left hand on the trigger and right hand on the wheel, quickly gauged the distance, and shot the front left tire of the Fiesta. A small cloud of smoke erupted from the blowout, and the driver had a look of shock on his face as his eyes locked onto the gun ahead of him. He threw the steering wheel in the direction of the now-flat tire, turning the passenger side of the vehicle towards Ian.

"Wrong move man…" Ian aimed at the Fiesta's visible gas tank and all it took was one shot.

"Holy shit!" One of the Delta Squad members exclaimed as a fireball erupted in front of them, encasing a grey, hollow shell of what used to be a compact car. The violent flame of debris tumbled down the highway, bouncing over, around, and on top of the still-in-motion traffic and took with it a slew of other cars.

SCREECH! All six government SUVs came to a halt as the highway ahead of them became clogged from the previous explosion and wrecks that followed it.

"Son of a bitch!" There seemed to be no way around the plethora of mangled steel and iron that now littered the entire span of the highway. "Team, push through the wreckage, we don't have time to stop and help." Each vehicle pressed their reinforced front bumpers against part of the wreckage and laid on the gas, steering through the injured civilians that would have to wait for help.

Ian looked back at the mess he had created and leaned back inside the vehicle. *That should buy me a few minutes…*He was gunning it hard now, pushing the Suburban to its limits and trying to keep as straight of a line as possible as he dodged traffic that was now slowing down due to the explosion in their rear-view mirrors. *Gotta get away. This is the last leg.* A deep breath exhaled from Ian's lungs as he focused his adrenaline and used it to tune into his surroundings.

Cloudless sky allowing the sun's presence…

High humidity causing sweat to bead on the brow…

Black asphalt, hard and punishing…

Warm breeze entering the car through the open window…

A police roadblock spanning the entirety of the northbound lane in a half mile…

Ian reacted as if he had been in this exact training scenario before. He hadn't. Ahead of him he counted four police cruisers each end to end except for directly in the middle. *There might be room to fit through.* As he was assessing the roadblock, coming up on it fast, he noticed several local-area police throwing cans out in front of the barricade. Three spurts of smoke began to create a visible screen in front of the cruisers, quickly escaping their aluminum canisters on the ground. Almost without thinking, Ian ripped off his sunglasses, reached in his lap, and placed the thermal goggles on his head.

Again he entered a world of blue, green, red, orange, and yellow. The smoke ahead was invisible now, and behind it, Ian learned just how cunning the policemen had been. As he rapidly approached the blockage, he watched as a greenish-orange human figure ran in front of the gap, dragging a blue contraption behind him. *Spike strip.* Ian scrambled for the glove compartment with one hand still on the wheel…*150 feet*…reached in and threw the medical kit on the passenger seat…*75 feet*…forcefully opened the kit…*25 feet*…

His sweaty right hand wrapped around the chiseled grip of the scalpel he had used earlier and he was dead set to run directly over the spike strip. The left hand, tight and secure on the steering wheel, threw it slightly to the left. Simultaneously, the scalpel hand came across the front steering wheel at the exact moment of impact with the parked police cruisers. A crunching noise fell in love with a sharp jolt as the Suburban penetrated through the road block at 100mph. The airbag exploded from the middle of the steering wheel and was quickly defeated by the scalpel that punctured it, saving Ian the whiplash and vision distortion after he had already braced himself for impact.

The armored and reinforced Suburban had crushed through the roadblock, narrowly missing the spike strip, and knocking one of the police cruisers onto it. Its front bumper was barely hanging on, but it alone had saved Ian's possibility for escape. The world jumped back to blue sky and black asphalt as Ian ripped the goggles off his head and calmly exchanged them for the sunglasses he had been wearing earlier. Placing the scalpel back on the passenger seat, Ian glanced back and was greeted with heartbreak as the remaining government SUV's crashed through the police barricade, easily avoiding the now-visible spike strip. Debris jumped from the edges of the solid black beasts as they blew through the gates made from police cars.

"Delta Squad, continue pursuit! Shut this motherfucker down! NOW!"

Ian had had enough. He slammed on the brakes, pulled the emergency brake, and yanked the steering wheel. The Suburban let out a neigh similar to a stallion as it switched directions and was slammed into drive. Smoke emanated from the tires as they dissolved on the hot pavement and added friction for the car to react against.

"What is he doing sir?" one of the squad members asked as Ian's car was charging straight for them.

Once the car was up to speed, Ian let up off the pedal and opened the sunroof of the vehicle. He grabbed the gun he had stolen off the agent in the hotel and reached his arms through the top of the sunroof, pulling himself up so that his left foot was standing on the driver's seat. He wedged his right foot in one of the steering wheel column gaps and kept the vehicle steady, heading straight towards his pursuers.

There was a SUV headed straight towards him. POW!

One shot exited the chamber, and the left front tire of the pursuer exploded, throwing the hulking monstrosity into the concrete divider. The back end of the SUV flipped up over the impact of the front end and the forward momentum unkindly created contact with a steel light pole located in the divider. Ian could not focus on the spectacle,

POW! POW!

A second and third shot shattered the next vehicle's windshield, revealing the two armed agents sitting inside. Their faces were covered in shock as a man sticking out of the sunroof of an out-of-control vehicle was shooting at them. Their next thoughts never came to fruition…POW! POW! The fourth and fifth bullets' vibrations echoed in the warm air as the two men crumpled, the shock permanently fused onto their faces.

Ian's Suburban was still headed straight towards the remaining, incoming SUVs. There was no way he would survive an impact with them, sticking half out of the sunroof…his right foot kicked to the left, again sending the car into a screeching left turn. His core muscles tightened as his body fought the lateral g-forces resulting from the sharp turning at high speed. Everything was slowing down; Ian had a pulsing reality in his head. Everything was clear, just as it had been in the hotel…the Suburban was turning to the left so Ian twisted his body to the right at the same pace in order to continue facing his pursuers.

POW! POW!

The sixth and seventh shot were the most efficient. The first shot of the two crashed into the front right tire of the vehicle on Ian's right. The second into the front left tire of the other vehicle on Ian's left. Both SUV's collided as their flat tires directed them into each other. Ian kept turning his body as the Suburban continued its reversal of direction to the left. The forces on his body were so strong he was surprised the car had not rolled over…yet. He watched his handiwork unfold as the third and final SUV that had been in the middle of the two now-connected SUVs tried to avoid collision, but to no avail. It slammed into the point where the two vehicles were connected and flipped over the barrier, landing on its roof; sliding, grinding, and spinning to an eventual halt on the seemingly now deserted highway.

Ian unwedged his right foot and popped back into the vehicle, controlling the remainder of the 180° turn with both hands, barely preventing a rollover. He was having a ball, but there was no time to bask in momentary glories. Just another task completed successfully. Now he had another: meet with the assassin, Daniel Brody, and kill him.

Like he had done several times before, Ian gave the vehicle some gas and continued northbound on I-95, leaving several miles of insanity and wreckage behind him.

"Sir." The short man inquired. "What do you want to do now?" Bryson was still staring intently at the satellite image of the highway massacre which had been unfolding in front of him for the last ten minutes. Whoever they were pursuing was skilled. In fact, "skilled" didn't even describe him with justice. This man was no common terrorist…*Who are you?*

"Sir?" he asked Bryson again.

"Just wait. See there?" Bryson pointed to far edge of the screen opposite the end the escaping Suburban was on. There, on the left edge of the image, was a small black rectangle slowly making its way through the wreckage. "There is one SUV left and I'm not sure that our guy in the Suburban knows…"

Ian had never forgotten anything…until now. The final black SUV had been creeping behind the other five pursuers the entire time and was finally turning and twisting itself through the wreckage littered around the highway. As it gathered speed the driver was careful to keep a large distance between himself and the Suburban. His partner in the passenger seat was busy readying a large, upgraded M24 sniper rifle. After the scope was properly adjusted he slid the small ammo clip into the bottom and unbuckled his seatbelt. The driver pressed down on the passenger window button and a rush of noise entered the vehicle's compartment.

"Wait until we are flat and have a clear shot!" He yelled as his squad mate leaned the top half of his body out the window. He brought the scope up to his face and peered through it. The only image available was that of highway pavement. "We are coming over a small hill, hold steady. I'll bring you within range!" His statement was greeted with a thumbs-up sign reaching inside the car. The squad member with the sniper rifle controlled his breathing, kept the scope to his eye, and loosened his grip around the trigger…relaxed shots resulted in the best shots. "Steady…" The driver commented long and casually. "Steady…" He said once more. The man leaning out the window knew he would really only have one shot at this. As soon as the man in the Suburban knew they were still after him, they would lose the element of surprise.

As he peered through the scope, highway wind rushing over his cheeks, the gray concrete rounded off and became flat, revealing a large, battered, black vehicle travelling away. The shot had to hit one of the back tires. *Cause a blowout or wreck; just keep the bastard alive…*

"Target is clear! Pick your shot!" The driver was yelling over the vacuum-sounding air ripping through the open windows of the vehicle.

Breath in.
Breath out.

The sniper rifle erupted with a deafening noise even over the rush of air. Travelling at over 2,500 feet per second, the large bullet crashed into the back right tire of Ian's Suburban, exploding the rubber and tire rim. Satisfied, the passenger of the vehicle slid back into his seat as the Suburban began to skid sideways down the highway…

Bryson and the short man watched on the streaming satellite image in the New York City N.E.T.S. headquarters as a small cloud of what appeared to be dust erupted from the back of the Suburban and the driver seemed to lose control…

"What the fuck!" Ian exclaimed as he heard and felt the vehicle's interaction with the bullet. Using only a half second, he glanced in the rearview and saw the last black SUV far behind him. The image in the mirror was quickly twisting as the car began to spin sideways, with Ian's driver door now facing the final pursuing SUV. Any second now, the Suburban would be rolling violently down the highway either taking Ian for the ride or ejecting him bloodily onto the concrete. He made his next decision in less than two seconds and threw open his door, making sure that he still had the handgun, and used his entire core strength to eject himself out of the vehicle. He prepared his body for the rough impact with the concrete, but natural physics had a slightly different plan.

The Suburban, now skidding horizontally down the highway, began to roll at the same time Ian had thrown himself out. His entire body was almost vacant of the rotating vehicle but the bottom step panel under the driver's door hit the end of Ian's feet. The world began to turn and he couldn't tell which way was up or down anymore. He had felt a slight knock on his feet and now he was slowly flipping through the air due to the rolling momentum of the SUV's impact.

This is going to hurt Ian thought to himself as he felt the handgun escape from the back of his waistline. A disgusting thud followed the thought as Ian's shoulders crashed into the pavement first and his head and body followed. Shock rocketed through the man's body as he was sure there had to be numerous bones broken. Ian thought he was paralyzed since not even his eyelids would open, but slowly they rose upwards revealing a humid day on the highway. The pursuing SUV was almost to his location, still travelling at high velocity. Ian had to make moves fast. A jet black object stood out against the gray pavement: a handgun. Focusing his energy into his appendages, he could feel muscular use travelling back into his motor skills and scurried on his hands and knees to the gun and picked it up. The roar of the pursuing vehicle's engine could be heard in the near distance. He released the magazine: three more bullets.

Bryson could hardly believe the man lying horizontally in the middle of the highway could even move. The Suburban had begun to roll from the shot to its tire and was now little more than a heap of metal further down the interstate. Somehow the man inside had escaped but it appeared as if the escape had nearly killed him as he now moved across the screen. With the final pursuing SUV closing in fast there was really no escape for the man, but Bryson still watched with fascination as he whispered to himself.

"What is he doing?"

The SUV was closing in fast and all Ian could think of was the phrase "*Karma's a bitch!*" Rolled over on his side in the middle of the road he aimed the gun at the SUV and pulled the cold, curved, metal of the trigger without a second's hesitation. Time had run out.

POW!

The bullet left the chamber and eagerly attacked the front left tire of the SUV. The vehicle lurched in the direction of the flat tire and the right side of the out-of-control monstrosity was facing Ian.

POW!

The second of the remaining three bullets sliced through the humid Interstate air, travelled through the rubber of the back right tire, and scrunched like an accordion against the hard metal rim. After losing another contact area with the road, the sideways SUV leapt into the air and began rolling and bouncing down the highway toward Ian, violently spitting metal and gravel debris every time its hull made contact with the ground.

Ian remained where he was: flat on the highway. There was no time to move out of the way. *I am meant to live.* Inside the SUV he could see the two squad pursuers bracing themselves as they rolled. The only expression on their faces was determination; determination that they would survive, that their mission of apprehending Ian still mattered. Ian also had the look of determination across his brow and a gun with one last bullet.

The SUV hit the ground and rebounded back into the air. Its frame blocked out the sun that had been shining on Ian's face. At the top of its short apex it seemed to freeze for a second…as if it was deciding if it wanted to fall back to the earth. Gravity eventually made the decision for it, pushing it back towards the ground. Ian followed the vehicle with his eyes as it crashed no more than a foot away from his body in front of him and once again rolled back into the air. The remaining front tire grazed his cheek as he pressed his body into the pavement as much as possible; it was going to be a close one…

With his eyes still wide open, he was staring straight up and could only see the side of the vehicle, twisting across the blue sky that outlined the black box above him. Instinctively, he switched the firearm from his right to left hand and extended the gun away from his body. Eyes still tracking the flying car, Ian realized it would land directly on its roof with his pursuers upside down. His focus shifted to the men in the SUV; the passenger's gaze catching Ian's. As the man rolled across the sky his look of determination turned grim. He saw the look in Ian's face and the extended arm with the gun pointed directly at his head.

Ian unleashed the final bullet.

POW!

Neither man in the vehicle knew that they had even hit the ground. As the automobile fell on the opposite side of Ian, he had aimed and fired the gun. The projectile from the simple handgun entered the head of the passenger, exited with a spray of blood, and continued on into the head of the driver. Both men were dead, and as the vehicle continued rolling and eventually stopped Ian could notice the crimson spurts scattered throughout the interior. There was no time for admiration as he began to stand up, soon realizing that his body had taken a major beating from his awkward fall. Once up, he began limping down I-95 in the direction which he had been going the entire time: north.

Only a few states away a stunned N.E.T.S. agent stared at the screen. What he had seen made no sense…the SUV had been rolling directly towards the man lying on the road. He had *seen* the vehicle go over the body, surely dragging the man with it…but yet…the man had gotten up and walked away. Bryson's head was racing. There were no more backups. The scene on the highway was already far too public for N.E.T.S. standards. He turned and began to storm out of the room.

"Keep the satellite image on that man. For God's sake do NOT lose him. Keep me updated through the headset as to what vehicle he gets into!"

"But sir, where are you going?" The short man cried out, just as beleaguered as Bryson. The door erupted open and Bryson answered before he left.

"This man wants to meet Daniel Brody? Then we give him Daniel Brody!"

Chapter X
Lost Love

Wednesday May 30th, 2012
St. Georges, Bermuda

"Bryson?" There was no response. Elena smiled as she sat up in bed having just woken up. She was gently holding up the covers under her arms as her back was exposed, breathing in the aura of romance that entranced the room. Only the soft "shush" of ocean waves could be heard from outside. It was midmorning and the light fell quiet on the floor and the end of the bed, warming Elena's feet that were under the thin covers. The lightest breeze entered the room through the open patio doors and licked the back of her neck sending a euphoric tingle up her spine.

Feeling sexy, she leaned down to her new, still-sleeping husband, barely pressing the edge of her lips on his ear and whispered, "Bryson. Wake up."

As if awoken by an angel, Bryson let out an early morning moan and rolled over only to be greeted with a long, passionate kiss from his wife. Elena reluctantly broke the kiss and opened her eyes. Bryson's lips transformed into a smile and he kept his eyes closed.

"Why are you smiling?" Elena inquired.

"With a wake up like that how can I not be?" Bryson opened his eyes as he propped himself up with his elbow and leaned in for another kiss from his wife. Before their lips touched both of them already knew they didn't want the moment to end. Lying in bed, not a care in the world, on their honeymoon in Bermuda; describing life as perfect was an understatement. Still in an adoring embrace, their eyes opened at the same time and each of them began to laugh. Elena leaned in for a short kiss, and then lay face down with her head hanging over the edge of the end of the bed, exposing her entire backside. Bryson copied her and similarly the sheets slipped off, their naked bottoms side by side like small foothills rising on the bed top.

"Oooo look at that one!" Elena pointed to a bright yellow fish with neon blue fin lines darting around in the ocean beneath the glass-bottom floor of their secluded bungalow.

"Look over there." Bryson removed an arm from under his chin and pointed opposite of where Elena had. There, on a grey rock with a flat vertical face, was a bright pink starfish.

The newlywed soul mates lay on the bed and watched the tropical fish swim, dart, and hide beneath them for forty-five minutes. They would point to a different fish and watch it for a while before a new one caught their attention. They reminisced on stories of their gorgeous wedding, each letting out a small chuckle as they remembered David Harper, head of N.E.T.S., dancing at their reception from one too many drinks. Bryson held Elena's hand in his as she played with each of his fingers, tossing them slowly in between her own.

Staring at the motion of life below him, Bryson's mind escaped him. He thought about how N.E.T.S. had paid for all of this. David had "moved some funds around" and paid in full for the small wedding ceremony for friends and family, the entire honeymoon and all expenses that came with it, and two weeks of time off for the both of them. In addition, and easily the most exciting to the both of them, was the promise that upon their return they would be considered partner agents within the organization, conducting every mission together. *I'll never be alone again...* and with that thought Bryson reflected on his childhood with only one word coming to mind: orphan.

His orphan story was not typical. He was a good natured child and was able to stay in one orphanage his entire childhood, but all around him other children, often times friends, would get adopted or transferred. For some reason, Bryson was never one of these children. His only friends ever really came when he began attending high school and he quickly lost touch with them afterwards. His grades were strong, he was socially capable, and he was athletic…just never loved by a family of his own.

After high school Bryson left the orphanage, bought a small apartment to himself, got a job as a waiter, and attended some classes at the local community college; all that he could afford. Life was dull for a couple years. Always working, same places, same faces, but Bryson kept putting forth the effort. For what reason, he did not know, but he knew he was destined for something more than what he was doing.

One day, a built African American man entered the restaurant where Bryson was working and was seated by the hostess in a booth by himself. He seemed to have an aura of authority about him but there was no discernable reasoning for the premonition. It was a Tuesday night which usually meant that business would be slow, often some of Bryson's least favorite times to work. He filled a glass of water, grabbed a set of silverware and approached the man.

"Hello sir. My name is Bryson and I will be your waiter this evening." Bryson placed the silverware down on the table and a coaster underneath the glass of water. "It is currently happy hour, all of our domestic beers are half off, as well as our appetizers. Would you like anything to dr – "

"I will just have water thanks." The man interrupted Bryson's recital.

"Do you need some time to look over the menu? I would recommend the king crab le – "

"Just give me a couple minutes please." The man's gaze hadn't even acknowledged Bryson; they were loosely concentrated on the menu.

"Yes sir." Bryson shrugged off the man's rudeness as he had dealt with much worse before. Returning back to the kitchen area, Bryson wiped down some counters and chatted with his coworker, Bill, as he gave the man at the booth an ample amount of time to decide what he wanted to eat. Four minutes and twenty-seven seconds later, Bryson returned to take the rude man's order.

"So what will it be sir?" Bryson asked cheerily. *Kill them with kindness…*

"Well for starters, I would like two minutes and twenty-seven seconds of my life back." The man said, looking up at Bryson for the first time. His eyes were stern, and his gaze induced a sense of power. But his facial expression was hollow; he looked neither mad nor happy.

"I'm sorry sir?"

"I told you to give me a couple of minutes, implying that I wanted two minutes. You gave me four minutes and twenty-seven seconds, which is two minutes and twenty-seven seconds of my time wasted as I sat here, waiting for you."

"Sir…" Bryson was astounded, this was a whole new level of rudeness in his experience. "I apologize sir bu – "

"Don't apologize, just sit down." The man pointed to the booth across from him.

"Sir I can't sit down, I will get in trouble. If you would like to talk I will remain standing."

"Sit down. You won't have a job here much longer anyway." Again the man pointed across the booth with a commanding energy. Bryson reluctantly accepted as he looked around for his manager but could not see him anywhere. As he returned his eyes to the man across the booth from him he noticed the man's gaze had returned back to the menu. "You know…if I were going to order, I would have gotten the king crab legs. Those do look delicious." Bryson remained silent, he was not sure of what to think of the man. "Bryson." The man let the name resonate off the tip of his tongue for a moment, "I knew your father. And your mother."

"What did you say to me?" He wasn't sure whether or not he should believe the man. He looked serious but how could what he said be true?

"I knew both your father and mother…"

"No you didn't." Bryson instantly replied.

"They both worked for me a long time ago, it's been about 25 years actually." His gaze was as serious as ever. Bryson was flabbergasted…he had never even known his parents' names much less their profession. Where was this man going with this setup?

"Sir…I really don't believe you, not to mention, I don't even know my parents. They died when I was just a baby." Bryson explained truthfully.

"I know." The man said with certainty. "I am the one who killed them." Silence ensued as he let the statement settle. He kept his gaze placed on Bryson who was instantly taken aback by this comment and leaned in closer to the man and replied in a vicious whisper.

"Fuck. You. I am done here. Get your own damn food." Bryson removed himself from the booth and turned to leave.

"Bryson, they were two of my best friends. They betrayed this country and I had no choice." He paused for a moment as Bryson had stopped walking away but still had his back turned to the man. "We worked for an agency of the U.S. government called N.E.T.S.; an organization which I am now the head of." Bryson whipped around and pointed a finger very close to the man's face, still whispering so as not to be heard by his boss or co-workers.

"Bullshit! There is no such organization as N.E.T.S. I've never heard of them and you have over stayed your welcome. Get the *hell* out of here." A slight smirk released across the man's face.

"Of course you haven't heard of N.E.T.S., you are a civilian Bryson. Not even the President knows of us."

"Who the hell are you?" Bryson demanded.

"My name is David Harper and I would like you to sit back down. We have a lot to talk about."

Bryson's consciousness returned to the present where he and Elena were on their honeymoon, lying naked and watching the tropical fish swim beneath their glass-bottom bungalow. The fish were mesmerizing as they jittered from place to place, surely busy with the day's chores. Elena had been watching the fish long enough and turned her gaze to her new husband as she rolled on her side and laid a hand on his back. She began rubbing his back and shoulders with just the very tips of her fingers – it was one of Bryson's favorite sensations. The feeling of Elena's skin barely gracing the short invisible hairs on his body soothed him and sent a comfortable chill down his spine. Embracing the amazingly light touch of his wife, Bryson closed his eyes and relaxed.

Elena's hands worked from the top of his shoulders down to the bottom of his back, and back up to his shoulders again. There was no exact pattern in the way she was moving her fingers across his skin, she was just drawing random curves of love along the canvas that was Bryson's back. And what a canvas it was…toned with nearly every muscle visible underneath his tan skin, but not grotesquely so. He had just the right amount of definition, Elena was noticing for what must be the hundredth time. Her eyes wandered along his body as she worked her gaze down towards his backside. Elena giggled to herself as she admired her husband's plump and slightly-less-tan buttocks. She was reveling in the fact that they could just lay here, together, without a care in the world as lovers, work partners, and best-friends. *I am so in love with this man.* As she continued to gently trace on his back she turned and looked at his face. There was no apparent look of sadness on his face but Elena could read him like a book. She knew exactly what he was thinking about.

"I'm sorry that your parents couldn't be at the wedding…" the way she said it was so light, so innocent. For a moment Bryson didn't respond. But then he turned his head towards Elena and looked deeply into her soft, sensual, and comforting emerald eyes. She was gazing back at him and her silky brown hair was resting on her shoulders and her back with a few sexy wisps inconspicuously crossing her face. A particular strand was curving down from her head, lightly resting part of its length on her bottom lip…those perfectly pink, soft, warming lips. *I am so in love with this woman.* Bryson rolled on his side towards Elena and placed the palm of his hand on her cheek, lightly holding her gorgeous face before leaning in and kissing her with as much love and passion as he ever had. This woman was his life, she had him memorized and she was what he thought about almost every second of the day. The term soul-mate didn't even begin to describe how Bryson felt about her and the feeling was mutual.

Bryson and Elena poured their hearts into their lips and continued the kiss; passion was their reality. Neither of them felt like they were half of a whole, or some clichéd way of love like that. They felt as if they were the two luckiest individuals of all time; living *for* each other. A perfect duo molded by friendship, careers, trust, chemistry, and a deep, true love.

They pulled away from the embrace at the same time and rested their foreheads on each other's. Each of them felt an unmatchable warming sensation on their contacted skin, as if the kiss was still happening. After a few moments of this Elena bent Bryson's head down and kissed it. He quickly returned the favor on her lips.

"Are you…" He quickly kissed her, "ready…" another kiss, "to get…" a third quick kiss, "the day…" a last quick kiss, "started?" Elena, enjoying her husband's cuteness, looked into his eyes and nodded. "All righty! Let's get up!" Bryson exclaimed as he playfully tapped Elena's bare bottom with his hand as he got up out of bed.

"Hey!" she laughed as she returned the favor, albeit with a smack rather than a tap. Bryson laughed and rubbed his left cheek where he had just been struck while he walked to the bathroom portion of the bungalow and started the shower. Elena sat up, got out of bed, and walked over to the shower where Bryson was waiting for the hot water to kick in, "Mind if I join?" she teased.

"Oh…I was going to take one first. I'll make it fast though so you can take one after me." Bryson replied kindly. Elena returned a confused gaze resulting in a smirk breaking out across Bryson's face.

"Ugh!" she said in annoyance from being tricked as she slapped his chest. Bryson was laughing as he was now rubbing a new red area of skin.

"Man we really need to find you a new reaction other than hitting." He joked as he leaned in and felt the temperature of the shower which was now hot. "After you…" He held a hand out towards the inside of the shower as a laughing Elena entered with Bryson following and closing the door behind them.

St. George, Bermuda had never had a more gorgeous day than this one. Bryson and Elena walked hand in hand through the streets, soaking in the relaxation of their honeymoon, effortlessly flirting with each other like true newlyweds. Clouds were nonexistent, the only thing that could be seen in a raging blue sky were birds flying in formation and the golden-white sun that warmed everything it touched. As if to counter the sun, a quiet breeze provided some relief as it flowed invisibly over the skin of the population of Bermuda.

Perhaps even more stunning than the weather were Bryson and Elena. Each had the honeymoon glow radiating from their faces, complete with smiles and laughter shared between them. Bryson was wearing a casual half-buttoned shirt along with a pair of boating shorts and shoes. His sun-soaked, brown hair was naturally tousled and his distinctive face was appreciated by a pair of rose-pink aviators which covered his baby-blue eyes from the bright and high sun. Elena was wearing a gorgeous sundress that was loose, but her features shone through. Her healthy curves commanded the dress to obey them; it was no surprise that she had been mistaken for a model many times before. Her tan and perfectly toned arms contrasted against the curved dress as she swung them more than normal out of joy of now being married. Light brown hair was exquisitely sun-bleached as it rested unorganized on her shoulders and slightly down her back. To shade herself from the sun, Elena had a sunhat that matched her dress. It was nothing too over-the-top, but she looked gorgeous in it as Bryson leaned in to kiss her and they continued to walk around town.

"Let's get something to eat…yeah?" Bryson suggested with his arm now wrapped around Elena and hers around him.

"Oooo let's go to that café we saw the other day! I think it's around here somewhere." The two of them continued their leisurely stroll, studying the stunning Bermuda landscape and population and soon arrived at the quaint café that Elena had mentioned. It was on a street corner directly across from the beach and since it was already noon it had a small line forming at the door. Bryson and Elena walked hand in hand to the end of the line and began to read over their options that had been colorfully drawn on a black chalkboard.

"Oh…that chicken Panini sounds so good right now." Bryson said half drooling. On the walk to the café he had realized that he was starving.

"Why are you so hungry Mr. Cooper? Working hard?" Elena teased as she shot him a sultry glance. Bryson smirked,

"You could say that."

"Well I'm hungry too so I think I'll get the St. George salad and a piece of chocolate chip banana bread."

"Those sound good. I might steal a piece of that bread."

"Next please!" The old man at the counter politely called. Bryson and Elena were up next and approached the counter. "What will it be?" the man's smile was endearing and emitted a feeling of friendliness towards the couple. He had a half-halo of gray hair on the top of his head, slightly yellowed teeth, and tan, leathery skin, but his voice was just as welcoming as his smile.

"Ladies first." Bryson encouraged Elena.

"I will have your St. George salad with the house dressing and then a piece of your chocolate chip banana bread please."

"Oh that's a very good choice dear" A voice from the side of the counter spoke as a cute, hunched-over, elderly woman emerged, clearly approving of Elena's choice. "The chocolate chip banana bread is Earl's favorite. He can hardly go a day without eating a piece!"

"HA HA HA!" The old man behind the counter let out a boisterous laugh. "It's true! It's how I packed on this gut!" He continued as he grabbed the edge of his belly and gave it a slight shake. "Somehow though, my wife has stayed just as lovely as the day I met her 60 years ago." He shot her a loving glance as she began to blush.

"Oh Earl! Stop it! You are embarrassing the new couple!" Elena was fascinated by the life-long partners in front of her and secretly grabbed Bryson's hand and gave it a loving squeeze. He returned the gesture.

"You're right Marty. I'm sorry sir, what can I get you?" His gaze was directed towards Bryson now. Bryson simply gave the man a reassuring smile that they were enjoying themselves and ordered.

"I'll have the chicken Panini without tomatoes please."

"Excellent choice sir. Why don't you two have a seat outside and we will bring your meals to you!"

"Thank you!" Elena said as she and Bryson exited the café and took a seat on a pair of wicker chairs that resembled royal thrones in the glorious Bermuda weather. In the perfect sun they exchanged glances, continued flirting, traded kisses, and began to talk about what they wanted to do for the afternoon when Marty waddled out and handed them their food.

"Here you go dears!" She placed the plates on the table that was between them, each with a set of silverware and a napkin.

"Thank you Marty!" Elena had fallen in love with the cute elderly couple immediately.

"You're welcome dear. You two just let me know if you need anything ok?"

"Will do, thank you." Bryson smiled as he replied and Marty returned inside. Sunlight continued to bathe the couple as they ate and talked and after ten minutes, they were both done with everything except for the chocolate chip banana bread.

"Mmmm! I am so excited to eat this delicious… scrumptious…decadent piece of chocolate chip banana bread *all by myself*." Elena teased as she reached for the fat slice of bread and tore off a piece. Making sure that Bryson was watching she seductively placed the piece of bread in her mouth, closed her lips on her finger, and slowly pulled it out of her now-closed lips. Bryson let out a chuckle.

"I hate you." He watched his wife reach for a second piece of the increasingly appealing bread.

"Oh I'm sorry! Did you want some of this delicious…scrumptious…deca –" Elena's teasing was cut short this time as Bryson and his reflexes snatched the piece of bread right out of her hand and plopped the entire hunk in his mouth. "Hey!" A giggle emerged as Elena surrendered and allowed her husband some of her dessert. Bryson struggled to talk through the enormous amount of bread he was chewing in his mouth.

"Uhhh mawww Gawww…thisis sawww guhhh." He leaned back in his chair as he closed his eyes and fully experienced the euphoria known as chocolate chip banana bread. Banana flavor laid the foundation within his mouth but the slightly sun-warmed and melted chocolate reached his taste buds and the bread became an entirely different animal. He released a bittersweet sigh as he finished chewing and opened his eyes again.

The two of them relished in what remained of the dessert bread, appreciating each and every bite they took. When it was sadly finished, Bryson grabbed Elena's plate, placed it on top of his, and swept the few crumbs on their table onto the top plate. He stood up from his comfortable chair and stuck out a hand towards his wife. She looked up at him from under her hat with a gaze that melted Bryson's heart. It was sexy and cute and gorgeous all at once; it was the look of an angel. She placed her hand gently in his and stood up with little assistance but then he pulled her close. They embraced right there in front of the café, in front of other guests, standing shamelessly in the early afternoon sunlight. It was always the unexpected, unique kisses that meant the most. They were the ones that Bryson and Elena would hold onto for a lifetime…

Slowly they pulled away from each other and opened their eyes. They shared a smile together and walked back into the café to return their dishes only to be greeted immediately by Marty.

"Oh hello you two! How did you like your food?"

"It was delicious thank you!" Elena kindly reported.

"Here are our plates and silverware." Bryson gently laid them down on the counter. "Thank you, everything was very good." He shot Marty a quick smile causing her to blush slightly.

"Oh you didn't have to bring those in! I could have gotten them!" She insisted. Elena waved her off almost instantly.

"Oh no it's fine! Plus we wanted to come back in here and thank you!"

"Well you are very welcome. Come back any time!" Earl mentioned from behind the register as Elena and Bryson started to walk their way out of the café. The two of them waved one last time as they approached the door when Earl called out, "Oh! What did you two think of the banana bread?"

Bryson thought about it for a moment and shouted back with the simplest and truest answer he could think of, "It was…magical."

Elena smiled at this statement and hugged her man close as they entered back out into the Bermuda paradise to continue their afternoon. Back inside the café, Earl walked over to his wife of 57 years, Marty, and planted a large kiss on her lips.

"You've got five minutes." Bryson was fuming as he sat in the restaurant booth across from this *David Harper* character.

"Fair enough." The man sat up straight, fixed his tie, let out a breath and began to speak. "I'll get right to it. As I said, I am David and I work for an organization called N.E.T.S. Trying not to sound too corny here, but we are an extremely…shall we say…invisible organization? N.E.T.S. stands for Non-Existent Task Squad, which is how the whole thing began at the height of the Cold War in the early 1960's: with a single squad. Shortly after the Cuban Missile Crisis it was decided by President Kennedy that this nation needed to know about foreign threats sooner and deal with them head-on, but with discretion from the knowledge of the rest of the world."

"I thought you said the President didn't even know of N.E.T.S.?" Bryson interrupted, trying to catch the man in his bogus story.

"Kennedy was the *only* President to ever know about N.E.T.S. which is precisely how he wanted it to be. When he, and the Secretary of Defense, Robert McNamara, and the head of the C.I.A., John McCone, all sat down and decided to create N.E.T.S., they agreed that it was to be their one complete secret. They needed a way to control the outcome of the world during a very tumultuous time. Assassinations, interrogations, tortures, spying; they required a process to accomplish all of these tasks and still allow the U.S. government plausible deniability. If a job ever went bad they wanted to be able to claim that it was some patriotic vigilante and back it up with the proof that they had no documentation of it whatsoever. But missions in N.E.T.S. never failed.

"Before Kennedy died in 1963, the three of them only accepted the best candidates for the job. Not just meatheads with brute strength. No…they wanted specifically talented individuals that could think on their toes, agents that could alter the course of any situation to be in their favor. To make a long story short, the 'task squad' eventually turned into 'task *squads*' and soon after, a full blown agency. We had our hands in cookie jars all around the world: Russia, Germany, Vietnam, Afghanistan and more recently, focused in the Middle East. And the best part was that the only people to know about it were the actual employees of the organization and the Secretaries of Defense throughout the past few decades." Bryson was still angry with the man, but his story was unquestionably intriguing.

"So the only person within the government to ever know of this agency at any given time is the Secretary of Defense?"

"Yes and the head of the C.I.A. The three founders figured that it was best for two individuals to know of N.E.T.S. That way if knowledge of the agency somehow found its way into the public spotlight, it would be obvious which person it had come from and consequences would be designated accordingly."

"Consequences?"

"Death, Bryson. Realistically, the individual who releases information on N.E.T.S. should be tried for treason, but then that would make it even more public. The only remedy that Kennedy suggested was that if N.E.T.S. was ever revealed it would immediately be covered up and denied and the person responsible would be disposed of by the agency itself. Harsh I know, but truly the only option in order to keep it as invisible as it has been for all these years.

"You see? N.E.T.S. is America's most powerful tool. It knows no rules of engagement, no international laws, and no U.N. regulations. We have singlehandedly been responsible for the assassinations of some of the world's biggest tyrants, preventing numerous terrorist attacks, and I know for a fact that World War III has been adverted by our actions on at least two different occasions in the 60s and 70s. We even had a large part in the creation of Facebook."

"Bullshit." Bryson had heard enough and began to get up out of the booth. *Facebook? Who is this guy kidding?* "You nearly had me there, but you kind of blew your whole 'secret agency story' with the Facebook claim. I'm going back to work. I'll send over another waiter to take your order."

"Tell me Bryson, where do you first learn of most national and international news stories? The news channel or your news feed? How much information about yourself do you have on Facebook? How much *personal* information? The advertisements on your Facebook relate to you don't they? Have you ever noticed how they are different from other people's advertisements?" The questions ran through Bryson's head as he stood there. "It may not be the type of work that you would expect from an agency - I assure you there is plenty of that going on as well - but how do you think the government keeps tabs on the general public? On the international public? Facebook allows them to see what the population as a whole is thinking…what they are fearing…what they are anticipating. It tells them who they are, what they want, what they think they want, and what they think they need."

"Who the hell is 'they'?" The inquiry shot out of Bryson's mouth before he had even thought of it properly.

"Does it matter? Frankly Bryson, I don't give a damn if you don't believe me right now. That's not the point."

"Then what exactly is the point sir? Because *frankly* I think your story is a load of bullshit and I technically kicked you out of this restaurant five minutes ago."

"The point is that I want you to work for N.E.T.S. Your parents were the two of the best agents that the organization has ever seen even right up until the end. We can only hope that some of their intuition and natural talent carried over into your blood."

"Oh you can't be serious." Bryson chortled at the man's reasoning.

"I'm very serious Bryson. In fact, I cannot take 'no' for an answer now that I have disclosed all of this information to you. This is really your only option." His eyes pierced Bryson with seriousness.

"What…so either I come with you or…you kill me? Just like you claim that you killed my parents? I apologize for being rude sir but Go. Fuck. Yourself." Despite Bryson's language, the man stayed cool and stern with his reply. What he said next would change Bryson's life forever.

"Son, your parents were traitors and heroes to this country. There was substantial proof that began to appear around the time of your birth that they were in the midst of becoming double agents for a growing terrorist cell, the name of which we never did find out. While they themselves did not commit any acts of terrorism, we did intercept a series of phone calls established between them and a contact located in Brazil. They were planning to give the contact as much information on N.E.T.S. as they could gather, which judging by their rank at that time, would have been a devastating amount." He paused for a second and noticed that he had Bryson's full attention. "What they were going to exchange the information for, we also never found out. But once I learned of this, I immediately sat them down and discussed it with them. They were some of my closest friends – no they *were* my closest friends and I had to know the truth. Our commanding officer, the leader of N.E.T.S. at the time, had no idea that I ever did this.

"Your parents claimed that they had been forced into the predicament, and in order to prevent a larger terrorist attack on the U.S., they had to give up the information. I told them that N.E.T.S. could help them, but they insisted that this was the only way. Of course, you can only imagine what the release of N.E.T.S. files would do to the nation. The public wouldn't trust the government anymore, we would be internationally crucified, and the U.S. government would almost certainly be put on a U.N. trial.

"I told your parents I would get all three of you out of the country and hide them. I arranged for your family to get new identities, and to go live in a completely different country. But then I was called into a meeting with the head of N.E.T.S. He knew of the situation with your mom and dad and told me that since I was closest to them, it had to be me."

"It had to be you? What do you mean?" Bryson was once again engrossed in David's story.

"It had to be me who," he struggled with the next words, "killed them…I'll never forget the night I went over to their house. I was supposed to be bringing them their new identities and plane tickets, but instead I had become an executioner. When I arrived, the two of them already knew what I was there to do. They were calm…your mother made sure that I promised her that I would take care of you. Despite the fact that I was a wreck, I made a promise to them. We said our goodbyes…God I can remember hugging them for the final time like it was yesterday…and then I brought out two silenced pistols. Your parents were very strong people, Bryson, and even in the end they were still in love. They knelt down in front of the pistols, shared one final kiss, and held hands as they closed their eyes." He paused and chose his next words with great care and spoke slowly, "I doubt you have ever had to kill someone you cared for, someone that you loved. But that night I had to do it twice. A part of me died that night along with them. They looked so peaceful, hand in hand, and here I was, the violent bastard who had come to ruin them.

"I don't even remember pulling the triggers. I just remember seeing them fall to the floor and an extreme… *hollowness* overcame me. I didn't feel human. I didn't even feel. I think I sat there for hours that night. You were up in your crib sound asleep. I just remember staring at the same brick around the fireplace for a very long time. It was a reddish brick with a divot on the left side and smooth everywhere else…I wasn't even thinking of anything. I was numb; my mind was simply pulsing blood and nothing else." There was a long pause. "I have killed quite a few people in my life but none haunt me like that night."

A tear formed in Bryson's eye and the black man in the booth finally seemed human. He wouldn't hold a gaze anymore because he didn't want the boy to see the tears welling up in his own eyes as he finished.

"The murders were classified as a double homicide and the killer was never caught. The surviving child was taken to a childcare facility." The story of the past continued. "At least that's what the local papers stated. Nobody would ever know that your parents died honorably for this country. They were beautiful people Bryson, and you deserve to know what happened to them. And I'll never forget what your mother told me when she was knelt down in front of me with her eyes closed: 'Tell Bryson that we will always be with him. Forever.'"

Bryson quit his job at the restaurant and joined N.E.T.S. by the end of the week.

The beach upon which Bryson and Elena were making love was secluded. After the café, the two of them had set out for the Bermuda coast nearby. They arrived at a public beach that was fairly busy and they remained there for a bit, sitting in the soft, pink sand, people-watching the locals and tourists, and getting their feet wet in the alarmingly turquoise-blue ocean water. Soon enough, they decided to take a walk on the coast line. They walked for what Bryson thought must have been an hour. Passing gorgeous palm tree after gorgeous palm tree and walking in the sand which turned into shallow tide which turned into some small rock formations. The rock formations featured a small cliff hanging over the tame sea and underneath the shadow of the cliff was a small patch of fine Bermuda sand: their beach.

Two timeless hours later and they lay still, breathing heavily, looking into each other's eyes. Not out of love, but out of wonderment. Wondering what the other was thinking at this very moment; this moment that the two of them would never forget for the rest of their lives. *Where will we be in 50 years? What will our kids look like? How many will we have? How long do we plan on working for N.E.T.S.?* No 'I' thoughts were present amongst their minds, just 'we'. Elena, on top, eventually laid her head on Bryson's chest and the two of them remained there motionless…listening to each other's breathing and feeling each other's skin against their own. Few words were exchanged for a while, each of them were too in love to speak much.

Bryson glanced upward towards the sky on either side of the overhanging cliff above them. Judging by the position of the sun in the sky it was late afternoon. As the sun moved closer to the horizon, the blue sky started to darken ever so slowly.

"Hey! Come on, follow me." Bryson said as he slowly sat up and pulled himself out from underneath Elena.

"Where are we going?" She grabbed his hand and stood up.

"You'll see."

Bryson and Elena walked out from the shade of their beach and he then turned to begin climbing up the side of the cliff. The side was not extremely tall, nor was it vertically steep, so for Bryson and Elena climbing it was effortless. On top, the dark, jagged rocks created interesting patterns and formations. Bryson turned and looked to the ocean and the two began to walk over to the overhang that had provided them shade for most of the afternoon. Near the edge of the overhang was a section where the rock formations and patterns ended and it became flat except for one small boulder in the middle, slanted comfortably backwards. Motioning Elena over to the rock, Bryson extended his arm and the two of them sat down and leaned their backs against the smooth surface of the lone boulder. Bryson put his arm around Elena and she curled up under him, holding his hand in both of hers.

As the sun began to set, ripples of pink stretched across the sky. Soon orange, yellow, and red joined in. It was a tropical sunset unlike any other. Bryson could tell Elena had something on her mind; she had been fairly quiet ever since they had sat down.

He began to speak, "Wha – "

"Bry – " They had both tried to speak at the same time and cut each other off.

"You go." Bryson suggested.

"Ok, I was just thinking…you've never told me about how you met Harper." She paused. "How did you get into this business?"

"Well…" Bryson, shocked that they had not discussed this before, replied with the truth. "He found me. I was pretty much not going anywhere doing what I was doing and one day he walked into the restaurant where I was a waiter, the one I told you about, and offered me a job."

"And you just took it? How did he convince you?" Bryson didn't dare tell her about how David had been the one who had been forced to kill his parents; he would never reveal that personal detail to anyone, mostly out of protection of David.

"He basically just gave me a history of the agency, made a lot of enticing promises, and offered me the job." Technically it wasn't a lie. "So yeah, I pretty much just took it. It was better than what I was doing at the time."

Slightly disappointed, as if looking for a more interesting answer, Elena replied, "Oh I see."

"What about you? I don't think I've ever asked you how you met him either."

"Kind of the same story." Elena explained. "I was pretty successful and preparing to go into college when he approached my parents and I one day. He convinced them that he had the 'job of a lifetime' for me and told them about a modeling job that I would be doing all around the world. Of course it was a fake job and in a private interview he told me what the real job was. At first I was hesitant but he claimed that he saw something in me. He promised that if I didn't enjoy it, I could leave at any time."   The irony was that the two of them knew that wasn't true. N.E.T.S. would never let a low level recruit out of its grasp for fear of being revealed. Bryson even wondered if he and Elena would be allowed to leave if they wanted to right this moment. Despite their closeness to David, he highly doubted it.

"David is a good man. Think about it…if it weren't for him we never would have met." Bryson furthered the conversation and smiled over towards Elena. She responded with silence. Across the ocean the sun was being cut in half by the horizon and the colors blazing across the sky were in their truest form. Bryson couldn't help but stare at Elena. She didn't look worried, she looked like she was calculating something: focused and picking exactly what words she wanted to use. A few moments passed before she finally spoke.

"Bryson, what if one of us dies?" That was certainly not what he thought she was going to say and his face revealed the surprise. This was a side of Elena he had never seen before. She seemed afraid and that was very unlike her. "I know that we are both really good at what we do and that when we go back to N.E.T.S. we'll be partners, but the fact is that we have a dangerous occupation." A pause followed the reasoning as she continued to calculate what she was going to say. "I just don't know how long I want to do this Bryson. When I first started off I thought I could see myself doing this forever but then I met you and…and…my life changed." Bryson had never seen Elena cry before but there was a tear running down her cheek now. Immediately she wiped it away as if she was embarrassed that she had done such a thing. "I know you are going to think I'm being all corny and girly but Bryson…I don't know what I would do with myself if I lost you."

Multiple tears were coming down her face now and she refused to make eye contact with Bryson, pretending as if she was watching the nearly-finished sunset. Bryson could not really think of what to say; he was in a state of shock. He always knew that Elena had loved him but it was this moment that he grasped the concept. This person sitting next to him just revealed that she would not be able to live without him? He had never had anyone feel that way about him…*he* had never felt that way about anyone. Bryson leaned forward into Elena's vision and kissed her in a way that he had not experienced yet. It was a kiss that promised he was alive now and he would do his best to stay that way so long as she was living. It was a kiss that a man who finally realized what love *really* feels like gives to the woman responsible for making him feel that way.

The sun was disappearing behind the horizon as he broke the kiss and he promised, "Elena, I will always be with you. Forever."

CHAPTER XI
THE STATE OF A NATION

"Vice President Greyson gave a midday address to the nation today, assuring the population that the terrorist cell, now known as the Dead Scorpions, will be brought to justice.

"The Dead Scorpions have claimed responsibility for the sudden and very public assassination of the President and issued a threat against the people of the United States less than 48 hours after the murder. In addition, they were responsible for the mayhem that occurred in southern Australia last week.

"It is believed that the man seen giving the threat in the video, known as Abd Al Aziz, a former Saudi oil lord, was captured and is now in U.S. custody. But neither the C.I.A. nor the F.B.I. have commented on this speculation as of yet.

"Since the President's assassination and the imminent threat of a large-scale terrorist attack, the nation has been in a state of panic. For that report we go to Shawn Holmes who is live at Times Square..."

The news anchor ended his introduction and the picture on the TV immediately transitioned to a well-groomed man standing in the iconic crossroads of Times Square, microphone in hand. The once heavily-populated area behind him was eerily deserted...and quiet. When he was positive that the camera was rolling, he began his monologue.

"I am here at Times Square where just a couple of days ago, the nation's and world's history changed forever." A typical news station video package began to roll, replacing the scene of the reporter with a variety of images and video clips as he continued his voice over. "This week has quickly become a very scary one for many Americans. No one would have expected that a speech designed to unite the nation would have ended in such bloodshed." A video of the President giving his last sermon began to play. "And now there are more questions than answers with the American people feeling as if they are sitting on a time bomb." Soon a stock market image showed up on screen.

"In the days since the assassination and the threat, the Dow Jones has dropped by 10% and shows no signs of slowing while the NASDAQ has dropped a similar 13%. Investors say that it could be the single worst drop since the recession of 2008 and speculate that it is because consumers are no longer buying what they want, only what they need." Transition to a video of multiple stock markets throughout the world. "Meanwhile, the global economy is feeling the threat of the Dead Scorpions as well. Around the world, stock markets are experiencing significant drops, although, not nearly on the same scale as the U.S. markets." An image of the British Prime Minister shaking hands with other diplomats appeared on the T.V.

"The British Prime Minister has made it clear to the world that the war on terror is still very much alive and that the U.S. has the support of the British Nation…" The reporter's voice trailed off and was replaced with a British accent coming from the video clip of the Prime Minister's address to the world from earlier in the week.

"The United States has always been our biggest ally. They have supported us in our times of need, and over the last few years I have become very, *very* good friends with the President. It saddens me to see him taken at the hands of such a cruel act and it also saddens me to see the American people threatened by such a coward.

"The British nation will continue to support the United States of America, now more than ever. It is my strong belief that the war on terror is the world's *most* important issue and I urge all of my fellow world leaders to take a step back and look at what really matters. A nation needs us now, in the face of an evil foe, and

I fully intend to do anything and everything that I can do to assist them in order to defeat this villain. The American people are not alone."

With that final sentence, the Prime Minister's face lit up as the media snapped image after image and the video package continued on its intended path with the original reporter's voice returning.

"Several other nations have voiced their support for the United States in the past few days including Australia, Canada, France, Germany, and Israel. Many more are expected to show their support within the week.

"While there is growing support globally against the Dead Scorpions, there is mounting turmoil within the nation." The video package began a steady stream of local news videos that all coincided with what the reporter was describing at that time. "In Kansas, an elderly woman was trampled in a Wal-Mart during the nation-wide rush to stock up on batteries, food, and other necessities. She died hours later at the local hospital.

"There have also been riots and protests in major cities throughout the nation. New York, Washington D.C., Chicago, Denver, Los Angeles, and San Diego have all had to call in local law enforcement in order to contain the often-violent protestors. Many protestors are calling for the government to 'save them' from the threatened attack, and in most cases the protests turn to panic which have been leading to the riots. In the Denver protest, an entire block of parked cars were flipped on their sides and in L.A. four people are dead, three of whom were officers, when an extreme protestor opened fire on the police control blockade. The Vice President addressed this in his speech today telling the American people that, 'we are doing everything in our power to prevent the attack.' He continued with, 'We do not want enter the situation where we even *have* to save you'.

"Also across the nation there have been increased reports of robbery. Among the list of most popular items stolen are firearms, leading officials to believe that a new internet site has started to gain traction.

"Earlier in the week, a website called EOD.com cropped up and within a few hours its Facebook page had over 5 million views. EOD is said to stand for 'End of Days' and has not helped emergency officials in containing the spread of panic that has gripped the nation since the assassination and terrorist threat. The site's main goal is to prepare people for the impending terrorist attack on our nation by featuring suggestions for what to stock up on, how to make survival kits – many of which include weapons - how to defend one's self, etcetera. Many believe that it is a good resource, but government officials disagree." An older man featuring a receding hairline and a tie standing in front of a mundane building was displayed on the TV screen.

"People need to realize that this terrorist threat will not come to fruition. We have knowledge of it and that right there is half the battle. Preventing it will be our absolute top priority for the foreseeable future and we urge citizens to continue on with their daily lives. Sites like EOD.com do not encourage anything but panic and violence. If people are truly concerned, we suggest that they visit the Red Cross website. Thank you, everyone that will be all for today."

The man's face was brightened with flashes as the media at the scene again took hundreds of pictures within minutes.

Finally, the video package ended and the reporter at Times Square was back on. He quickly glanced down at his papers and then back up at the camera, trying to pour as much fake urgency and emotion into his face as he could.

"So there you have it, Peter. The state of the nation is not a good one and the citizens are not viewing any promises or statements that government officials make as genuine. It truly is a dire situation and we will keep you updated as things unfold across the next couple of days. Shawn Holmes, NBC Nightly News. Back to you Pete."

The anchor, safe in his news studio, came back on the air.

"Coming up after the break we have the F.B. – " he was cut short as the channel changed.

And changed.

And changed.

And changed.

A man was sitting in the dark of his own lofty, expansive apartment somewhere within the continental U.S. His 50-inch HDTV practically lit up the room on its own; there was no need for lights. The couch upon which the man sat was leather – black – and was usually very cold to the touch because of the professional AC system that kept the apartment at a chilly 65° F. But right now, the couch was rather warm. The man on the couch had been getting excited watching the news reports of the current issue in the United States. His quickened pulse was causing him to get hot, not uncomfortably so, but enjoyably so. He felt as if he was in control of something…something big. And in all honesty, he was. The feeling of power was emanating from his pores. He liked it and continued to change channels on the TV, only stopping for a few moments when a news station came on.

The HDTV displayed image after image of the horrors that had compounded around the nation in the last few days. Abd Al Aziz's face, digital red numbers and downward-pointing arrows all over Wall Street displays, overly crowded supermarkets, empty shelves where canned goods used to be, stores that had been broken into, protestors, picket signs, rioters, police barriers – all were accurate images of the current state of the nation. The TV changed images every few seconds as the man continued to press "Up" on the channel button, but he abruptly stopped when he was captivated by what he saw on the screen.

A woman, with dirt on her face and a trail of blood running down her right cheek was being interviewed in the streets of Los Angeles. Behind her was a burning car with dying flames and the flashing, pulsating, red and blue lights of emergency vehicles. Far away, sirens were audible and the reporter was speaking strongly in order to be heard. The woman's eyes were red and puffy indicating that she had been crying. As the interview continued, her eyes got glossy and shone strongly into the camera, indicating that she was about to cry again.

"Why are you protesting ma'am?" The reporter asked. "What are you trying to accomplish?"

The woman stood there, bewildered by the question. She didn't have an answer for the reporter. Or maybe she did, she was just too ashamed to admit it. Finally, a tear rolled down her right cheek, mixing with her blood, and dropped to the ground once it reached the bottom of her chin.

She replied in a shaky tone, "We are all just so damn scared..."

And somewhere in the U.S., the man sitting on the black leather couch smiled.

Chapter XII
Connecting the Dots

Metal to the floor. Bryson slammed the gas pedal of his Camaro as he got on the entrance ramp of southbound I-95. It seemed like all of the other cars were moving in slow motion as he dangerously swerved in and out of them, eager to get out of the city traffic.

Jerk left around an 18-wheeler in one of the middle lanes.

Riding the backend of a Camry until they get out of the way.

Swerve right across three lanes to find the quarter-mile opening in the right lane.

Bryson was steering the Camaro with little effort or thought dedicated to the task. His mind was elsewhere. What he had witnessed in the N.E.T.S. headquarters still astonished him. The man on the screen seemed to be numerous steps ahead of his pursuers and when he wasn't…well when he wasn't was when he was at his most dangerous. Singlehandedly he had destroyed the agents following him and according to Harper, who had spoken to Bryson before he left, the hotel room in D.C. was in a similar state of dismay. *This man is insane. Where did he come from? Where did he get his training?*

Drive on the shoulder to get around a couple in an old, plodding Cadillac.

A green dot on Bryson's phone was positioned permanently in the center. Underneath, a map of Bryson's current position translated itself appropriately as he drove. He glanced over at the device mounted in the dashboard and zoomed out several times. There, on the bottom of the screen, was a blue dot moving slowly towards the center – towards Bryson's dot. Within the hour the two dots would be touching and Bryson had a plan of action.

The man wanted to see Daniel Brody, the President's assassinator, but he was dead. Bryson had to assume that the individual who had called earlier had never actually seen Brody. This worked well in Bryson's favor and he planned to exploit it. In fact, it was his only plan. He just hoped that the techs back at N.E.T.S. could figure out what number the man had called Brody from while they were in the interrogation room. It had read "Restricted Number" but Bryson knew that there were workarounds to that.

Once he was within a few miles of the man he would call him, tell him that he was Daniel Brody, and suggest that they meet somewhere off of the interstate. From there, Bryson knew he would have to act fast in order to subdue him and get him back to N.E.T.S. *What is this man's hand-to-hand combat like? He murdered two entire teams in Washington D.C!* Bryson had his doubts, but at this point it wasn't up to him. This mystery figure, this impossible man, was the last known connection to the Aqarab Mayta. If Bryson failed here…he didn't really want to think about that.

A quick head shake got his mind back in focus and he continued darting through and around the remaining traffic on I-95.

162 miles from the blue dot...

Ian was severely injured. He knew that he had at least three fractured ribs, numerous bleeding cuts, a possible broken collar bone, and most likely a concussion. He felt like shit and he guessed that he looked like it too. But he had to tie up loose ends. He had to finish what he started and kill Daniel Brody. With him gone, the strongest-known link to the Dead Scorpions would be eradicated and Ian and his superior could continue with their preparations.

A metal piece of shrapnel from the totaled SUVs slipped out from underneath Ian's foot as he walked north on I-95. The slight unbalancing pulled at his abdomen and a searing pain shot up the left side of Ian's ribcage.

"GAH – FUCK!" The exclamation came out and he gently rubbed the area of pain as he approached the Suburban he had been driving…or at least what remained of it. It was completely totaled and lying on its side. The roof was crumbled inward, one of the back doors was no longer attached, and most of the side paneling was hanging by a thread. A pungent smell of gasoline coated everything and the only other smell Ian could pick up on was burnt rubber. He glanced behind him at the massacre that littered the road. Mangled SUV's could be seen far off in the distance and there were jet-black tire marks re-telling the story of the horrifying end to the chase.

Ian was looking for his cell phone that had been on the passenger seat, if memory served him correctly. Where it was now was anyone's guess. Ian hoped he wouldn't have to look long for it. He needed to steal a car and get back on the road as soon as possible.

Several more stumbles led Ian to his unusable vehicle and he peered inside for the small, black rectangle that was his phone. After a thorough analysis of the front seats, he moved on to the back seat with his hope of finding it slowly fading. The back seats proved useless as well so he finally moved on to the trunk but again, his efforts came up empty.

"Shit!" He stood there, in the middle of the road, knowing he didn't have much time until backup and emergency crews would arrive. His eyes closed and his lungs filled with a deep breath. Ian exhaled as he calmed down and simply turned and started walking north as briskly as he could.

Within ten paces, lying all alone on the sun-beaten concrete was his cell phone. Ian let out a smile, glad that some force of nature had been watching out for him, and reached down to pick up the cell phone. "Ah! Oww!" the simple exclamation came out softly as his extended arm gripped the cell phone and he straightened back up. *Sometimes I just wish this would be a little bit easier.*

Ian only had to walk for two minutes before he saw a blue compact car travelling south. As if it were a chore, he lifted himself across the interstate median to the other side and stood in the middle of the road. *Let's hope this isn't the police…*

Slowly the car came to a halt in front of Ian. The gaping, shocked expression of the driver said it all. Here was a man standing in the middle of the road looking like he had just crawled out of hell; his clothes were ripped, he had blood flowing from several cuts on his body, his posture made him look exhausted, and his stare looked determined. Regretfully forgetting caution, the driver placed the car in park, opened the door, and started walking towards Ian.

"Sir, are you OK? Do you want me to call 911 for you?"

"Give me your car."

"Uh…I can drive you to a hospital if that's what you're asking." The man stopped walking once he reached Ian and gestured back to his car as he offered the kindness.

"Sonofabtich" Ian muttered under his breath, getting irritated with the man's good manners.

"I'm sorry, I didn't catch that. What did you say?"

"Nothing." Ian replied. He reached for the driver's head with both hands and snapped his neck. A searing pain climbed up his side after the rapid use of his arms.

"ARGH! AGH! AGH! Dammit!" Once Ian's small temper tantrum was finished, he reached down, slowly as to not agitate any injuries again, and took the car keys. *I did him a favor. He won't want to be alive for the next few weeks anyway.*

Ian made his way over to the car, got in and started it up. He found a break in the median divider of the highway and got on the correct side of the road, continuing his journey north on I-95.

150 miles from the blue dot…

Driving at a high speed on the highway, Bryson couldn't help but think about Australia. So much had happened in the last week. *What am I doing?* He slid the Camaro around the light traffic that was in front of him and pressed onward. There was a tingle in his palm and he remembered the wound he had there. He also remembered how much pain he *hadn't* felt when it happened. Bryson thought to himself why that was. Adrenaline? Shock? Anger? Love? It was curious to him how he could be in so much more pain now than when he had had a knife completely through the palm of his hand. As Bryson zoned out his thoughts travelled to Elena and her skin, and hair, and eyes, and smile…her laugh. He missed her laugh. The way her nostrils flared when she giggled and how her eyes smiled like you had just said the funniest thing in the world.

A sharp noise of a cell phone ringing jolted Bryson out of his memories and he pressed the "answer" button on his steering wheel.

"Yeah?"

"Hi Bryson…" It was a female's voice. It sounded just like Ele – "It's Rachel." She paused. "David told me what happened in the interrogation room and showed me the video of this guy." There was silence once again. "Are you okay? I mean you're still injured and…well you've been through a lot lately. There is no shame in sitting this one out and letting a larger squad take this guy down."

"I'm fine Rachel. Plus there isn't time for a task squad. This guy is on the move right now and I'm already halfway there."

"I know it's just that…I…" There was hesitation in her speech. "Just be safe Bryson. This guy seems really dangerous."

"I will, Rachel." Bryson was smiling. He had always liked Rachel. She was sweet and you could tell she genuinely cared for everyone she worked with. Bryson heavily valued her friendship. "I'll see you a little later. Keep me updated with any new info you guys get."

"Will do. See you later, Bryson." The car speakers echoed a click signaling the call had ended and Bryson glanced at the GPS on the dash.

97 miles from the blue dot…

Adrenaline was in its final stages of wearing off and Ian could feel the pain even while sitting still. He figured that he had to have bruised some additional ribs and was now certain he had a concussion due to the incredible headache he had. Stains of his blood were all over the stolen car: on the steering wheel, the center console, the radio and air conditioning dials, and on the driver seat and seatbelt. Ian wasn't positive as to where he was losing blood from, and he knew that it wasn't a dangerous amount, but regardless, he couldn't wait to find a hotel and clean himself up.

Despite his injuries, Ian found a smile creeping across his face. For 20 minutes now he had seen no tail. The single police vehicle that he had passed was speeding off in the opposite direction towards all of the mayhem he had left behind. Ian punched the radio dial and found a local station.

"And that was the newest song from Br – I'm sorry ladies and gentleman, we have a breaking news story and a traffic report to bring you. A stretch of Northbound I-95 has been shut down following a large accident which we are being told by officials was fatal. That's all the information they are giving us at this time. Please be advised to find an alternate route if you are headed that way." The DJ continued on, "That's unfortunate Gretchen, you hate to hear when someth – " Ian turned the radio off.

So the officials are covering it up? Of course they are. Keep the American people in the dark...no matter. All that stands between me and a hot shower is Daniel Brody. With that thought, the smile on Ian's face disappeared somewhat. He was in bad shape and he had to go kill an assassin without a weapon. He wasn't scared to kill the assassin; he was confident that his skills and remaining energy reserves could take care of it. It was just going to take some effort. *And it's probably going to hurt like a bitch.* Ian was soon realizing that taking out the assassin in his current state was going to be less of an easy joy and more of an annoying chore. *Gotta take out the trash from time to time I guess.*

Silence was Ian's copilot for the next 15 minutes. He let his mind drift while he directed the vehicle to where he wanted it to go. It had been a long time since he let his mind just…wander.

He was always so concentrated on the methodology of his life; what he needed to do next, when he needed to do it, and how he needed to do it. This new, or rather forgotten, ability was refreshing to Ian. It relaxed him and made him forget about the pain he was in, if only for a couple minutes.   But it was terribly inefficient. *What am I even thinking about right now?*

And with that, he returned back to his concrete way of structured and ordered thinking. *Maybe once this is all said and done I can relax somewhere...Now, what to do next?* Ian thought about a strategy to try and catch the assassin unexpected. These injuries were getting more and more painful as time went on and his adrenaline reserves were nearly tapped.

He wanted to gauge where the assassin was at mentally. Would he be expecting anything? *If he's smart he already knows that I'm coming to kill him. He knows he is a loose end.* Realizing the only option he had was to call the assassin, Ian reached for the cell phone and hit the button. The phone began calling the same number as it had before.

Does he know? The cell phone connection had reached four, long rings by now. *Is that why he isn't picki –"* his thought was interrupted by the other line's answer and a voice that had clearly undergone computer alteration.

"There is a N.E.T.S. agent coming to kill you. He is on his way right now and is posing as the assassin, Daniel Brody. He will claim that he is still in Brody's apartment in New York. This is not true.

"You don't know who I am and you never will. Just know that I am a friend on the inside. Pretend like you never heard this call. When I forward this call to the agent, you still assume he is Brody. We will take care of the rest. Acknowledge."

Ian's reply was calm and short, "Acknowledged."

49 miles from the blue dot...

An unexpected ring emerged from a cell phone in Bryson's car. For the second time this drive, he pressed the answer button on the steering wheel, but nothing happened. A second ring was coming from somewhere and Bryson's blood turned cold. *Brody's cell phone.* He reached into the pocket where he had placed the disposable phone, pulled it out, and was greeted with the caller ID of:

RESTRICTED NUMBER

Fumbling, Bryson accepted the call and brought the phone to his ear making sure that his first words were stern.

"Yes…father?"

The reply came quick and equally as delivered. "No need for the code anymore. We will be parting ways soon enough."

"Understood. What's the plan?"

"Where are you now?" the man on the other end of the phone seemed to be hasty but Bryson was confident that there was no risk of him knowing that he wasn't speaking to Daniel Brody. Bryson answered the question with a lie.

"Still in New York City. Just waiting for you to get here so we can complete the money transfer and go our separate ways, as you stated. Where are you?"

"It doesn't matter where I am." Ian answered with a tinge of annoyance in his voice. "I'm on my way to you, just sit tight."

"Understood. Call me when you get ne – " Bryson's reply was drowned out by the sound of a honking horn. He had just cut off somebody on the highway and they didn't seem all too happy about it.

"What was that? I thought you were in your apartment?" Ian was suspicious of this N.E.T.S. agent now. *He is driving. How close is he? Will they take care of it before he gets to me?*

Bryson felt a small sense of panic. He had to make sure the man didn't think he was lying.

"I…uh…I'm walking around the streets. Cars honk their horns all the time here." And then he had a moment of realization. "I never mentioned anything about being in an apartment." The statement lingered on Bryson's mind as he heard a click in his ear. The call was over, the man had hung up. Bryson knew he had flustered him enough to make a mistake.

37 miles from the blue dot…

"FUCK!" Ian knew he was acting unwisely. The N.E.T.S. agent had to be suspecting him now. His injuries and dwindling energy were starting to cloud his judgment; he wasn't sure that he could take this approaching agent in his current condition. Ian only hoped the "friend" that had answered first was going to take care of it. *Who was that guy? Was he an insider at N.E.T.S?* It almost seemed like he had to be. *Could it even be a* she? Ian hadn't thought of that, the voice had been far too modulated. Either way, he hoped that whatever they were going to do, they were going to do it fast and to completion. He had an uneasy feeling that the N.E.T.S. agent was closer than he presumed and there was no guarantee that he was alone.

Ian continued to drive and regained his nerves. Whoever had intercepted that call was on his side and he figured they were capable of handling the situation. *There is just so much on the line.* He did not know the endgame of the Aqarab Mayta; that honor was reserved for a man that even he had not met, despite his high position in the organization. All he knew was the imminent attack would be extensive, unexpected, and future-altering.

Through way of anonymous contact, Ian was informed that he would be spared and rewarded greatly for his efforts upon the completion of the attack. He believed it too. Anytime the Aqarab Mayta wanted something of him, they provided him with anything and everything he needed: top notch gear, plenty of ammo, trustworthy firepower, and even high-end food and boarding. There was no shortage of money within the organization but Ian didn't dare inquire where that money came from.

All he knew for certain was that he wanted to be far away from the United States when the Dead Scorpions planned to strike…

20 miles from the blue dot…

Bryson was actively scanning the horizon for the man's car. The blue dot was rapidly approaching the center of the GPS screen as both men were intensely making their way towards each other. Bryson knew that at least he had the element of surprise by how close he was. All he had to do now was keep an eye out for a possibly speeding vehicle and his GPS in case he overshot the guy.

Despite this confidence, Bryson was still shaken up by the phone conversation. Why had the man called in the first place? How did he know about the apartment? Why had he just automatically hung up? These were all questions that were cycling through Bryson's head that he would have to get answered later. For now however, he needed to focus on apprehending the man as quickly as possible and keeping him alive…no more situations like the one that had played out in the interrogation room.

Traffic had picked up slightly on both sides of the highway but was still relatively light. It was early afternoon so it could have been a combination of late lunch rush hour and people heading home from work early. Bryson glanced around at the scenery and realized that it was a gorgeous day outside: very sunny, some low lying cirrus clouds looking like misplaced paint strokes on a blue canvas, and luscious greenery on the side of the light grey interstate. *A typical American summer day.*

High above him Bryson noticed several black dots scattered across the sky moving slowly in various directions. *Will their attack utilize airlines again?* Bryson stared at the planes for a moment longer and redirected his attention back to the GPS seeing that the two dots were very close now. He would be passing the man at any moment now.

Ian was in a lot of pain, but that didn't matter. He just kept driving…it was almost a mindless activity at this point. New York City was still quite a ways away. After a short while he noticed a black car travelling southbound at a high rate of speed. To him it looked like a new Camaro with a man driving. Ian almost shrugged off his intuition but something about the car was making him anxious; it seemed like it was on a mission. He kept his eyes on the driver as he got closer and knew his feeling had been correct when he found himself staring directly into the agent's piercing blue eyes…

Bryson's eyes were rapidly switching back and forth between the GPS and the road. The dot was in the middle now so the vehicle had to be visible. He glanced to his left and saw a blue compact car driving faster than most. From his current position it looked like a man behind the wheel and as Bryson got closer something seemed odd about the situation. There was a gut feeling deep down inside of him that was trying to say something. *That's him.* Bryson was staring intently at the man while he approached and their eyes instinctively locked as they proceeded forward in opposite directions…

Their mutual gaze was interrupted by a loud roar and a bright flash. The only thing that followed was darkness.

0 miles until the blue dot…

CHAPTER XIII
A DANGEROUS THIRD PARTY

An ocean covered the inside of the vest. But there were no fish in this ocean, no breeze to create waves, and no ships. Just spheres. Silver, metallic spheres that were spread evenly across the landscape and reflecting everything around them, including the bomb maker's face.

He knew he didn't have to spread the metallic balls evenly throughout the baby blue, glue-like gel. *"The explosion doesn't care if the shrapnel is spread evenly. It aims where it pleases."* He had once been told. He didn't care; he liked the control he had over where the balls were placed. He liked the exactness of his methods. He liked the patterns.

Several more spheres landed on the gel with heavy thuds as they pushed the viscous liquid out from underneath them and stuck in place. The bomb maker was making a grid this time…he wasn't sure why, he just wanted to make a grid: rows and columns. There had been times before where he had made flowers, clouds, crosses, swords, and random pattern designs. His work had certainly picked up in the last few months…he had made over 300 of these vests exclusively for the Aqarab Mayta. The deal was that he would make as many as they needed and they would pay him extremely well. The second that he began to ask questions was the second they would kill him.

So he didn't ask any questions. He knew the bombs were going to be used for terrorism…to kill innocent civilians, but he tried not to think about that. *Perhaps that is why I make the patterns?* He thought to himself. They calmed him and gave him more of a sense of purpose than just creating tools for death.

As he finished placing the last corners of the grid on the gel, a man walked into his work place. His skin was dark and brown, his face was clean shaven, and his clothes were civilian,

"Good evening, Abdullah." The bomb maker stated as he looked away from his task and gave the visitor a nod. The man replied with a nod as well and put a hand on the bomb maker's shoulder. A gentle quiet crept over the room as usually happened in these situations.

The men would come to the bomb maker when they had been instructed to pick up their vest. The bomb maker was responsible for explaining the device to them and then to send them on their way. With vests in hand, the men would be called at any time in the future to do as the Aqarab Mayta bid. When this calling would come, they did not know. All they knew was that once they picked up their vest, they were one step closer to death. *But a "glorious" death in the name of Allah, supposedly,* the bomb maker reminded himself as he glanced at the man and gave him a gentle smile. Abdullah seemed half a world away and didn't even notice so the bomb maker picked up the final, deadly spheres and finished his grid pattern.

Once he was satisfied with his artwork, he reached into a highly organized drawer and grabbed a chip no larger than a credit card and placed it on the inside of the vest where there was a special opening for it. Again reaching over to the drawer, he pulled out a cable and connected it to the port located at one end of the chip. He began to weave the cable through the vest where it was designed to go and as he did so, he started to explain the bomb to the man as he had done many times before to other men.

"Basically, you have to do nothing for this bomb to be effective. In this chip there is a piezoelectric sensor that withstands normal stresses but once it senses an *extreme* stress, it will activate. For example, simply tripping and falling with this vest on will not activate it, but getting shot will.

"Once this piezoelectric sensor detects a high stress event it sends a signal through this wire which will ignite the gel within the vest. Due to the high pressure within the vest, this ignition and burning of the air will cause this metal to explode." He pointed to the metal lining that encased the gel and grid of sphere balls as he continued to explain, "The whole process only takes one microsecond from the extreme-stress event sensed by the piezoelectric device." He let that settle for a moment before he started up again. This next part was always his least favorite to explain.

"The vest explodes outwards and upwards. It is designed to kill the user as fast as possible by taking part of the force of the explo – "

"Decapitation" the man finally spoke.

"Yes…precisely. You will not feel a thing. That I can promise you." The bomb maker felt remorseful that this tool of destruction, this selfish "career" of his, was the device that would take the lives of so many young, brave men. *I will have to pay for my sins someday.* "Do you have any questions?"

"What do I have to do once I put it on?"

"Ah yes, good question, I forgot to explain that to you." He felt clumsy for leaving out the most important part. If the user didn't turn the bomb on, then it wouldn't go off in the first place. "Once the vest is on, you will notice a Velcro pouch over the left breast. Open it, and inside there is a button poking through the fabric." As he explained he opened the pouch, showed Abdullah the button, and pressed it. A small green light filled the inside of the pouch and a small *Beep* preceded it. The bomb maker noticed his guest twitch slightly once he had activated the bomb and thus continued explaining.

"After the button is pressed you will hear a small signal and a green light will turn on. This means that the bomb is active. If you just so happen to accidentally activate the device, all you need to do is open the vest like so…look on the inside of the left breast pouch, find this red cable, take it out of the port to the chip, and re-insert it into the same port. Would you like to put it on and try?"

The man nodded and stood up from the stool which he had been observing the bomb maker's instructions. Carefully, the bomb maker handed him the now-disarmed vest and watched as Abdullah slowly put it on, one arm at a time. Every time one of these young men would come to retrieve their weapon the bomb maker could not help but think about what it must feel like to be wearing the very instrument of your death around you. *The weight must be immense…on the body and the mind.*

He continued to watch as the man opened the pouch and pressed the button. The bomb maker looked up and the two men's stares met, holding for what seemed to be a while. There was an immense amount of sadness behind Abdullah's eyes. All the birthdays he would never have, the women he would never bed, the children he would never raise…it was a large price to pay, being a terrorist, regardless of what anyone believed would happen in the afterlife.

The bomb maker could tell that this was a *real* man. So many other men had come into his shop just as silent but twice as arrogant. They were proud to be getting a weapon of terrorism. The thought of killing innocent civilians and dying in the process, all in the name of Allah, excited them. Travelling to the afterlife and acquiring a plethora of virgins motivated them. And hatred for a country that they did not know fueled them. But there was something different in this man's eyes. Determination still shone through as it did with all who were to carry out the Aqarab Mayta's will…but there was…something. A deep pain, maybe an enormous regret or a dying dream, that coated this man's, nay, this boy's eyes as if it were a gentle blanket. The bomb maker's heart wept for Abdullah.

As if knowing that his soul was being weighed, Abdullah broke the gaze and opened the vest to pull the wire out and place it back in. He glanced in the pouch to make sure the light was off and removed the vest, handing it back to the bomb maker who had since tried to busy himself by putting all of his tools back in their proper place.

"Ah, thank you." The bomb maker grabbed the vest and walked it over to a table where he had a ragged JC Penny's gift box lying open. He placed it in the tissue and covered it, making sure that none of it was exposed and placed on the top of the box. There was a roll of Scotch tape on the table and the bomb maker took several partitions from it and taped down the gift box as if it was a present for a friend. After all, it was only travelling a short distance on land before it would be placed in a much more high-security container. Abdullah held out his hands to take the box and the bomb maker extended it towards him, but then pulled it back and asked, "Would you like to pray with me?"

The man stood silent for a moment - the bomb maker couldn't tell if he was surprised or annoyed - and then replied with a gentle nod. The bomb maker returned the gesture with a small smile and placed the gift box back on the table. He walked over to a dresser on the far end of the room.

"Will you need a sajjadah? I have an extra…"

"That would be most appreciated."

So the bomb maker grabbed an extra prayer mat and walked back into the room, removing his shoes at the entry way. Abdullah walked over and did the same. The bomb maker grabbed a bronze basin from atop another cupboard and filled it in the nearby sink, grabbing a towel from the counter on his way back. He placed the basin back on the same table as the bomb and both men began to wash their hands, face, and feet. Neither of them were saying a word; there was no need to. The bomb maker finished scrubbing away his sins first and gently dried himself with the towel and handed it to the young man next to him.

Once both men were clean and dry, the bomb maker unrolled both mats onto the hardwood floor and faced them Southwest, towards Mecca. Their gaze met again as they stepped onto their separate mats.

"Would you like to lead?" Abdullah acknowledged the question once more with a nod and began by lifting his hands to either side of his face with palms facing forward.

"*Allahu Akbar*" God is most great

The men continued through the ritual, following the process of reciting prayers, lines from the Qur'an, and stretching and kneeling as appropriate.

"*Ashadu anna la ilaha illa Allah*" I bear witness that there is no god but God

"*Ashadu anna Muhammadan rasul*" I bear witness that Muhammad is the prophet of God

"*Allah*"

"*Haiya `ala al-salat*" Come to prayer

"*Haiya `ala al-falah*" Come to wellbeing

"Al-salat khayrun min al-nawm" Prayer is better than sleep
"Allahu Akbar" God is most great
"La ilaha illa Allah" There is no god but God

At the conclusion of the prayer, as both man sat on their knees with their backs straight and arms extended forward, the bomb maker continued aloud.

"Allah," he paused, piecing together the right words that would help to comfort the troubled man next to him, "please bless Abdullah in all of his future. His sacrifice is great and please remember that all he does, he does in your name, the absolute holiest of names. He is a young man, yes, but a brave one, full of courage and faith, given to him as gifts by you. Watch over him now and always and when the hour comes, may you welcome him into heaven with open arms. *Allahu Akbar*."

"Allahu Akbar." Abdullah replied to conclude the prayer. After a short moment of silence both men stood up and rolled their sajjadah, with Abdullah handing his back to the bomb maker once he was finished. The bomb maker took both mats over to the place where he had gotten them and returned to the table. For a second time he picked up the JC Penny gift box and extended it towards Abdullah, this time letting him take it. He placed a hand on Abdullah's shoulder and gave it a soft squeeze.

"You will do great things my friend. I just know it." Abdullah smiled once more and turned and gave the bomb maker a hug. Several pats on the back later and the young man was on his way out the door. It would be the last time that the bomb maker would ever see him.

Now alone, the bomb maker let out a heavy sigh. *Sigh all I want, it will not lighten this burden of guilt off my shoulders...* He picked up the basin full of sin-stained water and walked over to the kitchen to rinse it out. Looking for a distraction, he turned on the TV and a news cast instantly appeared. He did not particularly care for the news and tuned it out as he completed some odds and ends in the kitchen. But he did catch one peculiar tidbit.

"We have reports tonight of mayhem breaking out in southern Australia..."

And with that, the bomb maker let out another sigh.

It was early in the morning and Abdullah couldn't sleep anymore. The little amount of sleep that he had gotten was poor; every 45 minutes he kept on waking up for no reason other than an odd premonition that hung over his head.

It had been this way since the President was assassinated a few days ago. Abdullah knew that this was the start of the Aqarab Mayta's plan even before the tape of Abd Al Aziz had surfaced a couple days later. What was once deep buried in his consciousness was now at the forefront of his daily thoughts: *any moment now they will call on me to put on that vest…* It was weighing on him heavily and beginning to affect him. He knew he wasn't afraid of dying. In fact, he wasn't even afraid of killing. Whatever target he was designed to take out deserved it and he truly believed that. America was a stain on the history of the world and a nation full of corruption, sin, and idiots. What the Aqarab Mayta was doing was cleansing history of that temporary blemish.

No…what he was afraid of was his regrets, his own sins; the ones that he would have to face when he died, which he assumed would be sooner rather than later. As he lay in his bed in the dark, tears began to well up in his open eyes; he missed them so much. So much that it just…hurt. They had been his entire world. *They were just one of your worlds, you bastard.* He remembered as he ridiculed himself. He knew it was true. He had lied to her ever since they had met and as a result his other life had destroyed his real life; the one in which his soul was located. His eyes were still open but he was dreaming as he travelled the painful road back into his memories…

A bright glare blinded him as he walked to the market to purchase some fruits and vegetables for dinner for his family: his beautiful wife and his four year old son. The sun was setting and its rays were gently receding deeper and deeper into the Mediterranean Sea. The Palestinian city was calm and the thousands of buildings seemed to be basking in the final sprays of heat coming from the sun.

He was very excited for dinner with his family tonight. He had been away a lot the past month and had been gone the last six days on business. Business? Keep telling yourself that. *His mind mocked him but he quickly shook the insult away; he was too happy to finally see them to care.*

After finishing picking the food that he needed he paid the vendor and began the walk back home. It really was a beautiful day. Even now that the temperature had gone down with the gorgeous departure of the sun, it was still tepid and comfortable. A minuscule breeze felt warm as it ran through his hair and across the skin on his arms; he could not help but smile. This night will be perfect *he thought.*

The rest of his walk home was spent thinking about what he was going to cook and how he would cook it. He glanced in the bag to remind himself of what he had purchased and started to plan out the process. He always had fancied himself a rather talented cook, certainly no master chef by any means, but a fair step better than many of his male counterparts. He turned the final corner on his journey home, walked up the steps and entered the front door.

"Daddy!!" His little boy came rushing to greet him and he reached down and scooped him up. "What took you so long at the market?"

"Maybe I was busy buying you a present?" Abdullah hinted and the boy's face lit up. "I'll show you after dinner okay?" His son's excitement deflated proportionally and he nodded. Abdullah set him back down on the ground.

"Dad you have a visitor! Come see who it is!"

"A visitor? Who did he say he was?"

"Ummmm I don't remember but he is in the kitchen talking to mom. Come on dad!" The boy took his hand and led him through the small living space and dining space into the kitchen. As Abdullah came around the corner his heart sank. He could see the confusion and slight worry on his wife's face as she tried to be a good host to their unexpected guest. He's not unexpected. You always knew this was a possibility. *The man standing across from her was Abd Al Aziz, Abdullah's ranking officer and general in the Aqarab Mayta.* What is he doing here? He questioned himself,

positive that the same inquisitive look was plastered on his face. You know damn well what he is doing here, idiot. *Abd Al Aziz finally broke the growing silence.*

"Greetings, Abdullah! Sorry to have stopped by unexpectedly...your wife tells me you are to cook them quite the meal!"

"Uhhm..uh yes...I plan to. I was just at the market getting some of the final additions." He really had no idea how to respond. Does he want to be invited? Maybe he is just here to check up on me? *His wife was slightly more reassured knowing that her husband actually knew the man who was in her kitchen.*

"Abdullah, who is your friend? I don't believe I have ever met him."

"Oh my goodness, how rude of me. Here I am in your home and I don't even have the decency to introduce myself. I am Nazeem, your husband and I work together at the law firm here in Haifa. Nice to meet you." Abd Al Aziz extended a hand to the wife and she shook it and returned a small smile. Everything seemed to be okay now that introductions had been made, at least on the surface. Abdullah was still a nervous wreck and wondered how Abd Al Aziz had found him and his family.

As he prepared dinner he kept a cautious eye on Al Aziz as the man told a long, very detailed, and very fake story to his wife about their time together at the law firm. Abdullah would have been impressed if he hadn't known that lying was just one of the many talents required of his and Al Aziz's profession. The motions he was using to create the meal were being carried out subconsciously; there was too much else to think about. Why is he here?!

45 minutes passed and dinner was finally done. It smelled divine and filled the home with a warm, delicious scent.

"Abdullah, that smells great! When can we expect it?" Al Aziz called from the living room.

"Five minutes!" Abdullah split the meal into four portions on the clean, white plates. The meals were noticeably smaller than they would have been had there only been three guests, but nonetheless, he made it work. He made sure to turn off the stove, grabbed all four plates, and brought everything into the living room where Al Aziz, his wife, and his son were all sitting at the table ready to eat. The sight was jarring...as if Al Aziz had replaced him

as the head of the household and he was having an out-of-body or alternate reality experience. Before he could let the oddity's emotion show on his face, Abdullah continued to the table and placed everyone's plates in front of them.

"Thanks dad!"

"Yes, thank you dear. This looks delicious." Abdullah sat the final plate down in front of Al Aziz and the uninvited guest looked up and smiled at him. It was not a smile used for thanks – it more accurately conveyed: "Enjoy this. It is time."

After that smile, Abdullah couldn't concentrate. He didn't taste his meal at all, didn't participate in the table conversation that was being led by his wife and Al Aziz, and didn't make eye contact with anyone. Abd Al Aziz recognized this and respectfully didn't force Abdullah to participate in the discussion. In fact, he aimed it away from him and spoke more about his personal history. Again, more lies.

Dinner lasted about 20 minutes and eventually everyone finished what was on their plate. The conversation also began to dwindle but Abdullah still remained inactive. A great worry had come over him; he was becoming anxious.

"I have a game we can all play!" Al Aziz stated loudly as to excite Abdullah's son and wife.

"What is it?!" the child asked innocently.

"It's very simple. The first step is to close your eyes. Everyone shut their eyes, you too Abdullah." Al Aziz completed the sentence with a smile as if he was actually about to begin playing a game. "OK! Now...I want everyone to think about the word 'paradise'. Try to picture it in your mind; it can be anything! But don't tell me what it is! Keep your eyes closed and just imagine it." He paused for a moment to let them create their own images. "A tan beach with warm, moist air and a blue sky? Or is it a truck full of candy?"

Abdullah went to his paradise. He was at his family's favorite park and they were enjoying a sunny weekend afternoon. Not a care in the world. His son was smiling and laughing and his wife was radiant in the comfortable rays of the sun. He held the thought and felt at peace...he did not take notice of Al Aziz anymore and it seemed like an eternity that he had been spending in paradise. And then he heard it.

BZZP!

BZZP!

Two silenced shots rang out in the room and the sound of bodies softly crumpling followed. Abdullah did not feel dead, but he kept his eyes closed. He tried to travel back to his paradise and lose himself to it but ultimately his emotions took over. Tears started rolling down his cheeks as he slowly opened his eyes. But he never saw the bodies. Before he could turn to look at them, Al Aziz took him in his arms.

"Shhhh, shhh, shh, sh. Don't look Abdullah. I don't want you to see. Just know that they are gone."

"Wh-y-y-y-yyy?" Abdullah was drowning in his own tears as he lightly thrashed in Al Aziz's strong grasp.

"You know why, Abdullah." Al Aziz replied gently. "I need you strong. I need you focused for what is ahead. What we have been preparing for – it is almost upon us." Abdullah reluctantly accepted the truth that he had always known in the back of his mind and cried into Al Aziz's shoulder. After several minutes, Al Aziz broke the sound of misery with a question, "What was your paradise, Abdullah?" For a while there was no reply.

"I was with them…in a…in a park. It was a beautiful day."

"Hold onto that thought. Once you have completed your task, your paradise will become your reality." Al Aziz held him and made sure that he didn't look back at the bodies of his wife or son for a short while longer. "Come, Abdullah. The time for weakness is over. You are stronger now. Leave them and come with me. It is all beginning."

That had been six months ago but Abdullah still felt the wound as if it were fresh. But Al Aziz had been right; it had made him stronger. The past few months of training had been grueling and Abdullah had been pushed to his limits several times, but he never broke. With nothing to live for other than glory for the Aqarab Mayta, his limits were further than they would have been with a wife and child. Eventually he recognized this fact and that had been the moment when he had died inside…until the President had been shot just a few days ago and he realized that the end was getting closer by the day.

Visceral and deadly skydiving training had been his life for the last six months. Day after day after day he and his brothers were required to act out scenarios, all of which were tests. The first few weeks had been practicing on land – replicating certain falling and diving positions over and over until they were part of his muscle's memory. Shortly after this came the first skydives that were in tandem with brothers who had done it many times before. Abdullah had rather enjoyed this part. The feeling of falling with no stress or responsibility at all, not even to pull the parachute, was a miraculous feeling. But then the real training began.

The very first time they practiced out of tandem their chutes had been rigged to not work. They were required to pull the emergency chute. One of Abdullah's brothers had not made it. His body was collected and disposed of as if it had never produced a conscious thought. Another time they threw all of the men's parachutes out of the plane and forced them to jump after them. In Abdullah's group six men had jumped. Only five parachutes had been thrown out.

It had continued like this until eight days ago when Abdullah had been sent to pick up his explosive vest back in Pakistan. He had passed all of their vicious tests and was now deemed acceptable to be a martyr. He sat up in bed and finally stood, stealing a glance at the box that contained the vest as he did so. *Is today the day?*

The morning routine which he so often and mindlessly completed began its motions. Stretch. Fifty pushups. Stretch again. Shower. Shave. Make breakfast. Wash dishes. Begin day. As Abdullah was walking away from the kitchen he heard his cell phone ring. It could only mean one thing: *It IS today.*

Slowly he picked it up, answered it, and brought it to his ear. The voice on the other end was one of the calmest he had ever heard and spoke with perfect annunciation.

"Brother, today we call on you and you alone. You will be the first in our plan and you *WILL* be remembered. Say your prayers and be at the destination at 1200 hours. Make contact with no one. Allahu Akbar." Not a second later the call was over.

Abdullah stood there with the phone still held to his ear, quivering slightly. His body was filled with an emotion, yet he had no idea which one. Fear? Anxiety? Sadness? Pride? Anger? He knew it was none of these and his mind thought of his dead wife and child. Relief. This emotion was relief and as soon as he knew that, there was no turning back. There was no final prayer. He just grabbed the box with the explosive vest in it and left.

His drive to the hangar had been swift and he arrived at 1145 hours. For a moment, Abdullah wondered if he should have enjoyed that extra 15 minutes more. He could have visited a park, or eaten anything he wanted; he could have *lived* an extra 15 minutes. This saddening thought was squelched as soon as his commanding officer pulled into the hangar at the same time. Abdullah had never learned his name over the last six months and he was to refer to him only as "Sir". The black town car that Sir had arrived in pulled away as he got out and glanced over at the small two engine plane that took up most of the tiny hangar. For him, this would not be a one way trip; he would land the plane several states away in order to avoid suspicion. Gracefully, the man who was also Abdullah's pilot for today walked over and held out a hand.

"How are you feeling brother?"

"Fine." The answer was short and quick.

"Good. Let's take you through the final preparations. We should be up in the air within the next hour."

They were taking off at 1301 hours and were at their appropriate 18,000 foot altitude by 1345 hours. Abdullah had been trained to jump from this height without oxygen and he assumed that their current height was another attempt at throwing off any suspicion of their purpose. Both men sat in silence until Sir informed Abdullah that he would give him the 15 minute heads up. Abdullah nodded and it was that moment that his mind went blank. It rushed back and forth with thoughts of his life and his coming death but none of them stuck; they were all fleeting insects unable to land on his solid consciousness.

He had thought about these last moments for a large portion of the past few days. Strangely, it was nothing like he had imagined it. His mind seemed to have an unusual sense of awareness, his mouth was moist, his sight was sharp, and his muscles were oddly relaxed. A single thought stuck in his mind and he held onto it: *I have accepted it.*

"15 minutes Abdullah." The pilot calmly said back to the hull. With the single thought still clear in his mind, Abdullah made the final, deadly preparations. There was a duffel bag in the hull next to him and he opened it up, already knowing what was inside: seven C4 charges. The wingsuit that he was wearing was designed to hold all of them. Slowly taking the first two, he put them in the pouches behind his calves, one on each side. Another two were placed in pouches on the outside of his thighs and another two were placed on top of his thighs. Carefully, Abdullah turned on his vest just as its creator had instructed him to a little more than a week ago. *That feels like a lifetime ago.*

He pulled the rest of the wingsuit up over his shoulders now that the vest was armed and made sure that it was securely tightened. There was one more C4 charge and he held it out in front of him. Out of nowhere he realized that there would be absolutely no remnants of his body. Seven C4 charges and the explosives in the vest would essentially vaporize him. *For you were made from dust, and to dust you shall return.* It was one of the few verses from the Christian Bible that Abdullah knew and he found it funny at this very moment for he knew that he wouldn't even be dust.

Finally he placed the last charge in the pouch at the front of his vest and double checked all of the others making sure they were absolutely secure. He removed the goggles from inside the duffel bag and placed them over his head, pressing a button on the side as he did. They were clear goggles but provided him with a minimal heads-up display. There was an altimeter in lime green on the left side of the screen that currently read 18,037 feet. The only other object being projected was a red target that indicated where he was to strike.

"30 seconds, Abdullah." The pilot turned back and looked at him directly. "Brother, we are so proud of you. You are the best of us and we will always remember what you started here today. It was my honor to train you and send you off this final time. Allahu Akbar." Abdullah stared at him for a moment realizing the magnitude of what he was about to do. It would be in the history books. He would be a hero to all in the Aqarab Mayta. He was a hero to *this* man staring back at him. A surge of confidence and pride came over him.

"Allahu Akbar." He replied sternly. *Today is the day that America begins to fall.*

A green light lit up on the side of the sliding hull door and without a second's hesitation Abdullah threw himself out into the blue abyss. He focused on his HUD and saw that the target was pretty much right below him, now 17,879 feet away. Abdullah pulled his legs close together, positioned his head downward, and pulled his arms to his side. Despite the fact that he was diving to his death, he was having the time of his life. He had never descended this fast and with this much freedom. There was no parachute to weigh down his cognizance with thoughts of pulling it. There was only falling and hitting the target.

The sky was a beautiful baby blue and the air, while cold as it rushed past him, had a warm tinge accompanying it. There were hardly any clouds and Abdullah realized that these used to be his family's favorite days. They would spend hours in the park together back in Pakistan and this was Abdullah's paradise. For the first time that day, he realized that he would be seeing them within 12,467 feet. An immediate punch of elation took over his thoughts like a blast of hot air. He knew he was going to enjoy the last couple minutes of his life and then be reunited with his wife and child.

As the ground came into view he could see its details. There was a highway with very few moving specks indicating the vehicles below. It became clear to him that his target was actually one of those moving dots and he figured that if he kept his speed up, he would land almost directly on the vehicle. He didn't care at all who was in the vehicle or how this would help the Aqarab Mayta, he just kept his dive position and enjoyed the ride.

The altimeter now read 6,233 feet and Abdullah knew he had only a few seconds left. The ground, which had appeared motionless before, was now rushing closer and closer to him. The red target was slightly off to his right and getting closer. Abdullah snapped out his whimsical state of bliss and felt fear. *This is it. This is where I die. Is this my last thought?* He made sure to answer that question by forcing himself to align with the target and forget about everything else but his wife and child playing in their favorite park: his paradise.

Cars were coming into vision with more clarity and detail. Abdullah could see the highway very clearly and it was violently and relentlessly coming closer. He took a long, deep breath. It would be his last one. His eyes were still open and the last things they saw were a gray surface, a black car on one side of the road, a small, blue car on the other, and a bleeding red target. Then his world went dark and his thoughts ceased to exist.

CHAPTER XIV
RESCUING THE ENEMY

MONDAY JUNE 26TH, 2017
N.E.T.S. HEADQUARTERS, NEW YORK CITY

N.E.T.S. headquarters was in an unusual state of disarray. A large explosion had just occurred on I-95 about an hour south. Local and national news stations were still confused as to what had happened, with some even calling it a gas explosion despite the fact that no gas lines were present around the area. David Harper knew better and immediately, but discreetly, declared the nation under attack from the Aqarab Mayta.

At the time of the explosion, several people had been in a large room that was presenting live satellite feed of Bryson's vehicle as he was on his way to meet up with this unnamed enemy. Two screen feeds had become one as the vehicles entered the general proximity of each other and when their paths crossed was when an immense fireball had filled the screen. The two vehicles had launched in opposite directions off the side of the road and Harper had ordered that both men be brought into N.E.T.S. for medical treatment rather than hospitals. Within a half hour the two of them had been wheeled in on gurneys through the N.E.T.S. service elevator and placed in separate rooms; the unnamed man's room surrounded by armed agents. Both of them had sustained injuries and were in temporary comas, but the unknown man had clearly taken the bigger blow. There were glass shards that had cut deep into his face and he had several broken ribs, bruises everywhere, a severe concussion, and a broken collar bone. Which of these had come from the blast and which had come from his handiwork on the highway earlier were not immediately clear to the medical personnel. Despite the injuries, the head physician had made it known that both of them would certainly live.

Back at the scene of the attack, many civilians were not so lucky. The explosion's shock wave had thrown Bryson and the other man's car sideways with little shrapnel embedded in their cars. A small piece had entered Bryson's leg but had since been removed. The few other cars that had been on the interstate at that time were mangled and scattered. Paramedics declared two dead at the scene and seven were taken to the hospital with serious conditions, three of which had suffered traumatic amputations of limbs. The only saving grace had been the time of the blast, which had occurred at a relatively low traffic hour. Had the event unfolded a couple of hours later during rush-hour, the toll would have been far worse.

N.E.T.S. knew that the explosion had not been a gas leak, but even their top operatives were confused as to exactly what had occurred. During the last couple of hours they had poured over the footage of satellite feed of Bryson's car moments before the explosion. As they slowed down the speed of playback several of them noticed a small, dark streak emerge from the top of the screen and travel to the point at which the explosion took place a single frame later.

Many believed it to be a small missile about six feet in length, but the analysts claimed there was no way that was correct. There had been no hostile planes even remotely close to the area and there was no detection of foreign objects in U.S. airspace immediately preceding the attack. Unless the Aqarab Mayta had created new, advanced stealth-missile technology then this had to be something else. Although, David had told them to not rule out that possibility based on what they had seen this organization produce so far.

That had been an hour and 15 minutes ago and there were no secondary attacks.

Zane Mlackish knew that there were would be no secondary explosions. He knew this because he was a mole within N.E.T.S., but not for the Dead Scorpions.

Aging muscles propelled him down a hallway that he had walked down many times before during his 30 years of service at N.E.T.S. Zane thought back to the days of when he had been an active agent in the field and gotten to see the world. He always missed it, but his current desk-bound intelligence position made his double-spy lifestyle far easier. He knew the inner workings of the entire organization; something that was only known to him *because* he was on the inside. It had taken him several years to figure out how to discreetly breach all of the extreme security measures at his place of employment but ever since then he had been consistently keeping up with N.E.T.S. operations, and non-N.E.T.S. operations. The only reason that he was putting his life on the line now was because of the man he worked for and the dark secrets he knew.

"Hey, Zane! Crazy stuff isn't it? The guys analyzing the footage right now think the Aqarab Mayta have a new type of missile!"

"Yeah...we will have to see." Zane replied to his overzealous colleague. *New type of missile? That's a certain way of putting it...* "Hey Henry, they brought both Bryson and that other guy into headquarters didn't they? Are they both going to make it?" he asked as they walked side by side down the hallway.

"Mhmm. Apparently this guy took out two Pentagon teams at his hotel and a bunch of their guys on the highway. I was talking to Shannon who was in the crisis room the entire time and the stuff this guy was pulling off made it sound like he was in a movie or something."

"That's great, Henry. Do you know if they are going to be okay? Where are they being held?" *I miss being able to pull off incredible physical feats* Zane thought as he looked down at an ever-so-slightly bulging gut.

"Yeah they should both be fine. Although I think the unknown is going to have a harder time than Bryson. From what I could find out all *Bryson* has is a bit of shrapnel in his leg. Poor guy...he has been through hell the last couple of – "

"Henry!" Zane was getting impatient as he interrupted the fairly green agent. "Location…of the two of them. Where is it?"

"Yeah, um…they are split up. Bryson is in the medical wing in his own room and the other guy is on the opposite end of the medical wing, right where that service elevator is, you know? And he has some guys watching him 24/7."

"Okay. Thanks, Henry. Now get back to work." And with that Henry peeled away from the conversation, walking the opposite direction down the hallway.

Zane continued on and turned right, toward his office. Several other N.E.T.S. associates ran past him without a second glance as the abrupt demand for everyone to do their jobs was still causing a commotion. His door was unlocked and he walked in, flipped a switch to turn on the lights and then a second one to make his office's glass walls opaque. Things were set in motion now and Zane had not prepared for this set of circumstances. *Why would they have tried to kill one of their own? And one of their best?* He pondered the possibility that the man might have just been collateral damage in order to take out Bryson, but his gut was telling him that the attack had been designed to take out two birds with two stone. *But which one was the bigger bird?*

Slowly sitting down into his chair, he continued to think about these questions as he woke up his computer and disconnected from the N.E.T.S. network. Normally, if an agent did this, they would have a technician at their office door within a few minutes to investigate, but Zane had reworked his computer to relay a message to the N.E.T.S. servers that still displayed his IP Address as "Connected" despite the fact that he was often offline. It was how he communicated with his contact. Their conversations were saved to a cloud that they had created and that only they had access to.

In the middle of Zane's computer screen, there appeared to be nothing but the N.E.T.S. background, but Zane clicked the invisible icon that was located there. His computer connected to a private network and an IM chat window popped up. Zane began to type:

Almost instantly a reply popped up from his contact.

Good. This does change things. Tango 1 will be fine. Tango 2 under guard?

Affirmative.

Damn it. You know what must be done?

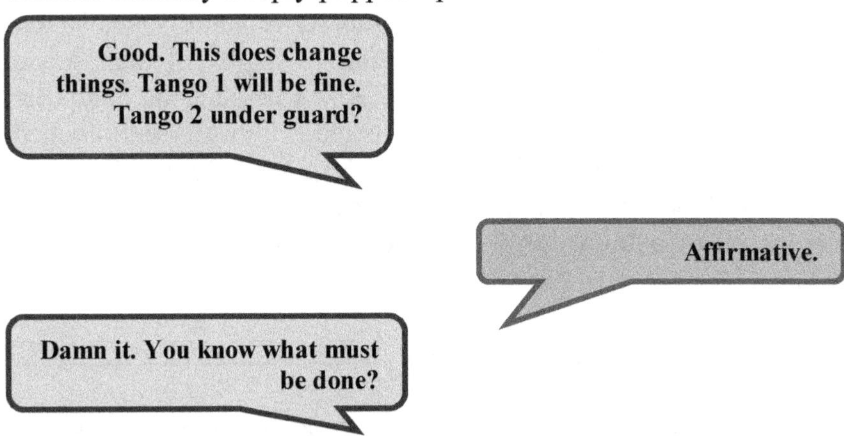

Zane had hoped that this was not going to be case, but he knew that it was the only option.

Affirmative. Time frame?

Tonight. I'm nearby. Method of extraction?

Service elevator. Tango 2 is near it and it seems like only viable option.

Confirmed. Will be outside at 0230.

You do know what this will mean don't you?

Affirmative.

The conversation ended and Zane's contact left the chat. He looked at his watch and saw that it was almost 5:00 P.M. A barely audible sigh left his lips; it had been a long day already and now it was going to be even longer. The computer screen eventually fell asleep in front of him, reminding him to logoff of the pseudo network and join back onto N.E.T.S.'s. As he shut the computer down, Zane glanced out through his frosted glass walls and watched the people walking around the office. *It's going to be a while*... and with that, Zane set his alarm, moseyed over to his couch, and slept. He dreamt of nothing, or at least he didn't remember any of his dreams.

A happy and irritating ringtone woke Zane up many hours later. Slowly sitting up, Zane reached for his phone and silenced the alarm noticing that it was 1:45 in the morning. He had given himself a half hour to scout out the area and get a cup of coffee. A gentle rub of his eyes cleared away the sleep that seemed to get crustier with age. Zane stood up, grabbed the mug that was on his desk, and exited the room. Outside his office most everything was dark. There were a few lights on at desks that still had occupants and desks where the occupant had forgotten to turn it off in the midst of the day's craziness. After a quick trip to the break room, Zane estimated that there were about seven people left on his floor. *Shouldn't be a problem.*

Dark black liquid quietly scorched the inside of his mug. When Zane was finished pouring, he placed the pot back on in the machine and went back to his office, again estimating that there were about seven people on his floor. *About seven to ten people on each floor...medical wing is about three floors up...21-30 people that could get in my way.* Luckily, he figured that the medical wing would be pretty empty except for the guards on duty at Tango 2's room. They would pose a problem and he knew that he would have to discreetly subdue them in order to rescue Tango 2. *'Rescue' is a strong word* Zane thought to himself. The man had committed several crimes against the United States today, but for some reason his contact wanted him out of N.E.T.S. custody. Much like the actions of the man who he was "rescuing", Zane figured he was just following orders and shrugged off the thought. He and his contact, his good friend, had been doing this for far too long to start questioning methods now.

After taking a sip of the steaming, delicious coffee, Zane got back onto his computer and opened up the surveillance camera system, quickly finding the camera set that pertained to his strategy. There were four cameras he would have to worry about. The first was inside Tango 2's room, near the back. The patient was on a mobile bed, and near the entrance of the room two looming shadows could be seen. A second camera was focused on the outside of the medical bay room and the tangent hallway. Zane's challenge was vivid in this frame: there were two agents by the entrance to Tango 2's room and another patrolling the hallway. A third camera was focused within the service elevator, currently empty and not being used. The fourth and final camera was discreetly capturing the alleyway's activities outside. It was here that the service elevator would take Zane and Tango 2 and his contact would pick them both up.

Working quickly, Zane set a recording device and captured the previous 20 minutes of footage that the cameras had fed to security. He figured that 20 minutes should be enough time to where no one would notice a loop in the video…or at least until they were looking for it. Once his computer had indicated that the loop was ready he fed the repeated feed of the four cameras back into the system on an infinite loop. *So far so good.*

Making sure the technological side of the rescue was complete, Zane moved on to the physical aspects. The bottom left hand drawer of his desk opened and revealed a contact Taser along with multiple syringes of tranquilizer. He knew how odd this combination would have appeared to anyone snooping through his desk but he had wanted it on hand in order to deal with N.E.T.S. agents, many of whom were his friends, non-lethally if and when push came to shove. And push was certainly going to come to shove within the next few minutes…

Zane grabbed the items, gulped down the remainder of his now lukewarm coffee, shut down his computer, turned off the lights, and left his office. As he closed the door behind him, he silently wondered if this would be the last time he would ever see his office again. *Presumably so,* he answered himself. Passing the few people still on his floor, Zane got in the elevator and headed up to the medical wing. The doors opened after the short ride and revealed a fairly dark medical bay that seemed to be deserted. Zane exited the elevator as normal and walked to the appropriate end of the building, stopping just before the corner that led to the hallway in front of Tango 2's facility.

Slowly, Zane bent his knees and began to think. *Two agents would have been a lot easier than three.* He wasn't entirely sure how he was going to incapacitate all three agents without one of them taking him into custody or calling for backup. But he had to get moving, it was already 0220. Still crouched, he strained his neck out around the corner and saw the two agents, still in front of the door, quietly chatting. The third patrolling agent was on the other end of the hallway walking back towards Zane. *Well...let's hope I still got it...*

Moments later, Zane could hear the third guard walk towards to corner where he was waiting. Amusingly, he was quietly singing a homemade tune.

"Guard duty blows! Guard duty blows! Guard duty blows, oh yes it does!" and so on and so forth. Zane felt a smirk form on his face and waited until the guard turned around and began walking the other way. Once he was halfway between Zane and Tango 2's entrance Zane made his move. Zane stood up and exited around the corner, walking briskly towards the guards as if he had something to report to them. One of the standing agents saw him.

"Agent Mlackish. What brings you to these parts?" All three agents were fairly close together now; Zane had timed his approach perfectly. The agent-who-hated-guard-duty turned around to see who was behind him now that his friend had spoken. Zane made no oral reply to the question; he made a physical one.

As the patrolling guard turned around, Zane swiftly brought the Taser into his neck, ducked to his left and jabbed it into the first standing agent's thigh. The second standing agent was now reacting despite his shock, but it wasn't quick enough. Zane got to him before he could wrap his finger around his gun's trigger by jamming the still-excited Taser into his stomach. All three men were still alive and trying to recover from their unexpected Taserings. Again, Zane Tased the agent that had been patrolling to keep him down. He immediately followed the re-Tasering to the neck with a syringe to the opposite side of the neck, releasing the powerful tranquilizer that was inside. He repeated this process for the other two men in order of who was attacked first. Within thirty seconds the whole ordeal had come to an end with all three guarding agents now taking some long and deep naps.

Moving forward without any time to take a breath, Zane reached down for one of the standing agent's IDs, held it to the keycard plate on the door, and dragged each body inside Tango 2's room one-by-one. His watch indicated that it was now 0226. Without hesitation, Zane walked over to Tango 2 and began to mobilize all of his medical equipment. He attached the saline bag to the mobile bed above the patient's head, turned off the heartbeat monitor and disconnected the wires leading to patches on the man's chest, and unlocked the bed's brakes. Zane took no time to look at the man; he had no desire to.

With ease he wheeled the bed out of the room, turned left, and approached the service elevator no more than 20 feet away, quickly pressing the down button. Some 30 seconds later the doors opened and Zane pushed Tango 2 inside, not knowing that someone had seen what he had done and was coming after him.

A soft thud was followed by the elevator doors opening to reveal a deserted alleyway. Carefully Zane pushed the man's bed out and started towards the left end of the alley. Behind him, he heard the doors close and the elevator start back up and head upwards. *Hmm…that's strange…*

The observation was overtaken by a small moment of panic as Zane looked around and did not see his contact. This panic quickly subsided as an ambulance backed into the end of the alley and swung its doors open in embrace. Inside was Zane's contact, friend, and boss ready to get out of here as soon as possible. As Zane approached the ambulance doors the two men nodded at each other and began to load Tango 2 into the back bed; there would be time for pleasantries later. While they were lifting the man's bed, Zane thought he heard a familiar soft thud but thought nothing of it. Moments later he would wish he had.

"Agent Mlackish!!" a shout emanated from behind him. Immediately Zane recognized who it was. *This was not supposed to happen,* "Zane! Wha – what are you doing?!" Henry's voice called out again, dumbfounded. Zane knew he had no other choice. He reached down for his gun and began to turn around not knowing that Henry's had already been drawn and despite his naïvety, he was still a trained N.E.T.S. agent.

A single shot rang out from near the service elevator and Zane Mlackish never took another breath. The bullet went straight through his head and into the ambulance, spraying the inside with a speckled mist of red.

During this time, The Contact had been securing Tango 2 inside the ambulance. He was sad to see his friend go but he knew that what he was doing was bigger than a single death. Almost as soon as the first shot had been fired, he grabbed his gun and shot Henry in the stomach without revealing his face. The young agent staggered in shock and finally accepted the wound by laying down in front of the elevator. The Contact pushed Zane's body out of the back of the ambulance, closed the doors, and put it in drive.

Within a few hours, he was hundreds of miles away where N.E.T.S. wouldn't be able to touch him…or Ian Tract.

CHAPTER XV
A CRUCIAL LOOSE END

There was a strong pull from behind his eyelids that was tearing him away. Away from nothing…away from everything…away from his dreams…away from this rest…away from *her*…Bryson felt the final snag as he left his scattered thoughts and immensely gratifying deep sleep. As his eyelids slowly rolled open he could feel their movement slowed down by the liquid that had collected on his eyelashes. He had travelled from one dark place to a slightly less-dark place and as he brought his arm up to rub his eyes he felt an uncomfortable presence of an IV catheter inserted in his right arm.

The ooze under his eyes cleared as he brushed it off and some small memories came back to him, who realized now that he was in a medical facility, most likely N.E.T.S.'s. His bed had been inclined to a comfortable position and part of him wanted to try and go back to sleep. But then he remembered the man he was supposed to capture. He had seen him hadn't he? And then after that he didn't remember anything. There was just darkness after a pair of determined eyes. *Shit! What happened?!*

Bryson felt a warm surge of adrenaline course through his chest as the lights to his room turned on slowly, allowing his pupils time to constrict comfortably. Bryson shifted a bit in his bed, trying to sit up taller and find any communication device he could to call someone in and get some answers. But someone was already on top of that.

"Bryson!" an angelic voice called from his room's entrance. The familiar face threw all of Bryson's worries out the door and he couldn't reply with anything but a smile. Rachel rushed over to him and gave him a gentle hug. Bryson let it last as he embraced his first smell of consciousness: Rachel's perfume. It reminded him of Elena. "I'm so glad you are awake. The doctors said that you would be perfectly fine, but I was still worried. How are you feeling?" Bryson struggled to form his first words and sentence as his brain continued to defog.

"I'm…good. Really good actually." It was true. As Bryson noticed his physical wellbeing he was astonished to find that he felt great. His muscles felt relaxed, there was no pain – not even in his hand, and he just felt plain well rested.

"Well that's good. You took quite a beating from that explosion the other day." Rachel stated with a soft smile.

"Rachel, what's been going on? What happened? How long have I been asleep?"

"Bryson, calm down. I'll explain everything in a few minutes. But first, the physician needs to check you over and you probably need to eat something. 20 Questions can come a little later."

"Yeah, okay. I am pretty hungry." Bryson replied reluctantly. He wished his body could have held off its needs a little longer so that he could get answers.

"I'll go get the doctor. Stay here."

"I'm not going anywhere."

He realized how glad he was that it had been Rachel who had been the first person he saw after he woke up. At least he knew that despite everything that had happened that he still had *friends*. Rachel, David, Elena…the pain in his hand may have subsided but thinking about Elena brought a whole new wave of fresh anger and sadness. Because of everything that had happened it had been a while since Bryson had consciously thought about her. *Just how long has it been?*

His attention gravitated toward the door as the head physician walked in with Rachel in tow bringing some food.

"Good morning, Bryson. Very early morning, but morning nonetheless."

"Hey, Paul. Yeah…what time is it exactly? How long have I been out?"

The doctor nodded at Bryson's request and replied in a typical medical tone, "Well right now it's 4:30 A.M. You've been out for a little over 36 hours." To his surprise Bryson remained rather calm at this announcement of the lapse of time.

"Ok. So what was the damage? I'm leaving this bed within the hour regardless, I'd just like to know what I'm dealing with."

"You suffered substantial shock from the explosion but your body has largely gotten over that. You have a very mild concussion, we removed a small ball of shrapnel from your leg, and while you were under we also did some repairs on the knife wound in your hand. Truth be told Bryson, you're in better medical shape now than you were when you came through these doors. It's really the N.E.T.S. vehicle that saved you from extensive injuries. Second one in a little over a week I hear?" Bryson smiled at this statement. It was true. He had certainly run up his company vehicle bill as of late.

A small chuckle escaped as he replied, "Maybe they should just give me a Vespa next time?" The doctor returned a smile.

"Now I don't think you would be very good at your job on a Vespa…you certainly wouldn't be alive."

"So I am good to go, Paul?"

"Yes, yes." The doctor walked over to Bryson's bedside and started unhooking him from the heartbeat monitor and his IV. "Just make sure you take it easy for the next couple of hours and eat what Rachel has for you here. Your body will need to adjust a bit, no different than waking up from a long nap. A normal doctor would suggest that after having come out of a coma to not leave the building but hell, you guys wouldn't listen to me if I was just a normal doctor."

"Thanks, Paul. I owe you one."

"Don't mention it, Bryson. Just be careful out there." He exited the room and left Bryson and Rachel alone. She walked over to him and placed some food and clothes down on the bed. Bryson was now sitting up with his feet over the side, realizing for a second time that he was ravenously hungry. Rachel had brought a sports drink, protein bar, some cheese, and a bag of mixed nuts.

"Sorry it's not a nice seafood dinner. I figured you should replenish some energy and nutrients. And here are some clothes to change into."

"Thanks, Rachel." Bryson answered with a smile. "Fill me in. What's going on? What happened on the highway? What happened to the guy I was tracking? Have the Aqarab Mayta attacked us yet?" After he was done rattling off questions he tore open the protein bar and took a bite followed by a large swig of sports drink.

"I'll start with what we know. The explosion was some type of missile. We have no idea how it surpassed all our radar technology and we really don't know where it originated. There are speculations that it was a dropped payload, but still nothing concrete. David privately declared the nation under attack by the Aqarab Mayta within a half hour after the attack. Only N.E.T.S. knows it was them." She released an audible sigh and continued, "But other than that, we are completely in the dark. The explosion killed two civilians at the scene, two more died in the hospital, and five are still there with injuries, mostly traumatic amputations. It's not good, Bryson. People were scared before this and now they are just downright terrified." Bryson finished his protein bar and continued onto the other snacks as he got up from the bed and changed clothes in the room.

"Ok…but we got the guy I was tracking right? He has got to be the key to all of this, or at least know who we can find to end it. Please tell me he wasn't one of the four that died."

"We took him into custody and he was healing up just down the hall from your room. He had it a lot worse and was pretty beat up."

"*Was?* What do you mean 'was', Rachel?" Bryson could tell something was tremendously wrong. Rachel's brown eyes held a deep truth.

"Bryson, sit down." She motioned to the bedside and he stopped getting dressed and sat down next to her sans a shirt and shoes. "Bryson…there *was* a mole inside N.E.T.S. and the man you were tracking isn't here anymore. It was Zane Mlackish."

Bryson's gut felt as if the protein bar were a monster trying to escape. *Zane?!* Bryson had known him ever since he had been at N.E.T.S. He was a veteran field operative and had been a valued asset to N.E.T.S. for decades. *There is no way.*

"Are you sure, Rachel? I mean…Zane? What happened?"

"We're sure that he helped the man escape. The three agents who were guarding him were all subdued and they identified him as the attacker when they came to."

"So I'm guessing that Zane escaped with the guy?"

"Zane's dead, Bryson. As they were loading him into an ambulance, he pulled a gun on Agent Cobble. Cobble returned fire and shot Zane in the head. There was a second, unidentified man driving the ambulance who shot Cobble in the abdomen."

"Henry killed him?! Is he okay?"

"He bled out by the service elevator for several minutes before the loop on the surveillance cameras ended and they found him. By the time he regained consciousness, whoever it was driving the ambulance was long gone with the guy you had been tracking. Henry will be okay, but just barely. Had that loop covered the camera feed for only five more minutes, we would have lost two agents yesterday."

"Son of a bitch, Rachel! We work for fucking N.E.T.S.! How do we lose the only chance we have at finding the Aqarab Mayta just like that?"

Unstartled by his sudden outburst, Rachel replied, "With the time delay of starting the tracking of the ambulance it was almost impossible, Bryson. We used all the traffic cameras, ATM cameras, satellite feeds, and mobile phones that we could but it's New York City. There are a lot of ambulances at any given time. They are gone. Zane knew exactly what he was doing and how to do it." She could tell that Bryson accepted this answer, but he was still frustrated.

"So where are we now?"

"I've been assigned the task of investigating Zane, posthumously. We're hoping that he slipped up somewhere and left some indication as to what he was up to. As of right now, that's our best lead, but David told me that he wanted to talk to you as soon as you woke up. He might have something that I don't know."

"Do you think Zane was a member of the Dead Scorpions?" Bryson wanted her opinion on the matter since she was the one who had actually been awake during the last day and half.

"It's possible. But my gut tells me no. Why would the Aqarab Mayta attack their own operative only to have to rescue him later? From our dealings with them, they seem a lot smarter than that."

"So why do you think he did it?"

"That's the million dollar question right now, Bryson." She joined her reply with a light smack on his thigh and a smile. "I'm just glad that you are okay. N.E.T.S. needs its best operatives right now and I need one of my best friends."

A gentle smile emerged on Bryson's face and he leaned over and gave Rachel a lasting hug. She was one of his better friends in this world, especially now that Elena…*I'd rather not think about that right now*. He kissed the side of her head.

"Rachel just be careful with this investigation okay? We can't be entirely sure that Zane was the only double agent in the office." They pulled away from their hug and she replied with a nod.

"I will, thank you, Bryson. I'll keep you updated with what I find. Now get dressed, David will want to see you ASAP."

"He's here at this hour?"

"Bryson, David hasn't gone home ever since the explosion. I don't even know how much sleep he's had."

"Ok, just give me a minute."

A frosted glass door opened up to David's office and Bryson walked in after giving Rachel one final hug goodbye. David was at his desk that was far more cluttered than usual. It was clear he was stressed and he hardly noticed Bryson enter the room.

"Sir. Rachel said you wanted to see me ASAP. What is it?" David's head remained looking at his desk where a plethora of computer files were displayed on the glass.

"I trust she filled you in on the situation? This *shit-show* of a situation?"

"Yes she did. What's our next move?"

"*Your* next move, Bryson. *Your* move." He answered matter-of-factly.

"Sir?" The confusion in Bryson's voice caused David to look up from what he was doing and remove his reading glasses in order to explain. He pointed the glasses in his hand at Bryson.

"You are going to make a move and you will not tell anyone about it. Zane was one of our most seasoned operatives and he just fucked us. Big time. I'm not letting anyone else in on this mission other than who I trust, which at this point is pretty much only you. What happened with Zane was bullshit, Bryson. That man was my colleague and my friend and he might have just fucked the entire country." Bryson noticed the emphasis David had placed on that last expletive and could tell he was not only angry, but hurt.

"Understood. You can trust me, David."

"I know, Bryson. I know." David sighed as if more weight had just been placed on his shoulders. "Before that bastard was rescued I met with him in the medical bay. He was only awake for a couple of minutes but I was able to get some information using some…creative…methods. It appears as if there is still one loose end that the Dead Scorpions haven't tied up yet"

"Rachel didn't mention – "

"That's because she doesn't know. I wanted to check the credibility of the info before I started to spread our plans for our next move. Then Zane did what he did and I've kept it close to my chest since."

"What's the information?"

"It's a contact with ties to the Aqarab Mayta, Bryson. There are even records of him having had dealings with Abd Al Aziz himself. I think you know as well as I do that this may be our last chance. We can't afford to fuck this up."

"Agreed. Where I am going?" the reply was quick and cold:
"Pakistan."

Chapter XVI
Scorpion Head

The older man entered the room in silence once again, and left in silence once again. Ian had woken up two days ago in a considerable amount of pain, but alive nonetheless. Twice a day, every day, this man had entered to bring him food and water and then left without saying a word. Sometimes he checked on Ian's wounds but other than that there was no interaction. The man was aged, probably in his sixties, or near there, Ian guessed. He could have been older but truthfully he looked remarkably in shape. He had a quick, spry stride, fewer wrinkles than one would expect, and a nearly full head of gray hair. But was he mute?

"Where am I?"

"Who are you?"

"What day is it?"

These were all questions that Ian groggily asked every time he walked through the locked door. One night Ian had tried to escape but he hadn't even made it to the door. His head pounded with pain, as did many other parts of his body, and he immediately passed out on the floor. When he woke the next day he had been placed back in bed. There was no way he was healthy enough to do anything right now and Ian figured the food was good so he would let this man have his way for a while longer.

During the day Ian mostly slept so that he could expedite the healing process. From what he could tell he had a severe concussion, broken ribs, and possibly a broken collar bone with a collection of cuts and bruises to go with it all. But when he wasn't sleeping he tried to get a bearing on his surroundings. The room he was in was air conditioned but there was still a weight to the air: high humidity. In addition, the days were almost exactly the same length from start to finish indicating that he was somewhere near the equator…or at least somewhere within the Tropic of Capricorn or Cancer. Based on the culture styling of the amenities, he ruled out Africa and had it narrowed down to somewhere around Indonesia, upper South America, or lower Central America. But it was really anyone's guess. *Hopefully I will get answers soon…*

It was the last thought he remembered before he dropped off into another deep sleep. The dream he entered was more of a nightmare…a familiar one. Ian was in a blue compact car driving on a highway, but he had no control over anything. For some inexplicable reason his arms were bound to his torso and his legs were rigid. The only part of his body that he could actually move was his neck and head. It was Ian's worst fear: not being in control.

He glanced down at the speedometer and was shocked to see that his car was going over 140 mph. The concrete divider in the middle of the road was nothing but a blur and somehow, despite not having a driver at the helm, the car was weaving effortlessly in and out of the copious amounts of traffic. All of the vehicles travelling in his direction were black cars, but Ian couldn't tell the make or models from his superior speed. On the opposite lane of the highway he was mesmerized by the fact that there was no traffic…just a completely empty road. The emptiness worried Ian's gut but something else caught his immediate attention: several large, black SUV's barreling down the highway towards him – on his side of the highway.

The SUV's made contact with the river of black cars that were many car lengths in front of him and took no damage whatsoever. They threw the smaller vehicles into the air extravagantly, almost poetically, and continued their aim towards Ian's blue compact.

Black cars were shooting off in every which direction as the SUV's plowed through them like a battering ram. As the tidal wave of flying vehicles began to approach closer and closer, Ian was frantically struggling to escape, or better yet, wake up. *Just let me move my damn arms!* He could physically feel the muscles in his arms, but as hard as he flexed them to force movement, they remained in the same position crossed across his chest.

"Argh! Son of a bitch!" Ian was screaming through his teeth as the destruction came closer. At the moment when Ian thought that it was over and he was going to die, his blue compact car pulled its emergency brake, cast the steering wheel to the right, and entered into a spin. Ian's dream went from frantically fast-paced to super slow. Almost every full spin of the car felt like it took greater than a minute. Ian craned his neck as much as he could and looked out in every direction of the car. On all sides of him were projected cars blotting out most of the clear blue sky. To his right was one of the SUV's barreling past – driverless. On his left was another SUV and a shower of sparks from impact with one of the black cars which he now recognized as Camaros. Above him was a chilling image: the tire of a Camaro within centimeters of the exterior of his vehicle, flipping end over end as he spun under it.

The slow spin continued on for what felt like an immense period of time but eventually the car was behind all of the SUV monstrosities. Oddly enough, there was no carnage behind them. All of the cars they had destroyed earlier had vanished and all that was left was open road and a clear blue sky. Ian's self-driving compact car eventually came to a halt after the spin and time regained its usual pace. The car corrected itself and continued forward the way it had originally been driving before its miraculous stunt.

A weighty amount of time passed in the dream and Ian consciously began to realize that he might actually be sleeping. But he still couldn't move his arms, torso, or legs in the slightest. After some time trying to wrangle his arms free again, his eyes caught a glint of sun shining off something in the distance…on the other side of the road. What had been a deserted landscape of interstate concrete this entire time now featured a single black vehicle approaching Ian's position. It was another black Camaro. Ian watched it intently, squinting his eyes so that he could try and make out who was inside. His gut was telling him something, something very familiar, as if from memory.

His concentration was ripped away from him as he felt the earth beneath his car vibrate and noticed an enormous explosion in his rear view mirror…and then another…and another…and another. The gargantuan fireballs were emanating from the median between the interstate and catching up to Ian's vehicle. Surprised he was still facing forward, Ian tried to brace himself as the vibrations in the cabin became deafening. *I have to see who is in that car!* The thought screamed across his head as the car was approaching him quicker and quicker – but so were the explosions.

By now he was frantically trying to escape the invisible restraints and take control of the car. *This is bullshit!* Ian just wanted control, but he knew it was too late. The continuous line of explosions were almost on him and the Camaro was an equal distance in front of the car. *Fuck it.* And with that calm sentiment he felt his arms regain control of themselves. He instinctively shot them up in front of his face as an explosion flared up on the side of him, blocking his view of whomever was in the Camaro and showering him with a shockwave of glass, heat, and flame.

Ian twisted in bed and woke up, sweating profusely. Breathing rapidly, he shot his eyes around the room and eventually got his bearings. Outside his window he could tell that the sun was setting which led him to believe that he had been sleeping for quite some time. Slowly, his adrenaline came back down to normal and his heartbeat settled at a healthy rate. *I fucking hate that dream.* Ian couldn't remember the last time he had had nightmares before this one and he couldn't figure out why this one haunted him so. It was like it was trying to tell him something, something about control, something about the man in the other car, but Ian had no idea what that hidden implication was. As he was trying to forget about it, the older man entered the room again. He walked over to where Ian's bed was, placed a tray, and turned to leave.

Ian didn't know if it was the pestering dreams, the humid air, or the fact that he simply had no idea what was going on, but he stood up out of bed. To his immense surprise his headache had largely subsided and he felt somewhat like him old self again despite the broken bones.

"Where am I?" he asked the man again. But he ignored the question and continued back towards the door. "I asked you a question. Answer it. Now." His voice was stern and no longer weak with pain as it had been the past few days. The man noticed this and slowly turned around, looking Ian in the eyes for the first time. Ian was shocked when he felt an emotional tug deep in his chest; there was something there. *Do I recognize him from somewhere?* He shook the sensation away. The man's eyes spoke for themselves. They were handsome, but heavy. There were years of secrets behind them, years of lying, and years of loneliness.

"Where do you think you are?" he asked calmly as he entered back into the room. He made his way over to the chair on the other side of the room and dragged it across the floor, placing it near the side of Ian's bed.

"I have no idea. My best guess is Pacific-Asia or Central/South America."

"Well you aren't wrong. You're in Costa Rica."

"Ok…and what am I doing here? Who are you?"

"You are here because I extracted you from N.E.T.S. headquarters in New York City. After the explosion on the highway, they took you there to treat your wounds and I'm assuming they were planning on interrogating you. I got you out of there inside of 12 hours. Or rather, my associate did."

"And where is he?" Ian was rather intrigued now. He knew that doing anything under N.E.T.S.'s nose was not easy.

"He's dead. Took a bullet to the head as we were getting you out of there." The man kept that stoic look on his face as he said it, but Ian could tell there was a deep sadness there of a friend lost. He didn't care.

"So who are you then?"

"Call me Someone."

"Seriously? Someone?" The man stared directly into Ian's eyes.

"Yes. Someone. I have rescued you, lost a friend doing so, taken care of your wounds and night terrors, fed you, and now I am answering your questions. You will call me *exactly* what I tell you."

"I never asked for any of that."

"It wasn't your choice." Someone half-whispered.

"What do you mean 'it wasn't my choice'? Tell me what the hell is going on, right now."

"Or else what?" Someone challenged Ian.

"Or else nothing, clearly. But I'm in pain, frustrated, and really not up for games right now. Either tell me what I'm doing here or I get up and leave right now."

"Fair enough. Let me ask you…have you ever met the head of the Aqarab Mayta? Have you ever spoken with them? Seen them?"

Ian felt an immense chill shoot from tailbone to neck. *He knows I'm in the Dead Scorpions? Is this the provost of the organization?*

"How'd you – "

"First things first, Ian. I know who you are and who you work for. I've known for some time now…that's all beside the point for right now. Answer the previous questions please." Shocked at this declaration, Ian began to collect his thoughts.

"No. I have never met the guy. I've never really even had direct contact with him per say. Basically everything has been through secured, voice-altering phone conversations, letters, and emails transferred on a protected network. To be honest, we don't communicate all that much. Why do you ask?"

"I just wanted to make sure that you were willing to tell the truth. I already know all of that."

"Are you the – " Ian was cut off a second time.

"Don't be ridiculous. No I am not the provost. But I know who is and he tried to have you killed today."

"I think you are mistaken, old man. He was trying to kill the N.E.T.S. agent who was coming to get me. It just so happened that I was right next to him at the time of whatever that explosion was."

Someone pulled out a small device and pressed a button. After a few seconds it began to play a recording:

"There is a N.E.T.S. agent coming to kill you. He is on his way right now and is posing as the assassin, Daniel Brody. He will claim that he is still in Brody's apartment in New York. This is not true.

You don't know who I am and you never will. Just know that I am a friend on the inside. Pretend like you never heard this call. When I forward this call to the agent, you still assume he is Brody. We will take care of the rest. Acknowledge."

"Acknowledged."

Someone followed the recording with a question, "Sound familiar?"

"Yeah, I got that when I was driving…ummm how many days has it been exactly?"

"You have been in and out of consciousness for about three days now. As you were saying?"

"I got that call about an hour or so before the explosion when I was driving *about three* days ago."

"Before you ask: no, this was not me warning you. This was the provost of the Aqarab Mayta." Ian was shocked that he had had almost direct contact with the man, but he hardly believed this random person. Why would the Dead Scorpions want him dead? Someone continued, "They 'took care of the rest' by trying to kill both you and the N.E.T.S. agent on that highway. It was a suicidal human missile loaded with an explosive vest and a substantial amount of C4 that landed in between you two."

"Why would the Aqarab Mayta try to kill me? I'm one of their best." Ian fired back.

"Because they don't need you anymore, Ian. Things are progressing quickly now and they see you as a loose end. They figured that they would take two birds out with one, explosive stone."

"How did they know the N.E.T.S. agent would be there?"

Someone took a deep breath and a moment to focus. Ian knew the information he was about to divulge was critical, but would have never guessed what he was about to hear.

"Do you know who the director of N.E.T.S. is, Ian?"

"Yeah. David Harper. He's been there forever, thinks very highly of himself and his organization, and is an overzealous patriot."

"Yes…well…*about three* days ago you spoke to him on the phone. *About three* days ago he tried to have you and his own agent killed."

Ian felt as if he had been hit in the gut. An organization he had been trained to hate, just like the F.B.I. and C.I.A., was run by the person he feared most. Despite never fully buying into the Aqarab Mayta's more extreme views and reasoning, Ian still respected the man. *How on earth?!* Ian took a breath and tried to accept this intelligence:

David Harper was both the director of N.E.T.S. and the provost of the Aqarab Mayta. The most skilled and secretive intelligence agency and the most dangerous and powerful terrorist organization in the world were run by the same man.

Ian's shock and sporadic mental calculations were interrupted by Someone reading off a piece of paper, "*Our operative and the N.E.T.S. agent will both be there at the same time if everything goes according to plan. Our operative is the key target and the agent is secondary. But I want them both dead. Neither of them are of any use to us anymore.*" Someone removed his reading glasses and looked back up at a still-reeling Ian, "This was an email sent from Harper's N.E.T.S. office four days ago."

"You're lying." Ian just could not accept this extreme shift in the game.

"I wish I was. But I assure you I am very serious."

"How has he not been caught then? How on earth did he create the Dead Scorpions with no trace?" Ian interrogated Someone.

"He certainly had help. But they never knew who he was. No one did. And N.E.T.S. never thought to look at the head of their own organization. David is the most respected man there; no one would have ever guessed. From a technical standpoint David pretty much has unlimited government funds. He most likely has two untraceable networks running out of his office and he leaves a lot of the delegating to his more…'stereotypical terrorist' inferiors."

"Why on earth would he do all of this? All of the intelligence that we ever gathered on him led us to believe that he was an undying patriot." A sickening feeling crept into Ian's throat and stomach as he asked the question. He realized that so many of the things he had been told could now be lies. Or it was this guy that was lying…

"It's anyone's guess really. I'm betting that it's just the sheer power he stands to gain. If you hold all the cards in the deck, in this case N.E.T.S. *and* the Aqarab Mayta, who's more powerful than you?" Someone stared off as he spoke, seeming bothered that he didn't know the exact answer to Ian's inquiry. He continued to surmise, "He's creating a war and managing both sides. Seems to me that there is likely a great deal of monetary and political power that can come from that, depending on how he orchestrates it."

Ian still wasn't buying it; it was just all too preposterous. He had always imagined the provost as some powerful menace…a wealthy Arab man…a powerful, shady Russian businessman…an angry North Korean political figure. But a revered American who bleeds red, white, and blue? It seemed like the farthest thing from the truth.

"How do you know all of this? If N.E.T.S. is as secretive as they say and the Aqarab Mayta were practically invisible until a week ago, how do you know everything?"

"Because I used to work at N.E.T.S. A long time ago."

"That doesn't mean anything." Ian retorted.

"You didn't let me finish…I worked at N.E.T.S. a long time ago and I knew David Harper before he was the director of the organization. Long story short, N.E.T.S. was beginning to act omnipotent and I got out. David changed into something that I didn't want to be around. I contacted one of my good friends who stayed, the man who lost his life rescuing you, and he and I have been working together on the inside for the better part of three decades."

"What did David do?"

"He killed two of my best friends and fellow agents at their home on nothing less than a rumor."

"Ok…" Ian replied rather heartlessly, "So that still doesn't really explain how you know everything that you do."

"My associate and I spent the first decade setting up everything. Tracing phones, expenses, etc. There were hints of David's plan back then.

"Once the Internet exploded, we had to spend another few years capturing all of that new media, but for the last decade we have kept up with everything that N.E.T.S. has improved from a digital-security perspective. I've been reading messages from *both* of David's inboxes for about seven years now…and his phone calls, computer files, text messages, video feeds, etcetera. We took our time and made sure not to get caught, Ian; it was a 'slow and steady wins the race' mentality."

Ian contemplated everything that Someone was telling him. He didn't like it at all. On one side of the coin, he didn't believe this guy. *Who tells people to call them 'Someone'?* But on the other side, he was incredibly angry. Deep down he wanted to believe this man and if that was the path he chose then God help David Harper. *He betrayed me. After all I did for him and the Aqarab Mayta? He owes his success to me and he tried to repay me with a suicide bomb! No one attempts to kill Ian Tract from the shadows.* Ian hated this feeling: the inability to make a calculated decision. He was so used to being in control of every situation he was in and now that control was evaporating all around him. He didn't know who to trust, he didn't know who to answer to, and worst of all; he didn't know what *he* believed.

Finally he spoke, "What makes you think I will believe you?"

Someone had his answer ready, "Well you can either believe me or go back to the Aqarab Mayta. I got you out of N.E.T.S. headquarters, hid you, fed you, and cared for you. The alternative tried to violently kill you."

Ian knew he had a point. Something about this man made him at least *want* to believe him and the alternative wasn't a very enticing option. Ian saw that a war was starting, he was a key player, and he needed to choose a side.

He asked a final question, "Why *did* you rescue me?" Someone smiled as if he had been waiting for this particular question all along.

"Because I believe that you can help me."

CHAPTER XVII
TARGET DISCOVERY

It had been three days since Bryson had woken up in the N.E.T.S. medical wing and flown discreetly to Pakistan. He had been in the country for two days, closely tailing the man that David referred to as the Bombmaker. The process was routine and the less intense nature of the operation made him realize just how crazy the last couple weeks of his life had been.

The Bombmaker was a fairly boring individual. All he had done the past couple of mornings was travel to the local market to pick up food. Yesterday, Bryson thought the man might be going to meet a contact since he was taking a longer path home but in fact it was just a case of an old man taking a stroll in the sun. Other than those two outings Bryson hadn't seen the man leave his small home, nor had he seen anyone go into the home. It was clear to Bryson that the best time to apprehend him would be in his home during the day as he got back from the market. He would make the move tomorrow morning and have the Bombmaker extracted and headed to N.E.T.S. headquarters within 12 hours. *This almost seems too easy* Bryson thought as he continued his stakeout across the street from the Bombmaker's house. A small yawn escaped as he sent a simple text to David and only David:

Target extraction planned.

He knew he would receive no reply because David had wanted to minimalize conversation in case there was a second mole in the organization. Bryson was still in shock over the recent happenings within N.E.T.S. Zane and he had never been close but the man had been one of the best field agents during his day and had an impressive track record. What was even scarier was that Bryson shared Rachel's gut feeling that Zane hadn't been a mole for the Dead Scorpions. *But then who the hell was he working for? How many moles does N.E.T.S. have?* Just weeks ago, Bryson had so much confidence in the organization. It was an invincible and invisible hand of government with a tight-knit group of people. What could go wrong? If the last two weeks were any indication, a hell of a lot. Despite his growing doubts, Bryson knew that he could at least trust two people still: David and Rachel. *Can't I?*

As soon as the unconscious thought crept into his mind he realized he needed to air out, take a walk. He shut down his minimal surveillance equipment and walked out into the brilliant sunshine that was coating the coastal city of Karachi, Pakistan. The warmth felt welcome on Bryson's skin as he transitioned out of the heavily air conditioned room he had been in. Leisurely, he made his way down the roads toward the beach, passing a multitude of shops, stores, and people on the way.

Karachi was a busy city, with an extremely high density of people. It was renowned for its amount of education; one of the highest in the Middle Eastern region. Bryson could see why a terrorist organization would hide assets here: no one would expect to look for them in a fairly developed city such as this one.

His walk lasted a while and the peacefulness overtook him. It had been a long few weeks and right here, right now, felt like the first breath of fresh air after emerging from a near-drowning. Bryson methodically weaved his way through the Pakistani pedestrians and headed toward the coastline. Beads of sweat started forming on his darkened brow but the heat bothered him little.

A calm swept over him…almost gave him a high, and his mind was racing. Thoughts darting left and right, not about his mission, not about the current threat, about his life. And how much it had changed in the last few weeks. Hell, how much it had changed in the last several years. It wasn't long ago that he was an orphan doing well in high school, but never really connecting with anybody. Then David came into his life. Then N.E.T.S. came into his life. Then Elena came into his life.

Now Elena was dead, N.E.T.S. had at least one mole if not more, and David was acting paranoid. But even still, David was all he had left. And Rachel. Bryson's mind shot to her investigation. *I wonder how that's going?*

Before long, and after several subject changes in his mind, Bryson arrived at a beach. For a moment he just stood there and scanned the horizon, left to right. The Arabian Sea lay out in front of him, vigorously reflecting the same sunlight that was beating down on him. It felt as if someone had replaced his heart with a bag of sand. The weight in his chest was his first indication and the flood of emotion in his head was his second. *Goddammit I miss her…*

The sand felt like a mockery when it slid between his flip-flops and his feet as he walked down the beach. It was hot and its only purpose was to continue reminding him of the honeymoon he had shared with his perfect wife. *Elena.* The name was visible in his mind, more so than her face. *Am I forgetting what she looks like?!* His mental question was answered with the immediate memory of the two of them lying naked on their honeymoon bed, watching the fish swim by. *And the way she looked in that dress. And the banana chocolate chip bread. And the older couple that served us…Marty and Earl. And the sex we had on that beach…that rock we sat against…that sunset…her vulnerability.*

Bryson realized that it had been the only time he had seen her that way. Scared almost, but more like concerned. *Oh, Elena…*Bryson hadn't been this deeply saddened since the funeral. He was walking along the beach, alone, half hoping that he would find a cliff overhang with a small beach under it, and a natural boulder-chair on top, facing the West with Elena sitting there waiting for him. He walked for thirty minutes and no such landscape appeared. An audible sigh left his chest and Bryson sat down in the sand.

What am I here for? Why her and not me? Truthfully, he wasn't really sure who he was directing the questions toward. The Universe, he supposed. And as if the Universe had heard the rhetoric, a great sense of happiness overcame him. He realized that he had pinpointed the happiest moment in his life: sitting against that boulder, with Elena in his arms, watching the sunset in

Bermuda. What happened before and after didn't matter to him anymore…he had reached his favorite moment. *I have nothing left to lose, except my life.* And with that final thought, Bryson headed back to his stakeout position, angrily determined to take down every bastard in the Aqarab Mayta, no matter the cost.

A quick glance at his surveillance radar indicated that the Bombmaker was still in his home and from the lack of sound coming from the distance microphones it seemed like he was alone, most likely done for the day and staying in for the night. Bryson felt a smile flash on his face and he shut down the equipment. This particular bastard wasn't going anywhere. Tomorrow when he took his morning trip to the market Bryson would sneak into the house, validate his identity, apprehend him, extract him from Karachi, and interrogate him on the way back to N.E.T.S. But for now he wanted, *needed*, a damn good meal. With the electronics shutting down, Bryson left his room in search of a good Middle Eastern restaurant.

The plan was set. The beginning of the end of this nightmare would start tomorrow.

Another beautiful day in Pakistan's largest city. It was still early, but sunlight was already encapsulating the entire floor of Bryson's room. Compared to yesterday at the same time it seemed a bit cooler which was nice for a change, but still hot and humid. Bryson rose out of bed without sleep trying to hold him back and got some breakfast, went to the bathroom, and shaved. In 30 minutes the Bombmaker would take his usual trip to the market and in 35 minutes Bryson would infiltrate his home. He kept himself busy during that time by cleaning his handgun and loading up. Before he put his phone in a secure pants pocket, he sent a text to David

Mission live: 10. Confirm: 30. Extraction: 60.

Based on the time frame that Bryson gave himself in the text, he expected the mission to be easy and brief. The phone slid tightly into a pants pocket and he zipped it shut. The knife strap around his ankle felt slightly loose so he rolled up his pant leg, tightened it, and pulled the knife out. Metal. Cold despite the heat. Dangerous. Weapon. *Tool.* Bryson took the end of the knife and pricked his calf. A small bead of blood formed but it wasn't enough to overcome surface tension and flow down his leg. He pressed his pointer finger against the blood bubble and quickly licked it off. *Metallic*...having completed this newly invented, savage routine, he was ready.

The magazine skated effortlessly into its cave and the gun was placed hidden away from open view. The door outside opened and closed behind Bryson. With a sharp "CLICK" the lock latched and the mission began.

It was another busy day outside his residence and it took a couple of minutes to inconspicuously cross the street toward the Bombmaker's home. For the time that he set foot in the house to the time that the Bombmaker returned home, Bryson had given himself 15 minutes. As he approached the side of the building, he realized that he had forgotten to check the radar of the home to make sure the Bombmaker had left. A slight jolt of panic rippled through his veins, but was overcome by the knowledge that if worse came to worst he could easily overpower the older target.

On the other side of the street now, Bryson made his way to an alley on the side of the home that featured a second entrance. Without wanting to draw too much attention to himself, he leaned against the wall next to the door and lit up a cigarette...just a pedestrian taking a smoking break. Slowly, he tested the door handle to see if it was locked. It was. With a forceful push downward, the mildly-aged door handle broke off and Bryson tossed his cigarette in the dirt as he entered the building.

The place was dark, unusually so, and also quiet. Bryson slowly pushed the door back into its frame behind him and drew his gun. With a crouched position he left the kitchen and entered the main living room. Nothing was there except for a few chairs, a low table, and some plants. All of the shades on the windows were drawn shut and Bryson couldn't remember if that had been a usual thing for the Bombmaker to do on his morning market runs. Now, as he crept onward through the building's first floor hallway, an unshakable feeling of foreboding crept into the back end of his subconscious. Something was not right here, but to what severity he could not estimate.

After several more minutes of clearing the bottom floor, he moved inaudibly up the stairs and began to check each of the rooms. The warming visibility being provided by sunlight was hampered by closed shades, creating a soft darkness. Finally, after a closet, a guest bedroom, and a bathroom, Bryson came to what he assumed was the main bedroom. The air felt slightly warmer as if someone in stress had very recently been here. There was a smudgy print on the brass door handle, indicating that a perspiring person had opened it, also very recently. And as the sense of miscalculation became a larger thought in Bryson's mind, he saw flecks of blood on the rug fibers below him. They were nearly invisible, but the small amount of light in the hallway had glinted off one in a way that it caught his attention and as he bent down to examine it, more came into view. None of them were very large, many smaller than the tip of a pen, but they were still wet.

Transitioning into a far more keen state than he had previously been in, Bryson opened the door to the master bedroom. There was a large amount of blood on the ground and lying in the middle of it was the Bombmaker, his throat slit grotesquely open and slowly oozing the brownish-red liquid everywhere. The room smelled metallic but there was something else…some other smell. Sweat. Bryson glanced down at the dead man and saw that he had no such evidence of perspiration on him. There was no glisten on his head or stains under his arms. He had died painfully, but he had died quickly. Which meant only one thing: there was someone else here.

Immediately Bryson began to retrace his steps and think where the killer could have been hiding. To his memory, the first floor was fairly open and he had checked it thoroughly. Admittedly, after spending so much time on the first floor he had rushed the second floor. There had been no movement towards the stairs behind him so the killer still had to be here…*but where?*

Guest bedroom – closet and under the bed. Both clear.
Master bedroom – closet, bed, window, bath. All Clear.
Hall bathroom – bath…curtains were drawn…

"Shit." Bryson whispered to himself. He remembered the aged, tan shower curtains had been pulled on the bath but he hadn't checked behind them. The killer was there, he was sure of it. With his back close against the wall of the hallway, Bryson crept silently across the carpet leaving a trail of dark red blood in the strands. He arrived at the bathroom entrance, still open from when he had checked it, and peeked in.

No one. Shower curtains still pulled shut.

If the killer was waiting in the tub for Bryson he would have the upper hand. Something had to catch him off guard. Something physical. Bryson would have to strike first. Carefully, Bryson peeked in again and looked at the hinges by which the shower curtain rod was hung into the wall. At first glance they appeared to be steel, but Bryson guessed they were really made of cheap brass. He hoped they were cheap brass.

Without making a noise he swung his foot around the entrance and into the bathroom, and put some weight on it to test for noise. Nothing. His other foot followed and he positioned himself facing the shower curtain. His hand crept up the back of his shirt and separated his waistband from his skin as he gently slid his handgun in. A ghost would have made more noise than Bryson in the last few minutes, but it was about to get loud. And violent.

A quiet exhale escaped Bryson's lungs and he stared at the curtain rod.

One.

Two.

Three. Bryson viciously swung his arms up, gripped the rod and pulled down on it, equally as aggressive. He pushed in at the same time and felt as the rod came out of the wall and made contact with something solid on the other side of it. Within less than a second Bryson saw the eyes of the killer wildly staring back at him as he brought the rod down on the man's extended arm. A muffled groan was swiftly outdone by the explosive sound of a gunshot. The gun had been aimed a considerable distance away from Bryson after the rod-to-arm collision and it crashed into the mirror to behind him. The musical chimes of shattering and falling glass echoed again and again like raindrops in a storm but neither of the men could hear them.

The man was pinned against the shower wall by the rod, grunting almost ecstatically. Bryson removed a hand from the rod, reached under to the other side of it and yanked the gun away. He tossed it up in the air, grabbing it by the barrel, and brought the butt of the handgrip down hard across the killer's cheek. A mixture of blood and saliva sprayed from his mouth against the brick walls.

ThumpThumpThump. Bryson unleashed three quick handgun-punches on the man's face, causing it to begin to swell and bruise. Bryson swore he caught the glimpse of a smile coming from the beaten killer, but he disregarded it.

"Why did you kill that man?!" Bryson shouted. "Do you work for the Aqarab Mayta?!" He demanded. "WHERE ARE THEY?!" He growled. The man was definitely wearing a smile now. Bryson didn't have time for this, he was coming with him. He pulled back the handgun for one more punishing blow. It never connected. The killer shot his knee into Bryson's groin. A painful fire spread between his legs and Bryson let out a moan that turned into a breathless gasp as the assailant drop kicked Bryson right there in the tub. The killer fell back into the tub awkwardly, but Bryson was thrown towards the wall where the mirror used to be. His back crashed into the waist high sink and he ricocheted to the floor, his face landing on the pool of glass.

A turquoise eye was staring back at him, his own, as the glass reflected the scene above its position on the ground. From the glass, Bryson could see the man getting up and trying to leave the bathroom.

His hand found the piece of glass under his eye and his reflection disappeared as he picked it up and reached, stabbing the man in the thigh as he made contact. The shard ripped out of Bryson's grasp, cutting him in the process but he had too much adrenaline to even remotely feel the pain. The killer let out a yelp, pulled the makeshift weapon out of his thigh, and threw it at Bryson. He bolted out of the room as the bloody shard entered Bryson's shoulder.

Still no pain. This was the last connection N.E.T.S. had. Bryson got up from his knees and followed the man out of the room as he yanked the now incredibly bloody shard out of his shoulder. The man was several paces ahead of him and ran back into the master bedroom. Bryson rounded the doorway's corner to hear a shattering of glass as a pair of feet exited the window. He rushed to the ledge and looked down, seeing that the man had rolled successfully onto a lower roof and was running across it. He came to the end of the roof where a three story apartment complex was separated by a small gap from a two story home. The killer placed his foot on the concrete of the three storied building and pulled himself up to the roof of the distant home. Trained in parkour.

You've got to be fucking kidding me. Bryson mentally muttered as he himself dove out of the window of the dead Bombmaker's home. All of the additional light now flooding into his eyes caused a moment of temporary blindness as he fell into the hot Pakistani weather. His landing was rough and Bryson felt a twinge of pain echo throughout his legs but he kept moving across the sandy roof and it was soon gone. Compared to a few days ago, Bryson felt phenomenal. On top of his recent emotional enlightenment, he felt physically unstoppable. The downtime of the mini-coma and the reflection period of the last 24 hours had done him good. *I could do this all day.*

As he neared the area where the killer had jumped up, Bryson repeated the same move he had witnessed and to equal success. Once he planted his foot vertically against the concrete, he pushed off from deep within his thighs and calves, propelling him across the gap and on top of the next building. He had managed to catch ground on the killer and was only ten paces behind him. Bryson's mind travelled to his gun, but discretion suggested otherwise. The last thing he wanted was to have the Pakistani police chasing after him for shooting a citizen. That was a mix-up that he didn't have the time to afford.

In front of him, the killer rocketed across the roof tops, many of which were used by the homeowners for gardens or patios. As he came to a set of table and chairs, he pulled his legs to the height of his chest and cleared the entire setup. Bryson kept his eye on the man and the settings around him to try and get an advantage. When he neared the table and chairs he ran around them, taking only slightly longer than the expert in front of him. The crunching of their feet on the medium grained, rooftop sand drowned everything else out and Bryson's mind had a temporary flashback to the rooftop in New York. He had been lucky then with the grappling hook but he had no such tool here. This man would have to be beaten on foot, or outsmarted.

The killer approached the edge of a roof where two buildings stood a body's length taller than himself on either side with a very narrow gap in between. *This is where I catch him* Bryson motivated himself.

That would not be true. Just before the man got to the edge of the roof he leapt, with what seemed like all of his might, into the narrow gap. At the apex of his jump he placed his hands on the top of the building structures which were now at his chest height, and used them as a fulcrum to give himself more than enough momentum to clear the gap and land on the roof below.

Bryson realized he had slowed down as he witnessed the gymnast-like move and increased his pace as he approached the gap. It was narrower than it had appeared but Bryson threw himself into it anyway; he had no other choice. The world immediately closed around him as the two walls blocked almost all sunlight. He fell unscathed for only a split second, but soon his broad shoulders caught the edge of the wall and he slammed into it as he continued his vertical descent. The rooftop below rushed to great him but Bryson knew it was coming this time and pushed off from the wall in the narrow gap as he exited, allowing himself to roll before the hit. He imagined that it had looked pretty impressive to anyone watching but it had really just been a testament to Bryson's athleticism and luck.

Coming out of the roll, his head shot up and he saw the killer staring wildly back at him. Part shock, part amazement, and part annoyance. The man's longer, dark hair was greasy and dripping with sweat. Beads of it flew off the tips as he turned on his heels and kept running, releasing an aggravated groan as he left.

"Get back here you son of a bitch!" Bryson yelled in a whisper to himself as he sprang back onto his feet. Together, they ran along the rooftops for a few more blocks before the killer jumped off to an alleyway below. He was trying to get into the public streets where it would be much easier to lose his pursuer. Bryson remained on the roof and anticipated one of the man's corner turns. He was nearly running alongside him now, looking down at the murderer who was selfishly running for his own life. Before the man got a chance to look up and see Bryson, he leapt down onto him like a panther on unsuspecting prey. Again, most of the sunlight disappeared as Bryson dove off the roof and soared into the alley.

His chest smacked hard against the man and the strong scent of another person's intensity and body odor conquered his nostrils. The man's salty sweat wiped across Bryson's face as the collision took both men down, hard, into the ground. The impact continued Bryson's forward momentum as he rolled off the top of the man, immediately turning around and grabbing him by the collar. Conveniently, the man's face had broken his fall…more specifically, his nose, which was gushing blood. His eyes met Bryson's and he spit a mixture of blood, sweat, and saliva into his face. Bryson reeled from a warranted reaction of disgust. Within that time the killer got to his feet, kneed Bryson on the side of his face, and tried to run past him.

Still partially blinded by the bodily fluid mixture, Bryson reached out for whatever he could find as he corrected himself from the blow. His hand grasped an archaic, wooden 2x4 lying on the floor of the alley and he slammed it against something solid. He felt it shatter beneath his grasp as what was once a wooden handle was now nothing but splinters.

"AGHH!" His hit had been successful and he quickly wiped his face off with his hands. The grime and loose wood that had previously been part of the 2x4 were now stuck to his face. It created a deep, dirty burgundy mixture with the blood that covered his cheeks, brow, and chin. Bryson's fierce appearance was now matched by his drive. When his vision returned a few seconds later he could see that the wooden plank had crashed against the man's ribs and he was struggling to move away from Bryson. He was moving slowly and grunting loudly, clearly in a lot of pain.

Without any sympathy, Bryson approached the man with a sterling resolve, ready to end the chase. Walking over to the killer, Bryson thought he caught another glimpse of a smile under the man's longer hair. Before he could confirm that he was right, the bluff had unfolded and the man attacked Bryson ferociously. Fist after fist connected with his head, shoulders, ribs, and stomach.

ThwapThwapThwapThwapThwapThwapThwapThwap ThwapThwap

THWAP!

THWAP!

Not one punch had been considerably painful, but it was more the summed force of all of them that caused Bryson to keel over, out of air, and unable to return any punishment for a few moments. When he brought his head back up to continue the fight the man was gone. Bryson was alone in the alley with nothing but stained-red sand, wood shards, activated nerve endings, and memories of the brutal battle. Still running on adrenaline, Bryson composed himself and ignored the pain. There were only two ways out of the alley and he hadn't heard a door open or close. *Left or right?*

After a quick glance of the fight area, the answer was vividly clear due to the noticeable blood trail left by the broken nose.

Left.

Bryson shot back out into the daylight where the streets of Karachi were packed with people slogging their way through the heat. Some Pakistani pedestrians furtively gave him alarmed glances and quickened their pace. The shirt he was wearing was ripped at the shoulder from his dive into the crevice, he was covered in dirt, and his face was still caked with the dark red pseudo war paint.

None of that mattered. Bryson was trying to keep calm but in the back of his mind he knew that there was a serious potential that he had just lost the last lead to the Aqarab Mayta. *Think. Fucking think!* He stood surrounded by people and dropped his head in order to get a grasp on the situation. There on the sand were small puddles of blood: the killer's blood. Bryson shoved his way through the busy sidewalk and followed it across the street. The trail was getting thinner by the meter, but it was still evident enough for Bryson to interpret it. After crossing the street Bryson continued onto a street corner of concrete and benches. It was easy to see the blood on the concrete and he increased his pace, adrenaline once again coursing tirelessly through his bloodstream. The blood trail led him past a small cloth vendor and perilously stopped. *He grabbed one of these cloths to stop the bleeding...*

This was it. This was where Bryson would either fail and lose the man for good or by some miracle, find him in this crowd. *What would I do?* Bryson demanded of himself. *What the hell would I do?* He took a deep breath and thought. *Disguise. Blend in.*

Double-back. Before the thought was entirely through his conscious, Bryson spun around and turned back and headed towards the concrete street corner. He scanned the benches. *Blend in.* There were dozens of places to sit and almost all of them were full.

A woman wearing a veil with a child on her lap

An elderly gentlemen eating something with great struggle.

A group of men, some sitting, some standing, talking loudly and passionately about something.

But one caught Bryson's eye. There was a man with everything but his eyes covered by a dark brown shawl. The clothes on his body were dirty and his pants had holes developing in the knees. Fresh holes. Bryson kept his distance to make sure the man would not see him. He was on his phone, talking through the shawl. He gave no indication of body movements or increased volume but instead spoke with his eyes. There was a fire behind them that he seemed to be attempting to push through the phone. The fire of fear. It was him.

Keeping a constant eye on the man, Bryson made a wide loop in front. The last thing he wanted to do was spook him and incite a chase again. He was behind the man and closed the radius of the loop. *Who's he on the phone with?* Bryson sat on a bench two rows behind the killer and took out his cell phone. The enhanced microphone had a tight cone of operation that could pick up sounds from several feet away, in this case, the man's phone conversation. First, a voice that was digitized; it was the one coming from the phone as the men began to speak in Arabic.

"What happened, Nasir? Calm down and tell me."

"The Bombmaker is dead…" He was breathing heavily. "But we have company. Not sure who. Some American agent."

"Did you lose him?"

"I think so. Haven't seen him for a while." He glanced over his shoulder nervously, questioning his own resolve, and Bryson turned his head away careful not to be noticed.

"Where are you now? What's your condition?" the voice asked calmly.

"Not sure. I got disoriented from running. Concrete street corner with a ton of benches. Ring any bells?"

"It's a big city, Nasir. I can't tell you exactly where you are. Figure out how to get back to here."

"Screw you, man! I'm a sitting duck out here with an American agent probably listening in to this call right now! How do you expect me to get back to headquarters?"

"Nasir! Shut. Up. The job you were sent to do is done. We leave in a few days' time to carry out The Will. Figure it out and make sure you aren't followed." The voice from the phone was unsympathetic to the killer's position and before he could respond, the call ended.

"Son of a bitch." Nasir whispered. Behind him, Bryson flipped his phone around so that the mirror-like backside reflected Nasir's actions. It was clear that Nasir was nervous. He was fidgeting a great amount as he sat on the bench, and despite the fact that nearly his entire face was covered, Bryson knew it had a look of worry and dread plastered across it. Soon, after a few minutes of concentrated thinking, Nasir got up and slowly turned, scanning his horizon for any signs of his chaser. Bryson pretended that he had to tie his shoe and spent a good little while with his head crouched downward. Cautiously coming back up, he held up his phone again to see that Nasir was walking away as normal. He hadn't been seen.

Remembering how hot it was now that his adrenaline had come down a few notches, Bryson wiped his brow with his hand and stood up, making sure to keep his face the opposite direction of Nasir. Again, he held up his phone and saw that Nasir was walking away from where he had been sitting, in the opposite direction of Bryson. It was a simple stalking game now…*Follow him back to his home base. Infiltrate. Not now, it's too light out. Infiltrate tonight. Gather any intel. Capture any high value targets.* The plan was set. Now all Bryson had to do was execute.

The crowds in Karachi were always thick, no matter the time of day. Tracking the man would prove difficult especially if Bryson wanted to keep his distance. Even right now it was hard to keep tabs on Nasir, even more so with the shawl that resembled so many others within the crowds. Bryson followed him into a market and saw a set of stairs leading to the rooftops and the edges of his lips curled upward. *You wanted to start this on the rooftops, I'm going to end it on the rooftops.* Swiftly, without losing sight of Nasir, he took the stairs to the roof and was thrilled to see that they were all fairly connected for the foreseeable distance, much like they had been during the earlier foot chase.

He set up a system for the edge of each new roof that he would stay two foot lengths back from the edge. This way he could still keep his eye on Nasir below him but also pull back if the man ever got the inclination to look up. Nasir stopped at a food vendor on the side of the street. He spoke Arabic with the man for a short while, nodded what looked like a "thank you", and continued in the same direction, eventually cutting into the buildings through a populated alleyway. Bryson figured that he was not familiar with this side of the large city and had stopped to get directions.

The two men walked onward, Nasir continually unaware of Bryson's looming presence, for around 45 minutes. During that time, Bryson only had to come down from the roofs twice when Nasir crossed larger roads. Finally, Nasir stopped walking for a moment and looked around, something that he had not done the entire time they had been walking. Bryson hunkered down on the roof. He could see Nasir's eyes through the slit in the shawl scanning for any imperfections on the horizon. Imperfections meaning American spies. Pleased with his observations, Nasir unwrapped the shawl from his head and entered through the iron gate to the two story home. He began talking with one of the guards who was behind the gate that Bryson could not see. After what seemed like an unpleasant exchange, Nasir headed into the compound. Bryson took a quick picture with his phone and sent it to David with the following text:

Complications. BM dead. "DS" associates at this location. Infil tonight – extract morning. Might have friends along for ride.

After the text had sent, Bryson saved the coordinates to his phone and put it in his pocket. It was midafternoon and Bryson realized he was starving. He walked away from the compound, making sure to stay on the rooftops until he was far out of sight. Back on the busy streets of Karachi, he followed the wonderful smells of the city and wandered around several street corners. He came upon a market that was selling everything: clothes, pottery, prepared food, spices, meat, and jewelry. In order to prevent being followed himself, and because he figured he would need it tonight, Bryson purchased a black shawl and fashioned it around his neck. Then he let his stomach do the talking. After listening to its growl he purchased some Lahori Beef Karahi with a side of tandoori naan. The dish was delicious, and a strong representation of the national cuisine.

With his gut more than satisfied, Bryson took the shawl and covered his head, nose, and mouth, leaving only the eyes much like Nasir had done. It was hot under the thin cloth, but the sun was setting and it would soon cool off. Based on recent memory, Bryson traced his path back to the compound and once again got on the nearby rooftops. The sun was setting too slowly for Bryson's liking; he was getting antsy. He passed the time by lying on the roof across from the compound with his binoculars taking notes.

One main entrance that I can see
Five windows
   Three on top floor
   Two on bottom floor
Three patrol guards in sight
   No helmets
   Protective vests likely
   Standard AK-47s

The list continued onward with notes that Bryson deemed useful and after a few minutes it delved into mental notifications that even he knew weren't necessary. But so was the nature of stakeouts at times. Finally, the sun was fully set and the city released its grasp on the final horizontal rod of sunlight. The moon and starlight took over, bathing everything in a softer, cooler light than had been experienced during the day. A gentle and refreshing breeze swept across the back of Bryson's hands and it felt good. He decided that he liked Pakistani nights.

Abruptly, he heard a stir coming from the compound across the street and brought his binoculars back up, flipping on night vision with a small switch on the side. Four men had rushed out of the entrance, each placing mags in their handguns as they crossed towards the gate. Without removing his gaze, Bryson reached back with one hand and retrieved his phone, once again facing the microphone toward the gathered men.

"Our intel tells us the American was located near the old man's home. Nasir thinks it might have even been right across the street. We travel over there and search the place." Another man lazily rose his hand as he spit into the sand.

"And what if we find him?"

"We're not sure how much he knows. We kill him on sight. No questions asked. Try to do it quietly, and keep the body. We will dispose of it later." He paused. "The dogs are hungry."

A small chorus of laughter rippled through the group but was interrupted when another man asked a second question.

"How many go there and how many stay here?"

"Six go there. Two teams of three once we split, each with their own point man. Three will stay at the compound. Two at the front entrance and one at the back entrance." The man who had asked the question nodded his approval and for a moment silence took over. "Ok. Let's go! *Allahu Akbar*."

"*Allahu Akbar*" they responded in near-unison. Two SUV's pulled around in front of the gated wall and they split up evenly. Within a half minute, the vehicles were off into the night, the distancing sound of their exhaust representing their impending failure of leaving the compound significantly more susceptible. Bryson couldn't help but smile as he climbed down, crossed the street, and crouched against the outside of the concrete walls. He contemplated using his night vision goggles, but there was more than enough light coming from the moon and the compound that they would most likely prove more of a hindrance than anything else.

With soft feet in the sandy road, Bryson quietly rounded the corner of the compound towards the back where there was apparently an entrance. The compound was at the bottom of a steep roadway that led up to another part of the city. Its back was against the wall of the rocky cliff and as Bryson made his way to the north-west corner, he noticed his "entrance". A horizontal drain gutter with a foot and a half radius travelled through the high concrete walls.

Still against the wall, Bryson removed the knife that he had pricked himself with earlier, realizing that he had forgotten to use it against the killer in their earlier scuffles. *All for the better I suppose. It led me here.* The ergonomic handle felt warm in his palm and the existence of small ridges in between his fingers made it feel secure. In the soft sapphire moonlight, the slightly-curved black and silver blade looked more than lethal; it looked angry.

Blade comfortably in hand, Bryson crouched even lower and entered the drain. There was a singular trail of water in the middle, not much wider than a hand, but Bryson made sure to not step in it. *Water makes noise and leaves tracks.* Instead, he angled his feet against the curved bottom edges that were dry. He could hear his heart pounding as he progressed through the infinite tube. Or at least it felt infinite. For what felt like the hundredth time that day Bryson reminded himself: *This is it. Don't fuck it up.* Bryson's mind wasn't focusing on breathing, blinking, swallowing, or any other non-essential tasks. What was essential now was perfectly infiltrating this building.

After what seemed like hours, the end of the drain that had always been in sight crept up on Bryson. Realistically, it had only been a little less than a minute, but in that time, Bryson's adrenaline had started up again. Everything was clearer now and he was exceedingly focused. *Invincible.* The quiet, paired pattern of footsteps was coming from further back in the compound walking towards the front, and was most likely going to pass directly in front of the drain exit. Inside the tube, Bryson flexed the muscles in his leg and began to rock back and forth in anticipation. Seconds later, two legs appeared in his circular vision, continued their paces forward, and were out of sight again.

Bryson leapt from inside the drain quickly enough that the man didn't have time to turn around. Bryson's left hand wrapped forcefully around the man's nose and mouth while his right hand plunged the blade entirely into his neck and ripped it out and across his throat. The process had been so quick that none of the hot red liquid got on Bryson's hands and the man hadn't made a sound. His AK-47 dropped to the ground with a considerable amount of blood on its frame by the time Bryson had begun to carry the body into the drain. Once the deceased was disposed of in the drain, Bryson wiped the crimson steel across the pant leg of the man in order to get the substance off. The blood of a terrorist was not worthy of his knife. Quickly, Bryson kicked some sand and gravel over the bloodiest spots, picked up the AK assault rifle and tossed it in the drain.

Luckily, and stupidly, the door at the rear of the compound was left unlocked. Bryson closed the door silently behind him and got a bearing on the inside of structure. *Where would there be information in here?* It was dimly lit except for a bright strip of light coming from a door that was ajar. He readjusted the grip on his knife and came to the door, revealing that it was a downward staircase that led to a basement. Once at the bottom of the steps, Bryson knew he was in the right place.

Sheets and sheets of paper covered the multiple tables basking in the light of a single, powerful light bulb hanging from the dirt ceiling. There was a calendar on the wall to the left and sealed steel chests to his right. He approached these first and it took only a few moments of looking them over to realize that he wasn't getting into them. Steel boxes with titanium locking rods, fingerprint scanner, and passcode entry. Whatever was inside must be important, or very deadly. *Or both.* Bryson took out his cell phone and began to take picture after picture. Nothing was off limits.

He brought his attention to the calendar next. Every day that had passed was crossed off with a large black "X" and there was a red circle three days from today's date. Next to the circle was simply the text: "THE WILL". This was it. This was the Aqarab Mayta's attack. Three days from now. Bryson took another picture, heart racing, and quickly turned to the documents on the tables.

Much of it was in Arabic and he didn't have the time to translate it right now. As he continued to snap pictures, the corner of a sheet caught his eye peeking out underneath the rest. Without moving too many of the other documents around, he slipped it out and saw that it was an airline confirmation for several tickets all leading to Denver International Airport. *Another 9/11?* His phone continued capturing everything in picture form and after a few moments he came across a second document that indicated two reserved planes at Centennial Airport, Colorado which he assumed was a smaller airport somewhere within the state. Panicked, but focused, Bryson checked the dates of the plane tickets to Denver International Airport and the small plane reservations at Centennial. It didn't make sense. *Why would they reserve planes at a smaller airport* after *their flight on a commercial airliner?* Bryson took some more pictures and placed things back where they had originally rested. His mind was racing with possibilities. He felt as if he had most of the puzzle put together but was missing the critical corner pieces.

One singular thought was at the forefront of his thoughts: *The commercial airliner travelling to DIA isn't the target…then what is?!* Bryson was mindlessly moving back through the compound, exiting out the same door, and back into the drain. Without a second glance, he stepped over the body and left the other side of the drain back into the street. Neurons were sending signals everywhere inside his head, but no concrete connections were being made. *And why Denver?* Bryson knew it was a big city, but not bigger than L.A., Chicago, or New York. *Military bases?* He remembered that there were several government bases there, several of which were classified. Could that be it? Through his frustration, Bryson entered a hotel and purchased a room for the night. Before he tried to get some sleep he sent a final text to David:

Attack three days from now. Codename: "THE WILL". Commercial airliners, small planes involved…different dates. Target: Denver. Back in NYC within 24 hours.

Over 7,000 miles away, David's phone lit up and he read the message he had just received from Bryson. A strong and unfamiliar sense of worry cascaded across his muscles and the warm, black leather couch that he so often sat on got a little bit colder.

Chapter XVIII
Mole Call

Monday July 3RD, 2017
N.E.T.S. Headquarters, New York City

Black, gray, and white. Lines and lines of the basic and depressing colors formed the images and video that she had been looking at for hours now. Just three colors and thousands of pixels, all trading places when called upon to create the media that displayed the mole.

Rachel leaned back in her chair and gently massaged her eyes. They blurred when she stopped and the alabaster ceiling haunted over her. It had been six days since Zane had helped the man escape, and given his life to do so. Since then, people had begun to refer to the escapee as "Target Zero" around the N.E.T.S. office.

These last days had been odd; Rachel had never seen N.E.T.S. experience such dysfunction. Most agents didn't know whether they should be hunting for Target Zero, solving the mole case, or focusing on the next Dead Scorpion attack. Even worse, gossip had spread about the possibility that Zane might not have been the only mole and no one trusted anyone. N.E.T.S. HQ had become cliquey and unprofessional. *Reminds me of high school* Rachel reminisced as she looked back on the last few days.

Luckily, she hadn't been involved with any of it. David had assigned her and her alone the task of tracking down what happened that night and she was to report to only him. He had been wildly erratic in the past few days. Whenever they talked he seemed rushed, almost worried, and he had no set schedule. There were times where he had been at HQ at 3 A.M. and another day where it was 1 P.M. and no one had seen him yet. She found it odd, but perfectly explainable given the current circumstances.

She continued her break from reviewing surveillance feeds and turned her chair around to look out at the city. It was night time and yet the streets and buildings were alive; lit up like lanterns for the night owls. Rachel tried to remember the last time she had danced…danced *with someone*. God, it had been ages. Subconsciously, an image of Bryson snuck into her thoughts and she wondered how he was doing. She looked at the clock and saw that he should be getting back from Pakistan within the next few hours. According to David, not everything had gone smoothly over there, but they ended up finding more information than they bargained for. She felt herself smile. *That's Bryson…always overachieving*.

More than usual, she was in complete awe of him. He had been through so much in the past couple of weeks and she questioned how he was even keeping it together. It was common knowledge around the office how much he loved Elena, but she was personal friends with *both* of them; she knew firsthand how real their relationship had been. "Once in a lifetime" is what she had always quietly called it. Sitting there, alone, and looking out at the city with all of its people, she longed to comfort Bryson. *Or maybe it's me that needs comforting? I lost a friend too*. Rachel felt guilty for the thought as she had found herself feeling more frequently lately. Her girly crush on Bryson had grown since Elena's death and she felt ashamed of it. She knew it was inappropriate but she couldn't stop herself from feeling that way. Rachel's thoughts felt foggy and she gave her head a good shake as she pushed aside the feelings in her head, heart, and loins. *Jesus, I need to focus*.

A slight groan came from deep in the joints of the office chair as she turned it back around facing the several screens that had dominated the last few days of her life. So many hours of surveillance, mainly from traffic cameras, pedestrian cellphones, and ATMs were all being compiled into a near-20-minute clip that detailed Target Zero's escape in the ambulance. A little more than five days ago, when Rachel had started this project, she had found herself overwhelmed. Eventually Agent Cobble had woken up and she had been able to speak to him, but it didn't lead to any new info. The green agent hadn't absorbed the situation like a veteran would have, but no one could really blame him.

"It all happened so fast, Rachel. All I remember is that there was a New York City ambulance with the lights off inside. After I shot Zane…I…I…didn't know what to do and the next thing I know I'm bleeding and laying down. I'm sorry. I'm sorry, Rachel." That was all he told her. She had comforted him; he was clearly upset after having to kill one of his superior colleagues and there was no reason for him to withhold information. Plus, she had it all on tape.

Zane had implemented a loop over the video feeds to give himself enough time to rescue Target Zero but he didn't know that they actually still recorded the data. And apparently neither did any of the specialists at N.E.T.S. until one of them stumbled upon the files through a backdoor coding a couple days ago. By then Rachel had found enough video evidence to track the ambulance from the alley way, but she had watched it anyway, mainly to see who the other culprit was. Unfortunately he had had his face covered and it seemed that some of his clothing made him appear larger than he really was. Based on the soles of his shoes, Rachel could tell what his height was fairly accurately, about 5 feet and 11 inches, and when he pushed Zane's body out of the ambulance a patch of white skin had appeared indicating his race. *A nearly six foot tall, Caucasian male. That should narrow it down.*

Frustrations had been mounting and Rachel felt like she was working against a ticking time bomb. Bryson was apparently coming back with information but that didn't mean that they were any closer as to figuring out who took Target Zero, and just exactly who Zane had been working for. The first 12 hours of her investigation had been combing through his life. Emails, texts, phone calls, college classes, high school classes, past girlfriends…nothing was off limits. She had found nothing other than the fact that Zane sometimes stayed late at the office, especially about a decade ago. She had to believe that if he was connected to the Aqarab Mayta that something, even something miniscule, would have shown up by now.

But rather than obsessing over the questions and mysteries of the dead, she focused on the living. She wanted to know where that ambulance had gone and where they were now. It had taken several hours of pouring through footage coming from cameras near the alley of N.E.T.S., but she had eventually found the ambulance from the feed of an ATM less than two blocks away. After getting the reports from nearby emergency stations, she had found out that this particular ambulance had been filed as missing only a few hours after the events that had taken place at HQ. She was positive that it was her vehicle.

From that point forward the process had become a grind. She continued to sift through gray, black, and white video feeds, compiling any that had the target ambulance in them into a sequential final cut. Luckily, N.E.T.S. had the technology to make it easier than she had initially predicted but it was arduous work regardless.

Based on the video feeds that she had found, the ambulance had left the alleyway and made its way directly out of the city. It obeyed all traffic laws and drove conservatively as it made turn after turn to exit the city. Rachel had hoped that she could maybe get a facial match with the driver, but he had kept his mask on while driving. Being that he was in an ambulance, people hadn't even given him a second glance, not to mention it had been early in the morning.

As Rachel had continued to follow the ambulance video feed trail through a fairly genius algorithm that she had discovered in the bowels of the N.E.T.S. operating system, she noticed the ambulance had driven a little more erratically near the end of its journey. After exiting the city and entering the suburbs, it was using its turn signal less, speeding slightly, and trying to anticipate stop lights; it had clearly been in a hurry. After what she estimated to be an hour of driving the ambulance was in the country and she had a hard time tracking it. On at least three occasions she had been convinced that she lost the damn thing, eventually finding it with traffic cam feeds each time.

But ultimately, she *had* lost the vehicle. Rachel thought back to earlier in the day and remembered how panicked she had been, frantically searching through video after video. It was a short break that sent her an epiphany that now seemed fairly obvious. *What is the saying? Hindsight is 20/20?* Much like her current break, she had turned her chair around to look out at the city. The weather had been slightly overcast, but still sunny and rather than looking at the street, she had turned her sights to the clouds. They had been just white, not gray or menacing, but they were tall and puffy. She remembered being amazed as a child learning how tall they actually were, some stretching out over multiple atmospheric layers. And then a sharp, metallic gleam in the sky had caught her eye: the sun shining off the hull of a passenger plane. Initially, she had ruled out the option that they could have gotten on a plane. N.E.T.S. had facial recognition programs implemented at every airport across the nation and not one had given a hint of Target Zero. But what about a small airport? Privately owned?

It was silly now. Of course they had used a small plane to get out of the country and Rachel had been beating herself up for having overlooked that possibility. She immediately began searching airstrips within a ten mile radius of where the vehicle had disappeared within the state of New York. Only one had shown up and it was privately owned: Kingston-Ulster Airport. Within minutes, Rachel had the owner on the phone,

"This is he. May I ask who's calling?"

"Hello sir. My name is Agent Trimble. I'm with the C.I.A. I wanted to ask you some questions about a plane that has recently flown out of your airport."

"Oh…" the man on the other end gained his composure as he spoke to Rachel's favorite cover name. "Uh yes ma'am. Please, ask away."

"I'll keep this brief, sir. We are on a time crunch here. Approximately five days ago, a plane left a hangar on your strip. The time was approximately 4:07 A.M."

"That was early Tuesday morning correct?" the man clarified.

"Correct."

"Ah, yeah. I…um…I was worried that's which one you were talking about." The man's tone piqued Rachel's interest.

"Sir, please tell me everything about the person that flew that plane." She was greeted with a rambling, flustered response.

"He insisted that we never meet. I didn't really have a say in it…he…he was paying me so well. And in cash! All he asked was to store his plane there for about a week and then take off without any clearance. I swear I would never allow that but…I mean, times are tough. With the whole thing with the President, and the attacks…I just figured I could use the money. Wait…" He paused, the gears in his mind turning so loudly that Rachel could hear them. "Is this about all of that? Did I just aid a terrorist?"

"Sir, please calm yourself. We aren't sure about the particulars and I'm not at liberty to discuss that. We are simply chasing down any and every lead. Now…" she realized she needed to establish a hold back on the conversation, "What currency was he paying you in?"

"Dollars…U.S. dollars that is."

"And how much was it?"

"Uh…um well he paid me $500,000 up front and then left behind a briefcase with an additional $750,000 from the hangar he was in."

"And you never met him?"

"Nope. Just a single phone call from a restricted number."

"Did he have any accomplices?"

"No, not that I could tell."

"What was his intent?"

"Uh…intent?" Rachel thought about how to rephrase the question.

"Did he give any idea as to what he was doing? Was he angry? Worried? Rushed?"

"Oh…um…none of those. When we spoke on the phone he seemed about as normal as normal could be. Strong voice, but not angry or anything like that."

"Ok. And which direction did his plane take off? Do you have any information about that?"

"I never inspected the thing but he had told me that it didn't have any ID numbers. I just sort of believed him. And the last reading we had on it indicated that he was heading south." Rachel remembered letting out a sigh. South most likely meant South America or something similar. It had been six days now; they were lost. She had responded with a defeated tone.

"Thank you for your time, sir."

"Wait! Am I in trouble or anything? I'll give the money to you guys!" He was clearly scared and Rachel could do nothing but rub her temples and respond.

"No sir. You aren't in trouble. Goodbye."

Now, several hours later, she was in her dark office with nowhere else to turn. The trail was cold, dead cold, and she had a feeling that no more epiphanies would be headed her way. She had passed the last few hours by continuing to rake over the video data to see if anything gave a clue but she already knew the answer. Target Zero was gone and no one knew why. Rachel was pissed off. She had really thought that finding the airport would have led to at least something…a name, a face, a bank account, a tail number. But there was nothing. She had lost and they had won, it was as simple as that. *Screw this*. The steam was rising to the surface and Rachel didn't want to be there anymore. She needed a damn break. As she began to exit the room, her desk phone rang.

"Of course it would." She said aloud. The light from the phone's screen gleamed ice blue in the darkness of the office and she walked over to see who was calling, half expecting it to be David or Bryson.

RESTRICTED

An excitement coursed through her veins for an inexplicable reason. *Who is this?* Emphatically, she reached for the receiver and answered the phone.

"Hello?"

"Hello, Rachel. I've been keeping an eye on you for quite some time. The world is becoming a precarious place. I think it's time I told you some things that you ought to know. I'm sending details via text to your phone now to come and meet me here." Rachel was baffled and was having trouble asking complicated questions.

"Where's here?"

"Costa Rica." The voice replied smoothly. The man had a strong voice.

"Who in the hell IS this?" she demanded. A cold aura had overtaken her voice and a sudden chill had slithered down her back. *Is he watching me now? In this dark office?*

"I'm the man who took Target Zero."

CHAPTER IXX
MOVING PIECES

TUESDAY JULY 4ᵀᴴ, 2017
N.E.T.S. HEADQUARTERS, NEW YORK CITY

An eerie quiet followed the elevator's high-pitched bell signaling its arrival on floor 'N'. Darkness was combated by a few splotches of light coming from workspaces and rooms in the distance that contained some lingering employees. Conversely, the icy blue lights shining from the front desk seemed to sensually entice the absence of light. Bryson stepped out of the elevator and as it closed behind him the main lobby of the New York N.E.T.S. headquarters got even darker. Disappointed that Rachel was not at her usual spot, he started a brisk pace to get to David's office. *Of course she isn't here right now, it's 1:30 in the morning.*

Coming back from Pakistan had been uneventful and Bryson had even managed to get a few hours of sleep. That is of course once his mind had stopped racing and trying to solve what seemed like an impossible mystery that he had seen only hours before. *The Will. Small planes…large planes. Denver?* None of it made any sense then and Bryson was even more confused about it now. He figured the commercial airliner tickets he found were going to be used for transportation purposes only; the likelihood of another 9/11 seemed preposterous. *We've seen it before…we know how to fight against it. Or is that what they want us to think?* His only possible guess was that they were going to fly the small planes into high priority buildings, but what would that do? Sure it would kill a few, but probably not more than a hundred. For such a public threat a hundred casualties would make the Aqarab Mayta the laughing stock of the terrorist community. And what had been in that high-security chest? A nuclear bomb? Guns? More files? Bryson continued his quick pace back to David's corner office so that he could get a second opinion.

The black door to David's office was closed so Bryson gave a polite but stern rap on the frame and entered the room. David had been sitting, or rather sleeping, at his desk with his head down. At the sound of Bryson entering the room he brought his head up and met Bryson's eyes with a scowl that could have turned Medusa to stone. Bryson, taken aback, slowed his pace and gave an awkward grimace back to his boss. Apparently he didn't like to be woken from his sleep. But…there was almost something more behind that look…a look of intense, new-found resentment.

Bryson tossed the thought aside and further entered David's office and took a seat on the opposite side of the large glass desk. The look had quickly faded from David's face, as if he never had meant to make it, and Bryson noticed that the glass walls of the room had all been switched to the "private" frosted mode. All of them except for David's magnificent windows that gave him one of the best views of the city. Bryson's admiration was cut short as David let out a short cough in order to clear his throat from his nap.

"Rough night, sir?" Bryson inquired, meant to be half joke and half serious.

"Cute." The answer was curt. David was not in the mood. Bryson took the hint and got straight down to business.

"Sir, here are the pictures I took from the scene." Bryson handed his phone to David and he placed it on the glass table, transferring the data over to his computer. "Total casualties on the mission equal two. First, the Bombmaker, who was killed by the man, Nasir. A fight ensued, followed by a chase, followed by another fight. I tailed the previously mentioned back to what I believed to be their compound. It is to my knowledge that I infiltrated the compound and retrieved the information without their suspicion. Upon entering the compound, casualty number two occurred. I killed a perimeter guard with my combat knife and hid his body. No shots were fired. My presence at the compound was most likely unknown until they found the man's body. By that time, I had left the country."

As Bryson gave David the typical debrief of a mission, the man swiped through the photos that were now displayed on the glass desk in front of him. The calendar with a circled date, the steel chest with the fingerprint scanner, the papers and airlines tickets; David was rattling through the files nonchalantly, as if he had already seen them.

"Also, sir I apologize for the text message sent after mission. I know that you said to keep any findings off the grid and I wasn't thinking straight."

"Hmm?" David was clearly distracted. "Oh yes, Bryson. Don't worry about it. What matters is that you didn't send these pictures." He was thinking for a short while and broke the silence with a question, "How many people have seen these?"

"No one, per your orders. Just myself and you."

"Not even Rachel?" he asked rather quickly. Bryson was somewhat surprised by the question but it was fairly common knowledge that himself, Rachel, and Elena were close friends.

"No sir. I haven't talked to her since I left actually." Bryson answered, feeling somewhat guilty for the answer.

"She wasn't at her desk? Or in any of the offices?" There was a trace of shock in David's voice.

"Um…no sir. It's half past one in the morning."

"Ah…" David hadn't realized this until now. "I suppose it is. She must have headed home a while ago."

"Sir are you okay? When's the last time you slept in a bed?" the inquiry contained genuine concern. David looked worse than Bryson had ever seen him. There were bags under his eyes, wrinkles around his cheeks, his skin looked exceptionally dry, and his tie hung messily loosened underneath the collar of his shirt.

"Yes Bryson. I'm fine." David snapped back. "Back to the task at hand." His eyes met Bryson as he raised the phone up in the air and placed it back on the glass table.

"Ok. So then where do we go from here, sir? I've tried to come up with an idea of what they have planned and I can't arrive at anything logical. I think the key to figuring it out is whatever was in that locked up chest but I didn't have the time to spend to open it."

"Terrorists aren't always logical, Bryson. But I agree…I can't connect the dots either. Let's assume they have a bomb in that chest…nuclear even. The question remains: why Denver? Sure the casualties would be catastrophic and the fallout across the U.S. would be great…" David's voice trailed off as the cogs began to turn. Eventually he made a comment that seemed more like he was thinking out loud, "But there is no evidence that they have a nuclear weapon. All of our black market contacts and Middle Eastern contacts have been reporting hourly since the threat on TV. And I assume that none of our nuclear-capable allies are assisting them."

"With all due respect sir, we *just* found out about the existence of Aqarab Mayta. 'Assuming' is something we cannot afford to do right now."

"True. Which leads me to believe that Denver is a diversion. We are trying to build a puzzle with none of the corner pieces."

"I thought of that, but what if we're wrong?"

"That's where you come in. They are supposed to arrive at D.I.A. tomorr – er…today I guess it is now." David corrected himself as vigorously rubbed his eyes. "We will have someone at Denver International keep an eye on the incoming passengers. Call it racial profiling if you want to, but if we get a significantly large number of Middle Eastern men coming into that airport at once then we ring the alarm."

"And if we don't?"

"You are going to go to that smaller airport in two days' time regardless. If we missed something and they really are planning something in Denver, you can be damn sure that we're going to stop it. Bring Agent Cobble with you. His wound is healing and I think it's safe to say that if he got shot, he isn't the second mole. Plus it will be good for him to get back out into the field. Lord knows he could use the experience."

"Sir?"

"Tell him it's an anonymous tip on a threat. Things of those nature never pan out anyway and it will keep him in the dark at the same time."

"Ok. Should we bring other agencies in on this?"

"No. They have their hands full as is and I want to play this pretty close to the chest. Plus, we don't need them sending agents out to sit at a slow airport and twiddle their thumbs."

"So instead I'm the one you're sending to twiddle his thumbs?" Bryson asked to try to get a smile out of his old friend. David looked up and returned the silent request with a small curl of his mouth.

"Exactly."

One day before The Will…

She looked at her feet as they travelled up the escalator and wondered if they would ever see another escalator. It was a curious thought, and a rather stupid one, but almost all at once she was realizing that this was one of the "lasts" of her life. Come this time tomorrow, she would be sailing through the air with several packs of C4 and a piezoelectric bomb vest strapped to her person.

It was the 4th of July today…she knew that it was an important holiday to Americans. One where they celebrated their freedom and diversity. *Let them have their final day of celebration.* Come tomorrow, July 5th, when they would be caught off guard by a terrorist event-free 4th of July, is when the Aqarab Mayta would strike.

Her months of skydiving training for the Dead Scorpions had been arduous, and she was told that she would never again see one of her classmates, for what reason, she did not know. She guessed that it was to prevent any socializing before the attack and keep up the extreme anonymity that the Aqarab Mayta enjoyed so much. She looked around the airport anyway. There were supposed to be twenty of them but she knew that she wouldn't recognize who they were. Instead she turned her attention to the marvelous airport. It was remarkably clean and natural light poured in through the pointed, lofty ceilings that were created to resemble the Rocky Mountains. She figured that if she was giving her life to a cause tomorrow, there could have been worse airports to arrive in than Denver International. Her craned neck gave her pause and she decided to stop gawking and get a move on to her hotel.

A seasoned agent from N.E.T.S. had assigned Todd to keep an eye on the incoming traffic at D.I.A. *This job sucks,* he quietly told himself. *There probably isn't even any reason for me to be here.* He took a bite from his granola bar and continued along the mental path he had created to remain inconspicuous while keeping an eye on incoming passengers. To his right he noticed a white female who was admiring the beautiful and unique D.I.A. architecture. He followed her gaze to the peaks of the building and by the time his eyes returned, she had walked off. He had missed her.

And the stout Asian male to his left…

And the young African American man who had exited the airport an hour ago…

And the elegant Middle Eastern woman who was coming up the escalator…

And the sixteen other terrorists that would come through the airport that day, all with a single purpose: to carry out The Will.

The day of The Will…

It was going to be a glorious Colorado day with blue skies, scattered cirrus clouds, and comfortable temperatures.
Currently however, it was dawn and the sun was rising in the east, electrifying the Rocky Mountains with extreme yellows, oranges, and pinks. As Bryson and Agent Henry Cobble drove southbound on I-25 they were both speechless as they tried to capture every glance they could of the beauty. Traffic was light for the most part and they seemed to be making good time on their way to Centennial airport.

"How you feeling, Henry?" Bryson stirred some conversation with the young agent.

"Pretty good actually. Turns out that the bullet didn't do as much damage as they initially thought. Plus our medical team is so good they might as well be using magic."

"Can't disagree with you there." Bryson responded as he remembered several occasions where he had been shocked with how good he felt after a trip to the medical wing, including his last.

"So physically okay…how about everything else?" There was a noticeable silence but Henry finally responded with carefully chosen words.

"It's weird. I've thought about it nonstop since it happened and I still feel guilty. I shot one of our own. I killed him. Questions keep running through my mind…did I act too quickly? Could I have just injured him instead? Would he have shot me? Would he have *killed* me?" He took a deep breath and continued, "I don't know the answers to any of those questions. And *that* is what's killing me inside. I keep telling myself that he was a mole, a traitor even, but it doesn't make it any easier. To answer your question, I suppose that I'm doing okay. Time heals everything right? I figure it's just going to take time to either forgive myself or learn to live with the guilt."

Bryson was taken aback by the mature response from an agent that he had always found to be inexperienced.
He found himself with a new sense of respect for the man sitting next to him. Henry had done something that Bryson never hoped he would have to do: kill another N.E.T.S. agent. Not sure how to respond, Bryson just nodded his head and they continued onward in silence.

Despite it being somewhat early in the morning, the small airport was still seeing some action. There were several fancy personal jets taking off and a few of the hangars were currently empty. Bryson pulled the car around to the hangar that N.E.T.S. had very quickly reserved after Bryson and David's discussion. It had a random single engine plane in it but they wouldn't need it as they actually wouldn't be flying. In fact, Bryson was fairly certain that this would be an uneventful trip with the highlight having been the sunrise. David informed him last night via text that the agent assigned to scope out D.I.A.'s incoming passengers hadn't caught anything suspicious. Even the facial recognition contact lens he'd been wearing hadn't tripped anyone. It was most likely that the terrorists had been using Denver as a diversion which begged the question, where would they be attacking instead? Something code named "The Will" was scheduled to happen today and N.E.T.S. was almost as clueless as the average citizen was.

Once the car was parked against the entrance of the hangar, Bryson turned off the engine and reached to the back seat for his binoculars.

"What do we do now?" Henry asked.

"Have you ever been on a stakeout?"

"Not that I can remember, no."

"Worst part of the job. We sit. We wait. And nothing will happen…probably." Bryson explained with a sly smile as he brought the pods of the binoculars up to his eyes.

"I'm fine with waiting." Henry reached for something behind his seat as well. "I'll get communications up and scan the area for any activity. If they are communicating with any physical media, we should be able to hear it."

"Sounds good." Bryson was again impressed by the often mocked Agent Cobble. So far, he didn't seem half as bad as everyone joked that he was. *Probably just a case of being the low man on the totem pole.*

Across the way, there were five hangar openings. Two were empty, one had a closed door, and two of them had twin engine planes in them. After making a mental note, Bryson reached down for the car seat's recliner, gave it a soft yank, and leaned back slightly. *Might as well get comfortable. It could be a while.* Several minutes later, Henry did the same as he continued to focus on what was being transmitted on his computer screen and through his headphones.

It was nearly 9:45 in the morning, an hour and a half after they had started their watch of the airport, when the silence in the car was interrupted by the ring of Bryson's cell phone. Henry shot a reflexive glance in that direction and took over binocular duty as Bryson pulled the device out of his pants pocket.

"Hey Rachel!" There was a measure of excitement in his voice.

"Hi Bryson! It's so good to hear you're okay!"

"You too Rachel. How is the mole hunt coming along?"

"It's going well actually. I reviewed every bit of data about Target Zero and tracked the ambulance to a small airport but then the trail went really cold."

"I thought you said it was going well…"

"Shortly after the trail went cold I received a call *on my desk phone* from a man who claimed to have Target Zero. He also said that there are 'some things I ought to know'. Bryson, I think this person, whoever they are, used to work for N.E.T.S. How else would they have gotten my desk phone number? It's nonexistent." Bryson pondered this as the fingers of worry began to creep into his thoughts.

"Rachel where are you now?"

"I'm in Costa Rica. I'm meeting with him in about 30 minutes."

"Do you have backup?" Bryson tried to refrain from the question sounding like a reprimanding adult, but it came out that way regardless.

It took Rachel a while to answer but she eventually let out a quiet, "No."

"Rachel…how do you know that these gu –" She cut him off.

"Bryson. I know. But we don't have the time for me to bring anyone else in on this and I don't even know who to trust anymore." He knew she was right but he didn't like it any more than he had a few seconds ago.

"Did you at least tell David?"

"Yeah, but he has been distant lately. Not himself. I told him I was following up on a lead with the mole here. Which technically isn't a lie." There was a bit of silence. Bryson knew that Rachel was scared not being able to trust anyone now and he cherished the thought that he was at least someone that she cared enough to trust. Eventually she continued, "Bryson, I'm field trained. And in case you forgot, I was near the top of my class. I'll be fine. Promise."

He smiled and remembered, "I know you are. It was Elena and I who trained you, remember?"

"See? I learned from the best. Anyway, where have you been? David wouldn't tell me much except that you were following up with something to do with the Dead Scorpions."

"Ah yes, I was in Pakistan. Originally I was supposed to capture a bomb maker but things took a slight turn. Ended up infiltrating a compound and found out that the Dead Scorpions are planning…" he chose his next words carefully, "they are planning to attack today, Rachel. Something called 'The Will'.

Henry and I are in Denver right now, but we have our theories that this is just a diversion. Either way, I think something is going down today and we don't have a damn clue as to when or where." There was another silence as Rachel took it all in. She knew this was serious.

"Okay. Well hopefully we are wrong for once or that compound's info was designed to feed you false info. How did we know about a bomb maker anyway, Bryson? I thought all of the leads we had escaped in that ambulance with Target Zero?"

"David told me that he spoke with Target Zero before he was taken from our custody. Apparently the discussion led to some info regarding *the* bomb maker for the Dead Scorpions and his location in Pakistan." Another silence pierced the sound coming out of the phone. But this one was different; Bryson could tell something was wrong. Something he had said…

"Rachel?"

"Bryson. No one had any contact with that man before he was taken. No one except the medical staff and all of those interactions were recorded. We had continuous surveillance on him from the second he was wheeled into the building. I'm not even positive if he ever regained consciousness while he was there."

"What are you saying?"

"Bryson, David never spoke to that man. I'm absolutely sure of it."

"Why would he lie about that Rachel?"

"I'm not sure. But that's a pretty big lie and a pretty valuable asset to pull out of thin air."

"Maybe he is protecting one of his sources?" Even as Bryson spoke the hypothesis he knew it sounded weak.

"Maybe. But this is cause for concern. If we can't trust David…" Bryson was worried himself. It wasn't like David to lie to him. The man was usually like a computer: factual and brutally honest. He tried to cycle through a million reasons as to why David would lie about talking to the man and getting information, *correct* information nonetheless, but could come up with nothing that satisfied him. Eventually Rachel broke his train of thought, "These last few weeks…" She sounded as if she was exhaling for the first time.

"I know." Bryson responded quietly.

"Ok. Well I have to get going. Bryson…I…" She was having a hard time deciding what she wanted to say. "Just be safe, Bryson. Please." Her plea seemed almost like a goodbye for some reason and Bryson felt a wave of friendly affection for Rachel come over him. She was one his best friends and now probably the only person that he could trust.

"You be safe too, Rachel. And you call me as soon as you're done meeting this guy. We'll figure this out together."

"Ok. Talk to you soon, Bryson."

"Talk to you soon, Rachel." Bryson ended the call and took a deep breath. He was liking this entire situation less and less. It used to feel like N.E.T.S. was three steps behind the Dead Scorpions at all times but now it felt more like a personal restraint, like he was the one who was being played. Something was off at N.E.T.S. and he was going to find out what it was.

"Sir, you're going to want to see this." Henry spoke up for the first time in a long time as he handed the binoculars to Bryson.

Across the way, several SUVs arrived at the two hangars with twin engine planes in them. The group that came out of the vehicles was certainly diverse, almost overly diverse, but all of them shared the trait that they seemed to be in shape. Every third person or so had what looked like a large duffel bag and based on the way they leaned in the opposite direction each bag had to be of considerable weight. Once they were all out of the vehicles and in the hangars, the hangar doors closed and the SUVs took off. *Well that's strange…*

"Let's keep an eye on them Henry. It doesn't appear to be anything, probably just an odd group of tourists, but since they are all we have in front of us I want you to track their communication."

"On it." Henry began to type away on his computer and very quickly had an update, "Nothing yet sir. It appears that they aren't using any electronic devices at this time." Bryson kept the binoculars focused on the hangar doors. As the seconds passed, the uneasy feeling continued to grow but he wasn't sure if that was because of what was happening in the hangars across the way or if it was due to what he had just learned from Rachel.

"Actually sir, a text message was just sent out from that area. It reads: 'Tell the kids I love them.'" Henry looked at Bryson. "That's it."

"Anything else?" This was getting very odd now.

"No. Nothing." A few more minutes passed before the hangar doors opened back up and the twenty people started boarding the planes that were now slowly taxiing out of the hangar. All twenty of them, except for the two pilots in the cockpits, were wearing bulky, black jumpsuits. It seemed as if they almost had something underneath. Judging by the way they were walking, whatever the clothes were covering wasn't exactly light, nor was it extremely heavy. It was still an odd situation to Bryson, but now he figured they were just a group of professional skydivers off to complete some crazy stunt in front of the Rocky Mountains on a beautiful day.

One plane was full and it proceeded to the runway. The other was still loading up people who were walking out of the hangar.

"Sir? What's our move?"

"Nothing. I don't think it's anything. They just look like a group of skydi – " Bryson abruptly stopped talking and became obsessed with focusing the binoculars. He thought it was a mistake, or just someone who looked remarkably similar, but the bandage on the man's broken nose confirmed the horrifying truth: the last man to board the second plane was Nasir. "Son of a bitch."

"Sir, what is it?"

"Get your gun and get out of the car."

"What are we doing?" Henry inquired, aware that something was serious now. Bryson got out of the car and glanced towards the runway as the first plane took off in front of them. He looked through the car at Henry with a deadly serious stare and pointed to the plane that was in the hangar behind them.

"You're going to fly this plane."

CHAPTER XX
REVELATION

WEDNESDAY JULY 5TH, 2017
PLAYA DEL COCO, COSTA RICA

"You be safe too, Rachel. And you call me as soon as you're done meeting with this guy. We'll figure this out together." Rachel barely heard the line echo out of her phone. She had an opportunity to tell Bryson how she felt and she had missed it. Would she get another chance?

She let out a thoughtless reply. "Ok. Talk to you soon, Bryson."

"Talk to you soon, Rachel." The phone clicked and the exchange was over.

It took several moments, but Rachel soon realized just how scared she was. *There is an attack scheduled for today? Why would David lie? Who is the contact that I am meeting? Should I have brought back up?* It seemed like everything in her life was a variable, a set of very scary and dangerous variables, and the only constant, Bryson, had just hung up the phone.

Calm down, Rachel.

Meet with the contact.

Hear what he has to say.

Kill him if he is a threat.

Call Bryson afterwards.

It will be okay.

Rachel glanced at her watch and realized that the man who supposedly had Target Zero would be showing up any minute. She had taken the quickest flight possible to the Daniel Oduber International Airport in Guanacaste, Costa Rica as it was the closest airport to their meeting spot: a coffee shop along the coast in the beach town, Playa Del Coco. The airport was small but surprisingly busy and well-run. Another surprise had been the humidity as she exited the airport; thick and hot, reminding her that she needed a break soon. She imagined that Costa Rica would have been as good a place as any but this was certainly no vacation. A taxi drove her straight to her resort from the airport and she slept, reviewed her somewhat-rusty field training, and continued to try and hunt down any clues about who the man she was meeting could be.

Making sure that she wouldn't miss him, Rachel arrived at her destination early. It was a dreary day with overcast skies, but still warm so she opted to sit with her cup of coffee on the beachfront patio that complimented the coffee shop. The darkened gray firmament, hot drink, and soothing ocean waves calmed her nerves and she felt relaxed. Ready for anything and focused on how important the information that she was about to obtain could be to the safety of millions.

Then she had decided to call Bryson and everything had turned to shit. Gray clouds suddenly seemed much more ominous and threatening than before, her gut was surging with auditory accusations, the once-fantastic cup of coffee now lost all of its taste, and even the ocean waves seemed to be strained and nervous. Despite her mental attempts to calm herself she noticed she felt sick, borderline nauseated, and was fidgeting incessantly; her leg hadn't stopped tapping up and down since Bryson had hung up.

For FUCK'S SAKE Rachel! She screamed in her head, *Get it together.* Consciously she placed her hands on her leg, steadying it and prohibiting it from bouncing up and down. *You are a trained N.E.T.S. agent. You're out behind the desk now...time to join the real world.* Her lungs took in and released two deep breaths and she reclaimed her grip on reality. She would take things one step at a time and the next immediate step was to hear what this mystery man had to say. Now, where was he?

"Ms. Monroe?" The question coming from behind startled Rachel. It had been a long time since someone had referred to her as 'Ms. Monroe'. Practicing caution, she turned slowly, almost seductively, to face the mystery. A pair of strong shoulders graced the fit, but geriatric man. He was an odd combination of youth and age. His stature, his body language, and that head of full, gray hair indicated a youthful spirit. But there was a tiredness about him; the wrinkles around his eyes indicated sadness and probably more than a few periods of hopelessness. For a small window, Rachel thought she recognized him. There was something familiar there, behind his features, but she couldn't place a finger on it.

"I am she." Rachel replied after her careful analysis. The hand she had reached into her purse clasped loosely around a handgun and she kept her eyes locked to his.

"Relax, Rachel. There will be no need for that." He nodded casually towards her purse and sat down with her on the bench. She kept her focus on him as he took a seat and tightened her grip on the gun regardless.

"How do you know my name?"

"That's your first question?" he half-whispered to himself but loud enough so that Rachel could hear the slight.

"Just answer it."

"No. There are more pressing matters at hand and by the time I get done telling you everything you'll know the answer." He leaned back on the bench and extended an arm towards the opposite side of Rachel. "Shitty weather huh?"

"Are we here to talk weather or why you stole the most important man in the world from us?"

"Oh…honey. He is far from the most important man in the world right now." His calm and insulting demeanor was starting to annoy Rachel.

"Where is he now?" she forced through slightly gritted teeth.

"Don't worry about that, Rachel. He's safe and his priorities have been…realigned. He's no longer a threat to you." Rachel was sick of the mystery and looked the man square in the eyes.

"Look…cut the cryptic bullshit. You called me down here to give me answers and so far you're about two replies away from me beating the hell out of you. If you have something to tell me, then say it. If I ask a question, answer it. It's either that or I call in my backup after you're good and bloody and we extract the info from you in a more colorful manner. Got it?" It had been a long time since Rachel had gotten so mad at someone but the stress of it all had finally made her snap. Inside though, she was proud of herself. It had been a healthy direction to point the anger.

The mystery man smiled as he looked Rachel up and down seemingly giving his approval.

"You're tougher than I thought. But I assure you a few things, dear. A) You couldn't beat me in a fight. Maybe it would be close, but you would never win. And B) I know you have no backup. In case you're wondering, this is me calling your bluff. But I accept your proposal. Time is wasting and we should get this show on the road. So, before I start, do you have any questions?" Rachel was dumbfounded and embarrassed by his reply but she didn't let him see that.

"You know my name. It's only fair that I know yours."

"Call me Someone."

"Seriously? Someone?" She asked tiredly. The man beside her just chuckled lightly.

"Yeah…I get that response a lot. Anything else?"

"Just tell me why you brought me here." Rachel demanded.

"Fair enough," Someone adjusted on the bench to get comfortable, "I brought you here because everything is not as it seems. A cliché statement I know, but true nonetheless. N.E.T.S., the Dead Scorpions, and the man you refer to as 'Target Zero'…they are not what you believe them to be." He paused and reached into his pocket and pulled out his smartphone, turned it on, and handed it to Rachel. "Here. Read this email chain." She glanced at him curiously and proceeded to scroll through the exchange of emails, reading them aloud quietly.

"She will eventually have to die too. She's just like him: loyal, honorable, and blind. In the meantime I have her looking into who took the operative that YOUR men failed to kill. Hopefully she can be useful one last time before this all ends."

She scrolled to the next email, confused and intrigued equally.

"Apologies provost. We thought the amount of explosives would be sufficient and they will be increased accordingly. But both

men proved difficult to kill. Any normal person would have died from that."

Another scroll downward.

"I don't give a shit what would have happened to a 'normal' person. I give you two targets that need to be dealt with and you fail on both accounts. Then I send one to Pakistan and your men FAIL again. Even worse, he knows the plan now. If Denver fails, that's on YOUR head you incompetent bastard!"

Rachel couldn't believe what she was reading but she continued to scroll before she asked any questions.

"Similar to how you failed to keep a hold of the man you wanted dead despite the fact that he was in N.E.T.S. headquarters? A mole helped him escape I hear. You should keep better track of your people, provost. Worry not about Denver. There are other plays in motion tomorrow."

One final scroll revealed the most recent string in the digital exchange.

"How dare you. Enjoy your power while it lasts."

Rachel's mind was spinning from the exchange of email. She had so many questions, *too* many questions, and the nauseated feeling had crept back. She handed the phone back to Someone and looked at him, knowing that she had an appearance of worry drenched across her face.

"What is your first question?" Someone asked her gently.

"Am I…am I the 'she' that they are referring to? Is Bryson the 'he'?"

"Yes." A blow to the chest is what the answer felt like to Rachel. Who would want her dead? Worse, who had been *planning* her death?

"Who is this conversation between? How do you have it? WHO ARE YOU?" The answers came out faster than she could think them but Someone took it in stride, again releasing a deep breath and explaining everything slowly.

"I do not know exactly who one of the people in the conversation is. My best guess is a high ranking member in the Dead Scorpions. The other, well, the other is the head, or provost, of the Dead Scorpions…" he paused, hoping that she would believe his next words, "And N.E.T.S."

Rachel's head had been turned toward the ocean but those words had caused a deep fury down in her. She turned back and gave Someone a stare that spelled both fury and an uncomfortable acceptance of that truth. She choked out a confirmation through a set of oncoming tears.

"David?" Her mouth was agape with pain. "David is the head of the Dead Scorpions?"

"Yes."

"And David…David wants Bryson dead?"

"Yes. He also wanted his own operative, the one whom I rescued, killed." Someone explained in a soft voice.

"And David wants *ME* killed?!" She choked out, both angry and frightened.

"It appears that way. That's why I reached out to you immediately."

"How do you know all of this? Why should I trust you?"

"You don't have to Rachel. We don't have the time to run through everything right now but basically I used to work for N.E.T.S. ages ago and always suspected David of something. I've been monitoring his activities for the past 30 years. Zane was my friend and *my* mole within the organization. Things are clearly coming to a head now and it may be the only chance we have to stop David."

Rachel was quiet and cold to the response; it seemed like too easy of an answer to give someone. It was clear he knew a lot, too much for a civilian or low level criminal, but she had known David for years. Was he really capable of such a thing? How had she not noticed?

Someone continued, "Look, Rachel. I know it's hard to believe. Hell, I wasn't even sure how to tell the people closest to David when the time came. But here we are. And I think you know it's true. I think you have seen change in David recently. A new hatred, bitterness, temper…it's because he is so close to the end of this game that he has been playing for so long. And when you're that close to the end, you're usually going so fast that one slight bump and you can crash and burn." Rachel considered his words and knew them to be true. As much as she didn't want to admit it, it made sense. Someone gave her a hidden glance. "I can see that you know I'm telling the truth. It's all crazy right now. You don't know who to trust and you don't know who your targets are. One thing is certain, Rachel: David is the villain here. He is the one we have to stop."

"We? I don't even know who you are! And why did you choose to divulge this information to *me*? There are a ton of other agents at N.E.T.S."

"My identity isn't important. Truly."

A snort escaped Rachel's mouth, "Talk about clichés…"

"And I chose you because I have been tracking everyone since they started working at N.E.T.S. It's one of the benefits of having complete access to everything that goes on in there. Again, the explanation of this will have to wait, but I can tell that I can trust you. *You* are an *honorable* person. You do what is right. You care about people."

Rachel was blushing slightly. *Is this crazy?* She asked herself. The world had just turned itself inside out and now she was being told by an old man named Someone that she was a good person. And that he wanted to team up with her to take down her longtime friend, David Harper. Head of N.E.T.S…and apparently the Dead Scorpions too. *This IS fucking crazy.*

"Fine." Rachel conceded. "You at least have my attention. But I need more proof than just a few email exchanges. I need to see Target Zero and I want your whole story. How you're doing this, who you have on the inside, everything."

"Perfectly fine. I was going to introduce you to Target Zero anyway. He seems ready to join my cause and if you decide to as well, you two will be working together." The smile on his face indicated that he was waiting for an adverse reaction from Rachel but she wasn't going to give it to him.

"We will see about that. I still haven't ruled out the possibility of arresting you both or killing you and arresting him. You had better have some strong evidence."

"Fair enough." He answered the threat calmly. "Let's get going then shall we? My residence is about 15 minutes away from here." They both stood up and Rachel extended her free hand, with the other still around the gun in her purse.

"Lead the way." She smiled sarcastically at him. As they began to walk away from the bench a question rang in her head and she blurt it aloud, "Who else at N.E.T.S. were you going to contact?"

"Bryson Cooper."

Another exclamation point went off in Rachel's head, this one much more lethal and grave.

"Shit!" She searched around in her purse frantically. "Shit, shit, shit. Bryson!" A hand found the phone near the bottom of the bag and she ripped it out, frantically waking it up and dialing Bryson's number. Her eyes were darting back and forth and a nervous pace soon emerged as she held the device to her ear. "Pick up! Pick up!"

Someone realized what was going on and proceeded to lean gently against a parked car as she tried to reach him. *She really does care about him.*

"Pick up the damn phone, Bryson!" It came out as a half shout, half beg. Rachel knew he was in trouble. *The emails, talk about killing Bryson, David isn't who he says he is. How did you not think of Bryson sooner, Rachel?* The internal stress was nearly as visible as her outward stress. A silence permeated from the phone indicating a missed call and instantly Rachel redialed.

She placed a final, seventh attempt to call his phone.

It was never answered.

Chapter XXI
A Born Hero

Wednesday July 5th, 2017
Centennial Airport, Colorado

"Bryson, just what do you plan on doing?" Henry asked desperately. Everything had been a blur for the last several minutes. Henry had pulled the plane out of the hangar as soon as Bryson had gotten in and within half a minute they had completed their unscheduled takeoff.

The skies were calm and easy to fly in, still a piercing blue with nothing but the sun to see. Bryson had taken a few moments to locate both of the terrorist's twin engine planes in the sky but eventually he spotted the small dots against the blue canvas.

He was watching them intensely as he replied to Henry, "You see those two dots on your radar? You follow those sons of bitches *exactly*. Not one degree different. Where they go, we go. Only difference is that I want you to add a couple thousand feet of altitude between us and them."

"Copy. Heading adjusted to follow theirs. They are at 15,000 feet. You want us at 18?"

"Yes. And speed up. I want to be right on top of them." The demand came without as much as a glance in Henry's direction.

"Won't they know we are on top of them?" It was clear that Henry didn't realize the severity of the situation.

"Most likely. But chances are that they are going to finish what they came here to do."

The altitude was increasing sharply and Bryson reminded himself to take deep breaths, treasuring the oxygen he was receiving. The pair of binoculars that had confirmed Nasir's face were in his hand and as their single engine plane surpassed the terrorist's planes in altitude, Bryson used it to track their location. *Why are they going so slow?* He brought the binoculars down for a second and noticed that the planes were making a conservative loop toward the downtown metropolis of Denver.

"Bryson, shouldn't we call the Air Force or something?"

"Go ahead and put the call through but they won't get here fast enough." Bryson replied with some confidence.

"Copy." Henry brought the radio receiver up to his face. "Centennial Airport this is…uh…well I actually don't know our tail number. But we need you to patch us through to the Air Force." There was a small amount of static and a quick, angry reply.

"Aircraft *Bravo Juliet Mike* you've taken off *without* authorization or clearance. Just what the hell – "

"Listen, this is an immediate and very real matter of national security. Patch me through to the fucking Air Force. Now!" Henry cut the airport air traffic controller off and there were a few more moments of silence.

"Aircraft Bravo Juliet Mike, this is Sam Georges of the U.S. Air Force. What seems to be the issue?"

"Air Force this is Peter Stines of the Central Intelligence Agency. Clearance code Alpha Charlie Niner Niner Seven Zulu November. We have an immediate terrorist threat that we are tracking several miles south of the Denver area. Two twin-engine planes flying at 15,000 feet. We are a single engine plane above them at approximately 16,500 and climbing to 18,000. Believed terrorist threat inside, possible nuclear situation. Scramble jets immediately to try and contain situation." Again, another static silence emerged from the microphone, this one seeming to take forever.

"Copy that. Jets have been scrambled. ETA 5 minutes."

"That won't be soon enough." Bryson said looking back at Henry. Their eyes made contact and Henry could see the fire emanating from Bryson's pupils.

Cautiously he asked, "Bryson, what do you intend to do? This is just a plane. No machine guns, no bomb bay…nothing."

The reply was simply Bryson holding up his handguns with a childish smirk on his face.

"Bryson, you can't be serious."

"I've figured it all out, Henry. That attack that sent me and Target Zero to the medical wing, the small plane rentals, the bomb maker, the locked chest in Pakistan, the bulky clothes. Henry…they are all suicide bombers. The vests and suits are outfitted with explosives that detonate on impact. We saw 20 people get on those two planes, that means there are 20 bombs about to rain down on that city and God knows how powerful they are or what they are targeting."

Our weapons will rain down on your cities in a way you never realized possible…the haunting prophecy from Abd Al Aziz in Australia was coming true. *Cities...plural. Is Denver just the opening act?* There was a deep ache in Bryson's gut. On faith and suspicion only, he knew that this was bigger than they had ever imagined. *No matter how this day ends, it will go down in history.*

"That still begs the question as to what you intend to do with those two handguns. I can get you close to the planes but I doubt that the guns are going to do much damage…unless…"

"Unless they hit one of the bombs inside" Bryson finished. His plan was simple:

Blow them all to hell.

The orange tint of the binoculars made it seem later in the day than it really was, but it gave Bryson the opportunity to see high amounts of contrast between light and dark. It took only moments of scanning the sky below them to zoom in on the planes once again. Holding the binoculars still he looked up to double-check how close the city was to their project path. This was going to happen fast.

"Henry, bring us down to 15,100 feet. Do it slowly until 15,500 so we don't spook them. Drop us that last 400 and we take them by surprise."

"Copy. Decreasing altitude now."

Dropping left a momentary weightless feeling in Bryson's stomach and he adjusted in his seat to get more comfortable. Judging by their current path to downtown he figured they had about a minute and a half left at their current speed.

"Henry, I'm opening the hull door. It's going to get loud."

To his left, Bryson grabbed a short strap that had a carabineer on both ends and hooked one end into a hook on the white wall of the plane and the other around his belt. He gave it a soft yank, felt the tug on his pant line, and reached for the door handle. The door slid back with ease and the cabin filled with white noise. Rushing warm air filled the cabin and ripped past Bryson's face. It felt so good that he couldn't help but smile a bit, like a dog with his head out the window.

Tears were forming in the corners of his eyes because of the velocity of the wind. Bryson turned around and searched the plane near the parachute that was behind him. Eventually he came upon a pair of goggles and put them on. The plane's body was sloped slightly downward due to the decent and Bryson had to stabilize himself with one arm against the opening's frame.

"17-5, Bryson!" Henry yelled back over the wind's audio. Bryson sat and listened as he again stared through the binoculars at the terrorist planes. All of the noise entering the cabin was telling Bryson something: *Shhhhhh*. He listened. Despite the events taking place, he was tranquil. The blue sky calmed his nerves, the sound filled his brain and pushed away thoughts, and the warmth of the air felt like an embrace. *Elena*. It was the only thought he could focus on.

Much as it had in Pakistan, a fire birthed in Bryson's chest. There was something about now, *right now*, which coursed through him. It wasn't adrenaline, although that too was beginning to travel into his veins. It wasn't chemical, it was something mental. The blood in his body felt on fire, and it excited him. It was like being drunk on a cold night, the only difference being that his senses were heightened. A sense deep down inside of Bryson told him that *this was it* and his body loved it.

Beneath him, his eyes caught the black dot that escaped one of the planes…and then another, and another. *Shit. It's started. We aren't close enough for me to shoot.*

"Henry, you follow what's left of these fucking planes! Redirect the Air Force to assist you. It's too late here!" Bryson screamed, making sure he was heard the first time.

"What? What are you talking ab –"

"They're jumping now!"

"So what are you doing?" Bryson barely heard the question as he grabbed the parachute and strapped it on. All he could hear now was the wind screaming at him: *FOCUS*. Bryson secured both pistols in his hand, undid the carabineer attached to his belt, fastened the parachute strap across his chest, and met Henry's gaze.

"I'm going to gun every single one of these bastards down." With a forceful leap Bryson exited the plane and left Henry alone, speechless.

Unfamiliarity.

Terror.

Speed.

Excitement.

Bryson had dived out of a plane before, but usually under much different circumstances. It was often the beginning of an infiltration mission, not the end of a stakeout. The emotions swirled within him but the fire his body had equipped before the dive was too much for anything as primitive as emotions; they were all expunged. Goggles on, parachute secure, and fully-loaded weapons in each hand, Bryson was experiencing a single effect:

Clarity.

Below him dots continued to exit the front plane. Guns placed at his sides, Bryson straightened his figure and sliced through the blue sky. It didn't feel like the ground or planes were getting any closer but he knew that was because of the distortion on depth perception that skydiving induces.

A quick glance around reminded him just how beautiful of a day it was in Denver, Colorado. There was sunshine absorbing the city's structures, a baby blue, empty heaven, and the Rocky Mountains shining with a lavender hue to his left. Any other time he would have been amazed. But not today. Not right now.

The air was warmer than it had been in the plane. Even screaming past his body it felt hot. The heat both externally and internally was satisfying to him. He realized that he yearned for this…this rush. Weightlessness was his world. Bryson knew he was plummeting through the sky, but he could not sense it. That's not what it felt like. The only object that seemed to be growing in size were the planes…

A black dot escaped from the second plane as the first peeled off its original course to escape. *So…close.* The second plane was almost in range. *Just a few…more…seconds…*
Three more attackers had jumped since the first when Bryson aimed one of the guns at the plane.

He felt the pull of the curved, cold trigger but the sensation of shooting while freefalling was immensely different. The gun kick seemed nonexistent with the lack of weight and Bryson lost track of the bullet completely until it struck and entered the hull of the plane. He saw the initial explosion and fireball before he heard it.

The blue sky was raped by the blackened metal and white light escaping from one of the explosive vests worn by someone inside the plane. Black smoke reached Bryson in seconds and he took a deep breath so as not to breathe any of it in. Shortly after, the air became scalding hot as Bryson punctured through the burning fireball of debris, explosives, and fuselage. A large hunk of the metal hull came within inches of his face and he heard its crackling moan as it passed. Just as quickly as the heat had started, it ceased and Bryson was met again with the Denver skyline, the sapphire sky, the Rocky Mountains, and fourteen human missiles.

In the back of his mind, Bryson calculated that he had likely less than a minute of freefall before he would have to deploy his parachute. *I'm going to have to do this fast* he stressed to himself. A diver was beneath him, seemingly oblivious to the immense explosion that had just happened above them. Bryson brought forth his pistol again and shot the person, aiming for their chest where he knew the explosive vest to be. Almost instantly an explosion transformed the falling individual into a ball of force and fire. Bryson had not been expecting the power of the explosion and its force threw him sideways across the sky, flames licking his body as he went.

The rushing air in his ears seemed to increase tenfold as he summersaulted continuously through the sky, twisting and turning and trying to get a grasp on what was up and what was down. Several moments passed before he regained his original diving position and he knew that his next thirteen kills were going to have to be from a considerable amount of distance away.

To his left were several bombers clustered together, but out of range for the handguns. Bryson could feel the endless vibration of falling on every muscle in his body and he knew that his range would be even less with that factor and the speed of falling affecting the bullet ever so slightly. Bryson lifted his right arm and leg, shifting himself leftwards across the blue. The terrorists were only half a hundred feet beneath him in the sky and as he shot closer towards their linear plane he counted four of them. His motion continued to propel him what felt like sideways across the sky, but he knew that he was also falling and time was short.

Several thousand feet below him were the downtown structures of Denver. Countless citizens at work, just like any other day, most likely unaware of the struggle for their lives happening above them. Bryson knew, as his figure continued to plummet, that he was their only hope. In his clarity he had one resounding realization: *Saving innocent lives. That is why I do this. That is why I took this job. That is why I am alive.*

Bryson meant to overshoot the group below him, and as he passed over top of them, he extended both guns towards the group and released two bullets. He could barely hear the pounding of the gunpowder ignition but the enormous explosion, followed by another, and another let him know that at least one of his bullets had hit their mark. A devilish fireball raced up towards his face as he fell into it, and instinctively he barrel rolled to his right, emerging from the fireball unharmed. That left at least ten more human missiles in the sky…Bryson hadn't seen a fourth explosion from that grouping. *Did it get swallowed up in the fire of one of the others?*

From the left corner of his peripheral vision, a black blur streaked across the blue towards him. Bryson had barely turned his head to look at it before the object collided with his gut. The hit was more surprising than painful and with the combination of twisting and turning through the air, it sent Bryson into a momentary daze. As he readjusted himself, a second hit came across his face from what seemed like above him. It had been from a fist. One of the terrorists was fighting back.

With little effort, Bryson twisted his body and brought his arms around, aiming for the man above him. Bryson could see the man had slowed his approach and was several feet above him, falling with his arms and legs spread to slow his descent. His eyes met Bryson's and the man locked his arms and legs and pointed straight down, ramming Bryson's gut with his head. Thinking quickly, Bryson dropped one of the pistols and grabbed the man's hair with every finger muscle he could conjure. In his other hand he held the pistol by the barrel and wailed the butt of it on the side of the man's cranium. Blood erupted by the fourth hit and he was frantically trying to escape by twisting his body around.

Bryson felt the man grasp onto his parachute latch in the front and roll him around. As the two switched positions, with Bryson now on top, they saw each other's faces up close. The man who was trying to kill Bryson had a recently broken nose, darkened skin, and sweaty hair. Nasir. Both men's gaze was reciprocated by a fiery hatred from recent altercations. Bryson struck first with a head-butt that left the terrorist blinking and squinting. But Nasir did not retaliate. They continued to fall and after a few moments Nasir simply smiled and moved his right hand slightly. He let go of the parachute pack's straps and closed his eyes, falling backwards. A strong tug on Bryson's back pulled him away, quickly separating the two men in altitude. Nasir had pulled Bryson's parachute and there were still ten human missiles falling towards Denver.

Smaller and smaller the dots became and Bryson's clarity had turned into an unclear crossroads. His descent slowed as well as his perception of time, as it had done so many times before. There would still be time to finish what he had started but…but…*I will die*.

The realization emerged from the fog in his conscious and became his only thought. Was his life worth a thousand? Two thousand? Ten thousand? Asking the question frightened Bryson because he already knew the answer and he already knew what he had to do. *I am not ready to die.* The parachute continued to pull him further away from the raining bombs. All Bryson wanted to do was escape the force pulling him away from saving innocent lives, but he had to make a decision first. *The* decision.

"**AHRGH!**" It was the loudest scream he had ever released and not even the sound of falling could cancel it out completely. It was his roar; the last cry of a warrior with his back against the wall. Inside his chest, his heart felt like it was trying to escape, trying to avoid what Bryson was about to do and stay alive. With his eyes closed, he tried to take a deep, peaceful breath.

His empty hand reached up towards his chest.

It grasped the parachute's latch.

And released it.

As the pack slid off the back of his body, he felt his speed pick up again. The fabric safety net was quickly far above him, now floating downward with no weight attached. For a moment, he was terrified; there would be no parachute to save him, no last minute miracle that somehow broke his fall. During these last minutes of his life there was one thing separating him between now and the moment of his death: the death of the ten other persons in the sky below him.

Bryson felt the fire consume him again. His skin was hot and his muscles were anxious. Once he placed his body in a rigid, aerodynamic position, the speed became blurry. Bryson was pissed off, furious at the fact that he had to sacrifice his life for the monsters below him. He was practically willing his body to fall faster even as it approached its terminal velocity. On the right of him, his eyes caught a glimmer slightly below him. It was his falling handgun that he dropped when he had grabbed Nasir's hair. Carefully, Bryson angled his body over to it and grabbed it around the grip, sliding his finger across the trigger.

There wasn't much time left and the ground was getting larger by the second. The sensation of falling was very much a reality to him now. *I've made my choice.*

He spotted his enemies even further below him. One grouping of three directly below him, two falling slightly to the right of them, a spread out collection of four underneath the two, and one, Nasir, to his left but not as low in altitude as the others. The plan of attack was set: *Two, then four, then three, then one.*

Bryson knew he was out of range of the two missiles below him, but he shot anyway. Out of anger, out of curiosity, and mostly because he just wanted them dead. Now. A brilliant flash of light escaped from the dots and another one right after. The fireball grew and evaporated into smoke beneath him and he glanced with raised eyebrows at the guns in his hands. *They're as angry as I am. This will be their last act too.*

Moments later, the group of four that had been beneath the two raced up through the smoke to meet him. The explosion above them had been an alert to the alien presence and they spread their limbs wide to decrease their speed. Forming the shape of a diamond, Bryson was poised to fall right through the middle of them within seconds. Before he got there, the Caucasian woman missile on the left twisted in air towards Bryson. He could see something in her hands but by the time he realized what it was, it was too late.

A single bullet struck Bryson in the hip and the pain seared down his legs. A mixed potion of adrenaline, anger, and acceptance suppressed it and the impact of the bullet forced Bryson to roll as he fell through the center of the diamond of terrorists. Like an angel extending its wings, his arms were fully protracted to each side and the woman, now on his right, made eye contact with him as he pulled the triggers of both handguns. Toxic ribbons of flame and light swallowed Bryson and the bombs whole.

Shrapnel from the vests entered along both sides of his body and he tried to release a cry of pain. All that came out was a disgusting blend of blood and saliva. Everywhere hurt. The impact of the explosives had most certainly caused some internal injuries and he could sense that his legs were torn up. There were fragments of hot steel implanted on the sides of his face and he could feel warm blood flowing down his neck.

Part of Bryson's soul wanted to cry, to be afraid in the face of his death. Part of him just wanted to die now. But the strongest part of him knew, that even with only a few moments left on this earth, he had four more lives to take. Or at least four more lives that he had to *try* to take, for the sake of all the naïve people just a few thousand feet below.

Painfully, he brought his sleeve up to his goggles and wiped the speckled drops of blood, leaving a thin red smear across his vision. The grouping of three terrorists was closer to him than he expected and he pulled the trigger towards their despicable existence. This time, he was too drained to even notice the resulting explosion and the slight kickback of the gun sending ripples of pain flowing through his mangled extremities. The gun that had released the bullet shot out of his grasp, across the sky; its mission was complete. Now his only two objectives were finding the last bomber and staying conscious.

Just…one…more. Stay awake. Stay awake.

Close your eyes, Bryson.

No! Just stay awake.

As much as he squinted and focused and searched, Bryson could not spot the final human missile. The skyscrapers beneath him were much closer now and it was hard to see the darkened speck against their brown, black, and blue windows. A sigh escaped his chest. *19 out of 20 isn't bad.* But Bryson was a N.E.T.S. agent. *Still one too many.* The worst part was that he knew the last man standing was Nasir. Their rivalry had clearly become deadly but Bryson couldn't let that man fulfill his wish. *My wish is to kill him.* He couldn't let him kill even one innocent person. *I am not an innocent person.* He couldn't let him win. As the thought processed in his mind, Nasir swooped over from Bryson's left and collided with him again.

It was a strange thing, dying. Bryson couldn't hear anything anymore. He hadn't noticed it moments ago but now as he was dropping out of the sky, tussling with a man who was clearly screaming at him, he realized that he was at peace.

There was no more roaring air.

Every punch, every movement of either man had no auditory consequence. Nasir had his mouth opened wide, pure hatred ignited in his eyes, sweat beading on his brow, hair slick with sacrificial moisture…he was letting out a final, barbaric war cry.

But to Bryson, he heard only one thing: Elena. Her voice filled him. He wasn't just hearing it, he was feeling it. She was all he could see, easily overpowering any visual data being received by his eyes. Tears poured from his eyes as she spoke to him.

"Bryson, I'm here." She was as beautiful as ever, standing in his mind with a glow that was holy. The smile on her face told Bryson that death couldn't be that bad. He choked out tears with a smile. Again, blood coughed out of his mouth and the intense joy plastered on his face bewildered the still-fighting Nasir. But for Bryson, time had completely frozen. He wanted to be here forever.

"Elena." He couldn't have contained the tears if he tried. But he didn't want to. "I've missed you so much." She began crying through her smile.

"I know, Bryson. It's been so hard watching you. You've been so strong."

"Am I dying?" Bryson asked, frightened.

"Yes, Bryson." She gave him a solemn, but comforting look. "Many people have their lives because of you. Do not be afraid." Bryson didn't know how to respond. *So this is it.*

"Bryson?" Elena asked quietly.

"Yes?" their eyes met in his conscious and hers grew dark.

"You still have one more thing to do." Her tone was serious and urgent. As was his reply.

"I know."

The vision ended and his eyes were his vision again. A baffled Nasir had been wrestling with Bryson's subconscious fighting skills and was choking Bryson from behind. The two men were dropping as they had before, but now the end was near. Tall steel structures swallowed them up into the city as they fell in between the skyscrapers of downtown.

One concluding objective.

Two absolute deaths.

His hand gripped the remaining gun tightly and pressed the exit of the barrel hard against his chest. With one final, weakened shout, Bryson pulled the trigger. The bullet passed through his body and entered the vest of the man on top of him, triggering the explosive.

Bryson Cooper's final thought was of Elena.

And then his world went black.

EPILOGUE I
THREATS IN THE RAIN

This environment was similar to one that Rachel had been in only a few short weeks ago. Skies were overcast and quietly leaking tears, the grass beneath her feet was green and lush, and the casket was both ominous and gorgeous. But there was a distinct difference she realized as the beads of moisture formed like domes on the glazed wood of the empty tomb.

Rachel had been naïve at Elena's funeral; completely unaware of what was really happening at N.E.T.S. What Elena had really died for…what Bryson had really suffered.

Now, she was at Bryson's funeral. Tales had quickly circulated about a man who saved Denver, and for the time being, the C.I.A. was taking credit that the "unnamed hero" was their agent. But that hadn't been the only attack that day. *I can't think of that now. Do what you came here to do.*

At *this* funeral, Rachel felt educated. No amount of inside information or conspiracy affirmation could erase the sorrow she felt from Bryson's passing, but what she knew now gave her faith that she could sure as hell make his death count for something.

But her grief and regret were crippling. As she stood openly in the soft rain, hair soaked from root to tip, she stared at Bryson's casket similarly to the way she had seen him stare at Elena's casket. There had been so much hatred and anger and sadness in his eyes. She remembered that she had left the burial ceremony early to return to work and hadn't had the chance to console him. *David probably took care of that. And probably set everything in motion at the same time*...Rachel glanced across the casket to the people gathered on the other side. There was David, pretending to be mourning for the life that he had purposefully meant to take. He was looking down at the grass as Rachel had been moments ago. They hadn't spoken since she had returned from Costa Rica after hearing the news that The Will had been carried out. But she was going to make sure that he remembered her next words *very* well.

Ian still wasn't completely convinced that all of this was right. Just about a week ago he had been one of the Dead Scorpion's most powerful tools. Now he was dead to most everyone that had knowledge of him and "working" with a man who still called himself "Someone", and a female agent from N.E.T.S. who appeared to be emotionally unstable these past few days.

He leaned against the tree to press further under the branches and avoid the rain. Across the graves and down the hill, he could see her, Rachel was her name, standing unprotected in the rain. *My, my. What the heart will put the body through when it's injured.* She had stubbornly insisted, Ian believed rather stupidly, that she attend this funeral. Someone had wanted them to both stay in Costa Rica the hours following The Will, but she refused and he urged that Ian go with her. Ian believed that the trust in him was misplaced. *I could easily run away and never have to work another day in my life.*

But he knew that something was keeping him here. It was a disgusting concoction of emotions. He was angry at the man down there, David, for thinking that he could so carelessly attempt to end Ian's life without repercussions. A small part of him was impressed by the sacrifice and skill that the N.E.T.S. agent, Bryson Cooper, had shown and felt ever-so-slightly obligated to honor him in some way, man-to-man. And perhaps most strange, was the inexplicable connection that he felt to Someone. He was sure that he had never met the man, but something about him made Ian sure that he was right and more confident about following him. *Damn these "gut-feelings". Clouding my judgment like that woman's feelings...*

Whatever the case of his inability to free himself was, Ian knew two things: that it was going to be a treacherous road to the finish line and that there were going to be more casualties.

Rachel had finished making her peace at the funeral, or at least she had stared at the casket long enough to realize that it wasn't going to change things. Her clothes were soaked through and she should have been cold, but she wasn't. She wasn't warm either. She was just numb. Half of this felt like a dream, a nightmare actually, and the other half was so startlingly real that it terrified her.

As the funeral proceeded, Rachel slowly made her way through the small crowd, around to the other side of the casket where David was. The lack of people at the funeral brought a new sadness to Rachel; Bryson Cooper deserved an enormous funeral and she guessed he would have had one if the people he saved would have known what he had done for them.

David was still looking down at the grass. *I hope he is ashamed.* Rachel came up on the side of David and stood next to him. The pitter patter of the rain seemed to be the only noise she could hear and it was especially calming right now. David did not acknowledge that she was right there; he remained completely quiet to the point that it enraged Rachel. *How dare he ignore me? After all he has done…*

She had her gun on her…she thought about killing him right then and there. For all he had done to Bryson, to Elena, to N.E.T.S., and hell, to the country! But she knew she had to be smart about the next steps they took. There was enough evidence for *her* to believe that David was the masterminding monster behind all of this, but there wasn't enough to condemn the man to death…yet. David would be dealt with in time. Of that, she was sure.

After a few more moments, Rachel inched closer to David and gathered her courage. When she was close enough to whisper, she quietly uttered the sentence she had waited days to say to him.

"You know I'm going to kill you, don't you?" The powerful sentence lingered on her tongue and she liked its taste. Soaking wet threats in the rain were erotic.

She expected a look of shock or a quick turn of the head from David, but was met with no such response. Rather, he kept staring at the ground for a few more moments and slowly turned back toward her. His eyes met hers and judged her worthiness, as if he were calculating if she was even fit to say what she had just said.

"Hmm." The small sound of acceptance of her statement barely escaped his mouth but his eyes did all the talking. They met with hers one last time before returning to analyzing the wet, lush grass. Screaming at her they replied: *You will try.*

Rachel knew that was all she was going to get from the bastard and slowly excused herself from the funeral. As she walked up the hill to rejoin Ian, she turned one last time to look at Bryson's casket. It all felt too fast. She had just been talking to him on the phone. How was it that Bryson and Elena Cooper, two of the best agents N.E.T.S. had ever seen, were now both dead? Emotions mixed inside of Rachel and created a confusing combination of anger, grief, depression, excitement, and loneliness. With a deep breath, she tried to leave all that behind. For this next leg, she would need to be as focused as possible.

Before turning and leaving the funeral, she closed the book on one of the best friends she had ever had.

"Goodbye, Bryson Cooper. I love you."

*W*hoosh...

Whoosh...

Whoosh...

Waves gently breaking on the shore were methodic and perpetuated his gentle sleep. Beads of moisture glistened on his skin and collected grains of pink sand as he shifted comfortably. Bryson Cooper was dead, in a deep and eternally relaxing sleep. There were no thoughts here, no agendas, no subconscious worries. This place contained only raw emotion and memories. There was no actual physicality but he was still in physical form. It was warm and effortlessly calm, almost creating a permanent buzz of contentment. This was Bryson's paradise. No matter what religion he would have believed in, he was where the human soul went after death.

Almost as if a second party had woken him, Bryson opened his eyes and saw the top of a cave. The brown rock hung down in random formations and Bryson followed the sight over to his right where he noticed that he was under an outcropping. On either side of him was sand and then softly rolling oceans with more beaches past that.

His vision was like it had never been before. Far, far distances were hazy and nearly blacked out while moderate and close distances were clearer than his vision had ever been. Bryson rolled over and looked at the sand and could clearly see thousands and thousands of pinkish grains. But he comprehended none of this. Rather, he was being controlled by an unannounced drive to stand up and move his body elsewhere.

Within a few seconds Bryson was overcome with emotions: joy and sadness, as he finally grasped where he was. This small patch of sand under an outcropping jutting into the ocean was his and Elena's beach. They had made love right there on their honeymoon. As his mind wondered back to that vacation dripping with perfection, he remembered his wife and more precisely, he remembered his wife talking to him just before he had died. *I died. I am dead?* The simple thoughts ran through Bryson's mind as if he was still conscious but their morbidity didn't cause him to worry.

Memories from then rushed back to him. It had felt only like a short time ago that he had been falling and falling…with so much physical and emotional pain. *How long ago was that?* Bryson realized that he, or perhaps the world, had no concept of time. Had it been only a short nap since he had died? Eight hours? A week? A millennium? This inquiry didn't cause him to worry either.

With the passing of the time, the sky began to streak with thousands of colors as the sun began its downward decent towards the horizon. Blues, pinks, oranges, yellows, and gorgeous purples all claimed their plots on the sky line and were reflected equally as beautifully on the rippling ocean surface. Bryson felt himself walking to the edge of the cave now, where the ocean, sand, and cave entrance met and he began to climb up the steep rocks on the side of the cave. It was just as he and Elena had done in order to go watch the sunset on their honeymoon.

The short climb was not hard. In fact, it was as if Bryson was gliding over the rocks. Maybe he was; he could not be certain. Deep inside of him he felt an excitement that almost brought him to the brink of tears and it grew as he climbed up and up and up. His traversal upwards felt like it took a while, but again, time was clearly not abiding by any rules wherever he was. The sun was still in the same place in the sky and the colors streaking across its canvas were still in their identical areas.

Once Bryson reached the top he glanced around and could not see more than a few miles in any direction. Much like under the overhang, his vision was precise up close but very far distances were blurry and eventually black, as if an artist had not finished that part of the painting yet. After performing a full view of his surroundings, Bryson's gaze caught an image that made him stop dead in his tracks. On top of the overhang that he had been under was the slanted boulder jutting out from the middle of the surface. Leaning against that boulder, watching the sunset, was a person with light brown hair hanging down around her shoulders.

The excitement in Bryson's stomach boiled over and he felt tears escape from his eyes. He was in pure disbelief and scared to walk any closer to find out that it may not be real. Without any thought into it, he seemed once more to glide over to the boulder where the person was sitting. As he was nearing the boulder the woman turned around and met his gaze with a pair of piercing, gorgeous, and perfect green eyes.

Elena Cooper stood up from the boulder, tears now streaming down her face, and threw her arms around her husband who returned the gesture with equal emotion. They embraced for what felt like multiple eternities, and who knows? Maybe they did.

"Oh, Bryson!" Elena released emotionally as she buried her face in Bryson's chest. He held on to her tighter than he ever had before. It had only been a few weeks with her gone from his world, but it had been the hardest time of his life.

"Elena…I…I'm sorry." He let out through the tears.

"For what, Bryson?!"

"You dying. I…I just feel –" before he could finish she placed her mouth on his and kissed him with all the passion that being separated by death prohibits.

When she released it she replied, "Bryson, do you remember what you told me, when I was so afraid of our future, sitting right here watching the sunset?"

"I said that I would be with you forever."

"And you were Bryson. And you are now. And I was always with you." She placed a gentle hand on his cheek and looked into his light blue eyes. "I saw how much pain you were in after I died, but I also saw what you accomplished. I was watching over you every step of the way, Bryson. And when it was time for you to come back to me I realized that I had never really been out of your life.” She paused and kissed him again. “I’ll always love you, Bryson.”

“I’ll always love *you*, Elena.” Bryson stated passionately. Elena was right. They had only been separated by a mere construct known as “death” and it had been no match for them.

So, with the realization that they would live in perpetual bliss in the comfort of each other’s arms, Bryson and Elena Cooper sat and leaned against the boulder, hand in hand, and watched as the sun drew its multicolored paint strokes across the heavens.

GONE WRONG

THE SHORT STORY THAT INSPIRED AGENTS & ANGELS

WRITTEN BY J.T. RATH

PROLOGUE
GONE WRONG
PART I: THE PAST

Five. He would never make it. Four. He was stuck for some reason. Three. He managed to break loose. Two. How did it get this bad? One. No more time to think…

An alarm went off in Sydney, Australia, fulfilling its only purpose by waking the man sleeping next to it. His eyes opened with a readied intensity; he was surprised that he had been able to get any sleep in the first place. The morning sun draped his face as he sat up in bed and observed that the city was cruelly gorgeous today. As if nothing was wrong, cars hustled across intersections, children played in the park across the street, and the cloudless sky, unusual for this time of year in the Southern hemisphere, was allowing the sun to play joyfully off the white tiles of the Opera House in the distance. *God that's a good looking building* he complimented in his mind. None of it mattered though. This was not a trip for pleasure, not even a trip for business. It was a trip that would most likely cost him, and the woman he loved the most, their lives.

The mission in Rome…it was supposed to be an easy one: a simple political assassination. The kill order was issued by the United States Non-Existent Task Squad, or "N.E.T.S." as it was often referred to as. The agency was unique, small, invisible, and most importantly, lethal. Despite their tall list of accomplishments, it would never receive any recognition from the government, President, or American public. For all intents and purposes, there was no such thing as N.E.T.S.

Abd Al Aziz was the assassination target, a relatively unknown oil businessman from the Middle East that N.E.T.S. had under surveillance for several years beforehand. It was a two-man operation and the team assigned had been the husband and wife duo Bryson and Elena Cooper, the pinnacle of success within N.E.T.S. Their track record was unmatched, even from the Cold War era teams, and it was the closest thing that N.E.T.S. had to a "sure thing" in a world that was so often filled with enemies trying to prevent that. *Make it look like an accident* had been their instructions. Their plan had been set before they had boarded the plane to Italy and had been perfected and run through at least half a dozen times by the time the wheels touched the ground.

"Bryson, we ready to go?" Elena inquired of her busy husband. In the sunlight her toned structure and tanned skin looked radiant while the athletic curves of her womanhood filled their respective articles of clothing. Her light brown hair was done up in a tight ponytail leaving her painfully gorgeous face and seductively perfect green eyes fully exposed. There was a twinkle in them that somehow never left.

"Yep. The semi is all set up and the oil tanker is filled and making its way around right now." Bryson replied. He too was an attractive human. His body was cut and muscular, but supremely athletic. He had a distinct jaw line, similarly tanned skin (although it was slightly whiter than Elena's, for which she always gave him grief), and crisp cheek bones. But his most endearing feature was his eyes, colored similarly to the clear sky they were under, they were nearly impossible not to look at directly.

"And both are rigged for satellite control?" Elena followed up, already knowing the answer.

"What is it? My first day?" The answer came out sarcastically, but was complimented with a warm smile.

"Yeah that's what you said in Chile too," Elena paused, "and we *both* know how that one turned out." Bryson leaned over and quickly shut her up with a kiss. She returned the gesture graciously.

"Fair enough." He agreed, and turned his gaze away from her. "All right. Let's go."

Sydney had always come across as an inherently friendly place to Bryson, but right now it was lonely. As he left the hotel lobby and emerged into the gorgeous winter day, he heard the sounds of the city first hand. A gentle breeze bouncing off tall buildings, the purr of automobile engines and their subsequent brake squeaks. He welcomed the company and took a moment to enjoy his senses. There most likely wouldn't much time for it later.

I would love to kill her right in front of you

A grimaced voice echoed the sentiment around his head, as if whispered by a ghost behind his shoulder. Slightly paranoid, Bryson glanced behind him knowing that no one specific would be there. *Just relax* he calmed himself.

Earlier he had been given instructions to meet at a warehouse a couple hours south of Sydney at 10:00 A.M. Despite the many clichés he conjured of going to meet bad guys in a warehouse, he knew that it was something he had to do. The thought had distracted him from his walking and he was quickly on the backside of his hotel, picking up his car from valet. As he reached into his pocket and transferred the keys to the young valet employee, a smile broke out across the kid's face that he visibly tried to contain, albeit rather unsuccessfully. Within a few seconds, Bryson could hear the distant humming of his "company car" and what he might qualify as the second love in his life. The Audi R8 Sport glided to a majestic stop in front of him and transmitted the sun's glare almost more effectively than the Opera House had.

There were small sparkles in its black, curved hull and the silver trim was nearly blinding.

"Whew!" The valet exclaimed as he stepped out of the car. "Tha's a mighty fine car mate!" He continued, half laughing.

Bryson appreciated his admiration and returned with the sly comment, "Yeah. It gets me from A to B." The statement was concluded with the shut of the door and the quick high peel of the tires as the vehicle pulled out into the downtown Sydney streets.

"Whatta prick! He di'nt even tip me!" The valet echoed to his buddy as he drooled watching the Audi disappear behind a corner.

Once Bryson was outside of Sydney by a considerable margin he began to wonder about the upcoming rendezvous at the warehouse.

What would happen if things went wrong again?

"Bryson, heads up." Elena warned as she nodded to a spot in the distance. The two of them were perched on the archaic rooftop of an apartment complex in Rome, looking down at the four-lane road that extended away from them where the "accident" would take place. In his peripheral vision, Bryson could make out the rounded, crumbling edges of the Coliseum. *Many died there once, now one will today.* He poetically spoke in his mind before he ran through the logistics of the plan a final time.

Abd Al Aziz would be travelling down this road in his customary Land Rover unaware of the satellite controlled oil tanker and semi-truck behind and in front of him, respectively, both with fully dressed human cadavers in the driver seats. Elena would have control of the semi-truck and drive it into oncoming traffic. Bryson's oil rig would jackknife, seeing the impending doom forthcoming; and all with the Land Rover stuck in the middle. Once successfully crashed in the middle of the behemoth vehicles, Bryson would blow a charge set on the oil rig to make sure the job was finished and additionally destroy any further evidence. The plan was simple. The plan was genius. And the plan would look like an accident.

"Here he comes." Elena said. It was hot on top of the building and she hastily wiped some sweat from her brow as if it were an annoyance. Both of them had their eyes firmly on the corner from where the Land Rover was supposed to be emerging, ready to put the plan in action at a moment's notice.

"Ready." Bryson confirmed. After a few more seconds of waiting, the Land Rover casually pulled around the corner just as planned. Its gleaming silver paint made it an obvious and bright target in the morning sunlight. "Go now!" Bryson ordered.

Elena obeyed by bringing the semi up to speed, and recklessly crossing the median into the opposite direction of traffic. The result was as expected, with pedestrian cars scattering like scared fish from the enormous disruption to their everyday lives. With a similar reaction, Bryson twitched the joystick of the control on the oil rig and after a quick left swerve it was sliding sideways down the road garishly, leaving hot black streaks of rubber from its tires. There was a loud crunch signifying the death of the Land Rover and Bryson pressed the explosive trigger.

A small shudder and a wave of heat made its way to the building top as an eye-catching column of gray-black smoke escaped the incident. Proud of how well the assassination had turned out, Bryson let out a quiet whistle.

"What a headline that will make..." He joked as he monitored the crash scene. He noticed that his wife had no smart quip to counter his lame jokes. "Elena?" Bryson turned over his shoulder and whipped around in alarm. Lying in a small pool of her own blood was his wife, a circular wound of open, torn flesh under her right shoulder blade. "ELENA!" Bryson scurried, half crawling, half running, over to his lifeless wife and threw two fingers onto her neck in search of a pulse.

A beat pressed outward against his skin; she was still alive. "Elena! Get up!" He had no more finished the sentence than the air pressure around his head changed drastically and a cloud of debris erupted to the side of him.

VOOT!

The sound of the bullet mocked him, assuring him that the next one wouldn't miss its mark.

"ELENA! It's time to go! N –"

VOOT!

Another bullet screamed into the building's surface and another typhoon of shattered matter escaped.

VOOT!

VOOT!

The next two had been the closest yet and Bryson knew he had to get out of there.

"Elena!" he pleaded one last time

Gray pavement cascaded under the driven rubber of his Audi – past car, after car, after car – exiting the city in a brisk gallop of horsepower and determination. The thought of losing her was too much to bear so Bryson didn't focus on it. Instead he focused on the stark black BMW M-series that had been following him for several miles. Most likely it was nothing more than an escort to ensure Bryson's path to the warehouse went as planned.

After 20 more minutes of accelerated weaving through the lessening traffic, Bryson arrived at the warehouse that was practically off a dirt road. The BMW pulled around the backside of the large complex while Bryson slowly pulled his vehicle into the complex. *So clichéd* he thought for the second time that day. The dull brown exterior couldn't hide the years of rust attacking the folds and corners of the rectangular box. Inside featured catwalks of a second floor and an open airiness littered with I-beams crossing in units under the ceiling. The floor was dank and moist, as if it had just rained…or it was permanently wet to live up to the bad-guy standard of warehouses.

Almost reluctantly, the audible caress of his car's engine stopped as Bryson exited the sports car, suddenly aware of how exposed he was and how silent the entire warehouse had become. As the final lingering of the V10's roar disappeared through the walls, leaving the uncomfortable silence, a calm voice broke through.

"Lay down your weapons, Mr. Cooper." Bryson couldn't make out exactly where the voice was coming from but he obeyed nonetheless. He reached for his weapon and 15 red laser sights simultaneously focused their attention on various vital parts of his biology. "As you can see, there's no room for funny business."

"No shit." Bryson muttered. He had done some pretty incredible things during his time as a N.E.T.S. agent but no matter which way he looked at it now, he was in deep. There were at least 15 different armed people in the room and here he was, giving up his firearm, and without his partner. *Could really use some help right now, Elena.* Bryson officially didn't have a plan and that worried him. "Where is she?" he demanded coldly, successfully masking his inner doubts.

"In time, Bryson…in time."

"It's awfully rude not to face your audience as you speak to them." Bryson japed. These type of pawns annoyed the hell out him. Always so omnipotent…so mysterious…so long-winded. And always ending up with a bullet right between the eyes.

"Did you bring what we told you?" The man pressed forward, ignoring Bryson's comment. "Did you bring the Redlist?"

"Yeah, I got your damn list." Of course it was a fake, but Bryson had to sell it as being the real one. The Redlist was supposed to contain all U.S. defense projects that were at least 5 years out from being implemented. The technology and scientific elegance it contained were worth billions of taxpayer dollars and many of the future projects would change the world permanently. In the wrong hands, the change would surely be catastrophic. Bryson prayed that this fake version would pass.

"Retrieve it from him." At that command, two guards walked cautiously and slightly crouched toward Bryson. Their laser sights on their weapons shortened as they kept the beams square on Bryson's forehead. Bryson reached for his back pocket; a gesture that was met with the overzealous sound of 15 machine guns cocking into place. Slower than he had been, he pulled a small, 10 terabyte hard drive out from the pocket and handed it to the guard closest to him. "Run it. Make sure it's the real thing. If not, kill him where he stands." The ghost voice ordered from afar.

"Oo gawd it!" the thick Australian accent chimed in from the lower floor of the warehouse. It sounded vaguely familiar to Bryson and when the boy came around the corner Bryson's jaw nearly dropped. Smiling, knowing that he had the upper hand, was the valet employee from earlier that morning. As he walked past Bryson he smiled. "Ooo shoulda tipped me, mate." He took the hard drive from the guard and walked a few feet further to the bottom of the nearby staircase and removed a laptop from the bag slung over his shoulder. He connected the hard drive and began typing furiously; his pungent keystrokes were the only thing that could be heard in the entire warehouse.

"Izz l'git sir." He said to the open air. "Poor bloke jus' 'anded over izz country's secrets." The typing continued as the kid was still looking through the various lists of potential scientific, military breakthroughs. "Tis ear is really interestin'. Izz a laser from Lock'eed Mar –" A thunderous eruption of sound filled the warehouse. A guard returned his sight to Bryson as the kid from the valet slumped over on the staircase, dead, dripping blood and adding to the dampness of the warehouse floor.

"I never liked that kid." The hidden voice took over. "Something about the accent…Now, Mr. Cooper. It seems that we have some business to attend to. I am often known as a man of my word. You gave us the Redlist, and I promised you *her* back. Let's hope she is still in one piece shall we?" The inflection of the coward's voice infuriated Bryson.

"If you did a single thing to her –"

"You'll what, Mr. Cooper?" The voice taunted. "There are 15 of my trigger-happy men ready to blow you away bit by bit, you're unarmed, and you have no idea where she is. Shut your mouth and realize that you are in no position to argue." He paused, as if he was wondering whether he should divulge the following information. "And consider yourself lucky Mr. Cooper."

"Why's that?" Bryson was getting fed up with the antics.

"You're lucky that the explosion threw off my aim in Rome. The shot I had intended was meant to kill." Bryson could tell the man was smiling somewhere right now. "Either way though, it was fun shooting your wife." A pause as he pondered his words further. "Yeah. It was very fun."

Bryson ran and ran and ran. The city of Rome was still in shock from the explosive accident in their streets and Bryson was the person running from the action fastest. Pedestrian after pedestrian was shoved aside as he lost himself in the crowd, mind racing, vision blurry, ears ringing, and heart exploding out of his chest. *She's dead* his consciousness screamed. This was not the way things were supposed to go. Abd Al Aziz was surely dead, but he wondered how much it looked like an accident with bullets flying around nearby rooftops. The mission had gone to shit and Bryson's life was following quickly after it. He stopped to compose himself and remember that he was a trained N.E.T.S. agent. Now was not the time to have a panic attack.

Alleyways became Bryson's momentary best friend as he twisted and turned through small openings all over, eventually getting himself lost which he hoped would mean the same for his tail – if he had one. He took a moment to gather his surroundings. Once he had, he walked briskly back to their hotel. Upon arriving at his room door, he removed his gun and slowly unlocked the handle, then crashed into the room, prepared for a fight. Much to his paranoid surprise, the room had been untouched from when they had left earlier. Rushing and fumbling, he gathered his necessary belongings: money, fake passports, and airplane tickets.

The nearest international Italian airport was a thirty minute cab ride away and he immediately got in line for the next flight to either Washington D.C. or New York City. The airport and the people it contained seemed so calm, the near antithesis of Bryson's situation at the current moment. Their days were normal, many leaving for vacations or just arriving into Italy. There were visits with family planned, tours of great monuments, plans to eat great food and create memories. Bryson meanwhile had just killed an international terrorist suspect, seen his wife shot, been shot at, and then run through the streets of Rome for nearly an hour. It was a memory he wanted gone.

As he fidgeted in line he felt the soft vibration of his phone in his pocket. *A text?* It vibrated again. And again. *A call...shit!* As he brought the phone out of his pocket he noticed that the number calling him was singular: "**0**"

What the fuck? Bryson answered the phone hastily. "Who is this?"

"Don't move an inch." The voice commanded. The voice was digitized, with low bass tones and randomizing modulations. "I have an operative with a gun trained on your left temple right now. He knows our cause and he isn't afraid to kill you in public." The threat caused Bryson to spin around in search of his executioner. "I said don't move Bryson. That is your only warning."

"Fine. What do you want?" Bryson asked, obviously pissed that he had corned himself like this.

"You took something very important from me today. One of my largest informants and buyers."

"Al Aziz?" Bryson guessed.

"Precisely. Our attempt to take something from you wasn't as successful as we might have hoped." The voice sounded perturbed. "But we might be able to help each other. Are you familiar with something called the Redlist?"

"I've heard rumors of it." Bryson stated. "What's the asking price?"

"Your wife."

"You son of a bitch! She's alive?" He felt his pulse quicken and his pores start to perspire. The thought alone forced him to catch his breath. *Oh my God.* Bryson was positive that she had bled out after he checked the pulse or that the assailant had shot her again.

"Yes, Bryson. And if I was truly a 'son of a bitch', she wouldn't be so watch your tone." Bryson remained silent in obstante compliance. "Be at this address at 10 A.M. in three days." Bryson's phone vibrated again, once, and he checked the address: Sydney, Australia. The bored voice came back on the line. "Don't be late, don't bring backup, and make sure you have the real Redlist." Before Bryson had a moment to gather any final questions, the phone clicked and the voice was replaced with a dead tone.

"Shit." Bryson muttered as he got out of line and dialed another number on his phone. It was N.E.T.S. headquarters in New York City. He uttered a single, coded line, "My mail never came." The call was automatically transferred.

"Bryson?" A strong male voice with an underlying current of worry answered. "We know the whole story. After you guys didn't rendezvous at the given time we tracked your phone. Your tickets for Sydney are already purchased and we have our best tech guys working on a fake Redlist. Your car will meet you in Sydney. Don't worry son, we *will* bring your wife home."

SATURDAY JUNE 17ᵀᴴ, 2017

"So what will it be Mr. Cooper?" The questions bounced off the empty warehouse walls. "Going to try something stupid?"

Bryson had been contemplating a plan during the pause in the man's recited threats. He had a few options in mind, but he didn't like the outcome of most of them. *Option C it is then,* he mentally murmured. Casually he found his keys with his hand on the outside of his pants and readied his finger above the alarm button.

"We'll see if it's stupid in about two minutes." The answer from Bryson came after a few seconds of tensed silence.

"Huh?" And with that final, confused inquiry, Bryson pressed inward on his pants. Quiet was replaced with the boisterous blaring of the car's horn, temporarily deafening anyone who hadn't been prepared for it. After a moment of delay and surprise, shots rang out from the guards' rifles, but were met only with air and the aluminum wall of the complex. Bryson had already taken action, dashing behind one of the thick, steel I-beams that supported the roof. The small knife located around Bryson's ankle slid out with ease as he thrust it at the guard nearest to him. There was too much noise from the alarm and gunfire to hear the thud as it entered the man's skull between his eyes, but Bryson knew it had stuck.

As the man fell forward, a thin path of blood tracing from the knife to his upper lip, Bryson reached out and caught him. Without hesitation he turned the deceased corpse into a shield placed between him and the other 14 guards in the room. Blood was spraying out of the man and onto Bryson, who dropped him once he was behind the beam again. For a brief second the firing stopped as many of the guards reloaded.

There was an assault rifle on the dead man, identical to the ones that were now firing at Bryson again. He grabbed it and blind fired several shots out from behind the beam. Many of the guards were making their way to the second floor bridge that hung high in the warehouse, attempting to get the high ground. *Shit!* Within a short half minute, they were all aiming down at Bryson. Each bullet ricocheting off the beam made a distinct ping of sound, failing to make a full melody, but making Bryson cringe when one came too close. A round, green object on the dead man's bullet-ridden corpse caught Bryson's eye: a fragmentation grenade. As the light bulb in his mind flashed, he reached down and pulled the pin.

Five…

Four…

Three…

Bryson pitched the ball of potential towards the guards from behind the beam and stepped out, bringing the gun to his face. The cold steel of the body brushed his cheek as his vision narrowed down the iron sights. Bullets passed by him and the forest green sphere floated closer into his gaze. Bryson felt the slight punch in his shoulder as he fired the weapon. A hanging fireball followed as the bullet broke through the hard shell of the grenade now soaring only feet in front of the fourteen men's faces. Hot, vicious shrapnel plunged itself into their skin with little disregard to the damage it was doing.

Two thirds of the men were screaming in pain and the other third was bewildered by the sudden change of events. 14 bullets was all it took as Bryson swept the machine gun from left to right, pegging each guard as he went along. The auditory rings from the puddle of his final shot's blast dissipated and the car alarm continued onward. Bryson, gun still at the ready and in hand, reached into his pocket and turned it off, bringing the warehouse back to the eerie silence it had been in before he had taken lives.

A steady rhythm of clapping was coming from somewhere and getting closer as it became more regular. The mystery man, the same one who claimed to have shot his wife in Rome, finally appeared from the shadows, as pathetic as Bryson had predicted he would look: short in stature and with a visible bulge around his waist line. Like his stomach, his face was also slightly pudgy, complimented by an ugly pair of glasses and a tussled mane of grayish hair that begged the question as to what hairstyle he was attempting to convey.

"Bravo, Mr. Cooper." He calmly stated as he stopped clapping and reached for a decently sized Colt .45 pistol and aimed it at Bryson's chest. A thin red beam from the laser on Bryson's machine gun was centered on the man's pale, large forehead, prepared to punch a hole through it. "I knew you N.E.T.S. guys were good, but *REALLY*?" The praise came across as mockery. "15 of my men dead within a matter of minutes and you! You hardly have a scratch on you! I am impressed!" A smile emerged but was replaced by a bi-polar switch to anger. "Too bad your fucking stunt will not only cost you your life, but *hers* as well."

"Where is she?" The demand came from behind the sights of the weapon that was becoming more and more prepared to end the little fat man.

The villain shrugged his shoulders and muttered, "Eh why not?" his eyes met Bryson's and narrowed. "You know the new tower they're building in Tasmania?" Bryson couldn't say that he had, but he knew that they had just completed a record setting bridge to the southern Australian island. "The Herman Tower?" The man asked from behind the comfort of his own weapon.

"I've heard of it." Bryson lied. "What about it?"

"Well, it's huge! We've posted up there and we're going to throw her off of it." The man chuckled thinking about the demise of Elena.

"Thanks." Bryson replied as he squeezed inward on the trigger, giving the man a one-worded eulogy. A small mist of blood erupted behind the man's now blank expression and his head lurched back violently, toppling over into a pulseless heap on the cold, damp floor.

Without any second thought to the mess he'd just made, Bryson got in his Audi, tossed the assault rifle onto the passenger seat, and tore out of the warehouse, leaving one last melody of the bass of the engine and the scream of the tires. It was a signal to all who lay dead in that building that they had failed. There was only one thing, one destination, in which Bryson was interested now: Herman Tower.

Australia had made great advances in the last several years to connecting their lower cousin, Tasmania, to the mainland. First came the growing economy of the island state, with its increasing international interest in tourism as well as a recent surge in mineral deposit findings there. Next had been the construction of the immense bridge that spanned slightly over 150 miles to cover the distance of the Bass Strait, finally connecting the two entities by land. The bridge was high and fairly narrow but an impressive feat of engineering in and of itself, easily taking the crown of the world's longest bridge. After the growth of Tasmania, Devonport (one of its larger cities) quickly became industrialized and subsequently its most populated city.

It was in Devonport that Herman Tower was being built. Not the tallest building in the world by any means, but still a respectable skyscraper nonetheless and it would officially be the tallest within the country of Australia. With regards to the new steps towards internationalization, this was one of Tasmania's largest. The building featured a gorgeous, narrow, concave design with blue glass from base to rooftop and if successful, it would pave the way for many like it within the city. The building was essentially complete, with corporations having already purchased and outfitted floors for their needs but within the last week there had been recent electrical issues that were requiring the building and some of the cities power lines to be redesigned to fulfill the excess power needs. Bryson was now assuming that this was a staged excuse and whatever terrorist organization was on hand here was using its vacancy to their advantage for the time being.

The drive to Devonport would still take a decent amount of time, but Bryson was travelling well above the speed limit at this point, hoping to shave crucial minutes off Elena's suffering and captivity. Traffic had picked up occasionally on his way to the bridge but all in all it was light as he stayed off the larger roads. Bryson had been driving for around four hours when the uncomfortable feeling in his stomach crept up. *Is she hurt?* Was his first thought and that led to thinking about scenario after scenario of him attempting to save her, most of which ended in a gruesome outcome for all parties involved.

The freedom of his mind executed a similar effect on his foot as the Audi was now travelling well over 120 miles per hour down the sun-soaked Australian highway. The air had a certain foreignness to it. Not because Bryson hardly every travelled here…it just felt heavy, like it meant something. It was the air of a very proud country that was special. Bryson painfully wished that he and Elena were here under different circumstances as the gorgeous continent of Australia had a calling to him, eagerly enticing him to become a permanent entity rather than a mere visitor.

A glimmer in front of his vehicle interrupted his day dream. At first it was a white dash in his vision, the object aiming its reflected sunlight into his eyes, but as it got closer he saw that it was a motorcycle travelling in the oncoming lane. A second glimmer of reflected sunlight in his rearview mirror…two more sport bikes and what looked like more BMW M-series. They had most likely been tailing him since the warehouse slaughter and decided to make their play here and now. As Bryson increased his speed to 140, he caught a road sign in his left peripherals stating that the bridge would be upon him within a few minutes.

His attention returned to the bike coming straight at him and Bryson saw the object on top raise one of his arms, most likely outfitted with a handgun. Unexplained instincts took over and Bryson gripped the leather handle of the emergency brake, now slightly moist with the sweat on his palms, and took it upwards. His knees came up to the bottom of the steering wheel and guided it into a spin, as if they were two fingerless hands. With his other appendage, Bryson pulled the driver door handle and let momentum take care of the rest. G-forces took a violent hold of the door and opened it outward as the vehicle came round to a reversing stance. The enormous rush of the outside air was cascaded briefly by the sound of twisting, collapsing metal as the biker from the front had collided with the inside of the Audi's driver door.

Some debris flew into the cockpit of the four-wheeled weapon as the door ripped off its hinges and Bryson continued down the highway in a high speed reverse. The metal of the bike and the door were almost indiscernible as they slid down the road, but as they collided with one of the second bikers, the bodies that had been driving the contraptions were very clear as they bounced down the pavement. Satisfied with his first strategic move, Bryson casually brought the emergency brake to a higher altitude and slid the car into a forward position again. *Three cars and one bike left.*

Without a door he had an easy opening out of which to rain destruction. His fingers grasped the cold metal of the assault rifle still in the passenger seat and he blind fired behind him. None of the bullets connected, but it had let his pursuers know, if they didn't already, that he was out for blood. Outfitted with special engines, the M series BMWs were catching up to him on either side and as they were about to pass him he cranked the leather rod of the emergency brake for a third time. The Audi went into yet another high speed slide and created a vacuum with the BMWs that had just passed its front and rear. Bryson's vehicle was sucked off the pavement and existed in the air space between the pursuers, the one who was in front of Bryson returned a baffled expression to the N.E.T.S. agent whom he had underestimated.

Gray lines and creations of concrete passed under the carriage of Bryson's sideways car as it floated between the other two vehicles…an equal product of chance, skill, and luck. Unlike his enemies however, Bryson had no time to revel in the physics of the situation and aimed the assault rifle at the front, inside tires of each vehicle, spraying them with round pellets and sealing their fate. Air escaped the punctured rubber of their tires as quickly as possible. The high speeds immediately chewed up the rubber and a yellow shower of sparks from each car's rim jubilantly skipped down the street behind them.

The vacuum was broken and the vehicles drifted towards each other, thus releasing Bryson's Audi sideways onto the pavement, making it skid until Bryson slammed the gas hard and gained traction. The cars that had once trapped him were now headed straight for each other and the third BMW that had been behind them, also marveling in the unlikelihood of the stunt, was going to make it a ménage a trois of destruction. Bryson's gaze met the pursuer's disbelieving expression until the man turned to watch his demise first hand. The BMW's all collided head on and metal, plastic, and body bounded into the air as if attempting to gain high marks in gymnastics. Groans, moans, and violent crashes echoed down the road as the Audi skidded to a stop with a front row view of the aftermath littered across the pavement.

Again, taking no time to sit in the pleasures of his abilities, Bryson slammed on the gas with gusto. His tires squealed in delight as they anxiously tried to make substantial contact with the pavement, finally leaping the car forward. After a few minutes, Bryson was up to 200 miles per hour and placed it in cruise control. The final thug on a sport bike was far behind, though being rather obstinate and not giving up after Bryson had made history of his fellow companions. It was loud in the cockpit of the Audi with the air from the missing driver door flowing in and deafening any other noise but the growl of the hard working pistons.

Something irregular caught Bryson's perceptive eye, located on the undercarriage of the vehicle. It was an impossible anomaly…there was no way it could be there. *How on earth?* A few more seconds of visual recognition confirmed the horror.

The bomb he was staring at was nearly out of precious time. What made the situation worse was that the final enemy had closed the gap and was right on his tail.

Ten. *How could there be a bomb?* **Nine.** *Did they place it in the warehouse?* **Eight.** *Ah...think Bryson!* **Seven.** *It was the fucking valet kid! It had to have been.* **Six.** Bryson reached for his seatbelt, but it was jammed. **Five.** *He would never make it.* **Four.** *He was stuck for some reason.* **Three.** *He managed to break loose and was on top of the vehicle.* **Two.** *How did it get this bad?* **One.** *No more time to think...*

Bryson had managed to scramble to the small roof of the Audi and prepare a beast-like leap off the back. He knew that it was a suicidal choice, but it was better than the alternative. Mere milliseconds had passed and he heard the boom of the bomb engulfing his car in force and fire. The resulting ball of flame licked the back of his neck as he soared toward the occupied sport bike. The force of the shockwave pushed Bryson further through the Australian sky and he began to make his play for the motorcycle. With grace, he began to level out and establish his figure, becoming nearly horizontal and twisting to face downward with his feet erect toward the man on the bike. A pungent smell of burning gasoline, scorched metal, and narrowly missed death lingered in the air and he began to lose altitude. The ringing of the explosion was steadily replaced by the high pitched hum of the bike. Bryson stiffened his muscles in his legs to brace them for impact and felt the punch of them hitting the man ripple through. His kick had landed straight in the man's chest, jettisoning him off the back of the bike and tumbling dreadfully down the road. Bryson's body slid effortlessly onto the cool leather of the black bike and he grabbed the handles, holding on for dear life. The speedometer on the bike read 180 miles per hour and the bike shook under the change in weight, eventually stabilizing itself once Bryson got comfortable. He slowed the bike to a halt, composing himself for a moment while looking at the mangled wreckage behind him. *How on earth did that work?* The stunt he had just performed was unbelievable, even to the man that had just completed it and he couldn't help but do anything but shake his head and smile.

A swift and warm Australian breeze tossed the lighter parts of his hair, feeling like nature's reward for defying its laws. Despite the calm elation that had come over him, he could feel his heart thumping inside his chest as he looked over the Kawasaki Ninja beneath him. There was a compartment in front of him, already unlocked. Bryson lifted the lid and found a fat, heavy pistol inside. Curious, he parted the barrel, much like a shotgun, and found that it had been outfitted with grenade rounds. Realizing that the man who was now scraped off on the pavement behind him had most likely almost used this, Bryson felt a surge of luck hit him knowing that things could have played out much differently.

After a quick cough to clear his lungs, Bryson revved the bike's engine and peeled away from the scene of the havoc, triggering the back tire to begin squealing like a hyena's laughter. The bridge was close now and Bryson knew that he had already wasted enough time; Elena needed him now.

Within 10 minutes Bryson was starting in on the miraculous bridge. The pylons holding it up were behemoth pillars of concrete and steel that utilized carbon nanotube composites; the first of its kind. They were tall, making the bridge a substantial height, but it was bare at the top, nothing but a fairly narrow four-lane highway from the mainland to the island of Tasmania. The low railings allowed for stellar views of the ocean and islands around it, but also made Bryson slightly nervous. Surprised and disturbed that there was no one else on the bridge, Bryson continued to rocket across it, leaning down on the bike to increase his speed. He had to admit, the thrill was exhilarating and had the speed been due to different circumstances he would have been enjoying himself right now.

As he neared what he guessed to be the $3/4^{ths}$ mark of the bridge, a shadow passed behind him and caught his peripherals. A slow but steady noise accompanied the shadow and was growing in volume.

CHOO
    CHOO
        CHOO
            CHOO
                CHOO
                    CHOO CHOO

The shadow became a reality as the massive black figure entered his vision and sunk his heart. A helicopter, with Australian sunlight playing on the glossy black hull, was now flying parallel to Bryson. *You have got to be kidding me right now.* He begged and then audibly retorted,

"It's never easy, is it?" Bryson's gaze averted from the empty bridge to the pilot almost collinear with him. Their gazes met, knowing that one of them would have to be dead in the next few minutes for the other to continue. Behind the guard, the slide door of the helicopter opened and revealed a second man brandishing a rather unfairly large light machine gun. Bryson, frankly annoyed at this point, reached for the small pistol he kept hidden in his sock and aimed at the bastard. The man had already readied his weapon and his shots came first, whizzing around Bryson's head and bringing back eerie sensations of Rome. Bryson kept the bike steady, carefully aimed for a few seconds, and pulled the trigger. With the speed of the bike and the noise from the helicopter blades, he hardly heard the small pistol's bark, but he *did* notice the spray of blood from the man's neck as he crumpled and slid out of the open door and into the lovely blue waters below.

As if the chopper had a personality and Bryson had just hurt its feelings, it lurched forward ahead of Bryson. Not quite sure what was happening, Bryson slowed the bike down to a reasonable speed and watched, exchanging the small pistol from his sock for the beefier, weightier, and deadlier grenade launcher. Once the helicopter was a considerable distance ahead of Bryson's position on the bridge it banked hard toward the center and continued to turn until it was facing Bryson. There was a slight motion on the front of the aircraft that caught Bryson's attention, subsequently causing him to speed up: two front mounted turrets began their rotations, gaining speed much faster than Bryson's bike.

Bright flashes of light appeared from two spots equidistant from the copter's center. *Shit! Shit! Shit!* Two straight lines of bullets echoed past either side of Bryson. The high caliber rounds plummeted into the pavement, creating a heavy dirt mist in the air. Frantically, Bryson brought the launcher up above his head, hypothesized the arc, and pulled the trigger, praying that it found its mark and ended the barrage of death flying around the speeding bike. Bryson could see the black grenade as it sailed towards the helicopter; its contrast standing out against the bright blue sky. It began its descent and landed with a miraculous explosion on the nose of the chopper. The vehicle began to descend, but the force of the explosion on the front had caused the back end to rear up and now the path of motion was irreversible.

Bryson could see that the grenade had done damage to the hull, but that the engines were still, for the moment, running as the copter was flipping, and very clearly headed toward being upside down. It would crash, blades first, into the bridge and either leave an impassable gap or an impassable amount of wreckage. The decision was made: he was going under it.

The bike screamed in agony as Bryson ripped the throttle. It was going to be close and if Bryson didn't make it the death would be horrific. Adrenaline was surging through his muscles and mind as the distinct WHOOSH of the rotors falling ahead of him were nearing. He was getting closer every millisecond, but gravity was just as quick. The falling helicopter was only feet ahead of him now and he knew he didn't have the height to spare. Bryson dropped the bike to one side and started a slide. *This is where I die* he thought as he heard the ghostly and deafening whirring of the blades in his ear and their breath cold upon his face. The blades churned above him, slicing bits of loose hair off, and then they were gone. Bryson, still sliding, felt a tremendous tremor beneath him and looked back to see that the helicopter had crashed through the bridge and into the ocean, leaving a considerable gap in its span. He had escaped the blades' wrath with only centimeters to spare.

His sideways skid eventually came to a halt and Bryson stood up, noticing that he was trembling. It had been an exhausting journey the past few hours and he needed a minute to take some deep breaths and compose. *All these years,* he reminisced, *I've never had to do anything quite like this without her.* Rather than feel sad for his captured wife, Bryson felt another emotion: pride. It was the knowing that he was a successful agent, with or without his wife that made him feel this way. Together they had been a complete force to reckon with, but by himself he was nearly as dangerous.

With pride, determination, and a hefty dose of adrenaline, Bryson picked up the battered and scraped bike and got on. He was going to Herman Tower and he was going to save his wife. God help anyone who would get in his way now.

SATURDAY JUNE 17TH, 2017

Herman Tower, and the city of Devonport for that matter, looked gorgeous on this Saturday. Even with a few miles left to go on the bridge's length, Bryson could see the iconic tower, not yet opened for business, standing tallest among the cities much smaller and emerging skyscrapers. The port town was where the historic bridge ended its run and soon enough, Bryson was pulling over the bike and walking towards the monstrosity's entrance.

The few individuals who were out and about shot sideways glances in Bryson's direction. In a few spots his pants and shirt were ripped, revealing now-dried cuts and his face and general appearance had an additional layer of sunbaked dirt and sweat. Now that he was here however, public image was the furthest thing from Bryson's mind. It was eerily quiet in the shadow of the tall structure and Bryson guessed that it was still closed. The city's electrical grid had not been prepared for such an increase and now required a bit of rework in order to provide enough for its citizens and businessmen.

As he approached the extravagant glass entrance, complete with revolving door, he noticed a white paper stuck to the door. The white paper was actually a small envelope with the word "**BRYSON**" written in red ink on the front. He turned the envelope over into the palm of his hand and out fell a small key with a stain of blood on its head. Chilled by the image, Bryson inserted the key into the revolving door's keyhole and entered the deserted tower. A grand sense of scale overtook his thoughts. Scale not based on the building's dimensions, but rather the scope of what was happening here today. *This* was his final destination. *This* was where his life's future would be defined.

He found the lobby to be eerie and as he rounded the security counter in the center of the hall, his feeling was confirmed, along with the question of where the blood on the key had come from. Two security guards lay crumpled behind their desk, each with a small entrance wound on their forehead. Feeling slightly guilty for their deaths, Bryson checked them over and took their 9mms for his own use. He slid one in his back pant line and kept the other out. As he approached the atrium of the building where the elevators were located his phone rang and echoed loudly throughout the deserted, yet gorgeous lobby. Bryson answered the phone already knowing who it was.

"We have a heat source on the 97th floor. Believed to be your wife and her captors. We have a crew in place already to clean up the bridge aftermath…we can reroute a helicopter to your location. Get yourselves to the roof and we will pick you up."

"Copy that." Bryson stated. "Sir?"

"Yeah. Go ahead."

"If we don't make it out of here, you make sure that all of these bastards go to hell. There is something bigger going on here than just the Redlist." Bryson had seen too much evidence in the last few days to think otherwise. There was some organization that they were unaware of and they had a substantial amount of resources: helicopters, guns, cars, bikes, and manpower. But probably most troubling was their knowledge of N.E.T.S. in the first place.

"Will do. Good luck." The phone clicked and Bryson was again alone, stepping ceremoniously into the empty elevator and hitting button "97". The box was gilded with mirrors from floor to ceiling with a pristine marble floor and gentle, dark yellow lighting. As cliché as it might seem given the predicament he was in, the elevator cubicle felt like a tomb. A gorgeous tomb, but a tomb nonetheless. Bryson caught his reflection in the mirror, the first he had seen of himself since getting ready this morning. What he saw in the mirror was not what he expected. Rather than a battered, tired, and desperate man, he saw a determined, angry, and strong individual. *Jesus, I look like shit* he smirked and his reflection returned the gesture.

About halfway to his vertical destination, Bryson reached up and found the hidden crack in the ceiling, removed the emergency hatch, and climbed on top of the speedy elevator. The dark atrium of the building was only lit by small red lights every 50 feet causing Bryson to have to work in the dark. He sat and wrapped his legs around the elevator cables and leaned near the open hatch, waiting for his moment.

The cool breeze from the shaft ceased to exist as the elevator slowed to a halt and signaled its arrival with the common "DING!"

"What the hell was that?" A gruff voice questioned rowdily from the 97th floor.

"Don't know sir. I'll check it out…Hey! You two! Come with me. Elevator!"

The conversation revealed that there were at least four people on the floor and the elevator's doors closed slowly after being open long enough for the ghost passengers to exit. Bryson grabbed the 9mm from his pant line and leaned into the cabin upside down, holding himself up with his wrapped legs. With pistols pointed at the door he anticipated the motions of the men on the other side. A quiet click of the button outside was followed by a second "DING!", opening the doors again. The armed men had made the mistake of sauntering over to the elevator and not taking the threat seriously, with two of them just turning their backs as the doors slid open.

"POP!"

"POP! POP"

Three successive shots painted the floor red with the ceased thoughts of less trained men. Bryson remained hanging for a second longer in case the fourth man was on his way but was tempted by the submachine guns that had spilled into the elevator as gifts from the dead. Easily finagling his body through the hatch, he switched out his guns and exited the elevator.

A fist came out of nowhere and pounded across his face, leaving the guns sailing through the air towards the floor's other elevators. Bryson was left reeling and as he opened his eyes he saw his attacker. The beast of a man was easily six-and-a-half feet tall, decked out in various special operations gear: tactical vests, knives, ammo clips; the works. Muscles and broad shoulders nearly ripped through his Under Armor clothing with veins that looked like river networks snaking down his arm. Bryson assumed this had been the man that the others had been taking orders from. He approached Bryson and swiftly kicked him in the lower half of his right leg triggering Bryson to crumple. A powerful knee came forward and hit Bryson's head. A warm sensation cascaded onto his lip and he knew the blood had started to pour.

"Well, thees izz not the famous Bryson Cooper I was 'xpecting!" The man said sarcastically in a deep, Australian baritone as he slowly approached where Bryson was heaving on all fours. He reached for Bryson's hair but Bryson tucked and rolled sideways to avoid it. The man laughed and continued to sportingly hunt down Bryson as he came to his feet and gathered his composure. He threw a dangerous right hook but missed as Bryson sidestepped, spun right, and turned in place on his heels; heavily elbowing the man in the back of the neck. The man stumbled, clearly dazed by the blow to the top of his spine. Meanwhile, Bryson kicked the back of both of the man's legs crashing the animal to his knees. Bryson bent over him and reached for one of the tactical knives attached on the large vest, but the man reached over, grabbed Bryson, and threw him over his shoulder. Bryson crashed into a desk and it broke beneath his impact.

"ARGH!" The man charged as Bryson got to his feet, dodging and grabbing the back of his opponent's vest at the same time. He pushed the man forward with exhausted strength, sending him through a glass door leading to an office space. The corresponding crash echoed through the halls of the 97th floor as glass shattered, falling like rain; each piece making a different twanging noise as it landed on the ground. Bryson rolled over on top of the man with his knees crushing in on his sides. Relentlessly he began wailing on his enemy; fist after fist made contact with the man, slowly decomposing his facial appearance. After the assailant had had enough, he sharply jabbed Bryson in both sides of his ribs, releasing the hold he had had with his knees. Before Bryson knew what had happened, the man's distorted face made contact with Bryson's equaling into a resonant thud.

"Mmmph…shit…" Bryson moaned as he cradled his pounding head with a bloody hand.

"Tha' stung a bit di'nt it, brotha?" The man taunted as he got up. He looked horrible himself though. Bryson's punches had easily broken his nose and blood drained out of several gashes on his face down onto his tactical vest. "Gotta say mate, I am a little disappointed! I really thought you woulda fought 'arder to save the bitch…" Blood spat out of his mouth at the last word with a special emphasis. Knowing he was provoking Bryson, he continued, "Obviously she di'nt mean 'at much to ya huh?"

The man was greeted with a foot into his face as he finished the question and he fell to the floor on all fours. Bryson hustled over to the dazed fool, pressed his foot on the man's right forearm, and pushed down. With a fulfilling crack echo, Bryson brought that same foot in contact with the man's already-broken nose. The strong man had a high tolerance for pain, hardly letting out a yelp despite his bones breaking.

Breathing heavily, Bryson walked away, leaving the man on the ground. As he made it back to the elevator, he heard his assailant get up and start charging again, trying to make one final attempt to end Bryson's life. Nonchalantly, Bryson reached down to the ground, picked up the submachine gun, cocked the weapon, raised it in his arm, took aim, and pressed his pointer digit in on the rigid grip of the trigger. An eruption of bullets released from the muzzle and struck the charging, rhino-esque man all over his body, causing him to lose his footing. Still facing the place where the man had been and arm still extended with gun in hand, Bryson kept his gaze forward a moment as he felt a slight bump on his foot.

After pondering the events of the brutal fight for long enough, Bryson moved his sight downward to see that the man had slid across the floor, his face barely nudging Bryson's foot in the process. Bryson stared at the man's empty gaze a moment, making sure that he was dead. Once he mentally pronounced him gone, he tossed the submachine gun aside and picked up a second one, full with ammo.

The air was heavy with the precipitation of the altercation and it stank of sweat and death. Elegant and modern office spaces could be seen across the floor and the timeline of the vicious struggle was evident. Floor to ceiling windows were showing off their views, something that Bryson didn't have any time to indulge in. It was time to find his wife and get the hell out of Australia. He knew this was the right floor, now it was just a matter of finding where she was.

Swiftly checking room after room, Bryson made sure to note where the stairs were as he continued his search. Within moments he came across a large office, one that he assumed belonged to a C-level executive, with Elena tied up in an office chair. Bruises and cuts peppered her face and her arms, but there was still that undeniable twinkle in her eyes when she saw Bryson round the corner.

"Elena!" He whispered, "Elena!" She had begun to tear up at the sight of her husband.

"You came back for me." She choked out. "I thought you left me for dead in Rome. How did you…?"

"We don't have time for that right now, Elena. We need to leave." He finished untying her from the chair. "Can you walk?"

"Yeah."

"Alright. Let's get going then." He took her by the arm and they made their way out of the office.

"No, wait I have to tell you something."

"Elena, it will have to wait. We've got to get going." They were out in the hall and headed toward the stairwell.

"No, Bryson." She tore her arm from his determined grasp. "It can't wait. Something went wrong in Rome. He isn't –" she was cut short by another voice.

"Dead?" a Middle Eastern accent rang out as Abd Al Aziz rounded the corner out of an office, very much alive. Bryson stopped in shock and wheeled around to look at Elena, then back at the man they had blown up in Rome.

"How are you…but what happened…Elena what's going on?" The questions sputtered out of Bryson's twisted, agape mouth.

"The man we killed in Rome was an imposter, one of Al Aziz's look-alikes." Bryson was staring at a smirking Abd Al Aziz, still barely believing how wrong their information in Rome had been.

"I'm not an idiot like you pathetic Americans are convinced. I watch your media, Bryson. All they do is show barbaric images of the Middle East…western civilization thinks that all we are good for is rioting and burning." Al Aziz explained with an articulate grasp of the English language. "We have information providers as well, Bryson. I knew you were coming for me so I placed one of my men in the car instead. His sacrifice is appreciated and honored." Al Aziz left the words hanging in the air as the cogs turned in Bryson's head. The silence between the three of them had grown awkward and Al Aziz continued. "I'll let you in on a little secret Bryson. I am a wealthy business man, this is true. But more importantly, I am an elite member of a terrorist group…the Aqarab Mayta. In English, it translates to the 'Dead Scorpions'.

"You've most likely never heard of them. We are an invisible organization, much like N.E.T.S…that is…until now. Non-Existent Task Squad is it? Named that way to create that idiotic acronym? Anyway, you may not have heard of us, but that's the point. You haven't because we are far reaching and all powerful. Al-Qaeda is a toddler compared to our adulthood. Let me ask you," his cocky persona was beginning to annoy Bryson who had now recovered from his disbelief, "Do you truly believe you have killed anyone of importance today? Do you think that any of those thugs were anything more than pawns on a chess board? They weren't. You gave us the Redlist today, correct? We don't care. Again, the Americans think that their technology is superior. No…the main purpose of today, of capturing your wife, of all of this, is to make people aware. Aware of the Aqarab Mayta. And today is just the beginning."

"What the fuck are you talking about?" Bryson demanded.

"I'm talking about another September 11th, Bryson! Except this time it will be widespread, across the entire nation. Our weapons will rain down on your cities in ways you never imagined possible. The devastation will eat your country from the inside out and within decades the virus known as 'Americans' will be expunged." His smirk was devilish. Not because of its physical shape on his face but because Bryson knew, deep down, that the threat was genuine. To his left he could feel Elena drifting into unconsciousness, most likely due to the beating that she had taken and he knew that it was time to leave. There was a fire extinguisher to the right of Abd Al Aziz and Bryson had his play.

"You know what, Al?" The question rang out with confidence and arrogance. "I've had a long, shitty day and frankly,

I'm a little pissed off." Elena turned her head wondering what on Earth her husband was doing. "Your plan, even if it does come to fruition, has a gaping hole in it. It will piss of the American people. You'll be poking a monster that will deliver swift and excruciating consequences. And it will all blow up in…your…face."

A shot startled the other two parties as the bullet left Bryson's gun and exploded the fire extinguisher, sending a white, frosty cloud into the hallway. Bryson yanked Elena and pushed her toward the stairs.

"Keep running Elena! Go to the roof!" Bryson screamed. He hoped to God that the helicopter was there by now and shuddered to think what kind of events would take place if it wasn't. In the stairwell nearly on the 99th floor, Abd Al Aziz crashed through the 97th floor's door. A sound akin to a small explosion rang off a pole by Bryson's left ear. It had come from one of Al Aziz's Desert Eagles.

Sunlight erupted through the door way as Elena and Bryson slammed through it and onto the roof, with the helicopter in mid process of landing on the pad. *This is it. This is where this hell ends.* Bryson encouraged himself. Bryson took Elena's hand and ran for the helicopter.

Behind them, Al Aziz similarly crashed through the rooftop entrance and began to chase after them, firing at their evacuation. The amazingly violent sounds from the handguns frightened Bryson, but he kept their heads down as they weaved around the rooftop structures towards the pad. The helicopter was taking the brunt of Al Aziz's fire and began to pull away.

"Elena we have to jump! Let's go!" Bryson screamed behind him in instruction. He removed his grasp from her hand and sprinted towards the edge of the building, finding a solid place to plant his foot near the corner and leapt. The space between building and helicopter and building seemed infinite and the chasm beneath screamed at him to look down.

The hull of the chopper engulfed him and he wheeled around to see that Elena was further behind him than he had hoped. There was so much determination in her bruised face and Bryson was reminded as to one of the many reasons that he loved this woman. She grimaced her face with focus and leapt off the edge of the building…

Bryson heard the shot.

He saw a spray of blood erupt from her stomach and felt the air change as the crimson bullet entered the hull with a loud thud. Her body went limp in midair. Bryson grabbed the side of the hull and lunged for his wife's hand, caught it firmly, and pulled her into the helicopter. The pilot veered the chopper hard to get to a safe distance from the building.

"Elena!" Bryson pleaded with a shout. "No, no, no, no!" His eyes were brimming with tears as he looked at his wife's ghastly wound. She let out a high-pitched whimper as she coughed.

"Bryson…" She began crying and could barely speak. "Thank you for coming back for me." She forced a sad smile as her color became pale.

"Stay with me Elena! Don't leave me!" Tears streamed down his dirty cheeks and dropped innocently onto Elena's face.

"You were always there –" a second coughing fit interrupted her, "for me, Bryson and I'll always be with you." The next words she chose carefully and she wanted to use her remaining energy to complete her thought, knowing they would be her last words. "I love you, Bryson Cooper."

"I love you too, Elena. So much." Bryson choked out. He bent his head and gave her a gentle kiss. He pulled away and was met with a one last smile from his wife…that then faded into nothing as her stare went blank. The twinkle left her eyes and Bryson knew she was gone. The world pounded around him, thrumming against his temples. His emotions were failing him and he couldn't describe his feeling. Sadness, anger, adrenaline, worry, violence, and fear swirled around in his mind.

She can't be gone.

She's my wife.

She's Elena for GOD'S SAKE!

Anger and adrenaline had prevailed in his thought process.

"Turn the chopper around!" He barked.

"Can't do that sir. My orders are strictly evacuation and –" The pilot tried to explain.

"He just killed my fucking WIFE!" Spittle formed on the edge of his mouth. "Turn the goddam chopper around! NOW!"

Blind rage was consuming him as the pilot reluctantly obeyed. The warm Australian air rushing into the hull might as well have been scalding, the same temperature of Bryson's blood. Adrenaline and emotions swirled, creating a dangerous martini of future actions. *He will die. I will destroy him. He destroyed her. He destroyed me.*

The helicopter closed in on the roof of the tower and Al Aziz returned fire once he noticed. Spinning metal cylinders crashed into the hull with ferocity and Bryson stood tall, hanging out the door, daring the terrorist to hit him with one. Bryson leapt out of the aircraft once it was reasonably above the rooftop and walked towards Al Aziz.

An odd air of superiority overcame his senses and the world blurred around him. There was no rooftop, no chopper, no ground, no sky…nothing. Just a man who would die and his shining, silver weapons. One bullet nicked Bryson's arm but there was no reaction. Just more steps towards his revenge. The man was backing away and another bullet left the chamber and deeply grazed Bryson's left thigh. He stumbled momentarily but there was no such thing as pain, just ripped flesh and draining blood.

CLICK!

One of the weapons revealed its downfall and Al Aziz threw the empty device to the side, knowing that he didn't have many bullets left in the other gun either. Bryson was still crossing the rooftop and Al Aziz took steady aim. Bryson could see Aziz pull the trigger; even *felt* him pull the trigger and his anticipation forced him to step sideways out of its linear path. A gleam from the sun caught on the metal as the tiny missile came within inches of his face. The density of the air around the bullet ceased to exist and was followed by a wave of hot air sweeping across his glistening skin.

Al Aziz had fear and rage equally combined in his expression and reached down, grabbing a knife that had been around his ankle. Bryson saw the knife soaring through the air towards him and the Desert Eagle rising and releasing another shot. The bullet narrowly missed Bryson's neck as he attempted to catch the knife and it threw him off.

Cold, ashen metal slid through the meat of his left palm and pain once again entered into the equation, screaming across Bryson's mind. Carefully, Bryson removed the blood drenched knife from his hand and increased his pace to a near sprint towards Al Aziz, throwing it back at him with vigor. It struck the cowering man in the thigh and he fell to the ground, writhing and screaming in pain. Bryson finished his sprint towards him, swept up the Desert Eagle from his grasp and pushed it against his temple.

"Go ahead, Bryson Cooper. Kill me. Put a bullet through my head." Al Aziz spat out eagerly. "It would be a gift to the Aqarab Mayta if you shot me now. I am expendable and after all I have done for my brothers I will surely arrive at the doorstep of heaven."

"Change of plans. You're going to hell." Bryson stated coldly as he contemplated the man's words. *Is he really expendable? What kind of organization is this?*

The gun leapt in Bryson's hand as it barked out a bullet. Silence. Then a loud scream as the terrorist realized he was still alive and the bullet had entered and subsequently exited his other thigh. Bryson knew he was more valuable alive.

"You bastard! Why didn't you just kill me?" Al Aziz pleaded with tears streaming down his face as he attempted to clutch both of his injured appendages. Bryson got very close to his face, enough to feel the warmth of his breath and smell its stench. At the end of the day, Al Aziz was just another man like him. Skin and bones and a mind.

"You killed her. And you feel no remorse. One day, I will pay you back tenfold."

"YOU AMERICANS ARE PATHETIC!" Al Aziz insulted, saliva foaming on his lips like a rabid animal. "You are all so weak for the female race it makes me sick. Females are nothing more th–" Bryson ended the irrelevant argument with the butt of a gun across the man's head, knocking him out and shutting him up. He hauled the unconscious body back to the now-landing helicopter and chained it to a railing.

"Let's go home." The declaration was simple and the pilot nodded his approval as he began to take off. Bryson knew in the back of his mind that once he was back in America he would be debriefed and examined, just like normal. But things were not normal. His gaze quickly landed on Elena's covered form and he hung his head in his hands.

The tears came softly as pain overtook him; physically and emotionally. *Alone.* The single word echoed through his thoughts and he tried to accept his new life under this mantra. He would have to be his own savior, his own partner. His heart ached and he wanted to go back to his simple life before N.E.T.S., before Elena, and before all of this violence. But this was why he was here. He was good at it. She had been good at it. *And look where that got her.*

Alone.

Alone.

Alone.

It was his reality. He accepted it now. It was his reality after everything had gone wrong.

GRATITUDE…

It was a long road to get this book made. There weren't too many big speed bumps, it just got set on the backburner a lot with getting an engineering degree completed and what not. But there are so many people to thank.

First and foremost I have to thank some of my favorite action/spy movies. I'm a movie buff and I just love a great action scene. So to those movies that have dropped my jaws over the years, thank you immensely. This includes but is not limited to: the James Bond films (particularly *Skyfall* and *Casino Royale*), all of the *Mission: Impossible* films, the *Die Hard* films, *The Matrix* trilogy, *Wanted*, the *Fast and the Furious* franchise, etc, etc, etc. Basically any movie that got my blood pumping with some awesome car chases, sexy gunplay, or perfectly choreographed fist fights; thank you so much. I built from your ideas and I owe anyone who worked on those films a great debt.

Next I'd like to thank anyone who helped me to improve this novel. Lord knows it needed it in some spots. I sent my book out to a lot of people that couldn't make the time for it, but for those that did and gave me critical feedback and praise, your assistance is appreciated more than you know. Writing your first novel is scary as hell and hearing someone genuinely tell you that they loved your book is comforting and exciting beyond words.

Special thanks goes to my buddy Ryan Robles, a friend of mine in the Army, who helped me to make my book just a tad more realistic and pointed out some huge flaws early on that I had completely overlooked. We've been writing buddies for a while now and I value your opinion to an insane degree.

Maria Capecelatro, you were really the final driving force that got me to complete this journey. At a time when I was somewhat discouraged, not only by this book, you reinvigorated me to continue and even offered to read this novel not once, but *TWICE!* Your effort, efficiency, dedication, opinions, support, enthusiasm, and love are the reason that anyone is actually reading this right now. They should be thanking you, but I'll do it for them: THANK YOU!

Thank you to my editor, Lexi Richardson as well. The book had been through many editing stages by the time it got to you, but your additions were still critical (especially for catching my obsession with "towards"!). But it was really your words of encouragement and praise for the story that were completely invaluable. Receiving positive praise from you, your husband, and some of your family was incredibly uplifting as it was truly the first feedback I had received from strangers, for lack of a better term.

Thank you to Jared Stone and Pat Emmons, two of my most valued beta readers for their valuable input (especially with the organization of the different parts of the novel) but also for their constant encouragement and positive thinking. Each of your opinions really helped to shape the way that this book turned out, so thank you once again!

I'd also like to thank the shower. At least 80% of the ideas and plot lines for this story were thought of while in a nice warm shower. If I can give any writers out there a piece of advice it would be: think about your story in the shower. It's a surprisingly powerful tool to get your creative juices flowing and a great place to harness some strict concentration.

Another debt of gratitude goes to my 7th grade writing teacher Mrs. Littleford. I highly doubt that she would be reading this now but she should know that she had an immense impact on me not only for writing lessons but for life lessons. She was tough but that's because she knew how much we could achieve as students if we just stopped being lazy. Not to mention, she made writing sound like a very cool hobby. Despite what anyone who reads this book may think about the quality of my writing or storytelling, I still get a great deal of personal satisfaction from it and that all started with Mrs. Littleford.

Lastly, a big thank you to YOU. By picking this book up off the shelf (or ordering it online), you have placed a certain amount of trust in me to tell you a worthwhile story. That right there means a lot to me. I hope that the book does not disappoint and once again, thank you for giving me the chance to take you on a journey!

ABOUT THE AUTHOR

JORDAN RATH HAS A BACKGROUND IN MECHANICAL ENGINEERING AS WELL AS A MASTER'S DEGREE IN BUSINESS. HE CURRENTLY LIVES IN DENVER, COLORADO AND ENJOYS WORKING WITH POPULAR DIALYSIS AND HEALTHCARE COMPANY, DAVITA.

HE SPENDS HIS EXTRA TIME WORKING OUT, ENJOYING TIME WITH HIS NEARBY FAMILY, FRIENDS, AND GIRLFRIEND ON TOP OF HIS WRITING. HE ALSO REVIEWS CURRENT MOVIES AND VIDEOGAMES ON HIS WEBSITE: RATH'S REVIEWS (HTTP://WWW.RATHS-REVIEWS.COM).

JORDAN FINDS INSPIRATION FOR HIS STORIES IN MANY OF THE FILMS AND VIDEOGAMES THAT HE WATCHES AND PLAYS. THEIR CONTRIBUTIONS CAN BE SEEN SCATTERED THROUGHOUT HIS WORK.

AGENTS &ANGELS IS JORDAN'S FIRST PUBLISHED WORK AND HE IS CURRENTLY WORKING ON THE SEQUEL.

HE LOVES RECEIVING FAN MAIL, READER SUGGESTIONS, OR JUST HEARING FROM FELLOW WRITERS. IF YOU WOULD LIKE TO REACH HIM, PLEASE EMAIL: JORDAN.T.RATH@GMAIL.COM